Rose & Thorn

ALSO BY SARAH PRINEAS
Ash & Bramble

ROSE & THORN

SARAH PRINEAS

HARPER TEEN
An Imprint of HarperCollinsPublishers

HarperTeen is an imprint of HarperCollins Publishers.

Rose & Thorn
Copyright © 2016 by Sarah Prineas
All rights reserved. Printed in the United States of America.
No part of this book may be used or reproduced in any manner whatsoever
without written permission except in the case of brief quotations embodied
in critical articles and reviews. For information address HarperCollins
Children's Books, a division of HarperCollins Publishers, 195 Broadway,
New York, NY 10007.
www.epicreads.com

ISBN 978-0-06-233797-9

Typography by Carla Weise
16 17 18 19 20   PC/RRDH   10 9 8 7 6 5 4 3 2 1
❖
First Edition

To my sisters, with all my love
Katie O'Shaughnessy
Maude Bing
Winnie Edmed

STORY WAITS.

The hulking machine, its grinding gears—all silent, all still.

It was defeated once, long ago, but its time has come around again.

Story watches.

It sees a City that has forgotten that it once belonged to Story.

In the City's people it sees complacence and ignorance.

It sees a Forest that has grown wild and abandoned, its enchantments unremembered.

Story plots.

Its City can be used, as it was before.

Its people will play their parts, as they did before.

And there will be more: Story will take its first step beyond the Forest to wider lands. More people will come under its sway, and its power will grow.

Story sets out its cogwheels, its driving pistons. It plans its devices: a beauty and a castle, a rose and three curses. And thorns. Always thorns.

And now, to set it all in motion . . . it needs a Godmother.

SHE IS YOUNG, just a girl, married to a man much older than she is, and she has found that he is stern, cold, even cruel sometimes. She has no love, no warmth, no happiness. She grows desperate, and then wild with her desperation. There is no way out for her but death.

And then she finds a thimble—as such things are meant to be found. It is silver without a speck of tarnish, and engraved at its base with brambles, but no roses. The thimble offers her power and she, who was powerless, seizes it. Story teaches her how to use people as devices; she learns avidly, glorying in her strength, where before she had been weak. Under Story's direction she leaves the City and the Forest that surrounds it, and she causes a castle to be built, populating it with animal servants that her thimble has turned to people.

And then, and then.

The Godmother finds a man and a woman and with the cold touch of the thimble she takes their memories of who they were, and she breeds them to each other until the woman bears a child.

A GROAN, A howling of gears, and Story lurches into motion, and once it has begun, it is as inevitable as time and cannot be stopped.

Story will have its ending.

And this is how it begins:

Once there was a girl who lived in a forest cottage.

Upon her wrist she bore a birthmark in the shape of a newly opening rose.

A ticking triple curse was cast at the moment of her birth, and her

Time is running out.

CHAPTER

1

AT FIRST I THOUGHT THE VULTURES WERE FAT, ROTTEN fruit hanging from the branches of the dead tree. Then I blinked and saw their hunched feathers, their curved beaks as they watched me step out of the forest's shadows.

I paused at the edge of the grassy meadow and sniffed. There was no oily, tainted smell of death. Whatever animal they were eating hadn't been dead for very long.

One of the vultures dropped from its branch and spiraled to the ground. Half hidden by knee-high grasses, its naked head went down, jerked, came up again with something in its beak. Another bird followed.

The path would lead me across the clearing. I was searching for mouse-ear mushrooms, my guardian Shoe's favorites, and they grew only on old oak stumps on north-facing slopes.

Our cottage was farther up the valley, where there were only pine forests, moss-covered rocks, and ferns; I had to come down here with my basket for the oak groves. This path led to the village, too, though I'd never been there.

Well, vultures. They were just doing what vultures do.

"Hah!" I shouted suddenly, and waved my arm, and then took a corner of my apron and waved that at them, too.

Startled, they lifted from the ground and flapped heavily into the dead tree's branches again.

Shifting my basket to my other arm, I set across the clearing. I meant to look away, but as I passed the place in the grass where the vultures had been feeding, I caught a glimpse of something that was not the fur and bones I expected.

A boot.

I staggered to a stop, closed my eyes for a mere second, and then looked.

Looked away, fast.

A man. A stranger. Sprawled. A flap of a hood over half his face, a splash of rusty-brown blood covering the other. The same blood stained the front of his blue coat. And there was something strange about his hands.

All of the air rushed out of me, and I gasped for breath. I staggered back, the dry grass whispering around my skirts, and then sat down hard. Still panting, I wrapped my arms around myself.

Dead man.

His hands were . . . claws?

From the tree, the vultures craned their wrinkled, hair-less heads, watching to see what I would do next.

What I did not do was scream, or faint, or throw up. "All right," I whispered to myself, my voice shaking. "All right." There was nothing I could do for the man. His story was over, and panic wouldn't change that.

Carefully, keeping my head averted from where the body lay, I crawled out of the long grass, got to my feet, and the smell hit me—rancid, wild, dead.

Dropping the basket, my head spinning, I fled, picking up my skirts, my feet slipping on the steep, pine-needly path that led back to our cottage.

The dead man. Somehow he'd gotten inside the bound-aries that protected us from the outside world.

Growing more frightened, I splashed across the stream and continued, running past the cairn of moss-covered rocks that marked the edge of the cleared land around our cot-tage. The clearing had been carved out of dense forest and was edged with ferns and looming pine trees; on a low hill in its center was the stone cottage that Shoe had built, and like everything he set his hands to, it was well-made, cool in the summers and snug in the winters. The roof overhung the front to make a kind of porch, and on early autumn days like this, Shoe would bring his shoemaker's bench outside to work. Behind the cottage was a stone well, and a shed where our two goats and six chickens lived, and our garden. The clearing was bright with afternoon sunlight and smelled of woodsmoke from our chimney.

Out of breath, I staggered up the path to the porch. Shoe's workbench was there, but he was not. I darted into the cottage— empty. Out again, and around the back to the garden.

Oh, at last. "Shoe!"

He straightened, rubbing his back with gnarled hands. He wore his usual shapeless brown coat, and his gray hair needed cutting. Seeing me, his face wrinkled into a smile, and he set aside the shovel he'd been using to turn over the dirt. "I thought to have this done before you got back, Rosie," he said.

I stumbled up to him. "There was a man," I gasped.

Shoe's face turned grim. He grasped my arm to steady me and examined me intently. "Are you all right?"

"No, no." I shook my head. "I mean, yes, I'm fine. He isn't. The man isn't." I caught my breath. "He was dead."

Shoe frowned at me. "What were you doing outside the boundary?"

I knew why he was asking.

The valley we lived in was bound by protective magic, and that meant Shoe and I never saw *anyone*. In all the sixteen and a half years of my life, I had never seen anyone but him. When Shoe went to the village to trade the shoes he made for supplies, and to get medicine from a healer named Merry for his arthritis, he left me at home.

And that was all right. When I was small, our valley was enough. I knew where the magical boundary was, and during my wanderings I never crossed it, until I knew every twig and leaf and tree stump and moss-covered stone in the forest around our cottage. That was when the boundary began to feel like the high wall of a prison, keeping me in when I wanted to be *out*, exploring, meeting other people besides Shoe, seeing more than our tiny corner of the world. I had books, I'd read stories, and Shoe brought home letters from people outside—I *knew* there was more.

And so, not so long ago, I had crossed the boundary. Because I didn't dare go to the village, I went the opposite direction, following a deer trail that led up the high hill at the end of our valley. Stepping through the boundary had been like parting a curtain made of stinging sparks, but I'd done it, and climbed on up the steep, rocky path, my heart pounding. Two hours later, near the top of the hill, I came to a stone outcropping, and there I'd stopped, panting, and looked over the valley, seeing our cottage and clearing—just a tiny patch of land from where I was standing—and beyond, the village in its own valley, the river running through it a glint of silver, and a thread of road winding away from it. Dusk was falling. Way in the distance, where the forested hills opened to a plain at the very edge of sight, was a smudge of lights amid deeper shadows. A city. Maybe *the* City, the one Shoe had told me stories about. Its lights winked at me. It beckoned.

I can't come now, I'd whispered to it, as if the City could hear me, so far away from it on my little outcropping of rock.

My head full of new ideas, I'd stumbled back to the

cottage, wild with the night, my hair tangled, my hands scraped from when I had fallen in the dark.

That was when Shoe had sat me down, taken my hand, and gently reminded me about the curse that hung over me. The boundary protected us, he said. If I ventured beyond it, neither of us would be safe.

Safe from what, I didn't ask, and Shoe didn't say, but after that night, I didn't stray again.

"The dead man wasn't outside the boundary," I told Shoe.

He stared. "Where?" he asked faintly.

"The path to the village," I answered, "but well inside our valley. Before the turnoff to the oak grove."

One of the things I loved most about Shoe was the way I could always tell what he was thinking—his face reflected his every thought. But I'd never seen him look like this before. He went deathly pale, and closed his eyes as if he'd taken a blow.

Now I steadied him with a hand on his arm. "Shoe?" I had a tendency to fill up silences with words, but I swallowed down my chatter.

He shuddered and opened his eyes. They were a faded green, and shadowed by bristly gray brows. "The boundary has been broken," he said blankly. Then he seemed to see me again. "Rosie." He took a shaky step.

"You need to sit down. We should . . ." I looked wildly around. "We should go inside. Yes."

Feeling shaky myself, I let Shoe lean against me as

I guided him up the path from the garden to the cottage. Inside, I helped him take off his coat and sit on his rocking chair by the hearth, and added wood to the fire and checked the iron kettle. It was empty, so I hurried out to the well for water.

When I came back in, lugging the kettle, Shoe's face looked gray, and he sat with his head tipped back, eyes closed. He whispered something and put his hand over his heart.

My own heart trembled. "What should I do?" I blurted. With shaking hands I hung the kettle on its hook and swung it over the fire. "I'll make tea," I said to myself. "Oh, and a blanket." I hurried to Shoe's tiny room and pulled the red woolen blanket from his bed. Returning to the main room, I crouched before Shoe's chair and laid the blanket over his legs.

At last he opened his eyes. "Rosie," he said faintly.

I took his hand. It felt icy cold, and I brought it to my cheek. "Shoe, what's the matter? Is something terrible going to happen?"

"It already has," he said sadly. He closed his eyes. "I've told you . . ." He paused to take a breath. "About how the boundary was made."

"The Penwitch," I breathed.

Without opening his eyes, he nodded. "She created it, and it is tied to her. If it's broken it means that she is . . ."

It meant she was *dead*. I didn't want to say it out loud.

From the time I was a tiny girl, Shoe had told me stories

about the Penwitch, how brave she was, and powerful, and how she was always fighting to prevent some great evil from arising. He told stories about the Penwitch's friends Templeton and Zel, too, and the faraway kingdoms of the world, and the City. I still remembered the first time he'd told me how the Penwitch had brought me to him.

"A story is shaped by the one who tells it, Rosie," Shoe had begun. "The teller chooses where to begin, what to leave out and what to leave in, and where to end. Every time we tell a story, it is different." He gazed into the fire, musing aloud. "We have a kind of power, we storytellers. I wonder if it is enough . . ." He trailed off, then took a steadying breath. "We just have to be sure we're living our own stories, Rosie, and not ones laid down for us by . . . well, by something else."

"Do you have a story, Shoe?" I'd asked, leaning my head against his knee. His gnarled hand had stroked my hair.

"Yes," he'd answered after a pause. "But it's too long to tell you tonight."

"Because you're old," I'd said, with the wisdom of an eight-year-old child. "What about me? Do I have a story?"

"Everyone has a story," he'd answered. He'd gazed down at me, his face wrinkled and kind in the light from the flickering fire. "Maybe yours began when you were brought here."

It hadn't occurred to me that I'd ever lived anywhere but with Shoe in our valley. "Tell me!" I pleaded. When he didn't speak, I prompted him. "Once upon a time . . ."

Shoe picked up the thread of the story. "It was a dark

night, and the old man—"

"You," I interrupted.

"The old man," he continued with a nod, "who wasn't quite so old in those days, was working by candlelight on a pair of new boots, when a knock came at the cottage door. In stepped the Penwitch, rain-soaked and wild and holding a tiny baby wrapped in a blanket."

"Me?" I'd asked.

"You," Shoe confirmed.

"Where did I come from?" I asked.

"She didn't say. Out in the world somewhere."

This was new to me too. Before that I hadn't realized there was more to the world than our valley, and the forest beyond it.

"'She is under a curse,' is what the Penwitch said," Shoe went on. "She handed the baby to the old man. 'Guard her well,' she said. And then she used her magic to set the boundary around the valley."

"And then what happened?" I asked. In stories, something always happened next.

But not this time. "I think maybe that was just a prologue, Rosie," Shoe said, smiling down at me again. "The rest of your story hasn't really begun yet."

The Penwitch had returned a few times when I was still a baby, but had always been called away. She had been away for many years, though some of the letters Shoe brought home after his visits to the village were from her, I guessed.

But I had never fully realized it before. Shoe had *loved* the Penwitch. I could see it in the hunch of his shoulders and the pallor of his skin. For all that time he had loved her. And now she was gone.

At the hearth, the kettle boiled. Scrambling to my feet, I fetched the teapot from its shelf and brewed some tea, adding honey and bringing a steaming mug to Shoe. Carefully I took his cold hands and wrapped them around the cup. His eyes flickered open. He sighed. "You're a good girl, Rosie."

"If I am it's because you raised me to be good," I told him. "Will you drink some tea?"

He didn't answer. His face seemed set in deeper lines, weary and old.

"I put some honey in, just as you like it," I went on. "Or would you rather have some goat's milk?" Then Shoe's hands went limp, and the mug of hot tea tipped. Before it could spill, I caught it, and set it on the floor. I knelt and took his hand, gazing up into his clouded eyes. "What can I do for you, Shoe?" My heart was pounding now; he wasn't just stunned, he was really sick.

His hand moved. "I'll do better in bed," he said at last, his voice a whisper.

"Yes, yes, I can help with that." I jumped to my feet. "Just wait a moment, and I'll help." Feeling almost frantic, I went to Shoe's room and turned down his sheets and plumped his pillow, and then hurried back to him, to unlace his boots and take them off. "Lean on me," I urged, and he did, so heavily that I stumbled under his weight as we trudged into his room. He almost fell into his bed. I helped him lie down and pulled up the sheet and fetched his blanket from the floor by the rocking chair, tucking it gently around him.

"Is there anything else?" I asked, clenching my hands together. "What can I do?"

When he spoke, his voice was a whisper. "I'll sleep for a while, Rosie. It'll be all right." Then he gave a deep sigh.

I backed out of the room and closed the door softly. "It'll be all right," I repeated to myself. "It'll be all right." I felt twitchy with the need to do something. It was late afternoon; the setting sun shone in the open front door. "I'll make some dinner," I decided. "Maybe he'll feel better after something to eat."

We had a few mouse-ear mushrooms left, dried ones, and some carrots and sage from the garden, so I made soup. Leaving it to simmer, I went out and put away the shovel we'd left in the garden and brought in the goats from their tether and collected the eggs and fetched more water. By the time my chores were done the sun had gone down behind the sharp spires of the pines to the west, and their shadows had fallen across the clearing.

He would be fine, I convinced myself. Shoe'd had a shock, but he would be well in the morning. Then we'd figure out what to do about the boundary, and the dead man on the path.

* * *

BEFORE BANKING THE fire and going to bed I checked on Shoe, but he was deeply asleep, so I climbed the ladder to the cottage's attic. The ceiling of my room was slanted and low; I had to crouch while undressing and then slid under my patchwork quilt, where I lay for a long time staring into the dark and worrying about Shoe.

In the morning I put on my dress, buttoning it with shaking fingers, and climbed down to the main room. The board floor felt cold under my bare feet as I padded to Shoe's room and peered in.

He hadn't moved. His face looked even more gray, his eyes sunken, his hands bony where they rested on the blanket.

"Shoe?" I whispered. Tiptoeing in, I knelt by the bed and took his hand. It was cool, the skin papery and thin.

His eyes flickered open. "Pin?" he breathed.

"No, it's me." Who was Pin? Did he mean the Penwitch? "It's Rosie."

He turned his head and gazed at me. "They're coming, Pin," he said faintly.

"Who?" I asked. "Who's coming?"

"The trackers," he answered, and looked away, and as if he saw something that I couldn't, a spasm of fright crossed his face. "No, I already told you," he muttered, and his hand gripped mine. "I'm staying with you."

"Oh, Shoe." I gulped down a sob.

"Not without you, Pin," he whispered.

My heart shivered in my chest. He was far, far away from me. I didn't know what to do to bring him back.

There was only one thing I could think of. "Merry." The healer from the village. "She'll be able to help you. All right?"

He didn't answer. His eyes dropped closed and he gave a rattling sigh. I held my own breath until he breathed again.

"All right, all right," I babbled as I got to my feet and patted his hand once more, and then hurried from his room. Quickly I laced up my boots and flung myself out the cottage's front door, almost falling as I jumped from the front step and ran across the clearing and into the forest, panting, my unbraided hair tangling as I ran.

The pine trees were just a blur as I hurried along, and the ferns, and the moss; the path was slick with fallen pine needles. When I reached the clearing where the dead man lay I didn't even pause. As I ran past, the vultures rose from the body, more of them now, shedding black feathers as they flapped away. They would circle the clearing and then settle again, I knew, as soon as I was gone. Not far past that was the edge of our valley, the broken boundary of my world, where the oak trees grew, and I didn't pause there, either. My lungs gasped for air; the muscles in my legs burned; a stitch stabbed my side, but I ran on.

At last the path widened and—panting, my eyes blurred with tears—I reached the village. The trees thinned. Ahead was a cluster of low houses built of logs and roofed with moss-covered wooden shingles. I smelled smoke from the hearths and animal dung and fresh bread baking. A stone wall appeared next to the road, and horses—I knew what they were, though I'd never seen one before—shied as I ran past. At one low cottage a white-haired old man stood in a doorway and stared at me as I staggered to a halt. "Merry," I gasped. "The healer. Where does she live?"

The man pointed, his eyes round. "End of the path," he said.

With a nod of thanks, I raced away.

Merry's cottage sat at the edge of the village where it met the forest; heavy oak branches encircled it like protecting arms, and rested on its mossy roof. I stumbled up to the front door and pounded on it until it rattled in its frame.

A muffled voice shouted something from within.

"Hurry, hurry, hurry," I gasped, and knocked again.

The door was flung open. An old woman, as plump and fluffy as an owl, stood on the doorstep scowling up at me. Then she blinked her bright-button eyes and carefully looked me up and down. "My goodness," she said in a high, piping voice. "Look at you."

"I'm—" I caught my breath, and realized how desperate I must look to her. With shaking hands I brushed strands of hair out of my face. "I'm Rosie," I explained. "From up in the valley." I pointed, vaguely in the right direction. "I'm Shoe's . . ." Shoe's what? Not his daughter. Not his grand-daughter. "Shoe is my guardian."

Her gaze sharpened. "Yes, I can see very well who you

are," she chirped. "What do you want with me?"

"He's sick," I explained. "Shoe is, and I don't know what to do. He's just lying there in his bed and he looks sort of gray and sick, and I'm here because . . . because I hoped you could help. Will you come?"

While I'd been babbling, Merry had frowned, and now she pressed her lips together and nodded sharply. "Come inside," she said, and opened the door wider, and I stepped into her cottage. It was dimly lit and crowded, the ceiling low, just over my head, and hanging from it were many strings of dried herbs; against one wall was a row of shelves crowded with stoppered bottles and cloth bags and pottery bowls. It smelled of the wood fire in the hearth and of something green and springlike, and musty, an old-lady smell.

"Has he been ill for long?" she asked, and bobbed to a counter that was set against one wall, where she climbed onto a stool and started pulling things from the shelves.

"No," I answered, and smoothed my hands over the blue wool of my skirt, trying to compose myself. "No, it came over him suddenly. I think—" I gulped. How much did Merry know about Shoe, and about me? Enough, I guessed, and the Penwitch must have passed through the village when she'd visited Shoe. "He's had a shock. I think the Penwitch might be dead."

At the counter, Merry froze, then glanced over her shoulder at me. "Ah." Her eyebrows lowered. "It's his heart, then." She turned back to the counter. On tiptoe, she reached for a bottle on the highest shelf.

Quickly I stepped closer and reached over her head, seizing the cobweb-covered bottle and setting it on the counter before her. "Are you making some medicine for him?"

"Hush" was her only answer. She opened a bag, took out a pinch of a yellow powder, and sniffed it; with a nod she dropped it into a heavy stone mortar.

Nervous and worried, I paced to the hearth on the other side of the room and back again. My legs were still shaking from the long run from our valley. "Do you think he'll be all right?"

"I don't know," Merry answered crossly, and added a few drops from a bottle to her concoction, then dumped more herbs into the mortar. "I haven't seen him yet, have I?" She picked up a stone pestle and started grinding. After adding more of a pungent-smelling liquid, she tipped the contents of the mortar into a bottle and stoppered it. "Hold this," she said, handing it to me, and she clambered off the stool, then wrapped herself in a red-striped shawl. Muttering, she put the bottle and a few more things into a wooden box with a handle, then latched it and gave it to me to carry.

I followed her from the cottage and onto a narrow, rutted path that encircled the village. We saw no one except for a man leading a cow by a halter, who stared as we passed him. When we reached the path that led to our valley, my feet felt twitchy, wanting to run all the way back to Shoe, but I stayed so I could show Merry the way. She went along at a surprisingly fast pace. At the place where the boundary had been, Merry paused and looked around. I opened my mouth to ask her another question, but she scowled. "Shush. I have to think."

At the dead-man clearing, Merry stopped and stared as the vultures flew up, then picked up the basket I'd dropped the day before and handed it to me. Giving one of her brisk nods, she continued up the path. With an effort, I kept quiet as she'd asked. She was puffing, her steps slowing, as we reached our clearing. From the shed I could hear the goats fretting that they hadn't been milked and let out in the morning, and neither had the chickens. They'd have to wait a bit longer.

I went up the front step and clattered across the porch, opening the door for Merry; then my impatience got the better of me and I set down the basket, hurried to Shoe's room, opened the door, and stumbled over to his bed.

The skin of his face was still gray, and loose over his high cheekbones; his eyes stayed closed. "Shoe?" I whispered, and took his hand.

I heard the patter of Merry's footsteps, and she elbowed me aside. "Don't crowd me," she said sharply when I peered over her shoulder. She pointed. "Give me my box, fetch me a stool, and then go stand over there, by the wall."

Words bubbled in my throat—*Can you help him?*—but I swallowed them down again and did as she'd ordered.

With excruciating slowness, she unwrapped her shawl, set it aside, and started examining Shoe. She studied his hand, peering at his fingernails; she pried open one of his eyes; she groped under the blanket to feel his feet. From the box she pulled a hollow wooden cone, rested it on his chest, and put her ear to it.

"What—" I started.

She held up her hand to silence me. Her face settling into grim lines, she straightened and put the cone away. "His heart was broken long ago," she said with a sigh. "He's only just dying of it now."

Dying. The word hit me like a blow to the stomach. I dropped to my knees next to the bed and rested my head against Shoe's arm.

"There is nothing I can do for him," Merry said. Her voice sharpened again. "You understand?"

Without raising my head, I nodded. Tears overflowed from my eyes, and I gasped, trying not to make any sound. I heard the hinges of Merry's box creak as she closed it, and a rustle as she picked up her shawl and went quietly out of the room.

I choked back another sob. My whole body was shaking at the thought of losing Shoe. He had been fine yesterday. *Fine.* His blanket was becoming wet with my tears.

Then I felt a hand rest on my head. I looked up, sniffling, my hair sticking to my damp cheeks.

His eyes were open.

"Sh-shoe," I said in a broken voice.

His face softened, almost a smile. With a trembling hand,

he brushed the tangled hair from my face. His lips moved. "Rosie," he breathed.

Swallowing down sobs, I nodded and gasped. "I'm right here." I tried to hold back my next words, but they spilled out of me. "Please don't die, Shoe. I don't know what I'll do without you. Please be all right."

His hand moved to mine, then turned it over; his fingers brushed the birthmark on the inside of my wrist. "Rose," he said again.

"Yes, it's my rose." I pulled back the sleeve of my dress. The birthmark was blush-pink against the pale skin of my wrist, the shape of a petaled rose just about to bloom.

"You are . . . ," he started. His face sagged and his lips moved, but no words came out.

"I'm cursed," I finished for him. "I know that's what my rose means." Another sob threatened, and I choked it back. "I'll stay here, and the curse won't rise, and it'll be all right, don't worry."

His head moved on the pillow. *No*, it meant. His lips moved again and I leaned closer to hear. "You can't . . ." He took a rasping breath. "Boundary. They will . . . find . . . you."

"Who?" I asked desperately. "Who will find me?"

"The spindle . . . ," he whispered. "Be careful. Can't stay here." His eyes dropped shut.

"Where should I go?" More tears spilled from my eyes.

A few more rattling breaths, and he spoke again, his voice just a thread. "Rosie. Tell me a . . ."

"A story," I sniffled. "I can do that. You just listen, Shoe, all right?"

He gave me the faintest nod, his eyes still closed.

Every night from the time I'd been a tiny girl, Shoe and I had settled by the hearth, him in his rocking chair with a cup of tea, me on a pillow at his feet, leaning my head against his leg, and he had told me a story. Sometimes his stories were about people he knew, and sometimes ones he made up. When I was old enough, I started telling the stories, too. And he had told me *about* stories, about how we needed them, how they worked, how they made our lives make sense. And how they had power.

But he'd never told me his own story.

With my palms I scrubbed the tears from my eyes. Carefully I took his gnarled hand in mine. "Once upon a time," I whispered. The beginning words, the words that, like a magic spell, unlocked all stories. "There was a young man named Shoe. He was a shoemaker, which makes sense, given his name. He had green eyes and he was very handsome, but even more than that, he was kind." I really knew nothing about Shoe's life before the Penwitch had brought me to him. I should have demanded that story, I realized. I'd thought he'd have time to tell it to me, but now it was too late.

"One day," I went on, trying to steady my voice, "he met a girl called the Penwitch. She was bold and . . . and she could do magic, and she had . . ." I closed my eyes, trying to imagine the Penwitch. "She dressed all in black, and her hair was black, too, and she looked, perhaps, a bit frightening to most people, but Shoe loved her. Not immediately, of course, but over time, and she could hardly help but fall in love with Shoe, too."

Lowering my head, I rested it against Shoe's shoulder. "You and the Penwitch had a story together, didn't you? Some kind of adventure?" I whispered. "Something terrible, and also wonderful. And after it you lived happily together? Maybe you even had children, and you were a family. But not forever." No, there was no ever-after. Shoe had taught me that. Even if the adventure ended, the story went on.

"Maybe . . ." More tears welled up in my eyes. "Maybe Pen had to go off to fight again, using her magic. You missed her desperately, Shoe, and she missed you, but she was needed elsewhere. So she went, and you stayed here with me, because my story was only just beginning."

Just over sixteen years ago, the Penwitch had brought him a baby with a rose birthmark on her wrist and a curse hanging over her. And the Penwitch had gone away again. "But she always loved you, Shoe, and you loved her. That never ended." I sighed. After my frantic run down to the village, I was weary. I closed my eyes, just for a moment. There in the darkness I imagined a young Shoe and a sharp-eyed Penwitch standing together, then leaning closer for a kiss.

When I opened my eyes again, I was alone in the room.

CHAPTER

2

Griff leaned against a brick wall, keeping to the alley's shadows, and surveyed the run-down tavern. It was rumored the Breakers had been gathering there in secret to tell their twisted stories—stories that, when repeated, would threaten the governance of the City's Lord Protector and give strength to the City's most dire enemy.

"What d'you think, junior?" Quirk asked, from behind him.

Griff gave a one-shouldered shrug. It could go hard; or it could go easy.

"You hear that, lads?" Quirk asked. "Our loquacious colleague has spoken. Be ready."

Turning, Griff looked down at Quirk. His partner was almost twice his own age, but half his height, and, like his name, quirked. His face was lopsided, one eye all a-squint; his nose had a bend to the left where someone had hit him long ago, and he had a gap between his front teeth. His eyes were green, and his thick thatch of hair was straw-yellow. Like Griff, Quirk was dressed in the sober gray uniform of the City Watchers, but Quirk's had a simple stripe on one sleeve, an indication of his higher rank.

"Who are you talking to?" Griff asked him.

"The lads," Quirk said, flexing his short arms. When Griff shook his head, not understanding, Quirk blew out an impatient sigh. "My *muscles*. I've named them." He paused and looked at Griff expectantly.

Griff turned to keep an eye on the tavern. "What have you named them?"

Quirk stepped up beside him. "This one is *the Hammer*," he said, flexing his right bicep. "And the other is *the Anvil*."

Griff nodded, only half listening. Their orders were simply to make an appearance at the tavern, as a deterrent and a reminder that the Watchers were always, well, watching. He didn't expect any trouble, but the Breakers weren't always rational, especially in their dealings with those who enforced the City's laws.

A lantern hung by the tavern's front door, and light gleamed in its grimy windows; the cobblestoned street before it was slick with the day's rain. A few people hurried past, their shoulders hunched against a chilly wind, heads lowered, going home late from a factory shift, or carrying packages of food they'd waited in hours-long lines to obtain. Griff noted them, but focused on the tavern. It had, he guessed, a back door, an easy exit into the winding alleys of that part of the City, a way for any of the Breakers to enter without being observed. A perfect meeting place, really.

"You ready?" Quirk asked. Straightening, Griff checked the long knife sheathed at his back, gave Quirk a nod, and together they set across the street, opened the tavern door, and went in. As he'd been trained, Griff surveyed the room in one glance. At some subtle signal that he didn't catch, a plainly dressed woman got up from a table and edged out the back door. He tensed. "Go after her?" he asked quietly.

"No," Quirk answered. "Just observe."

Griff nodded and tried to relax. He stepped up to the bar that stretched across one end of the room; the rest of the tavern was crowded with rickety tables and benches, the ceiling smoke-stained, the floor sticky with spilled drinks. It smelled of sweat and sour beer and the smoke from the hearth, and was busy with workers just off a shift, all sullen and silent. With a nod, he greeted the tavern keeper.

She looked them up and down, then scowled. "Watchers."

"We don't want any trouble," Griff said quietly.

The keeper folded burly arms. "Oh, sure you don't." She pointed at the row of bottles on a shelf behind her. "An' if you're going to take up space here, you'd best order something."

Griff nodded. "All right." Turning to keep an eye on the

room, he rested an elbow on the sticky surface of the bar. "What've you got to drink?"

"Gin," she answered. "Small beer, cider."

All of it watered down, Griff knew, and foul-tasting. "Two ciders, then," he said.

With a nod, the keeper turned away to get the drinks. When she turned back, Griff held out two of the wooden tokens that the Watchers used as currency. Seeing them, the keeper's scowl deepened, but she didn't protest, just set two mugs of cider on the bar, and took the tokens.

Griff handed one of the drinks down to Quirk.

"She probably spit in this," Quirk grumbled, examining his mug.

"Maybe," Griff answered, taking a sip. Ugh, it was foul stuff, more vinegar than cider. Quirk said something else, but Griff ignored him; his ears were listening to the low talking between the men and women sitting at the tables. Absently, he nodded to Quirk and took another sip of his drink.

In the shadows at the back of the room, a burly man caught the eye of a young woman and gave a tiny nod; she stood up from her bench and made for the back exit. She had on a knee-length coat, but beneath it, Griff caught a look at a long, slim shape: a sheathed sword.

Griff let her get out the door, then he set down his drink. "I think we should go after this one, Quirk."

"Oh, all right," Quirk said with a sigh, and stood on tiptoe to put his mug of cider on the bar.

As they headed for the back door, the burly man, who wore the gray overalls of a foundry worker, pushed back his chair and stood up, blocking their way. Griff tensed, his fingers itching to reach for his knife. But a fight here was not what he was after. "Let us pass," he said evenly.

The worker glared at Griff from under one bushy eyebrow. "Stinkin' Watchers stinkin' up the place," he slurred. Griff stepped to the side to go around him, and the man followed. "Scum," he repeated, and loomed with rather convincing menace.

His breath, Griff noted, did not smell of alcohol; he was not as drunk as he was pretending. *"The Hammer,* Quirk, if you've got it handy?" Griff suggested.

"Better not, junior," Quirk answered.

But Griff was determined not to let the young woman with the sword get away, or at least to get a better look at her, or trail her to wherever she was going. As the worker made a fist and took a ponderous swing at him, Griff ducked it, elbowed the man in the gut, and made for the exit. He was almost at the door when the man roared and made a grab for him, catching his arm and starting to drag him back into the tavern.

Quirk shrugged, drawing his truncheon from his belt. "Off you go then." He stepped up and kicked the big man in the shin, following it with a punch to the groin. The man howled and let Griff go.

With a nod of thanks, Griff squeezed past the doubled-over man and made it to the tavern's back door. Quirk enjoyed knocking heads together; despite his small size, he'd have no trouble handling the tavern.

The door opened onto a dark alley choked with old beer barrels, broken bottles, and trash. The air was heavy with the stink of a privy. The woman was gone. Griff paused, listening, and caught the faint sound of receding footsteps. Silently he followed, avoiding a pothole full of muddy water, staying to the darkest shadows. Picking up speed, he trailed the footsteps around more corners and down a winding, deserted street that led to the river, and over one of the bridges that had, many years ago, been airy and beautiful and was now stained with soot and missing its elegant stone filigree. As the woman he was following passed a lighted window, Griff got a better look at her; she was wearing a hooded sweater under her coat and finer boots than a patron of that tavern could afford. That alone was suspicious.

As if sensing a presence behind her, the woman paused and cocked her head, listening. Griff froze. More slowly, the woman went on; after a moment, Griff followed, all his senses alert. Abruptly she went around a corner. Quickening his steps, Griff made the same turn, finding himself in an ill-lit, narrow alley blocked at its other end with a rusted iron gate. A trap. Before he could reach for his sheathed knife, the woman was on him, slamming him into a brick wall. Instinctively, Griff ducked and heard the hiss of her sword passing through the air over his head and clanging into the wall. Lowering his shoulder, he plowed into the woman, sending

BERLIN-PECK ○ BERLIN, CT

them both staggering across the alley until they crashed into the opposite wall. As Griff recovered his footing on the slippery cobblestones, he drew his knife.

"Bouchet," the young woman shouted, her voice urgent. "Here!"

Griff whirled as the burly man entered the alley; he saw the glint of a knife being drawn. Sensing movement behind him, he twisted aside and felt a line of fire along his ribs, the woman's sword. Without hesitating, ignoring the pain of the cut, he reversed his grip on his own knife and struck, feeling a solid *thunk* as the hilt connected with her jaw; she grunted and staggered back. Griff faced the man, flipping his knife back to block the man's sword thrust; he flowed into his next move, a blow aimed at the man's head. With surprising speed, the big man ducked and turned, and had Griff cornered, his back to the rusty gate.

Panting, they faced each other. The big man's face was in shadow; his shoulders were so wide he almost filled the alley.

"He got a good look at me," the young woman said in a muffled voice.

"Right," the big man said. "I'll do him, then."

Griff tensed. He'd been holding back, assessing the fighting ability of his opponents, but if they were willing to kill, he would be ready for them.

From the street came the sound of running feet, then Quirk's hoarse voice. "Hammer, this way! Come on, Anvil!" He appeared at the mouth of the alley, a short, dark shadow.

At the same moment, the woman lunged past the big man, striking at Griff with her sword. Griff blocked it easily.

"Here now," Quirk panted as he started toward them. "Asking for trouble, killing a Watcher."

The big man turned, staring down at Quirk. A subtle signal seemed to pass between them, and the man gave a huff of annoyance. "Right." Grabbing the young woman's arm, he dragged her past Quirk and out of the alley, and they raced away down the street, their footsteps echoing from the dark buildings.

Griff gripped his knife. "We should go after them."

"No," Quirk ordered, and reached up to put a restraining hand on Griff's arm. "We were only supposed to observe, remember? Would you recognize them if you saw them again?"

"Maybe," Griff answered. Carefully he resheathed his knife, wincing as the movement pulled at the cut across his ribs.

"Hm." Quirk eyed him. "You all right, junior?"

"Fine." Griff could feel blood seeping into his uniform. Not much blood, though; it wasn't serious. "The shorter one, the woman, had a sword."

"I suppose we'd better report it," Quirk said morosely. He knew the implications of the sword. Weapons—except for Watchers' knives—were illegal in the City; a sword would be very difficult to obtain, and the woman had clearly known how to use it.

Griff gave a grim nod, and they started up the dark street that led toward the citadel. Hearing Quirk's resigned sigh, he added, "I'll take care of it, if you like."

"Good lad," Quirk said, relieved. They walked in silence through the darkened streets of the City until the wall of the citadel loomed up before them. Long ago, it had been a castle with four graceful spires and a central tower. Since then the spires had been lopped off, leaving a squat, ugly stone building that served as the City's center of government, and the headquarters of its Watchers.

Going through the gate, they nodded to the Watchers on guard. "I'll save you some dinner," Quirk said as he headed for the barracks.

Without answering, Griff crossed a courtyard and went into a side door of the citadel, then up a narrow, poorly lit stairway to a stone-paved hall that ended in a double door. Two Watchers, the Lord Protector's personal guard, were leaning against the wall beside the door; at Griff's approach, one nudged the other and they straightened. On the left was a sly, harsh-faced, black-haired woman named Taira; the other was a smoothly good-looking man named Luth. They were both tall and well muscled.

Luth folded his arms and leaned against the door, blocking it. "Oh, look who it is," he sneered.

"Hello there, pretty boy," Taira said, pressing close to Griff.

There was no point in engaging with them; Griff tried

to lean past Luth to knock at the door, but the bigger man grabbed his arm. "Oh, look. The junior's been in a scuffle."

"Ooh." Taira poked at Griff's side, right over the sword cut, then inspected her finger. "Blood, even!"

"You know," Luth drawled. "I've been thinking." He leaned closer; Taira gripped his arm, and Griff held himself still. "I've been thinking," he repeated, "about requesting your transfer into my cohort." His cold eyes raked over Griff. "We would have so much to teach you, don't you agree, Taira?"

She smiled nastily. "Oh, I do."

"I am sure," Luth went on, "that the Lord Protector could be brought to see the merit in such an assignment."

He probably could. Griff gritted his teeth against a cold surge of fear. In addition to guarding the Lord Protector, Luth's cohort served as the wardens of the prison cells on the lowest underground level of the citadel. Prisoners tended to disappear into those cells and were never seen again; the Watchers who guarded them were a secretive group with a reputation for viciousness. The Lord Protector seemed to think Luth's cohort was necessary; Griff just tried to avoid them.

"What do you think, junior?" Luth asked. "Afraid to get your hands bloody?"

Griff jerked his arm out of Taira's grip and managed to knock on the door.

"Come," answered a deep voice from within.

Luth gave him a venomous look and stepped aside.

Steeling himself, Griff entered.

The Lord Protector was sitting at his desk, reading some papers; at Griff's entrance he didn't look up. He was an angular man with hooded eyes and a fringe of gray beard along his jawline; he was dressed in a gray uniform similar to the one that Griff wore, with no indication of his rank. With bony, ink-stained fingers he turned over a page and continued reading; after a few minutes, he picked up a pen, dipped it in an inkpot, and started writing.

Griff stood quietly, waiting. The tension from his confrontation with Luth and Taira ebbed. His stomach growled, not loud enough, he hoped, for the man at the desk to hear it. Much longer, and he'd miss dinner entirely. The sword cut along his ribs stung; the blood had congealed, and the cloth of his uniform was stuck to it, pulling with every breath he took.

The room was bare of all ornamentation, the desk a plain square, the walls plain stone, no rug on the floor. Despite the growing chill of the night, the hearth was empty, swept clean of ash.

At last the Lord Protector set down his pen, picked up a handkerchief, and began to methodically wipe his fingers. He glanced up. "Report."

Griff outlined what had happened at the tavern, and the chase that had ensued, including every detail. As he spoke, the Lord Protector finished cleaning his fingers, then sat listening, his hands folded neatly on the desk before him.

"Analysis," he ordered. "They were Breakers? Spreading their seditious stories?"

Griff considered the sullen silence that had fallen when he and Quirk had entered the tavern, the sense that its patrons had been leaning toward one part of the room, their ears open, listening. The young woman with the sword—she would have been the one speaking. But he hadn't heard anything specific, no betraying words. "I suspect they were Breakers," he said slowly.

The Lord Protector frowned. "Your response lacks precision. I expect clearer reports. I require evidence. Continue."

"They're getting better organized," Griff offered. "Now that we've identified their meeting place, they'll change it." He paused to consider his next words. "I'm certain that the young woman was from outside the City."

"You know how unlikely that is."

"Yes," Griff said.

"Hm," muttered the Lord Protector. "Go on."

"The man she called Bouchet was dressed as a worker." Griff gave a slight shake of his head. "But I don't think he was. He was well trained, a kind of bodyguard."

"Two of them in the alley. Could you have taken them?"

Griff knew he could not lie. "Yes."

"Then why didn't you?" The Lord Protector's voice was cold.

"I thought—" Griff started.

"*You* thought?" came the knife-sharp interruption.

"Our orders were to observe," Griff said carefully.

"Mm. And yet you chose to pursue them." The Lord Protector leaned back in his chair and studied Griff during a long silence.

Under that assessing stare, Griff had to control his every breath, his every twitch. The room grew colder, and he tried not to shiver. He kept his mouth shut, too. To attempt to excuse what he'd done would be to invite more criticism. Or make it more likely for Luth to advocate for his transfer into a new cohort.

At last the Lord Protector spoke again. His voice betrayed no concern. "You were injured in the fight."

Griff glanced down at the front of his uniform. The gray wool of the tunic was slashed, and blood had soaked into it. More blood than he'd realized before.

"You should have had that stitched up and bandaged before you reported," the Lord Protector said.

Griff didn't answer. He knew that if he'd visited the infirmary in the barracks first, he would have been chided for not reporting immediately.

The Lord Protector picked up a pen. "A rational report, on the whole," he pronounced, and added a platitude. "Right thinking will prevail over Story." He glanced down at his papers again. "Dismissed."

Stiffly, Griff turned and left the room. After evading Taira and Luth, he made his way to the Watchers' barracks, where Quirk was waiting for him in a nearly deserted, nearly dark dining room. Its stone floors had been swept and lights put out, but Quirk was sitting at the end of a bench at one of the long tables, his short legs dangling. As Griff sat down, Quirk pushed a half-full bowl across the table to him. "All right?" he asked.

Griff hesitated, considering whether to tell Quirk about Luth's threat. No point, really. "All right," he confirmed, and sniffed at the bowl. Fish soup. He picked up the spoon and took a bite. Cold, and made from lentils, moldy potatoes, and the bottom-feeders from the river that were more mud than fish.

"Let me guess," Quirk said, handing him half a piece of stale bread. "The Lord Protector saw that you'd been injured and asked if you were well."

Griff dipped the bread into the soup and took a bite. "You know he didn't."

Quirk shook his head, as if disgusted.

The Lord Protector, Griff knew very well, was a true believer in his mission to keep them free of Story, which once fifty years ago, and again more recently, had come so close to destroying the City and all who lived in it. He was incorruptible and absolutely committed to his purpose. "He's a rational man," Griff tried to explain.

"And a hard one," Quirk shot back.

Yes. His father was a hard man. Griff had known that for a very long time.

CHAPTER
3

WHEN I CAME OUT OF SHOE'S ROOM, THE HEALER, MERRY, was sitting in the rocking chair. A fresh fire was burning in the hearth, and a bucket of goat milk was sitting on the table next to her wooden box.

"He's gone?" Merry asked.

Wordless, I nodded.

"Hmm." Her face set in a frown, Merry looked me up and down again. What did she see? I knew, vaguely, that I had wavy blond hair and blue eyes that were swollen from all of my tears, but I'd never seen an image of myself in a mirror. Whatever she saw, she didn't approve. "I suppose you can't help it," she muttered.

"Help what?" I asked. My voice was hoarse from crying.

She shrugged and waved a hand as she got out of the

rocking chair. "Well, I'd better be off home," she said. "I'll send some men with shovels from the village to take care of that for you." She pointed with her chin at Shoe's door.

Burying, she meant. At the thought Shoe's body being put into the ground, my well of tears overflowed again.

"He said . . . ," I sobbed. "Shoe s-said I shouldn't stay here, now that the boundary is broken." He'd said something about a *spindle*, too. A warning? I wasn't sure what a spindle was, or what exactly I should be afraid of.

"*Tcha*," Merry tutted with annoyance. "You'll have to come with me then." She wrapped the shawl about herself. "Go pack up your things. I'll have the men bring the goats and the hens back with them. And they'll deal with that body we passed on the way up here, too."

I could only nod, and cry. I cried while folding my other dress, and choosing my three favorite books, and the three pairs of shoes that Shoe had made for me, and packing them all into the leather knapsack that Shoe had used to carry supplies back from the village.

Still crying, I stumbled after Merry all the way through our valley, and past the dead man, and, at last, onto the dirt road that led through the village. There, she stopped and gave me her shawl to put over my head. "We'll keep you hidden for as long as we can," she muttered, as she pulled a corner of the shawl lower to shadow my tear-stained face. "Come along," she added crossly.

When we arrived at her cottage, she brewed some tea that

made my eyes heavy with sleep. "You can lie down there, for now," she said, pointing to a low bed behind a curtain in the corner of the cottage's one room. "It's my bed, so don't expect to take it for your own."

"I won't," I mumbled, and fell down into a deep pit of sleep and grief.

WHEN I WOKE up I cried all the tears I had left in me, and felt wrung out, like a rag, dry and empty. It was morning, I realized, when I stepped out from behind the curtain and into the dim, cramped main room.

Merry wasn't there, but an animal was. It was small, with black fur and white paws and white-tipped ears, and it was curled on a cushioned chair by the hearth. I stepped closer to see. Without opening its eyes, it flicked its ears, as if telling me to go away.

"Oh," I breathed. "You're a cat, aren't you?" It was so pretty and sleek; I wanted to pick it up and stroke it, but cats, I knew, had claws, too, and could scratch if they didn't like you.

Circling its chair, I went to the door and peered out. Merry had wanted to keep me hidden away. I assumed it was because Shoe had told her that I was under a curse.

At the thought of Shoe, a feeling of desolation swept over me. Opening the door wider, I stepped outside, sat on Merry's doorstep, where no one from the village could see me, and found that I did have some tears left in me after all.

After a while, I gave a shuddering sigh and scolded myself. Shoe would have something to say about all of this weeping. *How can you see your way forward, Rosie, if your eyes are all smudged with tears?*

"You're right, Shoe," I whispered. Wiping my tears away with the hem of my dress, I sat up and looked around. A narrow dirt path led from Merry's cottage, through a gate in a stone wall, and then joined a wider path that led to the village. The air smelled of woodsmoke and animal manure, but I could still smell the fresh pine and fern scent of the forest, too. The houses that I could see were built of logs plastered with some sort of white substance, with small windows and low roofs. Getting to my feet, I walked to the gate to see better. The nearest cottages had little gardens at their backs, and a shed for animals, and had stacks of firewood piled nearly to the eaves. Winter was coming. Shoe and I had been chopping our own firewood, up in our valley.

"Stop it," I told myself, as tears threatened again.

I heard a squeak and a rattle, and looking to the left I saw, on a path leading from the forest, some sort of small horse with long ears pulling a wagon piled with logs. Next to it walked a young man.

I couldn't help it—I stared. He was the first person I'd ever seen who was even close to my own age. He wore a homespun brown shirt and leather trousers and ill-made boots—Shoe could have done better—and he was tall and had a wide, full-lipped mouth, and brown hair cut very short.

When he saw me, he stopped, staring right back at me. His horse—I didn't think it was a horse, really, it was something else—took two more steps and then it stopped, too.

"Who are *you*?" he asked bluntly. He came closer, then, slowly, examined me from head to foot, his gaze lingering on my face.

I wasn't used to being stared at. I crossed my arms over my chest—as if *that* was any protection—and looked down at the ground.

His footsteps crunched on the path, and then he was leaning over the wall, reaching out with a big hand to tip up my chin so he could see me better.

I flinched away from his touch.

"Well, well, well," he said. He spoke with a different accent from Shoe's, and from mine. The same as Merry's, I realized. As if he was speaking through a mouth full of pebbles, all blurred and drawling. "A visitor, are you?"

He was still staring at my face.

I wasn't shy—I'd always wanted to meet more people—but the hungry way he looked at me made me feel strange. Prickly.

"What's your name, you pretty thing?" he asked.

Rosie, I almost said, but that was Shoe's name for me. I didn't want this young man to call me by it. "Rose," I answered.

"You're a pretty one, ain't you, Rose?" he asked, leaning closer.

I was glad for the wall between us. "I—I don't know," I stammered. Was he making fun of me? I knew my eyes must be red from crying, my hair tangled, and my face smudged with tears.

"Oh, you know you are," he said. His mouth twisted into a smile that didn't seem very friendly. "I'm Tom. My da is the blacksmith." He nodded toward the village. "We live just down the—"

He broke off. Coming up the path from the village was Merry, carrying a covered basket and scowling at me. As she came through the gate, she turned her frown on him. "Get along with you, Tom," she said with her usual crossness.

"Been hiding this dainty one away?" he asked, jerking his chin in my direction.

"Tcha" was her only answer, and seizing me by the elbow, she dragged me with her into the cottage, slamming the door behind us. It was dim, the only light coming in through a small window. "I thought I told you to stay inside," she complained, handing me the basket and then lighting a lamp. "Here, make yourself useful and put these away."

The basket was full of food. "I didn't know you meant—" I tried to explain, but she interrupted me with another impatient *tcha*. I unloaded the basket, setting dried apples, a pottery bowl of butter, and a small loaf of bread on the table. I didn't know the proper place for any of it, so she slapped my hands and put it all away herself, on shelves next to the hearth.

I retreated to the window and looked out.

"Get away from there," Merry scolded.

The cat was still curled in the chair, so I crouched next to the hearth. The fire there had gone out, and the ashes were cold and dead. I sighed, feeling rather gray and chilly myself. Shoe had never spoken to me the way Merry did. I didn't know what I'd done to make her so cross.

THE NEXT DAY, Merry set me to dusting the shelves over her work counter and helping her sort through all the boxes and bags and bottles. I tried asking her questions about Shoe and the Penwitch, and about the City, because she seemed to know more about it than I did, but the only answer I got was a glare. For dinner, Merry made potato pancakes with applesauce, which we ate in silence at her small table. That night Merry took her own bed back again, and I slept on the floor by the hearth with the cat's cushion under my head. It was wet with my tears before I managed to fall asleep.

The next morning, there was a knock on the door. Merry went to answer it. Standing on her doorstep was Tom, along with another young man, who craned his neck, trying to peer over Merry's head and into the cottage.

"Can't your pretty visitor come out for a walk around the village?" I heard Tom's deep voice asking.

I jumped up from the hearth, where I'd been trying to pet the cat, who was just as cranky as Merry, putting its ears back and hissing whenever I reached out a hand to it. I was used to being outside for much of the day, working in the garden, or looking after the goats, or rambling around our valley. I hadn't much liked Tom when I'd met him before—something about the way he looked at me made me feel on edge—but Merry's tiny cottage was starting to feel like a locked box, and I was itching to escape from it.

"I'd like a walk," I said, shaking out my skirts. When I had woken up, I'd washed my face and combed and braided my hair, so I hoped Tom wouldn't stare at me as he had before.

Merry had been irritable all day; despite her intention to keep me in, she wanted me out as much as I wanted to go out. "Go, then," she said with a shrug. "But be careful."

It was too soon after losing Shoe for me to smile, but I brightened as I stepped into the brilliantly golden autumn day. The sky overhead was a deep blue, and the air felt clean and brisk as I breathed it in. I knew the village was tiny, but it seemed like an entire new world to explore, full of many new people to meet.

"Oh, you were right, Tom," said the other young man. He was shorter than Tom, and broad, and had thick, wavy black hair and a pockmarked face that was made distinctive by heavy black brows that overshadowed his narrow eyes. "Hello, Rose," he said, giving me a gap-toothed smile. "I'm Marty. You and I are going to be friends, aren't we?"

Friends. I liked the idea—I'd never had friends before—but I didn't smile back. "I suppose so," I answered.

Tom leaned closer and seized my hand, then placed it on

his arm. "Let's have our walk, Rose."

Marty took my other arm, and they led me through the gate and away from Merry's cottage. I glanced over my shoulder to see her standing in the doorway, scowling. Then she shook her head and went back inside.

Tom and Marty showed me around the village—I saw the smithy, and a mill, and a shop that sold everything from needles and thread to salt and sugar. We encountered some other people, but even though I wanted to stop and say hello, they didn't introduce me, they just dragged me on.

"This way," Tom said, and he was looking hungrily at me again. "You'll want to see this." He started pulling me down a path that led toward the forest.

I was starting to feel like the rag doll that Shoe had made for me when I was small. "No, thank you," I said, disengaging my arms from both of them. "I should get back to Merry's cottage. She won't like me to be gone for too long." This wasn't entirely true, but I was feeling less and less certain that I wanted to go along with them.

Tom stepped closer. "What, too good for us, are you?"

I blinked. "No, not at all," I said.

"Give us a kiss, then," Marty said from behind me.

"To show that we're friends," Tom added.

Before I could decide whether I wanted to kiss him or not, he grabbed me by the shoulders, leaned in, and pressed his lips against mine. I tried pulling away, but he gripped me harder.

"Here, give me a turn," Marty complained.

Tom released me. Before Marty could get close, I stepped back. "No," I said, rubbing the back of my hand against my lips, trying to scrub off the feel of the kiss. "No, I don't think so." I kept backing away. "I—I don't think I like either of you very much."

Tom's face twisted into a sneer. "Oh, come on, sweetheart. We like you a lot."

"You're not going to run away, are you?" Marty said, and he started to circle around behind me.

Suddenly I was frightened. As Marty reached out for me, I ducked under his hands and darted past him. Without looking back, I ran along the path, then down the rutted road that led through the village, until I reached Merry's gate. Panting, I went through it, then checked to see if they'd followed. The path was empty. Wearily I trudged to Merry's door. I didn't want to go back into the dark box that was her cottage, but I was starting to realize that I wasn't safe outside her gate.

At dinner she refused to speak to me, and when I tried to explain what had happened, she told me sharply to be quiet. I ate in silence, washed the dishes, and looked around for something else to do. Maybe if I made myself useful, she'd approve of me a bit more.

"I can see to the goats," I offered. Merry was sitting with the cat on her lap, staring into the fire; she didn't answer. Taking up the bucket, I went out the door. While we'd been eating dinner, the sun had set, but there was still enough light to see the gray outlines of the cottage and the little shed behind it. Stepping carefully, I went down the path to the shed.

"I should have brought a light," I muttered to myself. But Merry had only the one lantern.

At the shed, I fumbled for the latch at the door, then pushed it open. Inside, the shed smelled of hay and goat droppings. I stretched out my hand to feel for the goats' stall, and my fingers brushed cloth.

A hand grabbed me from out of the darkness; before I could cry out, another hand clamped over my mouth. I was dragged deeper into the shed and slammed against a wall, and a long, hard body pressed against mine, holding me there. I gasped for breath behind his big, callused hand. He panted loudly in my ear and started to shove his other hand inside the bodice of my dress. I tried to kick him, but his weight and my skirts pinned me against the wall. Frantically, I flailed with my hands, hitting at his face, his chest, yanking at his hair, but he leaned harder, groping at me. Sparks danced before my eyes; I couldn't get enough air.

"Stop," I gasped.

He leaned his full weight against me. "You know you want it," he rasped into my ear.

It was Tom. My *friend*. "No." I pushed at him, but he was too big, too strong. "No, I don't." I didn't know what he meant, but I knew I didn't want it.

He shoved his hips against mine. "You wouldn't look like that if you meant no." He nuzzled his face into my neck.

With a bang, the door to the shed slammed open; a dim light seeped along the walls. "Rose?" cried a querulous voice. Merry.

The only answer I could give was a strangled cry, but it was enough.

Tom grunted, then pressed himself against me again, his stubbled face, his mouth gaping against mine, and then he released me, hurrying from the shed, brushing past Merry, who stood in the doorway with the lantern.

For a moment I leaned against the wall, trying to catch my breath. My mouth felt bruised, scraped raw. My knees shook as the fright echoed through me and then ebbed.

"He was . . . ," I gasped. "He was waiting for me."

"You arranged to meet him," Merry corrected. She muttered something else.

"No!" I shook my head. "No, I didn't." Taking a shaky breath, I straightened my dress. The tie at the end of my braid had come off, and my hair straggled over my shoulders.

"Liar," Merry said. In the meager lantern light, her face was deeply shadowed and scornful.

"No," I said again, hopelessly. "What did he want? What was he trying to do to me?"

Merry huffed out an impatient breath. "Do you know anything about the world? Did Shoe explain nothing to you?"

At the thought of Shoe, all of my sorrow welled up again. Tears rolled down my face. Wordlessly, I shook my head.

"What a nuisance. Well, you'd better come along inside," she said begrudgingly.

In the cottage, she sat me down and made tea, and explained about what men wanted from women—and women from men, too. "It's supposed to be loving," she said. "But it isn't always."

I thought I understood—I'd read enough stories to know how people fell in love. "But why me?" I asked. "He said— Tom said that I looked like I wanted him to—to do that to me, but I didn't."

"It's because they've never seen anyone like you," Merry said shortly.

"Someone who is cursed?" I guessed. I knew my rose marked me as cursed, but maybe it showed in other ways, too.

"*Tcha.*" Merry set down her teacup, got up from her chair, and went to her work counter, where she climbed on the stool and took something flat and wrapped in cloth from a shelf. Unwrapping it, she handed it to me. "Look at yourself," she said.

I'd heard stories about mirrors, but I'd never seen one before. Never seen myself, that is. I held it up and looked into it. A young woman looked back at me. Blond, blue-eyed, her lips a little swollen from being kissed so roughly. But there was something strange about her, something different about her face, something that made me unable to look away. "I don't understand," I said slowly.

"You're beautiful, you stupid girl," Merry said, taking the mirror from my hands. "Stunning. Gorgeous. No one around here has ever seen anyone like you. Very likely you're the most beautiful girl in the entire world."

CHAPTER

4

In the gray light before sunup, Griff took out a clean uniform tunic; then, wearing an undershirt, he left the room he shared with nine other Watchers who were just starting to awaken. Quietly he padded down a long hallway past other rooms to the stone stairs that led to the lower level of the barracks, which held officers' larger rooms, the dining hall, and the infirmary. The sword cut had stopped bleeding, but it had bothered him all night, and he hadn't gotten much sleep. In the infirmary, the physician grumpily set aside her morning tea to deal with him.

"Sword?" she asked, as he took off his shirt.

Griff nodded.

"Hmm," the physician murmured, examining him. "Should have come in last night."

"Too late," Griff said briefly.

"Hmph," chided the physician. "Well, it doesn't look like an infection is starting here. You must have a strong constitution." She looked him up and down, noting the other scars on his chest and the long-healed puncture wound on his upper arm. "I've stitched you up before."

Griff nodded. Since he was seven years old he'd trained to become a Watcher, and once he'd become proficient he'd sparred with edged weapons. And he had encountered his share of trouble when on patrol. Injuries were expected.

"You might try being a little more careful." The physician went to a side table, where she prepared a needle with thick black thread. Coming back to Griff, she got to work. Her hands were cold, and she was not at all gentle, so Griff found himself gritting his teeth and staring hard at the bare wall to keep from flinching as she stitched him up. She finished by wrapping what seemed like an acre of bandage around his chest.

"There," she said, tying off the end of the bandage with a jerk. "You're the Lord Protector's son. I suppose that means it's pointless to tell you to skip training today."

Griff didn't bother answering. Stiffly he pulled on his uniform and hurried outside to the training yard that was next to the barracks. Quirk was already there, along with the eight others of his cohort, a mix of men and women, all older than Griff was, and more experienced. The Watchers trained in shifts of six cohorts at a time, the same number that would, after training and breakfast, head out for patrols of the subsections of the City. For the past five years Griff had been a Watcher; about every few months his father reassigned him to a different cohort. Griff figured the Lord Protector did it partly to educate him about the City, but also to keep him from getting too attached to anyone. His time paired with Quirk was almost over, and he dreaded his next assignment. He didn't want to leave Quirk, who was the closest thing to a friend he'd ever had, and he felt fairly certain his next assignment would be with Luth and the prison cohort.

As Griff joined his cohort, nodding to the others, Quirk handed him a weighted practice sword. "Ready?" he asked.

Griff nodded as the other cohorts fell into straight lines. A bored-sounding commander called out the moves, and the Watchers responded, like clockwork. They drilled for an hour. Griff was used to it, but the lack of sleep and his meager dinner the night before left him feeling light-headed, his arms heavy, his footwork slow. Next they ran laps around the edge of the training yard, still carrying their weighted practice weapons.

"Come *on*, junior," jeered one of his cohort, a rangy older man named Stet, who had never approved of Griff's early admittance to the Watchers.

Griff had worked very hard to qualify. He knew that he'd been admitted for what he could do, not because of who his father was, but he'd never convince the rest of the Watchers that being the Lord Protector's son did not give him an unfair advantage. With an effort, he picked up his pace.

After they'd run for twenty minutes, they had another forty minutes of sparring. As usual, Griff was paired with Quirk, who, despite his small size, was one of the best fighters of all the Watchers.

By the end of their session the sun was well up, but the yard was still deep in shadow behind the high walls that surrounded the citadel. After putting away his training blade, Griff leaned against a wall and closed his eyes. With the exercise, the cut over his ribs had opened again; he felt blood seeping into the bandages. The doctor would scold him if he returned to the infirmary to have them replaced.

"Breakfast?" Quirk asked, stumping up to him.

Opening his eyes, Griff straightened. "Definitely."

They headed across the courtyard toward the barracks, and the dining hall.

"D'you ever think," Quirk began, "about strict rationality and austerity, whether it really is the best defense against the rise of Story?"

Griff looked quickly around them to see if anyone had overheard Quirk's words. The other Watchers in their shift had already gone in; they were alone. He glanced down at his colleague. "It's worked so far, hasn't it?"

"I suppose it has," Quirk said musingly. "I just find myself wondering, now and then, what's so bad about stories. They're just stories, after all."

That kind of thinking was dangerous. "Stories that are

told give power to our enemy." Griff lowered his voice. "All stories serve Story."

"So we're told," Quirk said. "We Watchers enforce a rule of strictness, rationality, and silence, all to keep Story from gaining power. But what if we haven't got it right? What if the stories we tell, our *own* stories, have a different kind of power?"

Griff stopped and stared down at Quirk. "But we don't tell stories. Ever."

"Right. I know." He put his hands on his hips and gazed up at Griff. "You've been raised more strictly than anyone in the City. You wouldn't even begin to know how to tell a story, would you?"

Wordless, Griff shook his head.

"There's the irony," Quirk went on. "You're perfectly trained as a fighter, and so am I. But what if we're fighting Story with the wrong weapons?"

Griff found his voice. "Quirk, be careful," he whispered urgently.

"Ah well," Quirk said with a shake of his head. "Just thinking aloud, junior. Don't worry about it." He went on ahead.

Griff stared after him. Quirk's words were alarmingly close to treason. Of *course* he was going to worry about it.

As he caught up to Quirk at the dining hall door, a citadel servant intercepted them. "Message for you from the Lord Protector," he said to Griff. "You're to report to his office."

"Doesn't he have time for breakfast first?" Quirk protested.

"Immediately," said the servant.

Griff knew better than to argue. With a nod to Quirk, he headed for the citadel, then up the stairs and down the hall to the Lord Protector's office. No Watchers stood outside the door, for once. After knocking, he entered.

As usual, the Lord Protector was behind his desk, neatly dressed despite the early hour. He'd probably been at work since before dawn. Near the empty fireplace stood a soberly dressed older woman, with a younger woman flanked by Luth and Taira. The woman's hands were chained behind her back, and a cloth gag was bound across her mouth that prevented her from speaking. As Griff came into the room, the Lord Protector got to his feet. "Ah," he said. "Finally."

There was no point in protesting that he'd come as soon as he'd received his father's message.

The soberly dressed woman studied Griff. "This is him? He will lift the curse from my daughter?"

At the question, Griff's stomach clenched, and he was glad that he hadn't eaten breakfast yet. It had been months since he'd had to break a curse, and he'd thought—no, he'd hoped—he was finally done with that.

Despite what Quirk had been saying, it was the strict and austere practice of rationality, the iron rule of the Lord Protector, and careful patrolling by the Watchers that had, after many years, seemed to squelch any attempt by Story to reestablish itself in the City. One way they could tell that it was trying to rise again was when curses began to fall, at random, on ordinary

City-folk. If their curses weren't lifted, the cursed ones would find themselves entangled in one of Story's plots, at odds with the rational laws that governed the City.

But Griff himself had a special talent, one that the Lord Protector simultaneously abhorred and found very useful. He was a curse eater. Maybe it was because his father was the most rational person in the City, the one least likely to be cursed, and Griff had inherited that resistance to Story. Or maybe there was some other reason. At any rate, Griff could take on another's curse and somehow—he wasn't sure how he did it, exactly—negate it.

But it was never an easy process.

"What—" Griff started, then cleared his throat. "What is her curse?"

"It came on her three days ago," the mother answered. "She awoke in the morning, and flowers fell from her mouth whenever she spoke."

"Flowers?" interrupted the Lord Protector. He seated himself behind his desk again and picked up his pen. "Can you be more specific?"

"Well, yes," the woman answered. "She speaks daffodils when she is happy, marigolds when she is angry, and violets when she is sad." She shifted away from her daughter, as if she might be contaminated just by describing the curse.

"I see," the Lord Protector said, and wrote something in the book that, Griff knew, was filled with notes on Story's devices. Curses were a particular interest of his father's;

it was as if by analyzing every aspect of a curse, he could come to understand Story and how it worked, and thus destroy it forever. The Lord Protector also had notes about objects that were important to Story, things like glass slippers and poisoned apples and magical mirrors. Such items were rarely seen in the City—they were destroyed whenever they appeared. "Go on," Griff's father ordered the woman when he'd finished noting her words about her daughter's curse. "You responded appropriately, I presume?"

"Of course," the woman said primly. "But the house became filled with flowers. We had to start giving them away to the neighbors." She folded her hands before herself and cast her eyes down. "The irrationality of it was starting to be noticed. One of the Watchers who patrols our sector of the City told me to bring her here, and so I did."

Griff looked away, and found himself locking gazes with the gagged young woman. She was a few years older than he was, short, ordinary, with brown hair and mud-brown eyes that were shining with unshed tears. She shook her head, and the tears spilled over, rolling down her cheeks, soaking the gag. She gasped, as if she wanted to speak.

She didn't want to lose the curse. The cursed ones often didn't, Griff had found. Their curses made them special, different, beautiful. Magical. Wonderful.

And wonder had no place in the City. Not anymore.

At the desk, the Lord Protector looked up. "Get on with it," he said impatiently.

Griff knew better than to protest. He nodded.

"We'll hold her for you, junior," Luth said, gripping the young woman's arms tightly.

"The gag should come off, too," Taira said. She ran a fingernail along the girl's jaw, then jerked the gag away.

The girl gulped and gazed up at Griff with beseeching eyes. "Please don't," she whispered. As she spoke, rich purple violets streaked with gold tumbled from her lips, falling to the floor. Luth and Taira stared; the Lord Protector nodded and made a precise notation in his book. The girl's cheeks paled. "I—I promise not to speak," she went on, and the violets' indigo darkened nearly to black, their pollen dusting her lips. "Please don't take the curse from me."

I'm sorry, Griff wanted to say to her. But he couldn't. He had to obey his father's order. As he stepped closer, his feet crushed the violets, and their sweet, green smell filled the room. He raised his hands and rested them on each side of the girl's head. She tried to pull away, but Luth and Taira wrenched her arms back, holding her steady. "Please, please don't," she pleaded as more violets fell.

Griff felt her curse rise under his hands. It retreated, as if trying to evade him, then struck, slamming into him like a wave of darkness. The girl screamed, and ropes of bitter brambles studded with blood-red roses flowed from her mouth, surrounding them, ripping at Griff's hands. Bracing himself against the pain and the darkness, he held on.

The girl screamed again. A last petal fell, and Griff felt the curse fill his own head, a pounding, ripping ache. Letting his hands drop from the girl's head, he stepped back. Released from the curse, she hung limp between the two Watchers who held her, weeping hoarsely. Against the plain gray of the stone floor, the violets were a vivid splash of color.

With shaking, bloody hands, Griff unwrapped the roses that had twined around his arms. The thorns were curved, and wickedly sharp. Ignoring her weeping daughter, the older woman stared at him, her mouth hanging open.

"It is done?" came the Lord Protector's voice from the direction of his desk.

Griff didn't look up. "Yes," he answered, his own voice ragged. His mouth filled with bitterness, and he swallowed it down. Getting free of the last of the roses, he let them drop to the floor.

"That will be all, then," the Lord Protector said, the distaste clear in his voice. "You are dismissed."

His head spinning, dark spots gathering in his eyes, Griff headed for the exit. His shoulder hit the doorframe and he staggered, then managed to get out of the room, and walked dizzily along the hallway and down the stairs. The curse pounded in his head. Barracks, he thought vaguely. Breakfast, if it wasn't too late. That would help. Blinking away the darkness that edged his vision, he took a wavering step.

A stutter of footsteps approached. "You look like cold

porridge, junior," he heard Quirk say. "What happened?"

Porridge. Griff swallowed down a sudden surge of nausea. "Had to lift a curse."

"Ah." He felt Quirk's blunt-fingered hand on his arm. The sharp brambles had pierced the sleeves of his uniform; his skin stung at Quirk's touch. "Come on," he said gently.

Griff let Quirk lead him up the stairs to their cohort's empty room.

"Here. Sit," Quirk said, and pushed Griff down onto his narrow bed.

"I was thinking about what you said before," Griff mumbled. "About what we have to do to keep Story from rising again."

"Never mind that now," Quirk said.

"No," Griff said, and tried to steady himself. "The curse. The girl and the flowers. That's the Breakers' fault. They tell their stories, and the curses—"

"Ah, Griff, lad," Quirk interrupted, "your hands are full of thorns. Lie back now; I'll go for the physician."

The physician would be annoyed with him, injured again. *No, don't go,* Griff wanted to say. For a wild moment he thought flowers might fall from his mouth if he spoke. With trembling fingers, he checked to be sure they hadn't, and felt the curse writhing in his head. A tide of blackness washed over him and his hand fell, leaving a smear of blood across his lips.

CHAPTER

5

NOT LONG AGO, WHEN I HAD GONE PAST THE BOUNDARY and climbed the high hill beyond our valley, I'd seen the City, far in the distance. And I had asked Shoe about it.

"Well, Rosie," he'd answered. "I haven't been there for a long time. I expect it's changed quite a bit since then." And then he had described what he remembered—a graceful castle built of stone the color of the sunrise, the wide streets of the upper city, the lovely arched stone bridges, the narrower streets and houses of the lower city, and the place where the City's river flung itself over a cliff to fall in swags of lace to a lake far below.

I knew I couldn't stay with Merry. So that's where I would go.

"The main road from the village leads to the City, doesn't it?" I asked Merry.

She had agreed without hesitation when I'd said that I should leave, and was packing my knapsack with food, enough for a long journey, and matches, and extra socks, and other things that I would need. "The City?" She shook her head. "No. The road leads to East Oria, the royal city, where the old king lives."

"Oh." I examined the shoes that Shoe had made. I could feel his love for me in every careful stitch, but I couldn't carry all three pairs; there wasn't enough room in my knapsack. I sighed. Leaving the shoes felt like leaving Shoe himself behind. But I didn't have much choice; I had to go on. "Well, is there another road, then?"

"To the City?" Merry shook her head. "We're outside the Forest, and you can't get through."

We were quite obviously not outside the forest; the village was surrounded by trees, just as our valley was. I raised my eyebrows.

"Not this forest," Merry explained. "The *Forest*." When it was clear that I didn't understand, she went on. "The Forest changes when you get closer to the City. It keeps people out, like a wall, and keeps those who live in the City in. The Forest is evil. Dangerous."

"Magic?" I interrupted.

Merry gave an irritated shrug. "*I* don't know. But I do know that it won't let you through, and the City is just as bad—a bad place, from what I've heard."

"Oh," I said, disappointed and confused. The City that Shoe had told me about had sounded lovely.

THE NEXT MORNING, as the sky lightened from gray to pink, I stood on Merry's doorstep, hefting my knapsack and stamping my feet in my best boots, wearing my blue woolen dress and a long, brown, hooded cloak that Merry had given me. I felt like a hawk, keen-eyed, alert, ready to leap from my perch, stretch my wings, and fly out into the world.

Merry poked my arm. "Listen, girl," she said impatiently. "Shoe raised you as an innocent, up there in your valley, but now you've seen how some men can react to that." She pointed at my face. The beauty, she meant.

"Yes," I said. With hunger, wanting to possess. "I definitely understand."

"So, be careful. Be quick to run and slow to trust. Keep your face hidden when you encounter strangers. Try, if you can, not to speak every stray thought that comes into your head."

I felt a flush creeping up my face. I did tend to chatter, but I'd been quieter than usual, missing Shoe as much as I did. "I will," I said. Merry was not one for tenderness, but I leaned close and embraced her. "Thank you for helping me."

"All right then," Merry said, blinking rapidly and then pushing me away. "Off you go."

"Good-bye." Taking a deep breath, I stepped from the

doorway. Without looking back, I went through the gate and out to the road that, in five days of walking, would take me from the village all the way to East Oria.

I WALKED BRISKLY all that first day. The sun came up behind me and marched across a bright blue sky. To either side of the road, the forest was thick, shadowed, and crowded with ferns and mossy rocks. Halfway through the morning, the road from the village joined another, wider road, and I encountered a few other people, a man driving a cart loaded with charcoal, two children riding a huge, brown horse, and a man with a staff and a wide-brimmed hat who approached on foot and nodded as he passed me. Heeding Merry's warning, and wary of those who might think my face gave them an invitation to touch me, I kept the hood of my cloak up. I didn't talk to any of them, even though I wanted to ask them where they were coming from, and where they were going. As the sun leaned toward the west and the shadows gathered under the trees, I started looking for a place to camp. I hadn't seen any other travelers for a few hours, so I guessed that I'd be safe enough sleeping near the road.

At last I found a good place—a perfect place, really—a grassy clearing in a grove of oak trees, with the road on one side and a stream bubbling along on the other. It was odd that there was no fire pit, that no one had camped here before, given how nice a spot it was. Humming, I cleared a place in the grass and built a little fire, using dried moss to get it started, then adding bits of bark and twigs, and a few bigger pieces of wood that I'd found nearby. The sun went all the way down and shadows crept in from the surrounding forest. I wrapped myself in my blanket and ate some of the bread and cheese that Merry had packed for me.

I felt content in my circle of warmth and light, with the oak trees beyond. "You'd like this," I said aloud, as if Shoe was still with me, and felt a pang of sadness knowing that he never would be again. I told him about my day, and about what Merry had told me. That I was beautiful. I wasn't sure, exactly, what that meant. Shoe hadn't ever mentioned it; I'd always just been his girl, his Rosie. For Merry, the beauty had meant that I couldn't be trusted. With my fingertips I traced the line of my eyebrow, felt the feather-tickle of my eyelashes; in the firelight I examined the end of my braid, noting that my hair was a mix of gold and whiter blond, with even a bit of red in it. I studied my hands, the long, slender fingers. What was beauty, exactly? A sum of parts? A whole greater than that? Other people valued beauty, or wanted it, but it set me apart, too, made me different. It might not be an entirely good thing.

As my fire faded, I noticed a pale glow rising in the sky from the east, and after a little while a half moon peeked over the trees, turning everything in the clearing into shadows and milky light. "Time for bed, I suppose," I said. Adding another branch to the fire, and using my cloak as a second blanket, I lay down on the fragrant grass and fell asleep.

WHEN I WOKE up in the morning, the road was gone, the clearing was gone, and I was completely surrounded by trees.

I untangled myself from my blanket and cloak and sat up amid a rustle of fallen red-brown oak leaves. Pushing straggled hair from my face, I climbed to my feet and looked around.

The air felt strange. The trees were closer together. It was different from the woods I'd been walking through, different from the valley I'd lived in with Shoe. Wilder. More dangerous.

"Ohhhh," I breathed. This was the Forest. It had offered the clearing as a baited trap, I realized, and it had reached out to take me as I slept. Merry had told me that the Forest was evil, and maybe I should've been frightened, but I suddenly felt excited. Ready to go where the Forest led me.

It was, I realized, my story beginning. "Once upon a time . . . ," I whispered to myself.

I ate a quick bite of breakfast, rebraided my hair, washed my face in the stream—which hadn't disappeared, like the road—put on my cloak, slung my knapsack over my shoulders, and, ready to start, turned in a slow circle, looking for a way through the trees.

"Once upon a time," I repeated, "there was a girl who was searching for a path through an enchanted forest."

The trees were dark and tangled around me, the morning light cold where it filtered through the branches. Off in one direction I spotted a hint of golden sunshine.

I splashed through the stream and fought my way through knee-high ferns and sprays of bramble until I reached the lighter area. As I stumbled into it, I saw that a narrow path started from that spot, winding among the close-set trees. It wasn't a path that human feet had made—it wasn't trodden dirt, but soft, springy moss that the trees had left when they moved aside.

"Thank you," I whispered to the Forest.

It felt like a place where wonderful things could happen, but I wasn't sure that the Forest really welcomed me. As I walked, I stayed alert, ready. The path went up hills and across streams and through groves of birch trees whose leaves were turning gold as summer gave way to winter. My shoulders ached from the weight of my pack, but my feet weren't tired at all, thanks to the boots that Shoe had made for me.

In the late afternoon, long after I'd stopped for lunch and gone on again, the path brought me through a stand of huge pine trees that blocked the sunlight. The air under their heavy branches felt stuffy. No ferns or brambles grew here; the ground was covered with brown pine needles that slithered under my feet as I walked along. No birds sang, either; it was dead quiet.

Ahead of me the path turned, and I stopped and stared. A high wall had appeared among the pine trees; the path led beside it for as far as I could see in the dim light. Slowly I approached it. The wall's stone was weathered; it was very old, I guessed. Something the Forest wanted me to see. I followed the path until it reached a few tumbled square stones, all covered with moss, and a break in the wall large enough to drive a cart and horse through. Stepping quietly, I went closer and peered through the gap.

Across a courtyard covered with swags of brambles and crowded with saplings growing up through the stones was the ruin of a huge stone building, some sort of castle or fortress. It had square towers that had collapsed on one side, and empty, dark windows where glass had broken, and an air of forbidding desolation.

It might have made a good shelter for the night, but something bad had happened there, long ago. Something from somebody else's story—I could feel it. I didn't want to step through the break in the wall to go any closer.

The path took a sharp right turn, as if leading me away now that the Forest had shown me what it wanted me to see. Emerging from the dense pine grove, I took a deep breath, glad to be free of the stuffy air. Not long after that, as the sun set, the Forest gave me another clearing to camp in. Even though I was tired from a long day of walking, I lay awake for a long time, watching as clouds crept in to cover the waxing moon, and listening to the wind rustle in the leaves.

Alone, in the darkness, I was a little frightened, but I was excited to go on, too.

That's the way it was with stories—you went on because you needed to find out what happened next.

I WALKED FOR two more days through the Forest. On the second day, as a misty rain fell from a cloud-clotted sky, the path went down a steep hill and ran along a wide, smooth river. On the morning of the third day, the path ended.

"And then," I said aloud, "just when she was starting to worry that she would run out of food, she reached the City."

From where I stood at the edge of the Forest, I could see that the City was walled—a high, blank stone wall pierced by only one gate. Between me and the wall lay a wide stretch of blackened stumps and brambles and scorched ground where the trees had been chopped down and the Forest pushed back. Beyond that rose the City; I couldn't see the lovely castle Shoe had described, and the rest of it looked as gray as the clouds that loomed overhead, threatening rain. The river was there, and the waterfall. It looked grim, cold. Maybe it really was as Merry had said—a bad place.

A glance behind me showed that the path the Forest had given me had disappeared, swallowed up by the trees. The Forest had sent me here; I didn't really have any choice but to go on. "All right," I whispered to myself.

There was no road or path leading to the City gate; I had to trudge through brambles, trying not to trip over stumps and old roots. The wall loomed higher as I got closer, and the clouds lowered, until everything seemed gray and dead. The air grew colder and smelled of metal and soot. At last I reached the City gate. I stood studying it. The gate was more a door, really, twice my height, heavy wood, banded with iron, with hinges barbed and twining like thorns, as if to discourage people from entering.

I tried knocking, but nothing happened. I tried calling out, but no one answered. Was anyone in there? Finally I shrugged, put both hands on the door, and pushed as hard as I could. To my surprise, it swung open on silent hinges. "She stepped through, into the City," I murmured.

And the door slammed closed behind me like a trap.

CHAPTER

6

DESPITE A LONG SLEEP, THE CURSE STILL POUNDED IN Griff's head as he pulled on his uniform tunic. The physician must have taken the thorns out of his hands and bandaged them the day before, but he didn't remember it. Just as well, because she'd probably scolded him. She'd replaced the bandage over the sword cut, too, and she must have given him something to make him sleep through the rest of the day and night.

The cold, gray light of dawn seeped into the narrow window of the room. His cohort was getting dressed, a few of them talking quietly to one another, the rest silent, probably half asleep.

Quirk stumped over to him, fisted his hands on his hips,

and looked Griff up and down. "You still look terrible, junior," he pronounced.

Griff picked up his boots and socks and sat on the edge of his narrow bed. With clumsy fingers he put on the socks, then held up a boot to examine it, trying to blink away the blurriness that lifting the curse had left on his vision. Left boot. Went on left foot. He bent to put it on.

"Ready for training this morning?" Quirk asked briskly. "A good long run, some sparring, some extra drill?"

"Sure," Griff mumbled, without looking up. Had his boots always been this difficult to buckle?

Quirk blew out an exasperated sigh. "No, you're not."

Griff frowned. "I'm not?"

"No," Quirk answered. "Breakfast, then light duty. Cohort leader's orders."

Griff let Quirk lead him to breakfast—their ration of oatmeal and an extra piece of bread and cheese that was going rancid and oily—and then out of the barracks and the citadel gate and into the narrow streets of the City when it was time for their shift to begin.

He couldn't stop thinking about the young woman from whom he'd lifted the curse. Like an echo in his head, he heard her scream as he'd taken it, as if he had ripped away something incredibly precious. But curses were bad. That's why they weren't called *gifts*.

"Quit your chattering, junior," Quirk said.

Griff blinked.

Quirk grinned up at him. "You're quiet, even for you. Got something on your mind?"

"No," he answered. Even though he did—their dangerous conversation the other day, about weapons for fighting Story. He wasn't used to questioning the way things were in the City, and now his thoughts were strangely muddled.

Quirk gave him another cheerful grin. After a moment, Griff gave him a nod in return. Quirk had said not to worry about it, and if he couldn't trust Quirk, he couldn't trust anybody. They went on down the street that led from the citadel at the top of the City, passing plain-fronted houses and a few shops that already had lines of people outside them, waiting to get in to exchange tokens for their food rations. The road was pocked with potholes; the chilly air smelled of factory soot and insufficient drains. Clouds covered the sky, gray and heavy with rain.

Their usual patrol was in the warehouse district near the waterfall—aside from the single gate in the City wall, which was never used, the river was the only way in or out of the City, and it was where all of its trade was conducted with the outside world. When on duty there, they had to watch for smuggling and other illicit activities, so they were usually busy. Instead of that, Quirk led them toward the gate in the City wall. It was closed and locked, as usual.

Quirk poked his head into the empty guardhouse. "They've left fixings for tea. Fancy a cup?" He dragged a chair out into the small courtyard that faced the locked gate, then nodded back at the guardhouse. "There's a pallet in there, too, if you'd like a nap."

Sleeping on duty? No. Griff shook his head.

Quirk shrugged and went back into the stone guardhouse and, after calling Griff in to reach the teapot from a high shelf, and building a fire in the hearth, he set about making tea.

Griff went back out to the courtyard and leaned against the wall. The curse still pounded in his head, but the pain of it had receded a little, and his vision was starting to clear. He wondered how the young woman was doing today. When he closed his eyes, he could see her flowers. The City was gray soot, grim rain, stone. But the violets and roses she had spoken in her sorrow and fury—he'd never seen colors like that.

I STEPPED FARTHER into the City and carefully pulled the hood of my cloak over my head so that it shadowed my face. The gateway opened into a cobblestoned courtyard with a little house at its opposite end, and another arched opening that led to City streets, I assumed.

A young man dressed in plain gray was leaning against a wall of the house with his eyes closed. I reminded myself to be wary. Quietly I stepped closer, studying him. He seemed about my own age, maybe a little older. Taller by a hand than I was, and lean. Short dark hair. He was nice to look at, nothing at all like brutish Tom or Marty from the village.

"Hello," I said, hoping he'd be nice to talk to, too.

At the sound of my voice, he straightened from the wall and opened his eyes. "What—?" He glanced past me at the City gate, which was closed. "Where did you come from?"

I kept my chin tilted down so he couldn't see my face. "From the Forest," I answered. "Well, from a cottage in a valley, really, and after that from a village." I realized that I didn't know if Merry's village had a name or not. "It's four days' walk from here," I added.

Frowning, he rubbed his head; his fingers were bandaged, I noticed.

Another person stepped out of the square stone house. Like the young man, he was dressed in gray, but he was very small, the size of a boy. Seeing me, he stopped and peered up at my shadowed face with bright green eyes. "Well, look at you."

"You're not a child, are you?" I didn't really think he was; his face was too old.

"No indeed," he answered, and gave me a gap-toothed grin. "My name is Quirk. But you can call me Quirk."

The young man was looking more alert. "She claims that she came from the Forest," he said, and I could hear the doubt in his voice.

"I *did* come from the Forest," I said. "Or through it, rather." As I turned my head to glare at him, my hood slipped back, revealing my face.

He stared.

It wasn't the same kind of look that I'd gotten from Tom

and Marty, not hunger, not a desire to possess; no, it was pure astonishment.

The small man—Quirk—whistled. "Oh, she's a beauty, isn't she, Griff?"

The young man jerked out a nod, and then wrenched his gaze away from me.

"You're guards, I guess," I said. "Will you let me come in? To the City, I mean?"

"Ye-es," Quirk said, with a glance at the younger man, Griff.

"She'll have to go to the Lord Protector," Griff said, still not looking at me.

After a moment, Quirk nodded. "Yes, of course." And then he added, "I could take her, junior, and leave you here on duty. You could use the rest." He grinned up at me again. "He's been ill."

I smiled back at Quirk, suddenly liking him very much, and he blinked.

"He'll call for me anyway," Griff said.

Quirk studied my face intently, as if he was becoming more interested in me. "What did you say your name was?" he asked.

"I didn't," I answered. "But I'll tell you. It's Rose."

"Ah. Rose." He stared for another moment, then turned to Griff. "She's under a curse, you're thinking?"

"Yes."

I blinked. "How can you tell that I'm cursed?"

Griff's only answer was to shake his head.

"He knows curses," Quirk explained, and gave a resigned shrug. "At any rate, I can see that we haven't any choice in the matter." He nodded at me. "You'll have to come along with us, Rose." He pointed at my face. "Best if you hide that away again."

I pulled my hood up and they led me out into the City. It was absolutely nothing like what Shoe had described, and a lot more like the *bad place* that Merry had warned me about. As we walked up a steep street, the clouds lowered even more, and a misty rain started to fall. A dank chill seemed to rise from the cobblestones. I shivered. "It's awfully grim and gray, isn't it?" I asked Quirk. He was walking along beside me; the other one, Griff, was a step behind.

"What, the City, you mean?" he asked. When I nodded, he said, "It's because of Story."

That answer didn't make any sense. "Because of stories?" I asked.

"No. Not the same thing. *Story*," Quirk said, as if that explained it.

"I don't understand," I told him.

"Well, let's see," he said, and went silent for a few steps, thinking. "It was about fifty years ago, I'm thinking—"

"Once upon a time," I put in, which was how all stories should begin.

"No, not at all," Quirk said, startled, and glanced over his shoulder, as if worried that Griff was listening to our conversation, which I was sure he was. Quirk was the nice one, I decided, and Griff was the grim one. "Right, well," Quirk went on, more carefully. "Almost exactly fifty years ago, as I was saying, Story rose to power here." He waved an arm to encompass the rain-gray street we were on, and the City beyond it. "It had a Godmother, who created the City itself and collected all the people. They were under Story's sway, and they became like clockwork gears, serving only its will. Story forced people to play certain roles that led them through one of its plots to an ending that added to its power. In the end, the Godmother and Story were defeated, but . . . ," he went on seriously, "if Story had not been stopped then, it would have spread farther, into other lands. It was a near thing, and, by all accounts, a very bad time. Then, almost twenty years ago, a new Godmother appeared and again served Story, and again she was defeated. Because this is its City, Story is always watching, always plotting. It could rise again, if we're not careful."

"So this *Story*," I asked. "It's something different from . . . you know, the tales we tell when we're sitting at the hearth after dinner? Because those stories never hurt anybody, did they?"

"We-ell," Quirk answered with a shrug. "There's some disagreement about that."

"No there isn't," Griff put in from behind us.

"Ah." Quirk glanced over his shoulder. "I should say that rational people agree that stories of all kind are dangerous.

The City is different from the rest of the world, Rose. It was originally created by Story to serve it. The theory is that any story told here, even the common tales we tell around the fire after dinner, adds to Story's power and enables it to arise once again. To stop this from happening, we live here according to a rule of rationality. Strict, austere reason. That's why it seems grim to you," he finished.

"You tell no stories here at all?" I asked, astonished.

"None at all," Quirk confirmed.

"That's terrible," I pronounced. "Without stories, how do the City's people know how to make sense of their lives?"

"Yes, well." Quirk reached up to take my elbow, to steer me around a group of drably dressed people who were waiting in a line. Then he went on in a low voice, so that only I could hear him. "There are some who would agree with you, Rose, people who tell stories in secret. Breakers, they're called; they are a kind of rebel group. They think they can tell their own stories—*new* stories—and use them to make sense of their lives, as you say, and by doing so, fight Story's power in a different way. They use words instead of swords. But listen." He lowered his voice even more, and I bent to hear him better. "It's best if you keep quiet. Don't mention anything having to do with stories."

"You think I'll get into trouble," I realized.

He nodded, then reached up and took my hand in his, and turned it, pushing up the sleeve of my dress to expose the rose mark on the inside of my wrist. He nodded as if seeing my rose confirmed something he'd expected to see. "I'm afraid you already are."

Shocked, I straightened, pulling my arm away. He and Griff were guards, I knew that. They were taking me to . . . to a Lord Protector, I thought Griff had said. Somehow I had the feeling he wasn't going to welcome me to the City. Still, we went on.

"Here we are," Quirk said as we came around a corner.

Before us was a thick wall with a gate in it under a stone arch; beyond that was a huge, ugly, windowless brute of a building. I stopped short, and Griff bumped into me from behind.

"Sorry," I heard him mumble.

I didn't want to enter this place. "It looks like a prison," I said.

"It's not," Quirk said reassuringly. "Griff, here, grew up in the citadel. It's not a prison, is it, lad?"

Griff stepped up beside me. He was looking at the citadel, his face blank. "No," he said, after a worrying moment.

Feeling not at all reassured, but seeing that I had no choice, I let them lead me through the gate, where two guards stopped us. Quirk went to talk with them, speaking in a low voice. The guards glanced at me, and then one of them nodded and hurried away across the puddled courtyard and into the citadel. Now that I'd come closer, I could see that its forbidding walls were stained with soot and though it had windows, they were only narrow slits. The rain grew heavier, and I shivered.

Griff, standing silent beside me, took my arm and pulled me under the stone archway so that I wouldn't get any wetter.

"Thank you," I said.

His only answer was a nod.

The rain dripped from the edge of the stone arch. Griff avoided looking at me. I huddled into my cloak and felt glad for the snug, warm, and, most of all, waterproof boots that Shoe had made for me. After a while, the guard who'd gone away came back with two other guards, a black-haired woman and a man with chiseled features. At the sight of them, Griff stiffened; he seemed watchful. There was more muttered discussion. Finally Quirk came over to us, rubbing his hands, as if to warm them. "Right," he said, with a nod to Griff. "We're to report with her to his office." He glanced up at me. Every trace of a smile was gone from his face. "Come along, Rose."

With a feeling of growing dread, I went with them, the other two guards following, across the rain-wet courtyard and into the citadel. It was almost as cold and damp inside as the streets had been. We went up a narrow stairway and along a passage. It was all made of gray stone, with no decorations, not even a rug on the floor. No wonder Griff looked so grim; he'd lived here all his life.

We came to a door that was banded with iron. I heard

Griff take what sounded like a steadying breath; then he knocked.

"Come," a muffled voice called from within.

We went in. The guards who'd been following closed the door behind us and stood by the wall, arms folded, alert. Griff glanced at them, then away.

It was a plain, stone room—what a surprise. Sitting at a desk piled with papers was an austere-looking older man in yet another gray uniform. He frowned and set down his pen. "I've received a rather garbled report," he said sternly. "Clarify it now."

"Griff and I were on guard at the City's main gate," Quirk began promptly, his voice even and formal, "and, we, ah, apprehended this girl."

"You didn't apprehend me," I corrected. "I walked right up to you."

"Yes, that's strictly true," Quirk said. Then he poked my arm. "Take your hood off, Rose, so he can have a look at you."

I shook my head. "I thought you were taking me to the Lord Protector," I said to him.

"I am the Lord Protector," said the man behind the desk in a controlled, even voice.

"Oh." I'd assumed he was some kind of clerk, given his inky fingers. "So you're the one who rules the City?"

"I do not rule," the Lord Protector said sharply. "I govern. My role is to protect the City from Story." He pointed a bony finger at me. "Remove the hood, girl."

I did as he'd ordered.

"Ah," the Lord Protector said, rising to his feet. I was starting to get a good idea about what people were like by the way they reacted to the beauty. Quirk had been frankly appreciative, but he'd have been friendly even if I'd had a face like a lumpy potato. Tom from the village had been possessive. Griff, who was standing very stiff and silent beside me, hadn't looked at me again after his initial astonishment.

The Lord Protector's gray-eyed gaze washed over me like a cold wave, making me want to shiver. He examined me from head to foot, slowly, as if dissecting my parts and laying each one out on a table to be carefully assessed. "She came from outside the City, did she not?"

He hadn't asked me, but I answered anyway. "I came from the Forest. Through the gate in the wall."

The Lord Protector nodded, as if he'd expected my answer. "She is under a curse?"

After a silence, Quirk answered. "Griff thinks so."

"Mm." The Lord Protector sat down at his desk again. From under a stack of papers he pulled a book covered in brown leather, which he opened. A book, I thought wildly. So they *did* have stories here, despite what Quirk had told me. Then he picked up a pen and dipped it in an inkwell and wrote something on one of the book's pages. Not stories, then. Notes. Assessments. "What is the nature of the curse, girl?"

I blinked. "I—I don't know. I've always had it. Since I was a baby."

"Indeed." He flicked a glance at Griff. "Remove it."

I wasn't sure what they were talking about. "Remove my curse, you mean?" I asked.

The Lord Protector ignored me.

"Yes. Griff is a curse eater," Quirk answered. "Curses are a device of Story, and Griff has been raised strictly to fight Story. So he has the power to break them." He glanced at Griff. "How do you do it, lad?"

Griff's only answer was an uneasy frown.

"He doesn't know exactly how it works," Quirk explained. "What happens, Rose, is that he'll touch you, and the curse will rise in response to him, and then he'll take it from you. It won't hurt her, will it?" he asked Griff.

"I hope not," he said in a low voice.

"It's more likely to hurt him, really," Quirk said to me.

I didn't find that very reassuring. "But what if I don't want my curse removed?"

"Doesn't matter," Quirk said, looking away. "Sir," he said to the Lord Protector, "Griff's still recovering from lifting the last curse. It's too soon for him to remove another one."

The Lord Protector waved a hand, as if brushing away a pesky fly. "Get on with it," he ordered.

"But sir," Quirk protested.

"She is a danger to the City," the Lord Protector said. "You will remove the curse at once."

Quirk gave a resigned shrug. "I'm afraid you don't have any choice," he said to me.

I glanced at the door. Even if I could get past the two guards, who were watching me avidly, there was still the citadel, and the winding streets of the City, and its wall, and the Forest beyond, which might not let me back in. I tried to take a step toward the door, but the two guards had come up behind me; they seized my arms. "I shouldn't have come here," I said aloud.

Griff had turned to face me. He raised his hands, which were shaking, I noticed, and placed them on each side of my head, the thumbs against my temples.

"It's all right, Rose," I heard Quirk's voice say. "It'll be over in a moment."

"No, it isn't all right," I whispered. I gazed up at Griff's face. It was very pale, and set. For just a moment, his eyes met mine—his eyes were gray, I found myself noting, and bleak— of course they were—and then they flinched away again. His lips moved, but I couldn't hear what he was saying. There was a roaring in my ears. The room spun.

And then papers from the Lord Protector's desk were whirling around me and Griff; a wild wind battered at us; I could hear distant shouts. The guards holding me staggered, and released their grip on my arms. The wind's roaring rose to a howl; for just a moment the entire room was plunged into impenetrable darkness; there was a flash of brilliant light and a feeling of immense pressure.

For just a moment, Griff and I were connected. For just that flash of a second, I knew him. It was almost as if something inside of me recognized something inside of him, apart from his bleakness and silence. And then it was gone.

Griff's hands were jerked away from my head.

A sudden quiet fell. I blinked away the darkness. Papers settled like falling snowflakes around the room.

Griff was sprawled on the stone floor in front of me, eyes closed. A paper drifted down to land on his face, and I watched, hands clenched, until it moved with his breath—he was still alive. Both guards were braced against a wall as if they'd been blown there by the wind. They stared at me. The Lord Protector climbed from behind his desk, spared a cold glance for Griff, then bent to pick up his book.

"You all right, Rose?" Quirk asked, his voice shaky, but loud in the silence.

I nodded. The tie at the end of my braid had come off, and my hair straggled over my face. I brushed it out of the way to see better.

Quirk stepped past me and knelt beside the unconscious Griff. "Ah, lad," I heard him mutter. He took the paper from Griff's face and with his stubby fingers felt for a pulse at his neck. Finding one, he nodded and glanced up at me. "That's quite a curse you've got."

Griff's eyes blinked open. He squinted, as if he was having trouble seeing. Had he felt the connection, too? I couldn't tell. With Quirk's help, he sat up. His face was whiter, even, than the papers that were scattered around the room.

From the desk came the Lord Protector's cold voice. "Did you remove the curse?"

"I don't feel any different than I did before," I said.

"Report," ordered the Lord Protector impatiently, as if I hadn't spoken.

Griff climbed unsteadily to his feet. Quirk stood beside him and took his arm as if to brace him. "It's a—" Griff stopped and cleared his throat, then took a shaking breath and continued. "It's braided. Very strong." He squinted at me. "I saw something. A . . . spindle?"

Spindle again. Shoe had said the same word as he was dying.

Griff shook his head. "I couldn't—"

"You failed, then," said the Lord Protector. I could hear the disdain in his voice.

Griff closed his eyes. Nodded.

"Best if I get him to the barracks so the physician can have a look at him," Quirk said briskly.

"Yes, you are dismissed," the Lord Protector said without looking up from his note-taking.

Quirk and Griff started toward the door, Griff with his eyes closed, Quirk guiding him. "Is he . . ." I gulped. "I didn't hurt him, did I?"

"I'm all righ'," Griff mumbled.

"Oh, sure you are," Quirk said, with a wry smile. He glanced at me. "Likely he feels as if his head's just been split open with an ax. Watch the doorframe here, lad," he said to him, and they stepped out into the hallway.

The door closed behind them. Leaving me with the Lord Protector and his two guards.

CHAPTER

7

GRIFF AWOKE FROM A DREAM THAT SWIRLED WITH BLOOD-red flowers and the luminously beautiful face of the girl named Rose. Along with her came a looming sense of dread—of danger—and a sound of distant thunder and . . . something else. When he opened his eyes, all was gray again and the headache lanced into him. Wincing, he sat up and pushed back the one thin blanket on his bed. The barrack was empty; the light that filtered in through the single slitted window was gray. Morning or evening, he wasn't sure.

Stiffly he stood and pulled a clean uniform from the shelf over his bed. Pinned to the front of the tunic was a note written in Quirk's spidery scrawl.

The L.P. wants to see you when you're up.

He nodded. It was to be expected.

He found his father in his office, as usual, but had to stand waiting in the cold hallway for an hour before the Lord Protector had finished his other business and had time for Griff's report. As the time passed, his headache ebbed enough that he noticed how hungry he was. While asleep he'd missed . . . breakfast? Dinner?

"You're to go in now," said a clerk emerging from the office, laden with papers.

Griff stepped inside.

The Lord Protector stood before the empty hearth with his hands clasped behind his back. "Ah."

Griff was sure that he must look, as Quirk would say, like cold porridge, but he knew better than to expect any sign of concern from his father; for him to express such a thing would be weak and irrational.

From the time Griff was very young, the Lord Protector had been training him to live according to the austere laws of the City, to become the perfect Watcher, and perhaps, someday, his successor. In addition to his physical training, Griff had been taught to report, to analyze, to draw accurate conclusions. He'd always understood the necessity of all of this; he knew that his father had to set an example for the rest of the City. There could be no softness, no love, no wonder, no beauty. Those things were dangerous; they invited Story to rise again, to dominate the City and all its people. They couldn't risk that.

Living up to the Lord Protector's rigorous expectations

was difficult. It was supposed to be difficult. But Griff had never made such a serious mistake before.

The Lord Protector paced before the empty hearth. Reaching the wall, he turned. "Report," he rapped out.

"The girl's curses were stronger than any I've encountered before," Griff said.

"*Curses?*" his father demanded. "You didn't mention before that there was more than one."

Hadn't he? He couldn't remember. "She is under three curses."

"And their nature?"

I was too busy having my head split open by an ax to notice, he wanted to say, but instead he kept his face blank. "I could not tell."

"Something to do with a spindle, you said," the Lord Protector noted.

He couldn't remember that, either.

His father went to his desk and opened the book where he kept notes on all the elements of Story. Silently he read, then turned a page. "Ah, here it is. The spindle. It is a device from one of Story's most powerful tales. All the spindles in the City were destroyed long ago to prevent that story from being retold again." Closing the book, he pursed his lips. "You said the girl's curses were braided?"

"Yes." A silence indicated that Griff should continue. "Individually, the curses might be broken. Woven together as they are . . ." He shook his head.

"Are you making an excuse for your failure to lift the curses?" the Lord Protector asked sharply.

"No." No excuses. Ever.

"So." The Lord Protector took a few pacing steps before the hearth. "You failed to lift the curse. You failed to inspect the girl before bringing her here."

Griff blinked. "Inspect her?" He could hardly bear to look at her; inspection would have been impossible.

"She was marked," his father said. "Beyond the curses."

The rose-shaped birthmark that Quirk had noticed. He should have mentioned it during the initial report.

"It is an old ruse of Story," his father went on with unusual patience. "One we haven't seen in the City since Story was last defeated. A person who is meant for a particularly significant role will have a birthmark of some kind so that he or she will be recognized, later, and Story's plot allowed to continue. The girl's Story-mark was here." He turned his arm, pulled up the gray sleeve of his uniform, and tapped the inside of his wrist. "A rose. It has been excised."

The Lord Protector kept talking, something about a plan to repel yet another attempt by the Forest to infiltrate the cleared zone outside the City's walls, but Griff couldn't quite make sense of his words.

"Excised?" Griff interrupted.

"It is not your concern," the Lord Protector said coldly. "Now, the girl said she came from the Forest."

That information was incomplete. "She came through

the Forest," Griff corrected. "She said she's from a village four days' walk from here, beyond the boundary of the Forest."

"She lied," the Lord Protector pronounced. "The girl herself is likely a spy." Before Griff could ask what he meant, he went on. "Beauty such as hers is not natural. She serves Story. The Forest brought her to the City to protect the world outside. A kind of quarantine."

Griff shook his head. The girl had seemed completely and openly innocent to him. "I don't think—" he began.

"I did not ask you to think," said the Lord Protector sharply. "Only to obey. As a Watcher, you know that the City has been uneasy of late. Outside elements, subversions, attempts by Story's Breakers to overthrow the rule of rationality."

Griff nodded. The flower curse he'd removed from the young woman proved that Story was, yet again, attempting to rise. He was sure it was assisted by the storytelling Breakers, who had evidently brought in new people from outside the City to aid in their efforts. They were dangerous fools, the Breakers. Quirk had said they thought their simple tales could be a weapon in the fight against Story, but they were wrong—and so they served Story despite their own intentions.

"Very well," his father continued. "That is all I need to know. As you go out, call in my guards. I shall have them imprison the girl."

"No," Griff protested. The guards, Luth and Taira, would be eager to get the girl into their prison cells. And what they would do to her . . . he couldn't bear to think about it.

The Lord Protector paused and gave a disapproving shake of his head. "What did you say?"

He thought quickly. "She . . . the girl . . . if she was free, the Breakers would try to contact her, and we could catch them."

The Lord Protector stared at him for a long, unnerving minute. "Hmm." With bony fingers he tapped his lips, considering Griff's words. "Yes," he said slowly. "There are no spindles in the City to activate her curses, so it would be safe enough. You and your cohort leader"—Quirk, he meant—"have a new assignment. You are to guard the girl. She will live here, at the citadel, but she will be allowed out into the City. Given her nature, she will attract these dangerous elements, these Breakers. You will observe them, and report. The Watchers will then act, and we will wipe them out. This may be an opportunity to quash Story's malign influence forever."

Griff really did not want to spend any more time with the girl, Rose. But better that than knowing she was in the citadel's forbidding underground prison with Luth. He stood quietly, waiting to be dismissed, while his father paced, his head lowered, frowning down at the floor.

A knock at the door interrupted them. Quirk. He cast a quick, concerned glance at Griff, then gave the Lord Protector a competent nod. "You asked me to report, sir?"

"Yes." The Lord Protector seated himself behind his desk.

"The two of you will guard the girl. She is not a prisoner." He paused, and the word *yet* hovered in the air. "But you will not let her out of your sight. Once she has served her purpose, I will let my guards deal with her. Understand?"

Don't think, Griff told himself. *Obey.* He nodded.

"Yes," Quirk said.

The Lord Protector picked up a pen and started writing. "Dismissed," he said, without looking up.

They went out of the office, closing the door behind them. Quirk seemed distracted as he stumped along the narrow stone hallway.

In the silence, Griff went over the conversation he'd had with his father. "He said—" he started.

"What?" Quirk said, with a glance up at Griff.

"The Lord Protector said the girl's mark—her Storymark—was excised."

"Oh." Quirk nodded. "Yes."

"What does he mean by that?" Griff asked.

"Ask her," Quirk said.

Yes, he wanted to say, *but that would mean I'd have to talk to her.* Something he was going to avoid, if he could. He didn't think she was a spy, as his father did, but she was definitely dangerous. Still, he hoped *excised* didn't mean what he thought it did.

Quirk led him around a corner into the busier hallway where some of the City's public offices were located. They passed a dour-looking couple entering the Office of Marriage, a clerk carrying a stack of account books into one of the Tax Offices, and many gray-faced petitioners lined up along the wall outside the Rations Office. They'd probably been waiting there all day, and they would wait all of the next day, too.

Quirk remained uncharacteristically silent as they continued up some stairs that led to a part of the citadel that held unused offices. At the third door he stopped, took a key from his pocket, and put it in the lock. Then he knocked. When there was no answer, he opened the door and went in. Griff followed.

All of the chairs and desks that had filled the office had been moved out long ago; it was empty now, except for dust. Along one wall there were three narrow windows that admitted the pink and gray light of sunset. An hour later and the room would be completely dark. A hearth set into one wall had been swept clean; the air was chill and dank.

The girl had been sitting in the corner farthest from the door; as they entered, she got to her feet and came toward them.

"You," she said, glaring at Griff.

He stared back at her.

Her blond hair was tangled, and her eyes were luminous with tears. With the palm of her hand she scrubbed more tears from her face, leaving a streak of dust across her cheek.

None of it made her any less beautiful.

But the beauty didn't seem to matter as much as it had

before. When he'd attempted to lift the braided curse from her they had shared a connection, and it had offered him a glimpse of her true self, apart from the beauty. Just for that brief moment he had seen deep within her, not darkness, not the intricate coils of Story that his father suspected she was hiding, but something else. He wasn't sure what, but it was clear and light.

She had switched the glare to Quirk. "What sort of place is this?" she asked. "I haven't done anything wrong, at least not that anyone has told me, except for my curse, which is hardly my fault. And I've been locked up here like a prisoner. And . . ." She paused and held up her hand. Her wrist had been bandaged, Griff could see. "And . . ." Tears rolled down her cheeks. "My rose . . ."

"Now then," Quirk said awkwardly. He took a step toward her.

"I didn't even have any choice about whether to come here," she went on, her voice shaking. "The Forest gave me a path, and I had to follow it."

"Yes, well," Quirk said to her. He glanced up at Griff as if seeking help.

Beautiful crying girls were something Griff had no experience with. All he could do was shake his head.

The girl scrubbed at her tears again.

The short silence that followed was broken when Griff's stomach growled. Loudly.

The girl blinked and stared at him.

Quirk's mouth twitched, almost a smile. "When did you last eat, junior?"

Griff thought back. He'd failed to break her curses the night before and had slept most of the day away, recovering. He had to clear his throat before he could speak. "Yesterday."

"You're made of clockwork, I think," Quirk said, shaking his head. "You need to eat. Go down to the barracks kitchen and tell them to give you some bread and cheese and something hot."

"But—" Griff started to protest.

"Go," Quirk insisted. "If they give you any trouble, tell them I authorize that they take it from the cohort's ration."

Griff was not, in fact, made of clockwork, and he suddenly felt light-headed with hunger. He went.

CHAPTER

8

As Griff left my prison room, Quirk stepped closer and spoke in a low voice. "We don't have much time, Rose. The kitchen won't give him anything outside scheduled mealtimes, so he'll be back soon."

"Time for what?" I asked.

"Time for me to help you, lass," Quirk said. His lopsided face seemed kind and concerned.

Be wary, I told myself. But I *liked* Quirk, even though he was working for the Lord Protector.

Who I most definitely did *not* like.

After Griff had failed to break my curse, the Lord Protector had ordered the other Watchers to take me to an empty room. There, while the Watchers watched avidly, a thin, sharp-eyed woman had made me strip off my dress and underthings, and my boots and socks, and she had inspected me.

"Are you looking for this?" I asked, showing her the rose on my wrist.

She grunted, and went on to study every bit of me, while goose bumps crept over my skin and my face burned with embarrassment. Then she let me get dressed again, and the guards took me to a dark, smoky cell deep in the lower levels of the citadel. A stoked fire heated the room, and the walls were hung with odd metal tools. The cell's keeper was an old man whose beard was streaked with soot, and who had enormous, gnarled hands.

"This is going to be good," one of the guards, the woman, had said.

"Hold her tightly," the other guard ordered. His hands gripped my arms.

As I realized what they were planning to do to me, I tried to fight, but the Watchers held me, and the sharp woman yanked up the sleeve of my dress, and the cell keeper put some sort of tool into the coals of his fire.

I tried to kick him as he came closer with the red-hot tool and seized my wrist. The woman hissed an order, and the male Watcher snaked an arm around my neck until spots swam before my eyes. I could hear the sizzle of the hot iron as the old man brought it close, and then felt the white-hot pain of the burn destroying my rose. I screamed.

He took the iron away, but the pain continued, pulsing as if my whole arm was on fire. I sobbed and kept my eyes squeezed closed while someone wrapped a bandage around the burn. Then the Watchers dragged me up to the prison room. They shoved me inside and stood blocking the doorway.

"We could have some fun with her, don't you think, Luth?" the woman said, leering at me.

"We could indeed," the male Watcher, Luth, answered. He looked me up and down slowly, in a way that reminded me of Tom from the village. Hungry. Possessive.

The woman licked her lips. "Why not start now?"

I felt a sudden jolt of fright. These two were dangerous— far worse than Tom and Marty from the village.

"Taira, you're so intemperate," Luth said, with a kind of oily smoothness that made me shiver. "We can wait. She'll be sent to play with us soon enough. In the meantime, she can enjoy the anticipation of the pleasures that await her."

I shuddered and backed away from them.

With a last, lingering leer, they locked me in for a long time. I'd sat in a dusty corner, cradled my burned wrist, and cried. I wished I was still living in the valley, and felt desolate with missing Shoe, until Quirk and Griff had come.

But now I was done crying. "Quirk, what does he want with me? The Lord Protector said that I'm a danger to the City."

"Well, yes," he confirmed. "Story is always hovering in the air around those who are cursed, or marked, as you are. You're a kind of catalyst. Now that you are here in Story's

City, Rose, one of its stories *will* coalesce around you. Once that happens, the entire City will turn into a kind of giant machine, and the people who live here will become only cogs and gears, performing the roles that Story dictates. You won't have any choice about your ending, and neither will they. So you see, you are dangerous."

"No, I'm really not," I insisted.

"Well, the Lord Protector thinks you are, lass, and he will ensure that after they've used you to try to expose the Breakers, you will . . ." He shrugged. "Well, you'll disappear."

I stared at him. *Disappear?* As in they wanted me *dead?* Or, I thought with a shiver, I'd serve as a plaything for those two horrible Watchers, and *then* I would die. "I have to get away from here."

"Yes," Quirk agreed. "But now that the Forest has brought you here, it won't let you leave." He frowned. "Or maybe Story drew you here, through the Forest. It's hard to be sure. Either way, it will be very hard to get you out before Story makes its move."

My knees went weak with despair. "What am I going to do?"

"I can help," Quirk said. "The Breakers—they are fighting Story. In a different way from the Lord Protector." He glanced over his shoulder at the door, which was still closed.

"Will they help me escape from this prison?" I asked.

Quirk shrugged. "The whole City is a prison, lass." Then he nodded. "But yes, I think I can persuade them to help."

I realized what he was saying. "You're one of them, aren't you, Quirk? One of the Breakers?"

"No," he said firmly. "Or not exactly. It's complicated. At any rate, the leaders of the Breakers will want to meet with you first. Now listen—"

There was a sound of footsteps out in the hallway.

Quirk continued, speaking quickly. "It's going to be difficult. I'll try to set it up, but Griff is—" He shook his head. "He's very observant, very alert, and he's been strictly trained to stay loyal to the Lord Protector. You'll have to be ready."

"I will be," I whispered.

Quickly Quirk stepped away and looked up at the ceiling, as if bored.

The door to my prison room opened. Griff. I hadn't noticed it before, but Quirk was right—he scanned the room as he entered. His bleak gaze washed over me, then flinched away.

"No luck?" Quirk asked, going to meet him.

Griff shook his head.

"Right, well, we'd better get Rose settled."

By SETTLED QUIRK meant that he and Griff didn't take their eyes off of me. First they took me to their barracks in the other part of the citadel and requisitioned a cot for me, and blankets. Then it was time for dinner, so they brought me with them to their dining hall, where they had me sit next to them at a long wooden table with the rest of their cohort, who eyed me uneasily; two of them stared openly for the entire meal. The bland soup they were eating was made of fish, which I'd never had before and didn't like the smell of. The burn on my wrist throbbed with pain, and I was worried about the Lord Protector's plan to make me *disappear* into the cells below the citadel. I sat across from Griff, who ate all of his own dinner, and then what was left of mine.

"How do you eat so much?" I asked him.

He glanced down at his nearly empty bowl. "Well, one bite at a time."

"So literal," I grumbled.

Quirk, sitting next to him, winked at me and then dumped the rest of his own soup into Griff's bowl.

I watched him eat, feeling very tired. His fingers were still bandaged; when we stood up from the table, I noticed that he moved stiffly, as if he'd been injured. Quirk said he'd been ill before, and I knew that he'd been hurt when he'd tried to break my curse. Yet he seemed keenly aware of what was going on around us.

Quirk was right. Griff was going to be a problem.

THE COT QUIRK had ordered for me had been set up in my prison. The long, slitted windows were dark, but Quirk brought a lantern, which lit one corner of the room; the rest was swallowed up by darkness. Griff stood in the shadows beside the door.

"Right." Quirk stood with hands on hips, surveying the

room. "This will do you, Rose, won't it?"

The room was dank and chill, and I didn't like the idea of spending a night locked up in it. "Could I have some wood for a fire?" I asked.

"Ah, sorry, lass," Quirk said. "No fires allowed in the citadel until after the first snowfall." He beckoned to Griff, who stepped closer. "Now, junior, I'm going to leave you on guard here while I go see to our cohort." He pointed at him with a stubby finger. "And don't just stand in the corner like a post, either. Talk. Keep her company."

As Quirk turned to leave, he gave me a meaningful nod. He was going to contact the Breakers, I guessed, while Griff was out of the way, guarding me. He went out, closing the door behind him, and I heard the key turn in the lock.

The last time I'd been alone with a man, it was Tom from the village. But here with Griff, I felt safe. I was curious about him. He was a Watcher, yet somehow I didn't think he was a danger to me, not like the Lord Protector or those other Watchers, Luth and Taira.

Leaving my cloak on, I sat on my narrow cot and wrapped a blanket around myself.

Griff stood leaning a shoulder against the wall at the very edge of the circle of golden light cast by the lantern. He looked remote, his face in shadow.

"Why are you *junior*?" I asked him.

As an answer, he shrugged one shoulder without looking up.

"Quirk said you had to keep me company," I reminded him. I could see why Quirk had given that order; Griff didn't talk very much, I realized.

After a long moment, Griff answered, his voice rough. "The youngest in a cohort is always *junior*."

"How old are you?" I asked.

"Eighteen."

Hm. I'd come to Shoe's cottage over sixteen years ago, so I was at least sixteen, maybe older. "How long have you been a Watcher?"

"Just over five years."

"Quirk said you grew up here, in the citadel," I remembered. "Why here and not in the City? Is there a school for Watchers here?"

"Something like that," he answered. "Why are you asking so many questions?"

"I'm curious, mainly. I haven't met very many people before this. And I want to know your story."

"I don't have a story," he said.

"Everybody has a story," I countered. "Even you."

He said nothing.

"To prove it, I'm going to tell you my story." For just a moment I felt a pang of missing Shoe. This was nothing at all like our snug cottage, Shoe in his rocking chair, a fire in the hearth. Yet telling a story made me feel warm and comforted. This was what the Breakers did—they told stories, even inside the cold, grim City. "Once upon a time," I began, and because I was beginning *my* story, I felt sure it couldn't be bad, or wrong, or something that Story could twist into power for itself.

"I can't listen to this," Griff interrupted.

"I know," I said. "But I'm going to tell you anyway, unless you leap on me and put your hand over my mouth, and you're not going to do that, are you?"

Instead of answering, he looked away, his lips pressed into a thin line.

"No?" I settled myself more comfortably. "Then you might as well listen."

Griff slid down the wall and sat on the stone floor with his knees drawn up. I could see his face better now, the planes of his cheekbones, the smudges of weariness under his eyes. He was so distant, so closed off from me. Yet we had shared a connection when he'd tried to break my curse. I really did want to know his story. But first, mine.

"Once upon a time," I started again, "there was a shoe-maker who lived in a cottage deep in a forest. Not the *Forest* forest," I amended, "just ordinary pine trees and oaks in a valley not far from a village. He had been there for a long time, but he had not always been alone, for he had a true love, and he had once lived out in the world having his share of adventures. He even visited this City once, when it was still beautiful here."

I glanced at Griff. For once he was looking at me. "I thought this was supposed to be your story," he said.

"It will be," I promised, and took up my narrative again. "One dark and stormy night, Shoe was working on a fine pair of boots, when there was a knock on the cottage door."

"Shoe?" Griff put in. "The shoemaker's name was Shoe?"

I hadn't really thought about that before. "I wonder if he had another name when he lived out in the world," I mused. "He must have. Maybe he was Shoe because he was in hiding. That would make sense. At any rate, he's Shoe in this story. He opened the door, and in stepped the Penwitch, all wild and wet from the rain, carrying a bundle wrapped up in a blanket."

Griff was listening, his chin resting on his folded arms. I could see his gray eyes shining in the light of the lantern, as if he was seeing the things I was telling him about. That was one of the magical things about stories—if they were well told they could transport the listener to another time, another place.

"The Penwitch handed the bundle to Shoe," I went on. "He pulled back a fold of the blanket and saw that it was a baby. *She is under a curse*, the Penwitch said to Shoe. *Guard her well.* And then she used her magic to set a boundary around the valley so that Shoe and the baby would be safe. When Shoe started looking after the baby, he found that she had a mark on her arm. A perfect rose, just starting to bloom. And so he named the baby Rose."

"The Lord Protector said your mark was excised," Griff said abruptly.

"Don't interrupt," I scolded. Then I paused. "He had me taken to the cells below the citadel," I told him, "and a man there burned it off."

"Oh." Griff rubbed his eyes, as if tired.

"He's a horrible person, the Lord Protector," I said.

Griff shook his head. "He's just doing what he has to do to protect the City."

I shrugged. Griff was a Watcher, after all, and, as Quirk had said, he'd been trained to serve the Lord Protector. "Now, where did I leave off?"

"The baby named Rose," he answered.

"Yes, that's right. Thank you. Shoe, who was very kind, took care of the baby, and raised her to be a good girl, and told her stories every night, and taught her to tell stories herself. The kind of stories that make you feel warm on a cold winter night, or make you laugh when you need a bit of cheering up, or make you sad when you feel like having a good cry. Stories that seem like they're about something simple, like goats and wolves taking shelter in a barn during a blizzard, but turn out to be about something completely different, stories that make you understand more clearly who you are, and what the world is like."

He was staring at me, a frown line creasing his brow.

"That's what stories do," I explained. "That's what Shoe taught me."

He shook his head slowly, denying it. "All stories serve Story."

I studied his bleak face. "What a strange life you must lead," I said musingly. "So rational and cold. You have no stories at all about the things that have happened to you. I wonder how you even know yourself."

"I know myself," he said.

"What are you, then?" I challenged.

His gaze met mine, intense. "A weapon."

I shivered. Yes. He was. I tried to defuse the tension that had arisen between us. "If you are a weapon, then listening to me must take the edge off you."

He frowned.

"Because I am a rather fine storyteller," I said lightly, "and the story of me and Shoe is a good one."

"All stories serve Story," he repeated.

I released a frustrated breath. "Well, I'm not going to argue with you about it." Teasing him again, I said, "Should I stop now? Or do you want to find out what happens next?"

"I do want to know," he said soberly. "But that is Story at work. That is part of its power. Once it starts, it is very difficult to stop it."

Hmm. What he said made an odd sort of sense. But I'd just come to the most important part of my own story. The sad part. I couldn't stop now. "And then," I went on, "the boundary around our valley was broken. That meant the Penwitch had died, and so Shoe's heart broke, because he had loved the Penwitch so completely, and then he died, too." I blinked away sudden tears. "Rose had always wanted to go

out into the world, to live her own story, but losing Shoe . . ."
I took a shaky breath. "It was awful." Under its bandage, my
burned rose ached, and my tears overflowed.

"I'm sorry," Griff said quietly.

"It's all right," I said, sniffling. I was surprised that he
offered words of comfort, even though he disapproved of my
story. "Telling about it helps. I have so many stories about
Shoe; it means I'll never forget him." I wiped my face with
a corner of my cloak. "Thank you for listening. That helps,
too."

After a moment, he gave a brief nod in response.

I went on. "You can probably guess the rest of my story.
I had to leave the cottage behind, and went to live in the village for just a few days, but then I had to leave there, too. I
meant to go to East Oria but the Forest brought me here, to
the City, instead."

I sighed, and we sat in silence for a while.

"The end," I added. "For now, anyway."

Without speaking, Griff got stiffly to his feet and paced
away into the room's shadows. After a moment I heard him
moving again—quick footsteps, the sound of his breaths.

"What are you doing?" I asked, trying to peer into the
darkness beyond the lantern light.

"I missed training today," he said gruffly. "I need to drill."

And, I thought, after hearing my story he needed to
remind me, or maybe himself, of what he was—a Watcher.
A weapon. Trained to serve the Lord Protector, trained to

resist stories in all their forms. But even though he was grim and quiet, and I was, in a way, his prisoner, I was starting to like Griff. He was a good listener, despite himself. And I suspected that he thought in his head a lot more than he let himself say aloud. Huddled in my blankets, I listened to him finish his training until my eyelids started to droop.

At last he stepped back into the circle of light. He seemed exhausted, his face flushed, his eyes glittering with what looked to me like fever.

"All right?" I asked sleepily.

He gave me a brusque nod. Then he lowered his head and stared down at the stone floor. "Rose," he began.

It was the first time he'd called me by name. "Yes?" I prompted.

"I know part of your . . ." He paused. "Part of what happened before Shoe went to live in the cottage."

"You *do?*" I was wide awake again, and sat up straight.

He nodded, still not looking at me. "The Witch. Pen. She's been gone from here for a long time, but she was the first Protector of this City."

"Protector?" I asked blankly.

"Like the Lord Protector," he said. "She and the shoe-maker, your Shoe, gave Story its greatest defeat, fifty years ago."

"I don't believe it," I said.

"It's the truth." Then he added, his voice wry, "Not a story at all."

My mind whirled, trying to make sense of what he'd just told me. "My goodness," I said faintly.

"Story is relentless," Griff went on. "It is always waiting, always ready to find a weakness and rise again. All her life, the Penwitch fought against it, just as the Lord Protector does. When she brought you to Shoe she must have created the boundary around the valley to keep you in. Not to protect you. To protect the world outside. Shoe was guarding you because you're dangerous."

"What? No." I shook my head. "Shoe loved me. He took care of me."

"You are . . . you were marked by Story," he insisted. "The Forest sent you here because you're a danger to the world outside. And you're cursed." He frowned. "Something about a spindle . . ."

"I don't even know what a spindle is," I interrupted.

"It's a device of Story, my father says."

"Your father?" I repeated, my voice shaking.

"The Lord Protector," he said.

Oh, I could see it now. They had the same eyes. Gray, bleak, rational. Terrifying.

Shivering, I wrapped my arms around myself. "But . . . I don't mean anybody harm."

He shook his head. "It doesn't matter. It's what you are."

"What do you mean?" I demanded. Quirk had said I was a *catalyst* for Story, but I wasn't sure, exactly, what that meant. "What am I?"

He studied me carefully, and I knew he wouldn't flinch away from the beauty anymore. He saw something else, now. "The stories you tell about yourself are false. You don't know what you really are. The Lord Protector thinks you are a spy. A servant of Story."

"No," I whispered.

But Shoe . . . he had never told me that he'd loved the Penwitch; he'd never told me his own story. Was this why?

Was Shoe, for all those years, not my guardian, but my guard?

CHAPTER

9

As far as Griff could see, he had two choices. One, ask the Lord Protector to relieve him of this assignment.

Two, he could do his duty as a Watcher, and guard Rose, while interacting with her as little as possible.

So really he had only the one choice, for the Lord Protector would sneer at any show of irrationality or weakness. And then he would hand Rose over to his most favored Watchers, Luth and Taira, who would drag her down to their prison cells below the citadel.

In the morning, after Quirk had brought a tray with Rose's breakfast to her room, he sent Griff down to the dining hall for his own breakfast and then to the barracks physician to have the bandages on his cut replaced.

With her usual brusqueness, the physician looked him

over and pronounced him a fast healer. "But you need to eat more," she said, while taking the bandages off his fingers.

Everybody in the City needed to eat more. Then he asked the physician for something for Rose and had to wait while she prepared it.

By the time he dressed again in his uniform and ran back to the cohort's room for his patrol knife, he almost missed Quirk and Rose as they were hurrying across the citadel courtyard, heading for the gate that led out into the City.

At the sound of his footsteps on the cobblestones, they turned.

Griff thought he saw a look of dismay pass between them before Rose glanced away. As before, she was wearing her cloak over a blue dress. Her blond hair, neatly braided and pinned into a crown on her head, gleamed in the morning sun. As if she'd realized that he'd noticed it, she quickly pulled up her hood, hiding her face. Then she tenderly cradled her burned wrist; it was probably intensely painful.

"Finally, junior," Quirk criticized, frowning up at him. "I was beginning to think that you'd decided not to do your duty this morning."

"But I—" Griff began. He'd been doing as Quirk had ordered. No excuses, he reminded himself. "Sorry," he finished, and fell into step behind them.

Rose, it seemed, was curious about the City, and Quirk had agreed to give her a tour. Quirk, Griff assumed, was acting on their orders from the Lord Protector—Rose was being taken out into the City so that she would attract the notice of the Breakers, so that the Watchers could identify them and suppress them before Story used Rose to make its move. And after that, Rose would have served her purpose, and she'd be given over to Luth and Taira. Griff had seen the citadel prison; he knew what the Watchers did to the people who went into those cells. The prisoners came out empty-eyed and broken in spirit and body.

Meanwhile, Rose seemed to have no sense of her own danger; she talked cheerfully to Quirk as they went through the citadel gate. In response to her questions, Quirk explained about the Forest, how it encircled the City and blocked access to it so that if Story rose to power again it would not escape out into the world.

"So if you can't get out," Rose asked, "and travelers can't get in, how do you get all the things you need?" She waved a hand. "Food and cloth and firewood and . . . goats and chickens, and things like that?"

A better question, one she should be thinking about, Griff thought, was why the Forest had let *her* in.

"Ah." Quirk grinned up at her. "I will take you to the waterfall, and you'll see how it works."

Griff trailed silently behind them as they walked down the steep street. The houses they passed in the part of the City nearest the citadel had once been fine mansions, but in the long fight against Story they'd been abandoned, and most stood empty, their windows blank, the decorative stone scrollwork along their roofs and doorways hacked off. Some had been divided into tenement apartments; from those hung lines of gray-looking laundry. The air was crisp and cool, but Griff smelled the ever-present taint of factory soot, too. Not many people were on the street. The population had been going down—every year fewer babies were born in the City, and some workers were killed in accidents in the factories, and while no one actually starved to death, too many died of the diseases that preyed on those who had to depend on poor rations for their food.

As they walked, Griff felt strangely aware of every move that Rose made. Maybe it was because watching her was his assignment, or because of the terrible things he'd said to her the night before. He could feel her dislike of him in the way she kept her hood up and her face averted, the way she pointedly ignored him. Yet she seemed keenly interested in everything they passed.

She stopped at a wide, blank square of scraped dirt dotted by piles of rubble. "What is this supposed to be?" she asked.

"Long ago," Quirk answered, "it was a park. Grass, bushes, flower beds, a few trees, that sort of thing."

Griff had forgotten that it hadn't always been this way—dead and empty.

Rose surveyed it. "There's not a scrap of green in this whole City, is there? Why is that?"

Quirk shrugged. "Nothing will grow here."

Griff hadn't thought about that before. For nearly all his

life the City had been this way. Seeing it all through Rose's eyes made him realize just how barren it really was.

As they went farther into the City, the streets grew narrower, the houses blank-fronted, the alleys between them shadowed and clotted with mud and trash. They rounded a corner, and Griff caught a glimpse of movement; he stopped and looked back, but saw nothing. Then, as they passed an abandoned shop, he saw a cloaked figure duck into a darkened doorway.

"Quirk," he said, interrupting something Rose was saying. "We're being followed. Or watched." Breakers, no doubt.

Quirk paused and cast a cursory glance around them. "You're imagining it, junior."

Imagining? He'd been trained all his life *not* to imagine things. "No, I'm—"

"Over that bridge," Quirk said, ignoring him and turning back to Rose, and pointing across the sluggish, muddy river, "is the factory district. But we're going this way." He led Rose, with Griff following, into the familiar district where they usually patrolled: the warehouses, and the waterfall.

The warehouses were huge, windowless buildings with slate roofs. In some of them were stored raw materials, mostly bales of cotton and wool and hemp, and bundles of hides, and stacks of timber that were brought into the City for processing in the factories and workhouses; and in some were finished products: paper, leather, rolls of cloth and thread and immense coils of rope, all ready to be sent down the river and out into the world.

At last they came to the waterfall. The river narrowed here, squeezed between two steep, rocky banks, and quickened before hurling itself over a high cliff and into the long lake below, which was crowded with boats and barges, some heaped with coal for running the factories. Perched atop the steep cliff face on the near side of the waterfall were a scaffold and crane and a platform, with an immense pulley and cables turned by a turbine in the river. A lift for bringing up supplies from the barges, and for sending finished products down.

"This is the only way in and out of the City," Quirk said, speaking loudly to be heard over the roar of the river and the grinding machinery of the lift.

"Except for the gate in the wall," Rose pointed out.

"Well, yes," Quirk admitted. "You're the first to come in that way for a long time. The Forest blocks everything else." He looked down at the lift, which was cranking up the side of the cliff with a load of coal. "If the Forest decided to block access to the river, I expect we'd all starve."

All along the cliff's edge were iron railings; there were huge piles of crates and bales waiting to be loaded onto the lift; a gang of heavily muscled laborers waited to unload the lift when it arrived, and then load it back up again for a return trip to the lake. A cohort of Watchers in gray were waiting, too. They would inspect everything that went out and in. Still, smuggling happened. Nobody ever got out—the Forest made sure of that—but Griff was sure that people came in—he was almost certain that the young woman he'd chased a few nights ago, the one who'd given him the sword cut, had not been from the City, but from outside. Someone working with the Breakers, brought in by them to spread new stories that, secretly told and retold, would give new power to Story.

Rose said something to Quirk in a low voice. He nodded, and she edged around a crate and stepped closer to the railing, where she could look out over the lake and beyond, to the Forest. The wind was stronger there, and it pulled the hood from her head. Her beauty, Griff realized, was not just in her face. Her every move was etched with grace. She turned back, and he found himself noticing again the arch of her eyebrows, the sorrow that lingered in her eyes, the sweep of her lashes as she lowered her gaze. The sunlit glory of her hair.

He was staring again. He ripped his gaze away from her and saw that Quirk was looking up at him, hands on hips, his face uncharacteristically stern. "Do your duty, junior," he chided.

Before he could answer—he *always* did his duty, Quirk knew that—Rose came back to them, raising a hand to brush tendrils of hair away from her face. "Can we go down to the lake? I'd like to see it."

No, Griff wanted to answer.

He was forestalled by a resounding crash, as the lift docked at the top of the cliff. An iron bell rang. Immediately, workers sprang into action, opening the lift's gate and starting to unload the carts piled with coal.

"We'll go down on this trip," Quirk told her. "Hurry, now." With a nod, Rose started for the lift. The coal had already been cleared, and the workers were loading the lift with crates.

"Wait," Griff protested. Their orders were not to let her leave the City.

"Now then, junior," Quirk started, and then he frowned and looked past Griff, at the road behind him. "Is that . . . ?"

Griff turned to see what he was worried about. The road was busy with carts and a rumbling wagon, but he didn't see anything unusual. When he turned back, two workers holding an immense crate moved between him and the lift. Griff stepped aside to go around them, when a man with very broad shoulders, wearing a peaked cap that shaded his face, blocked his way with a barrel that he was carrying. There was a harsh clanging sound—the lift bell. "Junior!" he heard Quirk call.

"Let me pass," Griff ordered, reaching for the knife sheathed at his back. The man holding the barrel raised his chin to give him a baleful stare and slowly shifted aside. Griff paused—did he know the man? He seemed familiar, somehow. But his way to the lift was clear. Shoving past a lingering group of workers, he reached the gate. The lift had already started its rattling descent; the heads of its passengers were just below the level of the cliff top.

Griff stepped onto the lowest rung of the gate, intending

to climb over and jump down to the lift, to join them.

"Hold there, junior!" he heard Quirk shout from the lift platform. "Wait for us to come back up."

Griff gripped the gate, staring down at them as they descended lower. Quirk lifted a hand, as if to say *stop*. Rose, however, smiled sunnily up at him. She was probably glad to be rid of him.

He couldn't blame her, really.

CHAPTER

10

QUIRK HAD WARNED ME THAT IT WOULD BE DIFFICULT TO lose Griff. He'd caught up with us before we'd left the citadel, and he'd spotted the Breakers that Quirk had said would be keeping an eye on us as we approached the warehouse district. He was quiet as he walked behind us, but I was aware of him back there, poised and competent, and very alert.

The night before he'd told me that the Lord Protector thought I was a servant of Story. But Griff hadn't said if he *himself* believed it.

Well, he must. He was the son of the Lord Protector, after all.

I wanted to be sure that he was wrong about it, but I couldn't be, not quite. What if Griff was right—what if my own stories didn't tell the true story? The question filled my thoughts. After a night of pondering it as my burned arm throbbed with pain, I felt less certain of who I was, *what* I was. There was the problem of Shoe, and whether he had been my guard or not. It didn't make me love him any less, but I did wonder. Then there was the curse, and the spindle, and the beauty, and the fact that the Forest had sent me here—

—or maybe it hadn't. Maybe Story had drawn me to the City so it could use me as its catalyst or servant. That was a thought too awful to contemplate. If it had, then Griff was right, and I really was marked by Story and dangerous, too.

As the lift slowly jerked its way down the cliff face, I looked up at Griff, who seemed wonderfully frustrated as he stood at the railing, watching us descend. The Breakers' plan to get us away had worked perfectly. Quirk and I would have time to meet with them down below at the lakeside, before going back up to the City.

Griff looked desolate, too. One still, gray figure amid the busy activity at the cliff top. I had a feeling that he would stand there without moving until we came back again. Just doing his duty, I reminded myself.

Beside me, Quirk reached up to nudge my arm. The noise of the lift made it impossible to talk, but he gave me an encouraging, gap-toothed grin.

At last the lift thumped to a stop at the bottom of the cliff, at a dank dock wet with the spray from the waterfall; other docks reached like long fingers into the lake. Some were busy with workers and crowded with supplies waiting to be ferried out to the barges; others seemed abandoned.

As I stepped onto the slippery planks of the dock, Quirk turned to the lift driver, a gaunt man who was busy squirting oil from a can into a complex set of gears that stuck out the side of the platform.

"We need you to hold the lift," Quirk ordered. We couldn't have it going back up with a load, and bringing Griff down with it.

"What?" asked the driver, straightening. Oil dripped from the gears he'd been working on and into the lake. The water's surface was slick with oil, and dotted with trash; here and there bobbed a dead fish, adding to the stink in the air.

It seemed as if the City killed everything it touched.

Or the City itself was dying.

"We need ten minutes," Quirk said to the lift driver.

"What did you say, Watcher?" he said, and bent closer to Quirk with his hand cupped around his ear. He must be nearly deaf from running the noisy lift.

"Ten minutes," repeated Quirk, and held up ten stubby fingers.

The driver nodded, understanding.

"Listen, Rose," Quirk said as he hurried me along a dock. "Try to keep quiet, if you can." I nodded, understanding. With Griff's vigilance, Quirk hadn't had time to tell me much about the leaders of the Breakers, and we didn't have enough time for this meeting, either. We reached a shed that stood on stilts planted in the oily water of the lake.

At the shed's door we were met by a young woman only a few years older than I was, who had a nasty-looking bruise on her jaw. Her brown hair was cut into a short bristle; she had a wide mouth set in a scowl, and incongruously lovely brown eyes framed by long lashes. She wore trousers, a patched shirt, worn boots, and a leather coat down to her knees. She had a sword, too, in a scabbard at her hip. She blinked when she saw my face, then curled her lip in a sneer. "We've been waiting."

"Nice to meet you, too," Quirk answered with a grin. "I'm Quirk. But you, sweetheart, can call me Quirk. It seems my partner gave you a fine memory of your encounter in the alley the other night."

The young woman rubbed the bruise on her chin. "And I marked him too, didn't I?" she said, frowning down at him. "Do I dare hope that his wound was much more serious than it appeared to be?"

"So bloodthirsty," Quirk chided, and his grin widened. "Oh, and I'd like you to meet the Anvil here"—he flexed one arm—"and the Hammer," and he flexed the other.

She stared. "You've named your muscles."

He gave her a falsely innocent blink. "Of course, sweetheart. Haven't you?"

She gave a disgusted snort and stepped aside so we could go in.

"Hello," I said, trying to be friendly, but she turned the scowl on me, so I ducked my head and hurried past.

The shed was full of rusted metal and broken boards and moldy pieces of canvas; its windows were shuttered. The young woman stepped past us to sit on a barrel. Next to her, close enough so their knees were touching, sat an old woman with thin gray hair scraped into a bun. A third person, a bigger woman, leaned against a wall by the door, arms folded; as we entered, she squeezed past us to leave the shed. Even with her gone, it was four too many for the shed to hold comfortably.

The young woman with the bruised chin shifted aside to give the older woman more room. "Is Bouchet with you?" she asked.

Quirk shook his head. "He had to stay behind to deal with the other Watcher. Who, I might add, is recovering well from the scratch you gave him."

Griff, he meant. Bouchet must have been the big man with the barrel who had blocked Griff's way to the lift.

The gray-haired woman nodded and got stiffly to her feet. She was wearing a beautifully stitched knee-length coat made of dark-green wool, with an embroidered belt and collar. "That's fine." She pointed at the young woman. "This is Timothy. Sent from outside to help us."

Timothy was an odd name for a girl, I thought. "To help you do what?" I asked.

Ignoring my question, the old woman squinted, examining me. "So this is the girl."

"It is," confirmed Quirk.

"You're certain?" the woman asked.

"Absolutely," Quirk answered.

I opened my mouth to ask her name, but Quirk caught my eye and gave a little shake of his head.

"Mm." The old woman leaned closer, and I held myself still as she reached out with thin fingers to brush aside a tendril of hair that hung in my eyes. "Yes, quite lovely, Quirk, as you said," she murmured. Timothy gave another disgusted snort. The old woman took my hand and turned it over to see the bandage on my wrist. "Marked," she noted. "And cursed."

She hadn't yet spoken *to* me, I realized, only *about* me.

The old woman seated herself again on her barrel and stared musingly. "I don't know, Quirk. The Forest has never done anything like this before; it shouldn't have brought her here in the first place."

"Maybe the Forest didn't have any choice," Timothy put in, her voice rough.

The old woman nodded. "Ah, then Story drew her here. Perhaps we should just let the Lord Protector deal with her; that is likely what the Forest intended."

"No," Quirk said, and it sounded strangely like an order. But he wasn't one of the Breakers, he'd said. I wasn't sure why he'd decided to help me, but I suddenly liked him even more than I had before.

The old woman frowned. "It will be difficult to get her out, given what she is."

I knew what the Lord Protector thought I was, and it

seemed the Breakers thought so, too. Her words made me suddenly feel very small and a little frightened, caught up in things that I didn't understand.

"Don't worry, lass," Quirk said quickly, reaching up to pat my arm. "This is Precious." He pointed with his chin at the old woman. "She is the leader of the Breakers. She was one of those who fought Story when it first took power in the City, and she knew the first Protector, Pen."

"Oh," I said to her. "Then you must have known Shoe."

After a silent moment, she answered. "I did, yes, and I am sorry to hear that he is dead." With a thin hand she stroked the embroidery on her coat collar. "Shoe knew better than any of us the power of Story. He had the scars to show for it, too."

Us, she'd said. "Shoe was one of you?" I asked. "He was a Breaker, even though the Penwitch was the Protector?"

Precious frowned and glanced at Quirk. "Does she know nothing?"

As an answer, Quirk gave a shrug.

"Shoe told me stories every night," I ventured. "And I loved him very much. That's what I know."

Quirk nodded approvingly; I'd said the right thing. He lifted his chin and gave Precious a narrow stare. "Rose knows the kinds of stories that open up the world instead of closing our minds. The kinds of stories that Breakers tell." As he spoke, his voice grew deeper with authority and certainty. "Rose will not willingly serve Story, even though Story drew her here and seeks to use her to rise to power again. As I see it, Precious, you have a choice. Rose must either escape from the City or die. You could let the Lord Protector have her. Or you can help her get away."

"That was a very fine speech," Timothy said scornfully.

Quirk gave her a gap-toothed grin. "It was, wasn't it, sweetheart?"

"*Sweetheart* again?" she sniped.

"Always," he answered, with mock seriousness.

Behind me, the door opened, interrupting Timothy's angry retort. The big woman who'd left before stuck her head in. "Jem can't hold the lift any longer," she said brusquely.

"Very well," Precious said with a nod. "Go on, Quirk. We'll need a little time. You'll be contacted soon."

Quirk patted my arm and turned to lead me out of the shed.

"No," I said, refusing to budge.

"Move it," Timothy said, and bumped my shoulder with hers as she brushed past me to the door.

"No," I repeated. "You haven't decided yet. Are you going to help me, or not?"

Precious frowned at Quirk, as if it was his fault that I had spoken. "We don't have time for this."

Quirk glanced up at me. "It's all right, Rose. Just wait outside for a moment, will you? I want to have a quick word with Precious, here."

After a worried moment I nodded and stepped into the

bright day, glad to be out of the dark, stuffy shed, feeling a little shaky about confronting Precious, who had seemed very powerful. Timothy came with me. Facing me, she folded her arms, lowered her brows, and glared.

In return, I gave her a tentative smile. She was one of the Breakers, so she was allied with Quirk. I had never had a friend before. Well, Quirk was a friend of a sort, but he was at least ten years older. I had to try to become friends with Timothy, even though it was clear that she disliked me. I still wasn't sure why. "Timothy is a nice name," I ventured.

"Oh really," she said with a sneer in her voice. "Do you really think so?"

I nodded, and cast about for something else to talk about. "Oh, you're from outside the City, Precious said. So am I."

"Oh my goodness," she said with false sweetness. "We must have so much in common."

I gulped. This wasn't working. "Yes," I said shakily. "I suppose we do."

"Don't even bother, *Rose*," Timothy said roughly. "I know exactly what you are, and what you're up to. So save your little smiles and all of that"—she pointed at my face, at the beauty—"for someone else."

Sudden tears arose in my eyes, and I looked down at the rough boards of the dock. Evidently Timothy and I were not going to be friends.

From inside the shed came the low murmur of Quirk's voice and Precious's, talking. *No,* Quirk said loudly. *She isn't*—and then Precious's sharp voice cut him off.

The big woman leaned over and knocked on the door, reminding them about the lift.

In response, Quirk came out, scowling. Without a word to me, he stalked down the dock toward the lift.

"Well, good-bye," I said to Timothy as I hurried after Quirk.

The lift driver beckoned as he saw us coming, and Quirk picked up his pace.

"Quirk," I asked, as I caught up to him. "They do want to help me, don't they?"

He muttered something that I didn't catch.

It was too much. I stopped in my tracks. I didn't want to go back into the City—it was too dangerous.

Quirk reacted instantly, turning to face me. "What is it, lass?"

I glanced toward the docks, at the river, at the Forest beyond, looking for a way out. "They're not going to help, are they?" I waved at the shed where we'd met the Breakers. "If I go back up there"—I pointed at the top of the cliff—"the Lord Protector will toss me into the citadel prison. I should get away now, while I can."

"The Forest won't let you in, Rose, and the Watchers would catch you before you got a mile down the river."

Desperation welled up in me. "What am I going to *do*?"

"The Breakers will help," he assured me. "Just be patient."

From the end of the dock came a yell—the lift was waiting.

"Come on, lass," Quirk said. "Trust me, all right?"

A moment more of hesitation, and I nodded.

After hurrying from the dock, we stepped onto the lift, which was crowded with coal carts; the driver slammed the gate closed, rang the bell, and threw the lever to start the machinery. Gears clashed; the lift groaned and started crawling up the cliff.

Quirk tugged on my arm, and I bent so he could shout into my ear. "Don't worry, Rose," he said. "It'll be all right. I'll make sure of that."

AS THE LIFT made its rattling way down the cliff face, Griff remembered where he'd seen the big man with the barrel.

"Bouchet," he whispered to himself. The bodyguard he'd encountered in the alley with the Breaker from outside the City. He whirled away from the lift gate and scanned the crowd. *There.* Bouchet was just setting down the barrel he'd been carrying. Without looking up, the big man hunched his shoulders and slouched toward an alley that ran between the railed-off cliff and the brick wall of a warehouse. Griff followed, dodging workers who were readying the next load for the lift. At the mouth of the alley, he peered around the corner just in time to see Bouchet slip through a door in the warehouse wall.

After casting a keen glance behind him—no one, that

he could see, was paying him any attention—Griff entered the alley, hurrying on quiet feet to the door. He put his ear against it. Muffled voices were talking; one sounded deep, like Bouchet. The conversation continued for a few minutes. Then there was the sound of receding footsteps and of another door closing. After a few moments of silence, Griff lifted the latch and opened the door to the warehouse. The room within was dark, but smelled of candle smoke. By the light of the open door, Griff could see that it was empty. Carefully he drew the patrol knife from its sheath at his back and stepped inside.

The room was long and narrow; at its end, Griff found another door—this was where Bouchet, and presumably whoever he'd been talking to, had gone. He was about to open it when he heard, in the distance, the clang of the bell indicating that the lift was arriving back at the top of the cliff. He needed to catch it so he could rejoin Quirk and Rose.

Quickly he opened the door to have a brief look. To his surprise, it opened onto a stairway that went down a few steps and then bent left. *Toward* the cliff. A secret way down to the lake, it looked like. *This* was how goods were being smuggled into the City, and how the young woman with the sword had gotten in, too.

He shook his head, frustrated. He didn't have time to investigate it now. Sheathing the knife again, he made his way back to the alley, then ran to the lift gate. Quirk and Rose were standing to the side while workers unloaded the lift; catching sight of him, Quirk frowned.

Griff joined them. "Quirk, I saw Bouchet, one of the Breakers we followed the other night. I think there might be a secret stair down to the lake."

Quirk shook his head. "Is that your current assignment, junior?"

"No," Griff answered. Not exactly. "But—"

"I will report it," Quirk said sharply. "But you will not let Rose out of your sight again. You let yourself be separated from us just now. You will do your duty, Griff. Understand?"

His duty was to guard Rose, and nothing else. He nodded.

"Good lad," Quirk said approvingly. "Now, we will continue Rose's tour of the City. The factory district." He stepped closer and lowered his voice. "No more mistakes like the lift. No more distractions. Stay alert."

Griff swallowed down a protest. Was he ever not alert? No.

CHAPTER

11

GRIFF WAS TAKING QUIRK'S ORDER VERY SERIOUSLY. I HAD
to trust that Quirk would find a way of distracting Griff when
the time came, or the Breakers' plan to help me escape was
not going to work.

We returned to the citadel and my prison room at the
end of the day. After I told Quirk that I hadn't liked being
stared at in the dining hall, he left Griff on guard while he
went down to fetch us something to eat. I was tired from all
the walking and went to sit down on the cot. Griff leaned a
shoulder against the wall by the door. We hadn't said a word
to each other all day.

Well, I reminded myself, he *was* the son of the man who
had ordered my rose burned off.

With a sigh I took off my cloak, and then pulled up the

sleeve of my dress to have a look at the bandage that covered my rose. The burn still ached wretchedly.

Hearing footsteps, I looked up; Griff came to stand before me and took something from his pocket. Without meeting my eyes, he said, "This is from the physician." He nodded at my arm. "For the burn." He handed me a packet, which I unwrapped, finding a roll of clean bandage and a small stoppered glass vial. Taking the top off, I sniffed. A sharp, medicinal smell; some sort of salve, I guessed.

I bit my lip to keep myself from speaking to him and set the salve on the cot next to me. I picked at the bandage on my wrist; it was tied tightly, and I needed two hands for the job.

Without speaking, Griff knelt on the floor before me and took my hand, turning it so he could get at the bandage. Carefully he took it off and set it aside. The burn was puffy and red around the edges; it felt tender, exposed to the air. Very gently, Griff applied some of the salve, then wrapped the clean bandage around my wrist.

As he worked, I found myself gazing at his bent head, the line of his neck, his shoulders. He was lean, as if his training had pared him down to his essentials, but I could sense his strength, too.

He looked up at me, his face sober. "Is that any better?"

For some reason, my eyes filled with tears. Wordlessly, I nodded.

He got to his feet, then headed back to his post by the door.

"Thank you," I managed to say. But I couldn't tell if he'd heard me or not.

WHEN QUIRK GOT back to my prison room with our dinner, he sent Griff down to the dining hall. "I'll stay with her until you get back, junior," he said.

With a nod, Griff left.

Quirk set the tray down on the cot. "I've had a note from the Breakers." He put his hand into his tunic pocket and drew out a piece of paper, which he unfolded and squinted at.

I sniffed at the muddy brown soup. Fish *again*. With the usual half piece of grayish, gritty bread. With a sigh I picked up the spoon and started eating.

"It's encoded," Quirk said, looking up from the note. With me sitting on the cot, his head was about even with mine. He gave me a reassuring smile and then peered at the note again. "Ah. It's tonight."

"Tonight!" I repeated, and then inhaled a bit of watery, fishy soup.

While I coughed, Quirk peered at the note again. "Mm. Two hours."

"My goodness," I managed. It was happening so fast. "Quirk, what is *it* exactly? I mean, what is the Breakers' plan?"

"I'm sorry, lass. The less you know the better. I can't say anything more."

"Oh." I didn't like it, but I couldn't stay in the City, not with the threats facing me here. I didn't seem to have much choice but to flee with the Breakers.

Quirk went back to the note. "There is a secret way down to the lake." He frowned. "I knew about it already, but it seems Griff almost found it today."

Yes, Griff. "How are we going to get rid of him?" I asked. "So we can escape to meet the Breakers?"

"Tell him his father wants to see him, perhaps," Quirk mused, folding the note and returning it to his pocket. "But that wouldn't give us much time, and it would risk raising the Lord Protector's suspicion. We'll need to leave very soon to get to the lake."

"He's serious about his training," I suggested.

"An extra session, yes." Quirk nodded. "That could work."

I picked up the piece of bread and nibbled at a corner of it. Stale. A thought occurred to me; my stomach twisted with worry. "Quirk, if I get away from the City and the Forest while you and Griff are supposed to be guarding me, will you get into trouble for it?"

Quirk reached out and patted my knee with his small hand. "Well, lass, I've been thinking. It'll be best if I come along to be sure everything is all right." Then he frowned down at the floor. "As for Griff . . ." He shook his head.

"He *will* get into trouble," I confirmed. "But maybe it won't be too bad, since his father is the Lord Protector."

"That will just make it worse," Griff muttered. "He's likely to be tossed out of the Watchers for it." He leaned against the cot, his head lowered, thinking. "I can't figure any way around it, Rose."

My heart sank.

Unlike me, Griff knew what he was—a weapon. What if he had that taken away from him? What would he be then?

I was sorry. But there was nothing I could do about it.

WHEN GRIFF GOT back from dinner, Rose and Quirk were sitting on the cot with their heads together, talking quietly. As he came into the room, they looked up, and Quirk hopped onto the floor. "There you are, junior," he said briskly, with a clap of his hands. Then he looked Griff up and down. "You're looking a bit out of condition. You've skipped training a few times, haven't you?"

He was fit enough. But he had missed a few sessions, that was true.

"Well then," Quirk said. "Rose and I are having a nice chat here. We've some time before locking her in for the night. Go and report to Stet and ask him to drill you. Do some sparring, too."

"Right," Griff said, and turning on his heel, he left the room.

INSTEAD OF REPORTING to Stet in the cohort's room, Griff made his way through the citadel until he reached the Lord Protector's quarters. He'd never disobeyed an order before, but he was sure the Breaker, Bouchet, was up to something. Given some time, he could track down that lead and discover what.

His father wouldn't be around now—he always worked in his office until late. Griff had lived in these rooms as a child, but he hadn't been back here for years, not since he'd joined the Watchers. Checking the hallway—it was empty— he lifted the latch and went in. The rooms were as chilly and austere as they'd always been, and they had the same musty smell even though they were spotlessly clean.

The Lord Protector, Griff knew, did not often go out into the City as himself, but he liked to keep an eye on things, to get a feel for the mood of the people, and when he did, he walked the streets in drab clothing that wouldn't be noticed. Griff opened the closet next to the main door into the apartments and took a shabby sweater and trousers and a long, ragged black coat. In the back of the closet, he found a broken-down pair of boots. Bundling it all in his arms, he slipped out of his father's rooms and into the hallway, then found an abandoned office where he could change. Dressed in the rags, he looked down at himself. He must have almost reached his father's height; the clothes hung loose on his slimmer frame, but they fit surprisingly well.

Leaving his uniform, but taking his patrol knife, he went through deserted hallways and down a back stairway, and let himself out a side door of the citadel, one that led to a seldom-used gate barred from the inside. He unbarred it and, hoping it would still be open when he returned, went out into the dark streets of the City.

The night was chill and dank. Putting his hands into the pockets of the coat, he found a pair of woolen half gloves, which he pulled on as he walked. Few people were out at this time of the evening, and the ones who were kept their heads lowered as they hurried along. Doing the same, Griff made his way along the streets from the citadel and into the warehouse district, until he came to the waterfall. He headed down the dark alley nearby that led to the secret stairway he'd discovered earlier that day. He found a broken barrel in the alley and settled himself in the shadows behind it. There was no telling if Breakers would be using the stairway tonight, but he would keep his watch and see what happened.

CHAPTER
12

WITH GRIFF SENT TO DO HIS EXTRA TRAINING, QUIRK and I didn't have long to wait until it was time to meet the Breakers who would smuggle me out of the City. We left the citadel and hurried through the darkened streets until we arrived at the meeting place, an alley near the lift gate. The sound of water rushing over the falls seemed louder than it had during the day. Nearby, the lift and its pulleys were a looming mechanical skeleton a darker black than the night.

"The note said that Bouchet would meet us here," Quirk whispered.

I nodded and shivered, and pulled my cloak tightly around myself. My burned rose felt better, I realized; it was hardly throbbing at all anymore.

A moment later, I heard the sound of a door opening, and

a huge, shadowed figure approached. Bouchet, I guessed. Without speaking, he led us through an alley that was completely dark, into the warehouse, then through a room that smelled of dust, and through another door.

"Watch your head," Bouchet's deep voice muttered.

We started down a dark, narrow staircase that had been hacked out of the living rock, first Quirk, then me, and then Bouchet. The ceiling was low, and when I put my hand up to check its height, it came away wet and smelling of mold. Behind me, Bouchet's broad shoulders filled the entire stairway, like a wall. The stairs turned, and turned again, and after a long, dark time we reached the bottom, coming out into a bigger room full of shadows that was barely lit. Its floor was rough stone, and its walls were slick with moisture. It wasn't a room, I realized, but a long, narrow cave. We'd reached the level of the lake, and we'd soon come out to the shore where, I assumed, the Breakers would have a boat waiting.

As we went deeper into the cave, Bouchet gripped my shoulder with a big hand. I stopped. The air felt heavy, as if the entire cliff was pressing down over our heads.

"Someone's following," he breathed.

I glanced over my shoulder, seeing nothing but the faint lantern light glistening on the wet walls.

"Here," Quirk whispered, and reaching up to take my hand, drew me deeper into the shadows. Bouchet came with us, and, hidden, we turned to see who would come into the light.

I heard a quiet step on the stair, and a dark figure emerged into the cave. He was wearing a ragged coat instead of his uniform, and his hair, usually neatly combed, was rumpled, but I knew immediately who it was. Griff. He looked keenly alert, and held an unsheathed knife in one hand. I covered my mouth to stifle a gasp.

"Ah, curse it," I thought I heard Quirk say.

"I've got a sword," Bouchet whispered. "I'll do him."

"No," Quirk said quickly. He tugged on Bouchet's arm, and the big man bent so he could hear Quirk's whispered words. "Go for help. I'll get his knife, but he's very skilled. You'll need at least two others to overpower him."

Griff had come farther into the cave, and he paused, head cocked, listening.

"Go," Quirk breathed, and as Bouchet nodded, he took three quick steps out of the shadows and into the light. "Ah, junior," he said in a low voice. "It's some luck meeting you here."

Griff started to speak, when Quirk looked over his shoulder, as if hearing a noise. "Quickly, lad. They're coming. I need your knife."

Without even hesitating, Griff flipped the knife and held it, handle first, out to Quirk. "Three of them, I think," he said intently. "I heard their footsteps on the stairs. Breakers?"

Quirk reached up and took the knife and stepped away from him. At the same moment, Bouchet and Timothy and the other woman who'd been at the shed came out of the shadows, ready to fight. "He's disarmed," Quirk said softly, almost sadly. "Take him."

For just a moment, I saw Griff react—a wide-eyed look of shock and dismay—and the three Breakers set upon him, Bouchet with a knife, the big woman with a club, and Timothy with a sword. As they attacked, Griff whirled into motion. It was too fast—I didn't even see what happened, except that Timothy's sword clattered onto the stone floor and she had fallen, holding her side. Griff had already turned and, ducking a thrust from Bouchet's knife, he blocked the woman's club with his arm and elbowed her in the face. She fell to the floor, blood fountaining from her nose.

I could see why Quirk had told Bouchet to go for help. Griff didn't even need the knife—he *was* a knife.

"Block the stairs," Quirk shouted.

They might have been too late—he might have gotten away—except that Timothy reached out as Griff leaped past her and grabbed his leg, and he went down hard onto the stone floor. Before he could recover, Quirk was there with the knife. He held it to Griff's throat, his knee on his chest.

"Be still, lad," Quirk said.

Pushing Quirk aside, Bouchet dragged Griff to his feet and slammed him hard against the cave wall not an arm's length away from me. Griff gasped, almost a sob, and fought against Bouchet's hold until the big man grabbed his wrist and twisted his arm up behind him, pressing him against the wall with a hand against the back of his neck. Griff's eyes were closed, his teeth clenched as he struggled to catch his breath. The bigger woman, still bleeding from the nose, came up with a length of rope and quickly looped it around Griff's hands, tying them behind his back. Then Bouchet spun him around again, bunched his big hand into a fist, and swung it at Griff's head—but Griff evaded the punch and hooked Bouchet's ankle; the big man tipped over, and like a tree falling, crashed to the ground. Roaring, he lurched to his feet and managed to grab Griff by the collar of his coat. "You're in for it now, Watcher," he growled. He bared his teeth and cocked his big fist.

Griff glared daggers at him, but didn't speak.

"That's enough," Quirk said sharply, stepping between them.

Bouchet could have easily pushed Quirk aside, but he obeyed, dropping his fist while keeping his hold on Griff's collar. "We need to give him a knock on the head and drop him in the lake," he grunted.

Kill him? "No," I gasped.

Seeing me, Griff's eyes went wide; then he looked away, his face set and pale.

"We have to get rid of him," the big woman put in, swiping her sleeve across her bloody nose. "We can't have the Watchers learning about the stairs to the lake."

"Bring him with us," Quirk ordered.

After a moment, Bouchet nodded. "We'll let Precious decide what to do with him." Taking Griff's arm, he dragged him along with us as we went through the rest of the cave and ducked beneath a low arch that was concealed by a deep crevice in the cliff. We edged around that and came out onto the rocky shore of the lake.

The rush of the waterfall, not far away, covered the sound of our footsteps crunching on the graveled beach. While we'd been inside the cliff, a three-quarter moon had risen and hung low in the sky, giving enough light to see the deserted docks off to our left, and the barges that were anchored farther out on the lake. A boat was waiting, just a shadow against the glimmering surface of the water. Without hesitating, the other two Breakers pushed it deeper into the lake, the keel grating over the stones. "Get in," Bouchet ordered, and I awkwardly climbed over the side and felt my way to a seat at the front of the boat. A moment later, Griff had been shoved onto the seat next to me; his shoulder bumped mine.

And oh, I wished he hadn't followed us. "I'm so sorry about this," I whispered, but it was as if I hadn't spoken. In the moonlight his face was so bleak, like stone. He didn't speak; he didn't even glance at me.

A thump, and Quirk climbed onto the seat behind me. The boat tilted; the keel scraped the rocks again, and Bouchet and Timothy had climbed aboard, leaving the big woman to push us farther out into the water. Another bump, and Bouchet settled himself at the oars and started rowing us away from the shore; Timothy was at the back end, holding the tiller to steer.

We slipped quietly past the moored barges and the impenetrably dark and forested banks of the lake. The cliff face, a black, rough curtain split by the rushing swath of the waterfall, receded behind us; above it a few lights shone from the City, and then, as we entered the river, disappeared.

GRIFF FELT THE shock of Quirk's betrayal echoing through him. For six months they'd been partners; Griff had trusted him completely, had admired him. The Lord Protector's unremitting coldness had become easier to bear because Quirk had been there, with his named muscles and gap-toothed grin and steady approval. But it was a lie. All along, Quirk must have been using him to get closer to the Lord Protector, to discover information that he could pass along to the Breakers. Griff closed his eyes at the bitterness of the realization.

The Breakers would probably decide to kill him. He was of absolutely no use to them as a hostage, despite who his father was. Quirk knew that well enough. If they freed him they'd have to assume—rightly—that he'd go straight back to the City to report to the Lord Protector.

Gradually he became aware of his surroundings. Rose was a huddled warmth at his side. The Breakers had to be helping her escape from the City. They were criminals, but he couldn't help feeling relieved that she was getting away. Her head had tipped onto his shoulder; she breathed softly, asleep. The Breaker woman had tied his hands tightly, and his arms ached. In the fight the sword cut had opened again so that blood seeped into his sweater, but he didn't want to shift on the hard seat in case he waked Rose. Instead he watched the reflected moonlight flow in ripples past the boat. All he could see of the shore was a dark tangle of trees and other plants he didn't know the names of. It smelled strange—like green, living things, he guessed, along with the tang of the river and a hint of woodsmoke.

Griff had seen the river and the lake from atop the cliff, but he'd never been outside the City walls. He'd been focused on becoming a Watcher, and training, and learning from Quirk, and trying to please his impossible-to-please father. It had been a hard life, but he'd never questioned it. Maybe he should have.

Well, it was too late for all of that, now.

As they continued down the river, a mist rose from the Forest, flowing over the surface of the water until they were enveloped in a dense, shifting fog that glowed white with the ambient moonlight. Even if anyone from the City was watching, or pursuing, Griff realized, the boat would be hidden by the fog.

After another hour of rowing, Bouchet set the oars aside and the young woman at the tiller steered the boat out of the current. The shore appeared out of the mist, dark and silent. They hadn't gone far enough yet to get beyond the Forest, which let supplies in and factory products out by the river, but, as far as Griff knew, allowed nobody from the City to escape. And there was another outpost of Watchers farther down the river. The Breakers wouldn't get past that barrier, so they must have figured out some other way of getting through to the outside world.

Beside him, Rose sat up, awake, but she didn't speak. The boat glided, then bumped to a stop against the riverbank, and Bouchet climbed out and tethered it to a tree. The others followed, and Bouchet leaned in and jerked Griff to his feet, pulling him out of the boat. He'd hardly found his footing on the lumpy ground when Bouchet grabbed the collar of his ragged coat and brought him along with the rest of them. They made their way down a barely discernible path through the shadowed woods. As they walked, the fog lifted. Ahead Griff could see a flickering light through the trees; a few steps later they came out into a clearing that had a small cottage made of round river stones in its center; off to the side of it was a fire that had been built in a shallow pit in the ground. It burned brightly and had a pot of something strange-smelling bubbling over it. An old woman got up from one of the big logs around the fire and came to meet them.

The old woman was Precious, Griff guessed. The one who would decide what the Breakers would do with him. She had a sharp, lined face and gray hair that she wore in a thin braid down her back; she had on trousers and a long, green coat and sturdy boots. "You're late," she said sternly.

"Had some trouble," Bouchet answered, and shoved Griff ahead of him. Griff stumbled, then found his balance.

Precious studied him, eyebrows raised, but didn't speak.

"He's a Watcher," Bouchet said. "He followed us. Knows about the secret stair to the lake."

"Hm." Precious looked past him to where Quirk and Rose stood together just inside the ring of light cast by the fire. The young woman stood in the shadows behind Rose, almost like a guard. "And you've brought the girl," Precious said.

"I've come, too," Quirk put in.

"Yes, I can see that." Precious turned back to Griff, frowning. "Well, Watcher? What do you have to say for yourself?"

Griff stared at her. The words he would have spoken were stuck in his throat, like stones.

"He's not very chatty at the best of times," Quirk put in. "His name is Griff, and he's been my partner for the past six months."

The bitterness arose again. Griff gritted his teeth against it and looked away, at the tangled, dark wall of the Forest beyond the clearing. It was a lighter gray than it had been before; he saw that dawn was rising.

"We need to get rid of him," Bouchet put in. "He's a danger to our plans."

To Griff's surprise, Rose stepped closer; her eyes were wide, hands clenched. "You can't kill him," she insisted.

"Keep her quiet, Quirk," Precious interrupted. Quirk reached out and pulled Rose to stand beside him, muttering something that made her nod.

"Hm." Precious studied Griff, laying a thin finger across her lips, thinking. Then she stepped closer and spoke in a whisper that only he could hear. "I know very well who you are, boy. And I wonder what the Lord Protector would give to have you back again."

All Griff could do was shake his head. His father would give nothing at all.

"You are a curse eater, and, as Quirk reports, an extremely skilled and loyal Watcher," Precious went on. "Yet I am not quite sure what to make of you." Slowly she looked him up and down again. "You cannot stay here, and we cannot allow you to return to the City. And yet killing you . . ." She shook her head. "We are not murderers. And it would not serve our purpose."

Griff wasn't sure what the Breakers' purpose was, beyond overthrowing the Lord Protector's rule of the City. Rose would play some role in their plans; he didn't know what.

Abruptly Precious raised her voice, speaking so the others could hear her. "I am sending him with you."

"What?" Bouchet protested. "He'll just try to escape back to the City."

"No matter," Precious said with an elegant shrug. She beckoned to Quirk, who still held Griff's patrol knife. "Come and cut these ropes."

As Quirk approached, Griff tensed. The Breakers would come after him if he ran, but if he could reach the shore, and the boat, he could use it to get back to the City. He felt Quirk's small hand against his arm, holding him steady, then the rope was cut, leaving his hands free.

Immediately he pushed past Quirk, then paused, looking back. Precious gave him a nod, as if saying *go ahead*. Rose stood with her hands gripped together, her eyes wide—and just for a moment he hesitated. He wanted her to escape— better that than letting her end up in one of Luth's prison cells. But then Bouchet bellowed and lunged toward him; Griff ducked his reaching arms, whirled, and raced for the path that led to the river.

CHAPTER

13

Run, I wanted to shout after Griff. The big man, Bouchet, swore and took a few steps toward the path.

"Wait," Precious ordered, holding up a hand.

"But he's going for the boat," Bouchet protested.

Precious shrugged again. "Come and sit down and have some stew," she said. "You'll all need to eat before you set off again."

"Mm, stew!" Quirk said with a wink at Precious; he went to the fire and stood on tiptoe, peering into the bubbling pot.

With a huff of annoyance, Bouchet stalked past Quirk and sat down on one of the sawn logs. Timothy gave him a resigned shrug, went to the fire, and held out her hands to warm them.

"Help serve the stew, Timothy," Precious said. She stood

with arms folded, watching the tree line as if waiting for something.

As Timothy handed a bowl and spoon to Quirk, Griff suddenly burst into the clearing from the path. He was panting and trailing vines and leaves, with twigs tangled in his hair. He stumbled to a halt and looked wildly around.

I was strangely glad to see him. But why had he come back, when he'd only just escaped?

"Ah, there you are, lad," Quirk said. Bouchet had a dripping spoonful of stew halfway to his mouth; he and Timothy stared. Precious just looked smug.

Griff tensed as if he was poised to flee again, when his face turned bleak with understanding. "The Forest," he said, catching his breath. He glanced at the path again.

"That's right," Precious said with an approving nod. "It is our ally."

Oh. The Forest was what made the City a prison. It wouldn't let Griff escape. The same way it had given me a path, it had changed Griff's path to lead him back here.

I went to the fire to join Quirk, who handed me a bowl of stew. Precious entered the cottage; a few minutes later she came out with a loaf of brown bread, which she handed to Bouchet. He tore off a chunk and passed it around.

I tried the stew. It was fragrant and savory with sage and black pepper. The bread came to me and I took some and dipped it into my bowl. Mmm. Shoe had been a wonderful cook; this tasted like something he would have made from the vegetables and herbs that we grew in our garden.

"Ask him to come have something to eat," Quirk said quietly, pointing with his chin at Griff, who stood beyond the warmth of the fire, his face in shadows.

My mouth full of bread, I raised my eyebrows, a question.

"He doesn't trust me at the moment," Quirk said, with a wry twist of his mouth.

I nodded and finished my bite, then got to my feet. As I approached, Griff took a wary step back.

"I'm sorry you've gotten caught up in this," I said softly. "I know you don't trust any of us. I can hardly blame you, really. I don't trust us either." Not even myself, entirely.

He glanced at my face, then away. The beauty. It seemed to make him uneasy. Well, it made me uneasy, too.

"Here's the thing, Griff," I went on. "The Breakers do seem to want to help me."

He was silent a moment. "Why?" he asked, his voice gruff.

Maybe that's what I would call him—*Gruff* instead of *Griff*. It certainly suited him. As I looked up at him, I couldn't help smiling at the thought, and his eyes widened. "I don't know why."

He frowned and gave a skeptical shake of his head.

I was doubtful, too. But like him, I didn't have any choice in the matter. "Yes, well, come and have some dinner." I eyed the sky over the clearing, which was pink, now, with dawn.

"Some breakfast, I mean." I turned and went back to sit with Quirk.

After a few moments, Griff came to the fire, where Precious handed him a bowl and the heel of the bread. He nodded and went to sit on a sawn-off log across the fire from us.

Quirk gave my arm a companionable nudge. "Watch Griff's face when he tries the stew," he whispered.

"Why?" I murmured.

He grinned. "He has only ever eaten food from the citadel kitchen."

"You mean that horrible fish soup?" I asked.

"Lentils, oats, watery fish soup, stale bread, potatoes. No spices, no herbs," Quirk said conspiratorially. "Not even salt."

We both watched. Griff looked as if he was deep in thought—probably trying to figure out another way to escape back to the City. Absently, he stirred the stew.

"Wait for it . . . ," Quirk whispered.

Griff ate a spoonful. His eyes widened with surprise. He stared down at his bowl as if it had bitten him.

I felt a laugh bubbling up in my throat.

He froze and glanced across the fire at me.

I couldn't help it—I laughed aloud. And to my surprise, his austere face lightened into a wry smile.

At the same moment, the rising sun peeked over the trees, flooding the clearing with golden-pink light. I blinked, dazzled, and despite the uncertainty about who I was and where I was going, for the first time since Shoe had died I felt as if my story would again have a measure of happiness in it. Maybe only a wry smile's worth, but that, at least, was something.

ONCE THE SUN was fully up and Precious had packed another knapsack and blanket roll for Griff, we stood at the edge of the clearing, waiting for the Forest to give us a path, one that would lead us to the outside world. I was fleeing from darkness and sorrow into further darkness, and maybe danger, but I was eager to find out what would happen next, where my story would take me. Or maybe where I would take my story.

The big man, Bouchet, was carrying the biggest pack; he stood talking quietly with Timothy, who glanced at me, curling her lip in disdain. Griff stood alone, hands shoved deep into the pockets of his ragged black coat, gazing at the trees that surrounded the clearing. He'd been quiet before, in the City, but now he was even quieter, as if drawn into himself.

Precious stood with us, but she would stay behind in the cottage, with the big woman whose name I still didn't know. The Forest, Quirk told me, had made a place for her. She hadn't lived inside the City for a long time, not since Pen, as he called the Penwitch, had gone away and a new Protector had taken her place. After a few years, he had decided he was a Lord Protector who could keep Story from rising through the practice of strict rationality. And, apparently, by serving only very bad food.

"So the Forest is going to let us through?" I asked Quirk. "Even though it won't let anyone else out of the City? How does that work?"

"Ah," Quirk said, tapping his nose, which was crooked, as if it had been broken.

"Oh really." I tapped my nose back at him. "What does that mean?"

"That I know something that you don't know," he said.

"You know a lot of things that I don't know," I grumbled.

Quirk gave me a lopsided grin. Then he nodded toward Precious, who stood at the very edge of the clearing with her head bent and a fist over her heart. "Wait and see."

Bouchet went to stand near Precious, as if lending her his strength. Quirk sat on the mossy ground next to me, then lay back and closed his eyes, using his pack for a pillow. Almost as if she couldn't help it, Timothy wandered over and stood looking down at Quirk.

"Hello, sweetheart," he said, without opening his eyes.

With a huff of impatience, she turned and went away again.

The sun crept higher in the sky. A few birds twittered and hopped in the lowest branches of the trees.

"Over there," Quirk said suddenly, sitting up and pointing. I turned to look, and sure enough, there was a shadowed opening in the trees not far from where Griff stood. A new path.

"Finally," Timothy murmured and shouldered her pack.

Precious raised her head, shivered, and blinked as if waking up. "Good," she said in a rusty voice. She held something out to Timothy; I saw a flash of sunlight on silver as she dropped it into the girl's palm. Timothy stowed whatever it was in the pocket of her leather coat. Precious spoke to her quietly, and Timothy nodded, listening.

"What was that?" I asked Quirk.

"A thimble," he answered. "It's a kind of talisman; a thing of power. It doesn't command the Forest, but it will open a path for us."

Precious turned to the rest of us and cleared her throat. "It is a three-day journey to the edge of the Forest," she said briskly. "Do not linger. Stay on the path." She turned to Bouchet. "If the thimble fails," she began, then added something in a low voice.

"We'll see it done," Bouchet muttered in reply. With a nod to Timothy, who led the way, he stepped onto the path.

Quirk handed me my pack and took up his own.

"So this thimble," I asked him. "It's magic?"

Quirk nodded. "Yes. Magic of a kind."

"Oh," I said. "I thought that sort of thing only existed in stories."

He turned and squinted up at me. "Well, you are in a story now, lass, aren't you?"

"Yes." I nodded. "But not one of Story's making."

"Mm," Quirk said noncommittally.

I gave him a narrow look, which he pretended not to see.

Once I was beyond Story's reach I would try to prove that I wasn't a catalyst, or a servant of Story. I was determined to make the rest of my life my own, true, real story. Escaping from the City was a good start.

FEELING UNEASY, GRIFF followed the rest of the travelers. What would his father say if he could see him now? He'd be coldly disapproving, Griff knew. For half a blink, he hoped his father might be worried about him, missing from the citadel with no explanation. With a shake of his head, he pushed that thought away. The Lord Protector could barely bring himself to look at his son; admitting to worry would be impossible for him.

To distract himself from thoughts about his father, Griff paid attention to his surroundings. He had been trained to observe, and he felt a little overwhelmed by the abundant tangles of greenery that edged the path, so different from the sterile gray of the City. The Forest on either side of the path was impenetrably dense with plants he had never seen before.

He looked ahead and caught Rose glancing back at him. She'd been walking next to Quirk, but now she took a skipping step down the path to join him.

"Hello, Gruff," she said cheerfully.

He wasn't sure what she had to be so cheerful about. And . . . Gruff?

"Would you hold this for me?" she asked, and held up a length of string.

He took it.

She thanked him with a brief smile; with quick fingers, she started combing out her hair and then rebraiding it. "Quirk told me that you've never been outside the City before," she noted.

Quirk. He shook his head.

"Moss," she said.

"What?" he asked.

She pointed with her chin at the path. She'd come to the end of her braid, and then she stopped, looking up at him. He gazed down at her, completely unable to look away. It wasn't the beauty that held him; it was her. Her eyes were shining. "Could I, um, have the string?"

He held it out to her; for just a moment their fingers touched, and her cheeks flushed pink. He wanted . . . he didn't know what he wanted. The moment stretched, and then broke.

She blinked and pulled away from him. How had they come to be standing so close together? "We're walking on moss," she said brightly, wrapping the string around the end of her braid. "Green antler moss, to be specific." She flipped her braid over her shoulder. "It grew in our valley, too. The trees through here are hickory"—she pointed at one gray-barked tree—"and black oaks, with the occasional red oak and chestnut."

He was interested, despite himself. "What are those?" He pointed.

"Ferns," she said promptly. She parted the greenery, pointing to a cluster of pale, round things growing from the leaf-covered ground underneath. "And those are mushrooms." She grimaced. "But not ones you'd want to eat."

Mushrooms? And people ate them? It occurred to him that there might have been mushrooms in the strange soup he'd eaten earlier.

She started walking again, and he fell into step beside her.

"Quirk feels terrible about what's happened," she ventured after a while.

"I don't want to talk about Quirk," he said abruptly.

"No, I suppose not."

He stayed quiet for a few steps, but he had to warn her. "Rose—"

"I like it when you call me by my name," she interrupted. "Quirk calls me *lass* mostly, and Bouchet and Timothy don't talk to me at all. Shoe called me Rosie."

He forged on. "Rose, about Quirk . . . ," he began, speaking in a low voice.

She shrugged. "I like Quirk."

"Yes, he's very likeable," Griff said bitterly.

She frowned down at the mossy path. "He's the first

friend I've ever had, apart from Shoe."

Griff refrained from pointing out that Quirk had been his only friend. "Just . . . be careful." He'd been watching Quirk very closely. For now Quirk was working with the Breakers, it seemed, but he wasn't one of them, Griff suspected. Knowing Quirk—and Griff *did* know him, despite everything—he was up to something. Something that would make sense to Quirk, but to no one else.

CHAPTER

14

WE WALKED FOR THE REST OF THE DAY THROUGH THE sun-dappled Forest, our path winding lazily around the base of hills. Sometimes the sun was on our left, and sometimes it was on our right. The Forest, it seemed, was in no hurry to let us pass through.

Or maybe Story didn't want to let me go.

As the shadows lengthened toward evening, the path ended abruptly in a grove of tall pine trees. Bouchet slung his heavy pack on the ground, which was thickly carpeted with pine needles, and started scraping out a place for a campfire. "Go collect wood," he ordered. He jerked his chin at Quirk, who held one of the pots we'd use for cooking. "Find some water."

The pine trees had straight trunks, with needly branches

high above, and spiky, broken-off branches below. I edged around them, looking for firewood. Timothy was searching for wood, too, but ignored me. I caught glimpses of her between the trees. She was dressed more practically than I was, in her trousers and long leather jacket; her short, dark hair was covered by a brightly patterned scarf. I was curious about her. She didn't know me, but she disliked me intensely, and I wanted to know why.

As she bent to pick up a pine branch, I stepped up to her and smiled. "Hello."

She straightened and gave me a baleful stare. Then, without speaking, she turned her back on me and started for the campsite.

I hurried after her. "I've been wondering. Quirk said that you had a fight with Griff in an alley?"

She stopped and whirled to face me. "Yes, your boyfriend and I have met before."

I felt a blush creeping up my cheeks. "What? But he's not—"

"Oh, stop," she interrupted. "I saw the pair of you drooling at each other."

"We weren't—" I shook my head. Since our conversation, when I'd felt so awkward, I'd tried to keep my distance from Griff, and yet I seemed to always be aware of where he was, and what he was doing. It made me feel unsettled. There was no point in explaining all of this to her. "What happened?"

Timothy's smile was not friendly. It had an edge that

would cut through steel. "The Watcher and I had a disagreement." Her smile grew even sharper. "I gave him a little memory of our fight, too. A cut over his ribs. I wish I'd struck a little harder. He is the son of the Lord Protector, after all. I should have spilled his guts in the street."

She really hated him. "I don't think you could have," I reasoned. "He's a very good fighter."

"Yeah, well." She smirked, and seemed to be about to say something else, then shrugged, and turned away.

I followed her to the campsite, where Bouchet was on his knees by the cleared area he'd made for the fire. Quietly I piled my collection of wood next to him, then went to help Quirk make our dinner.

After we ate, we sat around the campfire while the pine forest grew dark. Owls hooted, one to another, and a nearly full moon rose. Bouchet and Timothy had their heads together, whispering, every now and then glancing at me, as if I was the subject of their conversation. Quirk seemed deep in thought, and a little sad; Griff was leaning against a tree, staring off into the darkness. I wanted to go talk to him, but I felt oddly shy. Ever since he'd tried lifting my curse, I'd felt a connection to him, and now something between us was changing. I just didn't know what, exactly.

I sat and watched the crimson and gold of the fire as it ate the wood I'd collected, and felt hollow with loneliness, missing Shoe. I turned over my wrist, thinking of him, and noticed that my burned rose barely ached at all. I closed my eyes and saw Griff kneeling before me in my citadel room, gently bandaging the burn. Yes, he was keen—a knife. But he was surprisingly kind, too, and so quiet and so serious. So . . . alone.

When I opened my eyes, he was sitting beside me.

"Oh," I said, startled. "Hello."

"Hello," he answered, his voice rough.

That was probably the first word he'd said to anyone since we'd spoken that morning. I smiled, thinking of it.

"You're happy," he observed.

"I suppose I am," I said, after considering it for a moment. Then I gave half a laugh. "I really shouldn't be, should I? Given the situation? But I can't help it. It's just how I'm made." I glanced aside at him. With his fingers he was breaking a twig into pieces that he was tossing into the fire. "You're not happy."

"No," he said quietly.

I thought about our conversation in the citadel room, when he'd said some fairly awful things to me. "You told me that my stories were false. You said that I was dangerous. Do you still think that?"

"I don't know," he answered.

Neither did I. We sat quietly, watching the flames. Across the fire, Quirk spread out his blanket and lay down.

"You were a weapon," I said at last.

He nodded.

"And now you're not, are you?"

He gazed at me, but didn't speak.

"If you really were a weapon," I said, reasoning it out, "you would have killed me already. You've had plenty of chances. So if you're not a weapon, what are you?"

"I don't know," he said in a voice so low I could barely hear him. "I don't know anything anymore."

What a thing for him to admit. He, who'd had such absolute certainty in his life. Away from the City, and his father's rules, he was completely adrift. I reached out a hand, just to lay it on his arm to comfort him, but he stood abruptly and retreated from the fire, back to the shadows beyond.

With a sigh, I prepared my bedroll and went to sleep.

The next day was much the same. We trudged through the Forest and I thought about Griff, but barely spoke to him.

We walked. Quirk watched Griff carefully; Griff kept a wary distance from both of us.

By the following day, we should have come to the end of the Forest. Our supplies were running low, Bouchet was snappish, and Timothy had started wearing the thimble on her finger, hoping it would point the way more clearly.

Quirk and I were walking together, talking quietly, when Bouchet, ahead of us, cursed loudly and whirled to face us. Beside him, Timothy took the thimble from her finger, glared at it, and shoved it into her coat pocket.

"What's the matter?" Quirk asked.

"Look at it," Bouchet said, hurling his knapsack onto the ground.

The path had led us to a clearing. Around us clustered pine trees with straight trunks, and in the middle of the clearing was . . . the blackened remains of a campfire in a pit that had been scraped out of the pine-needly ground. No wonder the path had seemed familiar.

"We camped here on the first night," Timothy said disgustedly.

"The Forest has been leading us in circles," Bouchet confirmed. "Even with the thimble, it won't let us through."

"It's because of her," Timothy snarled, and pointed sharply at me.

"Me?" I squeaked.

"If the Forest won't let her out into the world," she said, "it must have a good reason,"

Bouchet nodded. "Or Story is trying to draw her back to the City."

"It's because of what she is," Timothy added.

I heard a quiet step and knew that Griff was standing at my back.

"And what . . . what is that?" I asked. "What am I?"

Timothy's answer was a sneer. Bouchet folded his burly arms and looked away.

"Tell her what you think," Quirk said beside me.

"She's marked, and cursed, and there's the"—Timothy's lip did its usual curl—"the way she looks. That kind of beauty is unnatural. It's perfectly obvious what she is. She's a construct of Story."

"A construct?" I asked. "What does that mean?"

"They think that you weren't just chosen to serve Story, you were created by it," Quirk said steadily. "A construct is a thing, and not a person."

"What?" I gasped, staring at Bouchet and Timothy, my heart pounding. "You think I'm a *thing*?" Neither answered, but oh, it explained why Timothy hated me so much. I turned to Quirk. "Before, you said I was a catalyst, Quirk. Not . . . not this. Is this what you really think?"

He gazed up at me, his lopsided face sad. "Listen, lass . . . ," he began.

"You do?" I whispered.

And Griff. He had to believe it; he'd been trained all his life to fight Story. Shivering, I backed away, bumping into Griff's shoulder, then felt his hand on my arm, steadying me. I shook him off. "What—what are you going to do?" I asked, my voice shaking.

"We've made a good effort to do what Precious asked of us," Bouchet said, speaking to the others, not to me. "But the thimble has failed, and Story is drawing the construct back to the City. We should abandon her here and get out of the Forest."

"No," Quirk said, in the same way he'd given Precious the order.

"If we don't," Timothy replied, "the Forest will just lead all of us in circles until we run out of supplies."

My heart trembled. "Why don't you just say what you

mean?" I demanded. "You're going to leave me out here to die."

"We wouldn't really be killing her," Timothy reasoned, speaking to Quirk. Her hand went to the pommel of her sword.

At that, Griff's head jerked up, and he reached for something at his back. His knife—but he didn't have it, Quirk did.

Quirk raised his hands. "All right, that's enough," he said with uncharacteristic sternness. "It's getting late. We're all hungry and tired. We'll decide what we're going to do in the morning." He pointed toward the other end of the piney glade. "You two set up your camp over there," he ordered Bouchet and Timothy.

"Oh, I see how it is," Timothy spat. "The construct has fluttered her long eyelashes at you, Quirk, and at the Watcher, and now you're both willing to do her bidding."

To my surprise, Quirk grinned at her. "Jealous?"

Timothy's face went red. "No," she protested.

Quirk nodded toward their camping spot. "Now, go on, sweetheart."

Scowling, the two Breakers collected their nearly empty packs and made their way through the clusters of pines.

Quirk kept his eyes on them. "Don't worry, Rose," he said quietly to me. "I'll make sure they don't bother you tonight. But we'll have to work it out in the morning. Timothy has the thimble. We can't get out of the Forest without it."

I felt tremblingly full of tears, but I was *not* going to cry. Did Quirk *really* think I was a construct? He didn't speak as if he did. "I am not a thing, Quirk," I insisted.

He looked up at me and gave me his lopsided smile. "Ah, well," he said obliquely.

He had told me that it would be all right, and maybe it was stupid of me, but I still believed him.

With a nod he turned and went to his pack, which he'd dropped on the ground near the fire pit, and started rummaging in it. "Shall we have a fire, lass, and see what we can scrape up for dinner?"

"In a moment," I answered, turning to face Griff. He was frowning, his gaze fixed on Timothy and Bouchet as they made their way through the pine trees to a new campsite. "And what about you?" I pointed. "Should you go over there with them?"

He shook his head.

"I never fluttered my eyelashes at anyone," I grumbled.

For just a moment, his face lightened. Not a smile, but almost.

Well, that was something. I found myself smiling back. I turned away to help Quirk start the fire.

"Rose?" came Griff's voice behind me.

I stopped, but didn't turn to face him. "Yes?"

"I don't—" He paused, and I heard him take a deep, shaking breath. "I never believed it," he went on quietly. "I never thought of you as a . . ." He paused again. "A thing."

"Thank you," I whispered.

And this time I knew that he heard me.

LATER, AS WE sat around our campfire, keeping an eye on Bouchet and Timothy's fire, and eating the thin soup we'd made from some shelf mushrooms and fern tips I'd found, and chewing on our last heel of bread, I thought about what the Breakers had said.

They thought I was a construct. While I didn't think it could be true, there was still so much I didn't know of my own story. Only what Shoe had told me. I knew that the Penwitch had brought a baby to Shoe. *Where did I come from?* I had asked him once. *Out in the world somewhere*, he'd said. Now that I'd been out in the world, I realized how vague an answer that was. What had the Penwitch taken me away *from*? Did I have a mother and father somewhere? Or did I just belong to Story—was I its creation, as they all seemed to think?

No. I couldn't be. Shoe hadn't loved a *thing*, he had loved me. *Me*.

I had never expected my story to take such an awful turn. I wasn't sure what to do. All I could do was go on, and try to figure out what kind of person I really was.

And figure out what sort of people I'd ended up with.

I eyed Quirk, who sat across the campfire from me. He'd taken a little sewing kit from his knapsack and was busy stitching up a tear in my cloak. Griff was on his feet, leaning against a tree, but alert, as if on guard.

"How much of Quirk's story do you know?" I asked Griff.

He straightened, glanced at Quirk, then away. "Very little."

Quirk bit off a thread. "He hasn't been trained to think in terms of stories," he said to me.

"He's up to something, I know that much," Griff added.

Quirk gave an approving nod. "So you've figured that out, have you?"

Griff gave a one-shouldered shrug. But somehow, even though he was silent, he didn't seem quite so remote as he had before.

"Clever lad, our Griff," Quirk said, and winked at me.

I rolled my eyes. "Do you feel like strangling him, too?" I asked Griff.

"Usually," Griff said with a straight face.

"Now, children," Quirk chided, but betrayed himself with a happy smile.

So things were better now, between him and Griff. But not, I thought, all better.

As our fire burned down to embers, and the night grew darker, we decided that we'd take turns keeping watch.

"I don't really think we'll have any trouble," Quirk said. "But it's best if we're careful."

I curled up with my blanket, using my pack for a pillow.

Griff had the first watch; I could hear his quiet footsteps

as he circled our camp. I knew he was keenly alert. It made me feel safe, secure.

Hours later, Quirk woke me with a shake of my shoulder. "Your turn, lass," he whispered. I sat up and wrapped the blanket around myself and sat by our fire to keep my watch.

Toward morning, a wind picked up, and the high pine branches rustled, and the shadows between the tree trunks seemed to shift. Our fire was a glow of red and orange embers. Through the trees, I caught glimpses of the answering glow of the Breakers' campfire. It winked at me, a red eye opening and closing. At last, the sky lightened, but it was heavy with clouds. A fine mist rose from the ground, twining around the trees. All seemed quiet. Too quiet.

Stiffly, I got to my feet and peered through the mist, looking for the Breakers. Their fire had gone out.

I took a few steps toward their camp. "Hello?" I ventured, and my voice was swallowed up by the fog that swirled around me.

Then a shadow loomed out of the whiteness—another step, and I saw that it was Timothy. Her face was pale and her eyes were wide and frightened. Seeing me, she put her hand to her sword. "Where is he?" she hissed.

"Who?" I stepped back and raised my hands.

"Bouchet," she snarled, and pulled the sword from its scabbard.

From behind me I heard swift footsteps; a rush and Griff was past me, putting himself between me and Timothy. "I'm unarmed," I heard him say.

She gritted her teeth, but didn't lower her blade. "He's gone. Bouchet."

"All right," said Quirk, who had come up beside me. His feet were bare and his straw-yellow hair was tousled from sleep. When he spoke, he kept his voice calm. "You two were preparing to abandon the three of us, weren't you, Timothy? And the Forest took Bouchet, it seems. He'll end up back in the City."

"Curse it." Timothy glared at the fog and the trees, as if she wanted to challenge the Forest to a duel.

"But you, apparently, have been left with us," Quirk said carefully.

"Which means we're still stuck." With a shake of her head, Timothy straightened and thrust her sword back into its scabbard. "Obviously the thimble isn't working for me, Quirk. Either we throw it away so we can go back to the City, or the three of us and the construct are going to keep wandering around out here until we die."

"We-ell . . . ," Quirk said with a shrug. "I've had an idea about that. Come back to the fire, and we'll talk it over."

15

"OH, SURE YOU HAVE AN IDEA," GRIFF HEARD ROSE MUTTER as they followed Quirk and Timothy back to the camp. She turned to him. Even in the foggy dawn light, she glowed with beauty. "We're going to find out what he's been planning now, don't you think?" she asked.

She was like a flame, Griff found himself thinking, then shook his head ruefully. Quirk's odd way of talking was rubbing off on him, at last.

"Well?" Rose prompted.

What were they talking about again? Oh, Quirk. "Probably," he answered.

"Something devious," Rose said with a decided nod, and they joined the others around the coals of their fire. The fog among the pine trees started to thin, and the day brightened.

Timothy stood with hands fisted on her hips. "Right, so what's your idea, little man?"

Beside her, Quirk looked very small. "Well now," he said slowly. "What I'm thinking is that you might not be the best person to hold this particular thimble."

"I'm not giving it to *her*," Timothy spat, pointing at Rose.

"I don't want it," Rose said quickly. She pulled the tie from her hair and started combing it out with her fingers. Something she did when she was nervous, Griff realized.

"No," Quirk agreed. "Not Rose."

Timothy dipped into her coat pocket, pulled out the thimble, and held it out to Quirk. "So you want it, Quirk. Why didn't you just say so at the beginning?"

"No, not me either," he murmured. Putting his hands behind his back, he leaned forward, not touching the thimble, but examining it closely. "No roses," he said. "Just thorns." He slid a glance at Griff.

No, Griff thought. *Not me.*

"What is it?" Rose asked suspiciously. "What are you planning?"

"It seems we have no choice," Quirk muttered. Straightening, he nodded. "I have an idea," he said, "that if you put this thimble on your finger, Griff, and ask for a path to lead us to the outside world, the Forest will have to give it to us."

"I don't think so, Quirk," Timothy put in acerbically. "Griff is a Watcher. He's not our ally. He wants to take the construct back to the City."

"No, he doesn't," Rose said, her fingers weaving her blond hair into a braid.

"Yes, he does," Timothy insisted. She turned her glare on Griff. "Don't you?"

"No," he answered. He wasn't sure why Rose was so certain about him, but she was right.

"That's it?" Timothy scoffed. "Just *no*? Would you care to explain yourself further?"

Quirk laughed. "You're lucky you got that much out of him," he said to her.

Rose smiled sunnily at both of them. "If you think about it, it makes sense for Griff to take the thimble. He's a Watcher, so Story can't have much hold over him. If it's trying to draw us back to the City, he can resist it better than any of us, even better than you, Timothy. Don't you think so, Quirk?"

"Hm," Quirk said noncommittally.

"Oh, but wait a moment," Rose said. Griff saw that she was frowning as she finished tying off her braid. "Timothy was right about one thing." She pointed at Griff. "You're not our ally. You could go back to the City now, couldn't you?"

"Yes, but—" Quirk started.

"Be quiet, you," she said to him. "You've been manipulating us—all of us. Don't pretend that you haven't, Quirk. I don't have any choice, but Griff does. He shouldn't have to take the thimble if he doesn't want to." She gazed up at him, and her eyelashes did flutter a little. They were so long; she probably couldn't help it. "What do you want to do?"

Griff considered it. He wasn't used to it—getting to choose. For as long as he could remember, he'd followed orders, usually without question. What he should do was refuse the thimble and insist on returning to the City. On doing his duty. But now that he'd seen the Forest, and all its life and color, it would be hard to go back to the drab gray of the citadel, where he'd have to face his father's cold disapproval and a reassignment to Luth's prison cohort.

With the thimble, the four of them might manage to escape to the outside world; that is, if it had the power that Quirk seemed to think it did. Without it, Rose and whoever went with her would be drawn back to the City. And then, one way or another, Rose would die.

He couldn't let that happen.

"Well?" Quirk asked.

Griff frowned. To take the thimble and go with them, he'd have to trust them. He went on one knee, putting his head level with Quirk's, and studied his face. It seemed just as honest and open as it had before. But Quirk knew things that he wasn't telling, Griff felt sure.

"Don't look at me like that," Quirk said.

"Like what?" Griff asked, expecting Quirk to turn one of his characteristic phrases.

"Like you've lost your best friend," Quirk said sadly.

Instead of answering that, Griff looked away, staring blankly out at the Forest.

After a moment, Quirk went on, speaking in a whisper.

"Do you know what the thimble is, lad?"

Griff shook his head. "A device of Story?" he guessed.

"Ah." Quirk blew out a breath. "No. Not exactly. Will you take it? And here, lad." Quirk held the sheathed patrol knife out to him, handle first. "You'll need this, whatever you decide."

Griff got slowly to his feet. Going with them would be a failure to do his duty; it would mean he wasn't a Watcher anymore. He'd never be able to explain this decision to his father. It was like, as Quirk might say, standing on the edge of a precipice and then taking a step. But at least he'd have a good view, for a while, as he fell. And the feel of the wind rushing past. Before he hit the ground. "All right," he said after a moment. "I'll take the thimble."

"*Finally,*" Timothy said with an impatient huff of breath. She stepped closer and held up the thimble. Even in the dim, foggy light, it gleamed, almost like it was winking at him.

Reaching out with a shaking hand, he took it. It was sticky with cold and oddly heavy. Then he bent to take the patrol knife from Quirk, who gave him a searching look, then nodded and handed it over.

"Right, well," Quirk said, with a clap of his hands that sounded loud in the muffling fog. "We'd better pack up and see if this works."

Rose smiled up at him. "Thank you, Griff," she said.

He wasn't sure *you're welcome* was the right thing to say

in response, so he didn't say anything. Taking that first step off the precipice, he hoped that he'd made the right decision.

ONCE GRIFF HAD the thimble on his finger, the Forest gave us an absolutely straight trail. We hiked along it with hollow stomachs and light packs. I was very glad that Griff had decided to take the thimble and lead us out. I didn't want him to go; somehow I'd started counting on his steady, strong presence.

He led the way, ten paces ahead, with a hand in the pocket of his long, ragged black coat. And behind me stalked Timothy, glowering, with a hand on her sword.

Overhead, the sky was gray and heavy with rain about to fall, and the air had the kind of cold-iron chill that creeps down your neck and makes you shiver. On a day like this at home in the valley, Shoe and I would be sitting cozily by the fire drinking tea and taking turns reading stories aloud from a book, or telling new ones.

"Did Griff tell you my story? What there is of it so far, anyway?" I asked Quirk.

"You may not have noticed," he answered, "but Griff is not much of a talker."

"True. But I think you know most of it already, don't you?"

Quirk's answer was a rather Griff-like shrug.

"Typically evasive," I said. "So you already knew about

me and my curse and my rose, or you guessed it, maybe from the first moment I stepped into the City." I assumed it was why he hadn't decided yet if I really was a construct of Story or not. But he was Quirk, and I couldn't hate him for it. "I think you knew about Shoe, too," I went on. "And you know something about the thimble. I wish you'd trust me enough to tell me."

"It's not a matter of trust, lass," Quirk said, his eyes fixed on the leaf-strewn path. "I just don't know enough yet."

"You know a lot more than I do," I complained.

He shot me a wry smile. "That's irony for you."

Above our heads, the tree branches that arched over the trail shivered in a sudden breeze. A few drops of rain fell. I pulled up the hood of my cloak. "Well, what's something that you don't know?"

"Hm." Quirk glanced up at the lowering sky. "I'm fairly certain we're going to have a wet night."

"That you *don't* know," I repeated.

"Yes, well." He walked quietly for a few steps. More raindrops pattered down. "I don't know enough about Griff," he said darkly. "He's not going to talk to me about himself, that's certain, and there's something very odd going on here." He brightened. "Lass, do you think you could—"

"No." In the distance, thunder grumbled. "I've asked him to tell me his story," I said. "But he won't." And I knew Griff was struggling. He wasn't any more certain of himself than I was of myself.

"Ah." As he spoke, his breath came out as a puff of steam in the chilly air.

It really had gotten cold; maybe we'd have snow instead of rain. I glanced behind me. Timothy had pulled up the collar of her coat, and had the scarf wrapped around her head; only her face peeked out.

The path grew narrower, so that we had to go single file. The rumbles of thunder grew more frequent, and the patter of rain became a drizzle and then a downpour. Droplets edged my hood, and the shoulders of my cloak grew wet and heavy. Keeping my head down, I trudged after Griff.

Then the rain turned to sleet.

As I was taking another plodding step, I ran into Griff, who had stopped on the path ahead of me. He steadied me with a hand on my arm. Blinking raindrops from my lashes, I looked up at him. The gray of his eyes, I found myself noticing, was the same as the cloud-covered sky.

"What's the matter?" I asked.

Timothy stepped up beside me. "Keep moving," she mumbled.

Griff shook his head and peered through the falling sleet, beyond me. I turned and saw Quirk's small figure, stumbling along the path, far behind us.

"He's littler than we are," I said. "He's gotten cold faster."

Griff was already taking his coat off. Handing it to me, he stripped off a thick woolen sweater; under it he was wearing a ragged shirt. He put on his coat again.

Quirk trudged up to us. Water dripped from his chin, his straw-colored hair was plastered to his head, and his teeth were chattering; he had the sleeves of his Watcher's tunic pulled over his hands.

"Here." Griff crouched and gently took Quirk's pack from his shoulders, then pulled his sweater over Quirk's head. It hung down to his knees. Quirk just stood there as Griff rolled up the sleeves. Then Griff took off his woolen half gloves and put them onto Quirk's small hands.

Standing, Griff frowned down at him.

"I-I'm all r-right," Quirk said. His face was bone white, and he clenched his teeth trying to keep from shuddering with cold.

"Oh, sure you are," Griff muttered. He took off his own pack and crouched beside Quirk. "Come on."

Oh, he meant to carry him. With clumsy hands, I pushed an unresisting Quirk closer to Griff, who hoisted him onto his back, then climbed slowly to his feet.

Our eyes met. Griff nodded wearily. We both knew how much trouble we were in. As he turned back to the trail, I saw him dip his hand into his pocket to put the thimble on his finger again. At its touch he shivered, ducked his head against the pounding sleet, and led us onward.

Twilight came on. The branches over our heads, I realized, had thinned. Instead of the impenetrable darkness of the Forest, the path wound through a last few trees that were tossing their branches in the wind. Wet leaves scudded past us. A few steps more, and we came to the end of the trees. Timothy stopped, and then Griff, and I stood next to him and Quirk, surveying what lay ahead. The clouds were lighter here; they spat out a few last icy drops of sleet. We stood on the bank of a wide, rushing river that ran shallow over a rocky bed. Ice crusted along its edges. Beyond it was a gray plain swirling with a low fog. In the distance was a huge shape, dark against the oncoming night, but with a few twinkling lights high up in what looked like looming turrets.

"Huh," Timothy grunted.

"It's a castle," I said through lips stiff with cold.

Quirk lifted his head from where it had been resting against Griff's shoulder. In the advancing twilight, his face looked gray, but his eyes glittered, feverish. "No . . . c-can't . . . ," he croaked. His lips moved, but I couldn't hear what he said. He wasn't shivering anymore; I knew what a bad sign that was.

"He's right," Timothy said wearily. "We can't go to the castle."

I turned to glance over my shoulder at the Forest. Like a door slamming closed behind us, the path had disappeared. "We have nowhere else to go," I said through chattering teeth.

Timothy shook her head. "I'm telling you, the castle is the last place we want to go."

That didn't matter. "We don't have any choice, Timothy. If we don't get Quirk warm soon, he's going to die."

In the dim light, Timothy's face was shadowed. "You care

about him?" She sounded truly puzzled.

I knew what she was thinking—a construct wouldn't care. I was freezing and close to despair, and I'd had enough. Reaching out, I grabbed the front of her coat, and dragged her closer. "Yes, Timothy," I said, trying to put some growl into my voice. "Because I am a person, and I care about the . . . the people that I care about." I wasn't sure I was making sense. "All right?"

"Yeah, all right," Timothy said, shrugging herself out of my grip. "You don't have to get all cranky about it."

"*Me*, cranky?" I gasped, and my outrage made me feel warmer. "Am I the one who's been glowering around, and pulling out her sword at any excuse? No."

"We'd better keep moving," came Griff's voice out of the gloom.

"*You* are the cranky one," I muttered to Timothy.

She gave a half shrug. "True enough."

"Oh," I said, surprised at her capitulation. "Then let's go." Onward. To the castle.

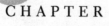

CHAPTER

16

J UST TEN MORE STEPS, G RIFF TOLD HIMSELF. A ND WHEN HE had staggered ten steps along the edge of the river, he set himself to take ten more. Quirk was a dead weight on his back; Rose stumbled at his side, Timothy a step behind her. Rose had pushed back her hood and peered ahead through the growing darkness. There was just enough light to see her face as a pale oval with dark smudges for eyes.

"I think we can cross there," she said, pointing farther along the riverbank.

Ten more steps.

"At least it's not sleeting any m-more," Rose said with forced cheerfulness.

"Is she always this chipper?" Timothy asked wearily.

"It's practically w-warm, don't you think?" Rose added.

Griff couldn't answer; all his words had frozen. The thimble on his finger was another source of cold.

Ten more steps.

He wasn't sure Quirk was breathing.

They came to a place where the river curved and the rocks along its edge gave way to sand that was pale in the darkness. They were closer, now, to the lights of the castle, but it was still too far away.

"Let's cross here." He felt Rose's hand on his arm. The sand shifted under his feet; he heard the crackle of ice, the grate of gravel, and then freezing water seeped into his boots. "Step where I step, if you can," she said, and pulled him deeper into the river. The water rose to his knees; he couldn't feel his feet anymore.

"Oh, goodness," he heard Rose gasp. Then a splash.

He stopped, the shallow river pulling at his legs. "Rose?" All he could see was a glint of frothing white here and there on the surface of the water. The castle lights seemed unutterably distant.

Timothy was a step behind him. "You all right?" she called.

"Yes, fine," Rose said, climbing to her feet, dripping wet. "K-keep to the left."

He followed her voice as she chattered on about the hole she'd stepped into.

"I th-think we're nearly ac-cross," she said, her voice thin with weariness. "Just here—" He felt her hand on his arm again. Something loomed ahead. "There's a bank," she said. "Wait a moment." A sound of scrabbling, and he could see her climbing. A few stones slid, then splashed into the water. When she spoke again, her voice came from higher up. He blinked at her. "Can you pass Quirk to me?"

He nodded, even though he knew she could barely see him. With heavy arms he shifted Quirk's weight from his back.

"Here," Timothy said, and together they lifted him.

"A little higher," Rose said, her voice strained.

"Careful with him," Timothy put in.

He and Timothy pushed, and felt Rose pulling, and together they managed to get Quirk to the top of the bank. He followed, his boots slipping on a steep slope that was mostly mud. Panting, he reached the top. He got to his knees and, after checking to be sure the patrol knife was still sheathed at his back, reached out; his numb hands brushed wet cloth.

"That's me," Rose gasped.

A moment later, Timothy joined them, sitting down with a wet thump. "Now what?" came her voice out of the darkness.

Rose tipped her head up, and he saw a glint of light in her eyes, a reflection from the castle windows. "We're so c-close," she murmured. He put his hand on an unmoving lump on the ground. Quirk. She and Timothy helped lift him onto Griff's back again. He was even heavier than before.

"There's a path just here," Rose said, and yes, he could

see it, too, a darker strip with lighter gray grasses to either side. Quirk's head lolled against his shoulder.

Ten more steps.

They were never going to make it.

Ten more steps.

He'd taken his step off the precipice, but the fall was going to be shorter than he'd hoped it would be.

Ten more steps.

And the wind rushing past him was a lot colder than he'd expected.

Ten more.

When he looked up again, they'd reached the castle gates.

THE CASTLE WAS surrounded by a high wall built of rough stone; it reminded me of the wall around the ruined fortress that the Forest had shown me on my way to the City. Where the narrow path ended there was a break in the wall, a dark arch. The wall was so thick that the gateway through it was a tunnel; at its other end was a faint glow of lantern light.

I was so cold from falling in the river and climbing up the muddy bank that I couldn't feel my legs, or my hands.

Griff stumbled up to stand beside me. I leaned my head against his shoulder for a moment. He had to be even more exhausted than I was after carrying Quirk for so long, and colder because he'd given Quirk his sweater. Glancing up,

I saw that his face was stark white, his eyes smudged with weariness.

"Break it up, you two," growled Timothy, who stood a pace behind us. "We need to get Quirk inside."

With a huge effort of will, I got myself moving; Griff followed.

We came out of the tunnel into a wide courtyard paved with stones that glistened wet in the light of the tower windows. One lantern glowed beside a door in a low outbuilding; another shone from a door in the castle itself. Without speaking, I headed for the castle; I heard Griff's stumbling steps behind me, and then Timothy coming last.

Reaching the door, I banged on it with hands numb from the cold. After a moment, it swung open.

And the castle reached out with embracing arms and gathered us in.

WE'D COME INTO a large kitchen, I realized blurrily. A fire burned in a wide hearth, but I could barely feel its warmth. I heard a babble of voices; hands stripped the sodden cloak from my shoulders. A white ceiling arched overhead; it was stained with soot, and shadows lurked in its corners.

"Here, lovey," a woman's voice said, and I was shoved into a chair. A mug of something hot was put into my shaking hands. I bent my head and let the steam waft over my numb face. I closed my eyes, too weary even to think.

But then—Griff. I jerked my head up and looked wildly around. There he was, leaning against the wall by the door, his eyes closed, asleep on his feet. He had a streak of mud smudged across one high cheekbone, as if he'd wiped his face with a dirty hand; his patched coat was streaked with mud, and water dripped from its ragged hem. Nobody was paying him any attention. Two women and a man dressed in blue were clustered around a small figure that lay on the floor. Quirk.

"Go fetch a blanket," one of the women ordered in a high, piping voice. One of the others hurried away. Another person came into the room, his arms full of wood, which he added to the fire.

"Timothy?" I said, and it came out only as a whisper.

"Here," she said, and I turned to see her sitting on a chair like mine, only a few feet away, with a towel draped over her shoulders. Her face was bone white with exhaustion, her eyes dark, the long lashes spiky with the rain. Like me, she held a steaming cup, warming her hands. She gave me a nod. Not friendship, exactly, but respect. "Be careful," she whispered.

I nodded and, raising my own mug to my lips, took a drink; hot, sweet tea burned a trail down to my stomach. All of a sudden I started to shiver; the mug dropped from my hands and fell, and I stared blankly down at the splatter of tea and shards of the mug on the slate floor.

A woman bustled up to me. "Nah then, lovey," she said in an oddly slurred voice. I looked up into her face. I blinked, and my brain couldn't make sense of what I was seeing. But her hands were gentle as she helped me to my feet. "C'mon alon' nah," she urged.

"But—" I said through chattering teeth. Timothy had warned me—be careful.

"A ni' baff lovey," she said, and pulled at me, and other hands pushed at me from behind, and I let them bring me out of the bustle of the kitchen into another, smaller, quieter room. A fire burned in a little hearth; before it was a metal bathtub full of steaming hot water.

"Ohhh," I breathed, and fumbled at the buttons of my dress with numb fingers.

The gentle hands pushed mine aside, and in a moment the chilly cloth of my dress was gone, and my undershift had been stripped off over my head, and the boots and sodden socks taken from my feet. I stepped into the bath. The water burned against my icy-cold skin, but I sank into it and closed my eyes, still shivering. The steam smelled of sweet herbs and flowers. The ice in my bones started to melt.

As my shivers faded, I drifted toward sleep. Gentle fingers touched my hair, unraveling my braid, then combing it out.

Soo preddy, a voice crooned. *So preddy.*

When all the snarls were out of my hair, the hands took my hand, then I felt them carefully unwinding the sodden bandage that covered the burn on the inside of my wrist.

I heard a sharp intake of breath. "Ah," I thought I heard the slurred voice say. "Rose." Other awed voices repeated,

"The Rose. It's th' Rose."

Yes, I thought. *I'm Rose.* But my rose had been burned off. How did they know my name?

I was too tired to think anymore. The sound of their babbling voices drifted further and further away, and I sank into the soft velvet of sleep.

CHAPTER

17

I WOKE UP IN A CLOUD THAT SMELLED LIKE MILDEW.

No, not a cloud, I realized, as I came to myself. Just a very soft, slightly damp bed. Somewhere in the castle, I assumed, remembering the end of our long journey through the Forest.

Timothy had warned me. She hadn't had time, or the energy, to explain why, but this castle was dangerous somehow.

I struggled to sit up, and pushed tangled hair out of my face. The bed was enormous, bigger than my entire attic room in Shoe's cottage, and had ivory-colored sheets covered by a heavy spread made of some sort of slippery ice-blue cloth, thickly embroidered; at each corner of the bed were posts of intricately carved dark wood that held up a canopy of the same blue cloth, with curtains edged with gold held back by gold-encrusted ropes. The sheets were the source of the mildew smell.

I peered past the bed—with its canopy and posts it was its own room, really, or would be if the curtains were closed. The room beyond was also enormous, with a high, arched stone ceiling; the walls were paneled in dark wood, and a patterned carpet covered the floor. There were various heavy pieces of furniture made of carved wood—a wardrobe, a few chairs, a table. A fireplace with an elaborate stone mantelpiece took up half of one wall; in another was a door with a carved wooden frame, and across from that was a pillow-covered bench set below a row of windows made of tiny diamond-shaped panes. Watery sunlight filtered through them—it was daytime.

I looked down at myself. I was wearing a nightdress with a row of pearl buttons down the front and a froth of lace at the collar, cuffs, and hem. It was, by far, the fanciest thing I'd ever worn. The lace at the neckline was itchy.

I needed to find out where Griff was, and Timothy, and be sure Quirk was being properly looked after. I hoped he was warm and sound asleep in a bed even more comfortable than this one. Moving stiffly—I was still tired from our long hike—I pushed back the coverlet and crawled to the edge of the bed. It was very high off the floor; I started to climb down, then slipped on the shiny cloth coverlet and slithered to the rug, landing with a thump on my bottom.

At the noise, the door opened and two odd faces peeked into the room.

I stared back at them.

Both women wore crisp white aprons over matching light-blue woolen dresses; uniforms, maybe. One had a frilled cap tied over her perfectly bald head; she had no eyebrows or lashes, either, and a straight, lipless mouth, and strangely round, golden eyes with a long narrow slit for a pupil. The other, plumper and shorter, had mouse-brown hair, a sharp nose, and furred, paw-like hands that were folded neatly at her waist.

"Hello . . . ," I said hesitantly. They didn't *seem* dangerous.

At the sound of my voice, the two women withdrew, and I heard a rush of nervous-sounding conversation; then they pushed the heavy door open and hurried into the room, the bald one carrying a tray and swaying sinuously, the other pattering on quick feet to where I sat on the carpeted floor. After the tray had been set on a low table, they both lowered themselves into abject-seeming curtsies.

I climbed to my feet and curtsied awkwardly back at them.

"Ooh," whispered the mouselike, plump one. "What do we do now, Sally?"

"Shhhh," said the other. Sally. "We're not s-s-s'posed to speak, only serve."

"You're not supposed to speak to me?" I asked. Straightening, I examined them more closely. The tall one, Sally, licked her lips nervously with a forked tongue. The other, the mouse, gazed up at me, her sharp nose twitching.

"What's your name?" I asked her.

Her black eyes grew round and she clasped her paws—her hands—under her chin and emitted a high-pitched *meep*.

"Settle yourssself, Dolly," Sally said sharply. She shifted, and I caught a glimpse of her shoe beneath her skirts. Shoes were something that I noticed, because of Shoe. Hers was made of snakeskin.

Or no. Her foot was.

They were so odd, but I hadn't seen much of the world, and for all I knew it had plenty of people like this in it, and I could see they didn't mean me any harm, despite Timothy's warning. "Well, Sally, Dolly," I said, nodding at each of them. "I'm Rose." I glanced down at my frothy nightgown. "If you don't mind, can you tell me where my clothes are? The dress I was wearing last night, and my boots?" I frowned. "I think it was last night, anyway."

They both stared at me.

"I'm worried about my friends, and I'd like to go and see them," I explained. More staring. I sighed. "If I have to, I'll wear this nightgown." I lifted the lacy hem and waggled my bare foot at them. "And no shoes at all."

Meep, Dolly said again; Sally blinked, the flick of a lashless lid across her eye. Then they both spoke at once, a flurry of sibilance and high-pitched squeaks. The gist of it was—*no no no, stay, we shall assissst you*—and then a few more deep curtsies. Then Dolly pattered away to the wardrobe; she flung its door open and started pulling things out—dresses, lacy underclothes, stockings, slippers, ribbons. Sally went to the tray and brought me a plate with a hot buttered roll on it. While I ate it, she reached out and with swift fingers started undoing the pearl buttons of my nightgown.

"I can do it," I protested, my mouth full. She pushed my hand away, took the plate and the rest of my roll, and then bent, seized the hem, and pulled the nightgown off over my head. I blinked, standing there naked for a moment, with the cold air of the room washing over my skin, and then Dolly had pattered over with a plush blue velvet robe and the two of them swathed me in it, tying it at the waist.

"Come along now, come along," said plump Dolly, pulling at my hands, leading me to a chair near the wardrobe.

"Shhhh," chided Sally, following.

"Do you know if my friends are all right?" I asked.

Instead of answering, Sally pushed me into the chair, fetched a cup of tea from the tray and gave it to me, then seized a comb, and started combing the tangles out of my hair; at the same time, Dolly bent and slid silky stockings onto my feet, tying them just over my knees with thin, pale-blue ribbons. As Sally's quick fingers worked what felt like intricate braids into my hair, I drank the tea. Dolly slipped low-heeled slippers onto my feet; then she tugged me up so that I was standing.

"Sahhh," chided Sally, still working on my hair.

"Blue," chattered Dolly. "Don't you think, Sal? The blue?

Blue to match her eyes?"

Sally shook her head; she was looping a braid and pinning it into place; she held a few more hairpins in her lipless mouth.

"No, not blue," Dolly said. "You're right, Sal. Pink."

"Yssss," Sally agreed.

The robe was whisked away, and the teacup; a moment later a lace-edged petticoat dropped over my head; I heard Sally's hiss of annoyance, and another petticoat settled around me and, before I could gasp out a protest, a corset clasped me around the middle. I'd never worn one before. From behind, as Sally finished with my hair, Dolly laced it up.

I stood there gasping for breath while the two women reverently lifted a dress. It was nothing like my plain dark-blue woolen dress, the one I'd worn on the long walk to the City, and the long walk away from it again, the one that had gotten a bit ragged around the hem, and worn at the elbows, and rather stained in places, and yes, it had a button missing in the back, too.

This dress was made of shimmering rose-pink cloth—silk, I guessed—and it was the finest, the most beautiful, the most elegant thing I'd ever seen. It had a heart-shaped collar embroidered at its edges with dainty roses a darker pink than the silk, and tiny green leaves; the same roses, but bigger, edged the hem. There was just a hint of lace at the collar, too, and a line of tiny pearl-pink buttons up the back. Dolly and Sally helped me into it. The silk slithered like cold water over the corset and petticoats; I felt Sally's fingers buttoning it; Dolly added a sash made of darker pink velvet ribbon, also embroidered with roses. I looked down at myself, wishing for a mirror like the one Merry had in her cottage, and ran my hands over the skirt.

"She likes it," Dolly whispered. "Don't you think, Sal?"

"Yesss," Sally hissed back.

"I *do*," I said to them, and smiled. Dolly beamed delightedly back at me.

I turned to feel the skirt and petticoats swish around my ankles. The shoes didn't fit quite right, I realized. A little pinch in the toes. No matter. I supposed that Shoe had spoiled me for other shoes, ones not made to perfectly fit me. I wondered what he would say if he could see me now.

Sally darted forward and dabbed a bit of something onto my lips.

Then they both stepped back and looked me over, head to foot.

"Ooh," squeaked Dolly, clasping her paw-like hands. "Lovely. Just . . . just lovely, don't you think, Sal?"

"Yesss," Sally said. "Spun sugar, so sweet."

I heard the door creak open, and a sarcastic voice said, "Oh, *very* nice."

I whirled; my skirts swished around me. Timothy stood in the doorway, her face set in its usual scowl. "Timothy!" I sped across the room. Seeing her was such a relief; I wanted to throw my arms around her, but she stepped back and raised her eyebrows. As she did, I realized that she wasn't wearing her old boots and stained leather coat; she had on a pink dress similar in cut to mine, made of a lighter fabric, not silk, and missing the rose embroidery around the collar, and with longer sleeves that covered the muscles in her arms. Her neck looked slim and graceful, she held her head proudly, and her short hair had been parted at the side and combed flat.

And around her waist she wore her leather belt, and hanging from it her sword in its scabbard. I grinned at her. "I like your belt better than mine." I held up the embroidered end of my pink velvet sash.

She looked down at herself. "This dress is ridiculous."

"No, you look beautiful," I said truthfully.

In response, she rolled her eyes.

"Have you seen Quirk or Griff?" I asked.

She snorted. "Caring about the people you care about?"

My smile widened. She was teasing me! Then I sobered. "I hope they're all right."

Timothy stared at me, then shook her head. "Huh."

"What?" I asked.

"You really are more than that." She pointed at my face.

"The beauty," I said. "Yes. I am. Timothy—" I started, wanting to ask her if we were friends now, as I'd hoped we'd be.

But a broad shape loomed in the doorway, interrupting us; we stepped back and a wide, heavy-browed woman with a streak of white in the center of her black hair came into the room. Her ears, I noticed, had a little tuft of black-and-white fur on their pointed tips. She had on the blue woolen dress that was clearly some sort of uniform, and she had a jingling set of keys on a ring at her waist. Like the others had, she swept into a low curtsy.

As before, I curtsied back. "I'm Rose."

"Nah then," she said, and I recognized her voice from the night before. She had put me into the bathtub and given me tea. "Y've found y'r friend."

I glanced aside at Timothy. Her face was blank.

"Yes," I said, after an awkward moment. I waited for Timothy to correct her, but she stayed silent. I went on. "I'm worried about my other friends, too. Griff and Quirk? The young man with dark hair, and the very short older man, the ones who were with us, before?" I took a step toward the door. "Will you take me to them?"

The two maids joined us. "She keeps asking, Keeper," Dolly said.

"A's well," the broad, black-and-white woman said. Keeper of what, I wondered. Her mouth stretched, revealing widely spaced, sharp teeth. Oh, she was smiling. "Come nah," she said, ushering me and Timothy toward the door. Sally and Dolly followed, and we stepped into a dimly lit corridor that had a polished wood floor with a faded blue carpet running down the middle of it, and walls paneled like the ones in the bedroom we'd just come out of.

I walked quickly, eager to see Griff and Quirk. Timothy

paced silently beside me, her hand on the pommel of her sword.

"Are we in danger now?" I whispered to her.

Her only answer was a shrug.

The corridor led to a balconied gallery; we went down a graceful curve of stairs to a wider corridor with high, plastered ceilings and no carpet. The three servants made no sound at all—their shoes were soled with felt, I guessed. We came at last to an arched double door; the Keeper threw the doors open and stepped aside so we could enter. "'S Lady Rose th'y want t' see," she slurred.

"I'll wait here," Timothy said tensely.

"All right," I told her. "I'll be careful."

The room was long with a very high ceiling encrusted with white plaster curlicues and flowers. White pillars were set along the walls, and the floor was black-and-white checkerboard tiles. At the other end of the room was a cluster of men and women, all finely dressed. There was a rustle of wide skirts and a murmur of whispers as they turned to stare at me in the doorway.

I paused, looking for Griff and Quirk.

"Go 'long," whispered the Keeper. The keys at her waist jingled as she motioned toward the end of the room where the people were, and also a pair of chairs set on a low platform beneath a blue velvet canopy; a man and a woman sat on the chairs, watching me.

The heels of my shoes sounded very loud on the tiles as

I walked toward them. The air of the room was chilly, and smelled of floor wax and flowery perfume. When I reached the cluster of people, they bowed low and curtsied as I passed; I heard more whispering. I reached the man and the woman.

The man, who had dull blond hair streaked with gray and a bland, lined face, wore a simple suit of black, but over it he had on a rich, dark-blue mantle edged with fur; a chain made of heavy gold links hung around his neck. The woman's dress was the same blue, and her mantle was black edged with fur, and she had a stack of jeweled rings on each of her fingers. Her face was heavily made up, the eyes outlined in black, the lips a very bright red, the skin powdered pale with smudges of pink on each cheek. As I approached, her mouth opened in a perfect O.

Everyone in the room, I realized, was staring at me. I glanced around, looking for Griff and Quirk. My heart started fluttering in my chest; I wasn't sure what was happening.

The woman gasped; she reached toward the man with one bejeweled hand.

Ignoring her, he nodded at me.

I nodded back. "Hello," I said, my voice sounding thin and nervous.

"Nah, show 'em th' arm," whispered the Keeper's voice from right behind me. I hadn't heard her following, in her felt-soled shoes.

"My arm?" I asked, turning to her.

She nodded, then pointed to her own wrist.

"Oh," I said aloud. The burn hadn't been bandaged up again, I realized, after my bath last night. "But it's been—" I turned my hand over, and there, on the pale inside of my wrist, was my rose. The burn was gone, and the rose mark, which had been just a bud before, had blossomed.

I turned back to the man and the woman on the blue chairs and held up my wrist. "Is this what you wanted to see?"

"Oh!" cried the woman. Her eyelids fluttered as if she was going to faint. She leaned back in her chair and held a trembling hand to her forehead.

The man got to his feet. "It is true," he announced, and leaned down from the platform. Seizing my hand, he pulled me up to stand beside him. "She has returned to Castle Clair at last. The birthmark on her arm proves it. This is our most beloved and long-absent daughter, Rose."

CHAPTER

18

W HEN G RIFF OPENED HIS EYES, A PIG-SNOUTED FACE WAS
peering down at him, baring fangs that jutted from a heavy
lower jaw.

He reacted immediately, finding himself tangled in
a woolen blanket and his coat, falling from a narrow bed
to the floor, then scrambling to his feet and backing away.
Looking wildly around, he saw he was in a narrow room
with whitewashed walls and a row of beds like the one he'd
just flung himself out of. Not so different from the barracks
in the citadel.

Quirk was in one of the other beds, lying quiet and still.

The pig-snouted man climbed to his feet.

Griff reached for the knife sheathed at his back, beneath
his coat, but didn't draw it; without taking his eyes from the

man, he edged closer to Quirk's bed.

The pig-snouted man took a lumbering step toward him.

"Hold there," Griff said tensely; he gripped the handle of the knife, ready to fight if he had to.

"Whoa, whoa," the man said in a deep, snuffling voice, holding up his hands. "Steady on. Don' mean you any harm."

Griff eyed him warily.

The man was wearing a leather coat with a blue vest under it; his hair stuck up in brown bristles. "No harm," he repeated. "M' name's Arny. I'm th' stableman. Ye're at Castle Clair."

Right. The castle—he remembered now. The night before was just a blur of exhaustion and cold. But Timothy had warned them to be careful, hadn't she? "Where's the girl, Rose?" he asked. "The one who came in with us?" He nodded at the bed where Quirk lay.

"Keeper has 'er," the pig-snouted man, Arny, answered. "She's well enough."

"And the other girl?" Griff asked.

"Well enough. No harm meant, as I said." Arny's face was . . . strange, but he wasn't, after all, threatening. Griff straightened and released the knife without unsheathing it.

He was, he realized, still falling from the precipice, but he hadn't hit the ground yet after all.

Keeping an eye on Arny, he stepped to Quirk's bed, then went to his knees beside it.

Quirk's closed eyes seemed sunken, and he was so still,

barely breathing. "Do you have a physician here?" Griff put the back of his hand to Quirk's forehead. Fevered.

"Healer's seen 'im," Arny said, with a heavy nod. "Gave 'im a med'cine."

Griff frowned down at Quirk's too-pale face. He would talk to the healer later. He got stiffly to his feet, feeling the lingering weariness and the ache of their long, freezing walk to the edge of the Forest. His clothes and coat were still damp and streaked with drying mud, and he was cold and needed to eat something, but first he had to be sure Rose was all right. "Take me to the girl," he ordered.

"Whoa, whoa," Arny said, and made a calming gesture with his broad hands.

Swiftly Griff stepped past him and opened the room's only door; he heard Arny's heavy footsteps following as he went down a bare, stone-floored corridor that led to an empty eating room with a scarred wooden table and benches running its length. He cast a look around the room, then headed for the door at the opposite end.

It opened onto the kitchen they'd come into last night. It was hot, with a fire in a huge stove, and another fire in a hearth, and busy with aproned cooks stirring pots and chopping vegetables; they all looked up when he came in, then went back to their work. Like Arny, they were strange. Not entirely human. Griff made his way to an arched doorway, and out a heavier door to a part of the castle that was suddenly very fine, with polished wooden floors and pictures in gilt frames. And lots of doors along the corridor. He stopped, disoriented.

"Best not to be in this part of th' castle," Arny puffed, catching up to him.

"Where is she?" he asked. When Arny didn't answer, he whirled to face him. "I'll open every door in the castle until I find her," he threatened.

"A'right, a'right." Arny made his calming gesture again. "They was goin' to take the Rose to see th' lord an' lady." He pointed with a blunt finger. "Great Hall, at the end there."

Griff paced along the corridor to a double door; a figure in a dress was waiting outside it. She turned: Timothy, and she had her sword with her.

He gave her a brief nod, as he would to another Watcher. "Is she in there?"

"Yeah," she answered. "Something strange is going on."

Stepping past her, he opened the door and scanned the room.

Rose was there, standing on a low platform with two other people. He started across the shiny black-and-white tiled floor, noting the other exits and the number of people in the room, and the decorative rapiers worn by three of the young men near the platform, aware of Arny's lumbering presence at his back.

There was a murmur from the cluster of people at the other end of the room. Rose turned, saw him, and said something to the woman and man who stood next to her, then hopped down from the platform in a swirl of pink skirts, and came to meet him. "Oh, Griff," she said, and gripped his hands.

"You're all right?" he asked, studying her face. She seemed all right. Tired, still. Her hands were cold. And she was even more beautiful than before, but the beauty didn't seem to matter as much, despite the new dress she was wearing, and the elaborate hairstyle. She was Rose now, not some lovely stranger.

"Yes," she nodded. "Yes, I'm fine. Is Quirk all right?"

He shook his head. "He's sick. A healer's seen him."

"Oh, goodness," she breathed. "I'm so glad you're here." She really was, he realized. Something had changed between them.

For just a moment, as he looked down at her face, he forgot that they were probably in danger; he forgot that he was plunging from a great height and that he didn't know who he was anymore. There was just her.

She gazed back up at him. Her lips parted, but, surprisingly, she didn't speak.

From beyond their bubble of quiet, someone cleared his throat.

Rose gave herself a little shake. Still holding his hand, she led him to the two people on the platform. They were finely dressed, Griff noted. The lord and lady that Arny had mentioned, he guessed. "This is Griff," Rose told them.

There was a rustle of whispers from the others in the

room. Griff felt suddenly aware of how muddy and ragged he was compared to all the finery.

Rose turned back to him. Excitement lit her eyes. "Griff, these are my parents. My mother and father."

Griff looked at them again, more carefully this time. The woman sat in one of the velvet chairs; the man stood beside it. They both seemed bland, ordinary—nothing compared to Rose. They seemed safe, too, not dangerous, not a threat.

Then he frowned. The Forest had just happened to lead them here? Or the thimble had? Timothy had been right—something *was* going on. "Rose . . . ," he said warily.

"I know it's strange," she murmured. "But I think it's all right, really. Or I hope it is." She tipped her head back to look at him, and her smile was glorious. "Don't you see what it means, Griff?"

What it . . . "No," he said blankly.

"My *mother*. My *father*," she answered, eyes shining. "I have parents. I'm not a construct."

"I never thought you were," he reminded her.

She gripped his hand with both of hers and gazed up into his eyes. "I know." Her lips trembled. "You were the only one." Giving him a quick smile, she released his hand. With a quick step and a hop, she rejoined the lord and lady on the platform. The man—her father?—leaned closer and said something to Rose.

"No, he's not a servant," Rose answered, with a quick glance at Griff. "He's my—"

"Oh," her mother said faintly, interrupting.

The lord made a dismissing gesture and spoke in a deep, commanding voice. "Deal with this, will you, Arny? See that our daughter's servant is settled appropriately."

Griff felt a big hand on his arm. For just a moment he tensed, ready to draw his knife and call Timothy to help fight to get Rose out of here. But Quirk was ill and needed rest. They couldn't leave yet.

"Come along wi' me, now," Arny said from behind him.

"But he's not a—" Rose protested.

"It's all right," Griff reassured her, and let Arny pull him from the room.

"SHOULDN'T 'A GONE in there," Arny chided as they passed through the doorway that led from the finer corridor to the kitchen. "It's not for th' likes of us." In the eating room he paused and scooped up a few slices of bread and cheese from a side table and handed them to Griff. "Here." Then he went to the door that led out to the courtyard. "Come 'long now."

Griff shook his head. "I want to be sure Quirk is all right."

"Your little friend, y' mean?" Arny asked. "He'll sleep for a bit longer, and that other girl's gone to see him. Nothin' to do f'r him now." He opened the outer door. "We've orders. Come 'long to the stable."

As they stepped outside, a few pigeons flew up and circled overhead. Halfway across a courtyard paved with smooth, square stones, Griff paused and turned to see what the castle looked like in the daytime. It was monolithic, a big central section built of black stone, flanked by asymmetrical towers, some taller, some shorter, some round, some square, all topped with pointed slate roofs. It had not been built as a fortress; its many windows were large and had lots of tiny, diamond-shaped panes. The pigeons had settled on a few of the windowsills. On one side of the castle, facing a large gate, was a huge arched door with a stairway edged by stone railings. The gate in the thick wall was open; through it Griff could see a stone road that rolled away into the distance. Oddly, there was no village, no sign of any people. Just the castle set alone in the middle of the empty plain they'd crossed the night before.

The stable was off to the side, a long building set against the castle's inner wall. As they went through its wide sliding door, Arny pointed to the left. "Tack room's there." And overhead. "Hayloft." To the right. "Stalls for eight horses, and I c'n use the help with 'em, that's for certain." He nodded at a bale of hay just inside the door. "Sit y'rself there and eat a mite." He bared his fangs in what looked like a smile. "Look half done, y' do."

And suddenly Griff felt half done, light-headed with hunger and leftover weariness. He could almost feel the wind of his fall from the precipice rushing past him, a kind of roaring in his ears. He sat on the hay bale, lined up the cheese on the bread to make a sandwich, and took a bite. The stable was warm and smelled of hay and what he guessed was horse droppings. He'd seen horses before, but only the small sturdy ponies that were used for pulling carts in the City. The horses that poked their heads out of the half doors of their stalls to look at him were much bigger than that, and had elegantly long noses and intelligent-looking eyes.

"Right," Arny said, sitting down beside him on the hay bale. Then he groped behind him, picking up a jug from the floor, resting it on his leg while he tugged out its cork stopper, then taking a long drink. "Ah," he said, wiping his fanged mouth with the back of his hand. He held out the jug to Griff. "Have a snort?"

Griff could smell the alcoholic fumes from where he sat. He shook his head.

Arny shrugged and stowed the jug behind the hay bale again. "So y'll be lookin' after the stable wi' me. Know anythin' about horses, do you?"

Griff swallowed down a bite of sandwich. "I'm to work here?"

"Y's," Arny said with a blink. "Settled *apporpritally* is what th' lord said." He gave a decided nod and another one of his fanged smiles. "Y'r the Lady Rose's servant, and she'll be looked after well enough, so y'll work wi' me instead."

Griff considered protesting—he wasn't a servant, he was a Watcher, except that he wasn't a Watcher anymore, was he?

"Right, so," Arny said, and leaned back against the stable wall. "Your name's Griff, is it?" At Griff's nod, he went on. "Whereabouts do you come from?"

"The City," Griff answered.

"Don't get many visitors from the City," Arny said. "Not usually. Not f'r a long time."

Griff was surprised they got any at all.

"Not a lot of call for horses, neither," Arny went on. "But y' got to have horses."

Griff nodded and took another bite of his sandwich.

"Huh." Arny reached for the jug again, drank, and belched. "Not much of a talker, are you?"

Without answering, Griff got to his feet and went across the hay-strewn entry to the first stall to have a better look at the horse that lived there. As he approached, its ears pricked toward him. Stepping closer, he rested a hand on its nose.

"Careful o' that one," Arny called from his seat on the hay bale. "It's a biter."

"Hello, Biter," Griff whispered, and leaned a shoulder against the doorframe.

The horse shifted closer and lowered its head, and Griff reached out to pat its neck. He could feel its solid warmth and strength. He and Biter were going to get along just fine, he thought.

So he would work in the stable, but only until Quirk was better and they'd figured out why the Forest had brought them here. Having access to horses might not be a bad thing, if they had to escape from the castle in a hurry. He'd have to see if Arny would teach him to ride.

CHAPTER

19

"ALL RIGHT, THEN," MY FATHER SAID, AFTER GRIFF WENT out.

My *father*. My *mother*. I was worried about Quirk, and about Griff, too, but the thought of it—I had parents! I belonged to them, not to Story!—made me smile widely at them. My mother blinked back at me. My father made a lordly gesture, and the other people in the room went out, whispering. Three of them were young men, who seemed completely fascinated, staring over their shoulders at me until the door was closed.

"I'm so happy to meet you," I said.

"And we are very glad to have you returned to us, of course," he answered. "After so long." He glanced down at my mother; I saw no sign of affection in his face. "Can you see that she is settled?"

My mother licked her brightly colored lips. "Yes, I suppose I can."

"Very well." He touched the gold links of his chain, as if for luck. "I have things to . . . er . . . see to myself." He glanced at me, cleared his throat, and looked away. "My dear daughter, I should say." He stepped from the platform and went out the door.

"I suppose we should see you settled, then," my mother said, gathering her skirts and climbing from her chair. She was shorter than I was, and seemed frail, and, behind the bright makeup, rather colorless.

She and my father were part of my story, I realized. The very beginning of it. I felt vaguely disappointed that they didn't seem all that happy to see me. Maybe they just needed time to get used to the idea. "I have so many questions," I said to my mother.

"I suppose you do," she said faintly.

"You must have known the Penwitch," I said.

She blinked. "The Penwitch?" she asked, and stepped from the platform, then started across the room.

I started to explain. "She was—" I stopped in the middle of the black-and-white tiled floor. The Penwitch had, maybe, stolen me away from my parents before bringing me to Shoe. But the Penwitch had been good. Hadn't she? She'd been fighting against Story. I *knew* Shoe had been good.

I didn't know what it meant, except that being returned to my parents was, perhaps, more complicated than I'd realized. This castle was a very strange place, I could see that much. I would have to be careful, as Timothy had said. And I needed to see Griff and Quirk so we could try to figure out what was going on.

My mother had paused four steps ahead of me and stood there without looking back. I hurried to her side and we continued to the door, where I looked for Timothy but didn't see her, to my dismay. We were met by the Keeper and Sally and Dolly, who curtsied to my mother, and then to me. "Nah then, m'lady," the Keeper said, baring her teeth in a smile. "Y'r friend Tim'thy is a' well. She went t' see the little man."

I nodded, relieved.

"This is . . . ," my mother started, then glanced up at me and blinked, as if remembering who I was. "This is Rose."

"Apparently I'm supposed to be settled," I said to the Keeper, smiling back at her.

"Th' pink room, m'lady?" the Keeper asked.

"Oh," my mother said, with another one of her blinks. "Yes, that will do."

The Keeper's keys jingled as she turned and led us, with the two maids trailing behind, up the curved stairway and along a corridor, through a door that led to another stairway that wound up inside one of the castle towers.

"Thisss is a sitting room," Sally hissed as we passed through one room. But we didn't stop; instead we went up another flight of winding stairs to an arched doorway.

The room inside was round, the shape of the tower, and it was called *the pink room* for a good reason.

I stepped in, and my feet sank into the pink carpet. A high bed had a pink velvet canopy and spread, all edged with gold, and faded tapestries stitched with pink flowers covered the walls.

It was the same color pink, I realized, as my rose.

The air of the room was chilly, and smelled of dust and mold.

Behind me, the Keeper was giving orders to Sally and Dolly about cleaning and building a fire and airing out the bed.

In one corner of the room was a cradle encrusted with lace. My mother had drifted over to it.

I went to join her. "Was this . . . when I was a baby, was this my cradle?"

My mother flinched, as if startled. "This was my baby's cradle. The witch stole her away. My Rosebud. My little Rose."

"Why did the witch take me?" I asked.

"She took my baby," my mother corrected. Her face contorted. "The witch was evil."

"I don't think she was," I said gently.

My mother's beringed hands clenched into jeweled fists. "She stole my baby." Her voice rose in anguish. "My baby!"

It had been a long time ago. Almost seventeen years. But

my mother's grief seemed immediate. She didn't seem to quite realize that I was that baby, grown up.

"Nah then," said the Keeper, jingling up to us. Gently she took my mother's arm. "It's time f'r your med'cine an' a nap, m'lady. Come 'long nah." Docile, my mother allowed the Keeper to lead her out the door.

I looked around the room. Dolly was at the hearth building a fire; Sally had gone out on one of the Keeper's errands. So much pink. It was cloying, stuffy. "Dolly," I said briskly, "I'd like to check on my friend, the small man, to be sure he's all right. Will you take me to him?"

Dolly, kneeling at the hearth, blinked up at me with round black eyes.

Before she could answer, there was a clatter of footsteps at the door. Dolly leaped up to open it, then sank into a low curtsy as two young women sailed into the room, followed by Timothy. The two women were both entirely human—no fur or fangs to be seen—and they wore dresses similar to Timothy's, so I knew they were ladies, not servants. As one they dipped into curtsies, then rose and stood beside each other as if presenting themselves for an inspection.

Timothy stood to the side. I glanced at her and raised my eyebrows; she answered with a shrug.

"Greetings, Lady Rose," one of the ladies said primly. She was very tall and had bony shoulders and brown hair, carefully curled; the other was shorter, plumper, red cheeked, and red haired. They were both very elegant. "I am Miss Amity," said the tall one in a high-pitched, nasal voice, "and this is Miss Olive. We are your ladies-in-waiting."

"Oh," I said. "Hello. What are you waiting for?"

Miss Amity wrinkled her nose. "We wait upon you, Lady Rose. The three of us are to be your companions."

Timothy, who still had her most unladylike sword hanging from her belt, crossed her arms and scowled.

"We are skilled in all the proper accomplishments," added Miss Olive, ignoring Timothy, and bestowing me with an ingratiating smile. "Embroidery, playing the harp, deportment, tatting, engaging in delightful conversation, painting with watercolors . . ."

"Playing cards," Miss Amity continued, "dancing, serving tea, behaving with perfect etiquette, and conveying only the most delectable pieces of gossip."

I couldn't do any of those things. I didn't even know what *deportment* was. Or *tatting*.

Timothy lifted her chin. "And I shall teach you proper etiquette with the sword," she said in a falsely mincing voice. "You must try not to get your opponent's blood on your dancing slippers."

"Oh *really*," said Miss Amity scornfully. Miss Olive looked down her nose.

"Well, it's nice to meet you," I said quickly, even though it wasn't really. I was starting to get very worried about Quirk, and I wanted to talk further with Griff, too. I was sure he had some ideas about why we were here. "I need to find my friend. He was nearly frozen when we arrived last night, and I want to be sure that he is all right."

Miss Amity shifted subtly, so that she was blocking the door. "I was instructed by the Keeper to assure you that your servant has been seen by a healer."

"Yes, I know," I said, not bothering to inform her that Quirk wasn't my servant. "But I'd like to see him for myself." I smiled at them. "It's all right; Miss Timothy will come with me, and you can stay here."

The Misses exchanged a glance. "It is our duty to serve as your companions," Miss Amity said with a sniff.

Miss Olive pulled a packet from a beaded purse she had looped over her wrist. "Perhaps a game of cards, instead?"

"No, thank you," I said, beginning to feel a bit desperate. "I'm going to visit Quirk." I started for the door, and I would have knocked Miss Amity over, but she scurried out of my way. "If you'll wait here," I said quickly, "I'll be back very soon, all right?" And without waiting for their answer, I opened the door. Facing me was an older woman—another fine lady—and the Keeper, and Sally, and a man carrying several bolts of pink cloth, and a plainly dressed woman holding a basket.

"Ah, Lady Rose," exclaimed the lady, sailing into the room. The others crowded in behind her, forcing me back inside.

Timothy stepped up beside me, her hand on her sword. "I could take them, easily," she hissed.

"No!" I said, shocked. I turned to face her. She looked so incongruously fierce in her pretty pink dress, a scowl on her face. "It's all right. Really."

Timothy huffed out a disgusted breath and went to stand near the door.

The fine lady was Miss Abigail, one of my mother's ladies-in-waiting, and she'd brought a dressmaker who would measure me and help me pick out ribbons and cloth, and new shoes, and stockings, and a reticule, whatever that was, and lace.

And unless I let Timothy have her bloodbath, I was not going to be allowed to visit Quirk, or talk to Griff, evidently.

Well, we would just see about that.

I SPENT THE rest of the day being measured for new dresses and underclothes, playing cards with the Misses, trading eye rolls with Timothy, and finding out that *delightful conversation* was also extremely dull, and then being primped and put into another dress—a proper evening gown, I was told. The ladies-in-waiting, including Timothy, were whisked away, and I was sent to eat a very awkward dinner with my formal father and abstracted mother, both of whom behaved as if the other did not exist.

At the table, my mother mechanically took one tiny bite after another without speaking, but after a long silence my father said something interesting.

"I am surprised, Rose, that you were not returned to us

sooner." He paused to fork up a bite of meat, chewed, swallowed, and then continued. "We sent servants to find you. To bring you home in time."

"In time for what?" I asked.

"For your sixteenth birthday," my father said.

I'd been sixteen for at least six months. Maybe longer. "Well, I never saw the servants you sent," I said. Because Shoe and I had never seen anyone.

"They must have expired," my father said.

I blinked. What?

Seeing my confusion, my father continued. "They were given an order. They would obey it unto death. If they didn't find you in time"—he shrugged and took another bite—"they expired."

And then I remembered—the dead body in the clearing in our valley, with the vultures. The man had been wearing blue; his hands had been more like claws. He must have been one of the castle's servants. A cold feeling gathered in my stomach. "How would they die, exactly?"

"As I said." My father took a sip of wine from a crystal goblet. "Unto death."

"I don't understand," I said.

My father stared at me without blinking, as if I was being stupid.

At last my mother spoke. Her voice was without inflection. "Once the servants left the castle, they could not stop to eat or sleep until their orders were fulfilled."

"Unto death," my father repeated. "If they fail, they die."

Oh. I wondered how long the servant had blundered at the edges of the magical boundary around our valley, slowly starving to death. Or maybe the lack of sleep had killed him first. And then the boundary had broken, and he'd stumbled in far enough to fall down in that clearing and die.

It was awful. I put down my silver fork and stared at my plate, at my half-eaten dinner.

My mother and father continued to eat without speaking.

After dinner, feeling very subdued, I let Sally and Dolly lead me back to my bedroom, put me into a lacy nightgown, and tuck me into the bed with its swags of pink velvet.

As soon as they went out, leaving me alone, I climbed down from the bed and found a robe and my toe-pinching slippers and settled on the cushioned window seat. The land outside the window was completely dark. It was odd, I thought, that no one lived nearby. The castle was so isolated. My parents were so strange, with their blankness, their mask-like faces. And the servants, half animal, half obedience *unto death*.

At last, when I guessed that most of the castle was asleep, I took a candle and went down the winding stairs of my tower. The corridors were shadowed and deserted. I crept along their edges like a mouse until I came to a door that I'd noted when going down to dinner. Servants had been coming out of it then; I went into it now, passing down a much barer corridor, coming out at last into the kitchen, which I remembered from . . . was it only the night before? My goodness.

It was mostly empty, the fires banked, with a lingering smell of the roast we'd eaten for dinner. On a stool at the scarred table sat the Keeper, drinking tea with an enormous man wearing an apron, who had nubs of horns at his hairline. Seeing me, the Keeper got to her feet.

"I'm sorry to trouble you," I said, before she could say anything. "I'm looking for my friend Griff. Do you know where I can find him?"

"Well nah, Lady Rose," she started.

"Please," I interrupted. "I really do need to see him."

She was shaking her head.

So I added, "A lady ought to look after her servants. I need to be sure my servants are well settled."

After a moment, she nodded. "A'right, m'lady. Come 'long. He's in th' stable."

With a sigh of relief, I followed her out of the kitchen, across the courtyard, to an outbuilding. She pointed at it, then bobbed a curtsy and went back toward the castle.

Lantern light spilled from the stable door. I padded over the smooth paving stones and peeked in. It had a large central room with a hay-strewn floor. Griff was alone in the middle of it. His coat was off and the sleeves of his ragged shirt were rolled up, and he had his knife in one hand, its sheath in the other. The knife was held back against his wrist; he spun and it flicked out to stab air, then he ducked and turned smoothly to block an imaginary thrust with the sheath. He was all deadly grace. Dark. Honed. Dangerous.

Oh, he was sparring. Practicing.

Because he was Griff, he could hardly fail to notice me there, lurking in the doorway. He spun, knife at the ready.

"Hello, Griff," I said awkwardly, stepping further into the light.

Seeing it was me, he straightened and sheathed the knife, one clean motion, and a smile tugged at the corner of his mouth.

Suddenly I was very glad to see him.

He observed me with his usual keenness. "You've had to sneak out."

"Yes," I said, and I wanted to tell him all about the waiting ladies and Timothy, and the pink room and my odd parents and the *unto death*, but first things first. "How is Quirk?"

"Come and sit down," he said. While I settled myself on a hay bale, Griff rolled down the sleeves of his shirt and put on his long coat again. Then he answered my question. "He's not well. Asleep, and still feverish."

"Oh," I said faintly. "Is somebody looking after him?"

"Healer's assistant," Griff told me. "And Timothy's checking on him every hour."

We were silent for a few minutes while I worried about Quirk, and Griff went to lean a shoulder against the frame of a door that led to another room in the stable, where he stared down at the hay-strewn floor.

"This is a very strange place," I said at last.

Griff looked up at me and nodded. "Have you figured out what it is?"

I hadn't had a chance to really think it through. But now I did. My oddly blank parents. The animal servants. Timothy's warning. The fact that the Penwitch had stolen me away from here and brought me to Shoe. "*Oh,*" I said, and felt stupid for not realizing it before. "This must be a place of Story." I frowned. "But the Forest brought us here, and it's Story's enemy. Why would it do that?"

"The Forest didn't bring us here," Griff corrected. He reached into his pocket and pulled out the thimble. It glinted in the lantern light as if winking at me. "This did."

"Quirk knows a lot more about all of this than we do. He knew the thimble had some kind of power," I said.

Griff nodded.

"I don't suppose he told you about it, did he?" I asked.

"No" was Griff's unadorned answer.

Of course not. I turned my hand and looked down at the rose that bloomed on the pale skin of my wrist. "I thought that Story's place of power was the City. I thought we'd be free of it once we got out of the Forest. Why is it here, too, in this castle?"

"It must have escaped."

"How?" I asked.

Griff opened his mouth as if he was about to answer, but instead he shoved the thimble back into his coat pocket and looked away.

"I wish you would tell me what you know," I said softly.

"I don't know much more than you do." Griff was staring down at the floor again. "But I can tell you this. In the City, we Watchers were trained to watch for signs that Story was rising again. One of its devices would appear, or a few people would be cursed, and Story would start to take shape around them, forcing them to act their part. All the Lord Protector's rules . . ." He gave a half shrug. "They were supposed to prevent Story from gaining power."

"Oh, I see," I interrupted. "Story's been thwarted in the City, so it escaped somehow and established itself here, outside the Forest."

Griff nodded. "There's a story that's supposed to happen here."

"One that's been told and retold, so that it gives Story even more power," I added. "And now it wants to retell it again."

"Yes. My father would know which one it is; he had his book of notes on Story's devices and plots. This story—" He glanced swiftly up at me. "It's something about a beautiful girl."

Me, unfortunately. "Shoe never told me about any of this. What should I do?" I wondered. "Or not do?"

Griff remained silent, pensive.

"And what about you?" I asked. "And Quirk and Timothy? Does Story have plans for you?"

Griff shook his head, as if he'd used up his allotment of words for the night.

"My parents are part of it, too." Feeling suddenly afraid, I pulled up my legs and wrapped my arms around my knees. "We have to get away from here."

"Quirk," Griff said, under his breath.

Yes, he was right. We couldn't leave until Quirk was better. "I don't think escaping is going to be easy."

"I don't either," Griff said.

"Now that Story's got us here, it's not going to let us leave. They've got me surrounded by ladies and servants and they're very . . . sticky." I shrugged. "I don't even know if I can get away again to see you, or Quirk. And I'm sure they'd come after us if we tried to escape."

He nodded, and we were silent for a while, thinking. Suddenly, Griff straightened. "You need to learn how to fight."

"It's hardly a ladylike accomplishment," I noted.

He shook his head, not understanding.

"I'm supposed to learn embroidery and to play cards, things like that. Polite conversation and *one lump or two* for tea." I rolled my eyes. "It's very boring." I got to my feet and tightened the sash on my robe. "But yes. I do want to learn how to fight. You'll teach me?"

He nodded.

At that, despite the danger we were in, I felt a sudden glow of happiness. He was so serious, so sober. He needed to be teased once in a while. "So you *did* run out of words just now."

He stared at me.

I stepped closer. His face was so finely drawn; he didn't have to speak for me to see what he was thinking. Now he had the faintest line between his brows, a frown gathering. "You might try smiling now and then," I said to him. I'd seen his smile before, and it transformed his face from something stern and austere, like his father's, to something completely different.

"Rose," he breathed.

And suddenly I felt a little breathless myself. "I'll . . . um." I gazed up at him. He had a faint line of stubble along his jaw. "I'll come to the stable for fighting lessons," I said in a rush. "Every day after lunch. Will that be all right?"

Yes, Griff's nod said, his gray eyes fixed on me. *It would.*

CHAPTER

20

ARNY, IT TURNED OUT, SPENT A LOT OF TIME WITH HIS jug, which meant he spent even more time snoring in the little room in the stable loft that Griff shared with him. He couldn't blame Arny for the jug, given what he was. Not quite human. But definitely not an animal, either.

And Arny's fondness for drink gave Griff more time to plan his escape, with Rose and Quirk and Timothy, from the castle. He had trained most of his life to fight Story. He knew what he had to do.

The horses had a fenced paddock outside the castle walls, where they could graze. While they were out, Griff took the opportunity, as he'd been trained, to scout the land around the castle. It was as he'd thought: empty grasslands, no place to hide. If they tried to run, the Forest would be their only refuge, and even with the thimble—he refused to think of it as *his* thimble—it might not let them in again.

After bringing the horses back to the stable, he cleaned their stalls, forking up heaps of manure and straw and carting it to a pile behind the stable, and lugging buckets of water to refill their troughs.

Once he'd finished, he had a wash at the pump outside the stable, put on his coat, and went to check on Quirk, who'd been moved by the healer's assistant from the other servants' dormitory. He found him in a closet that had been partly cleared to accommodate a small bed. It had one narrow window that let in a little light. After collecting a lantern and a cup of the herb tea that the healer had prescribed, Griff squeezed past a broom and a mop and sat down on the edge of the cot.

He rested a hand on Quirk's forehead. Still hot. Any plans to escape would have to wait until he was better.

At his touch, Quirk's eyes fluttered open.

Griff shifted so that he could lift Quirk's shoulders, then held the cup of tea to his dry lips. "Drink this, all right?"

Some of the tea dripped onto the pillow, but Griff thought most of it had been swallowed. He used a corner of the sheet to wipe the spilled tea from Quirk's face and neck.

Quirk's eyes were half open; his face was chalky white except for a flush over his cheekbones. His lips moved.

Setting the teacup on the floor, Griff leaned closer. "Listen," he said quietly. He wasn't sure if Quirk could understand him or not. "We're in the castle. The one Rose was taken from as a baby."

"No," Quirk said faintly. "Can't . . . go to the castle."

"It's too late for that," Griff told him.

"Too late . . ." Quirk blinked, then seemed to focus on Griff's face. "Ah. Junior."

"Yes," Griff said patiently, though he wasn't a junior Watcher anymore. "Do you understand, Quirk? We're in the castle."

A slight nod. "Get away. You must. Take Rose and Timothy and go."

"You're too sick to travel," Griff told him.

"Go anyway," Quirk said. His trembling hand groped over the blanket; finding Griff's hand, he clung to it. "Go," he repeated.

Griff wasn't going to argue with a sick man. Instead he picked up the nearly empty cup, gently raised Quirk's shoulders, and made him drink the rest of the tea.

"Something must have happened," Quirk mumbled, as Griff helped him lie down again. "She went back to the castle." His head moved on the pillow. "Why'd she go back?"

Was he talking about Rose?

Speaking of her . . . "Do you know what story Rose is supposed to be a part of?" Griff asked.

Quirk muttered something unintelligible.

"Do you know what she should be doing?" Griff remembered Rose's words. "Or not doing?"

Quirk blinked, as if he was fighting off sleep. "Spindle," he murmured. His blunt fingers gripped Griff's hand.

"Spindle," Griff repeated. A device of Story that had something to do with Rose's curses.

"Tell Rose." The feverish gaze settled on Griff's face again. "No, no, no. No. Careful."

"Be careful of what?" Griff asked.

"He has the thimble," Quirk whispered.

"No, I have the thimble," Griff told him. Seeing Quirk so sick was making him feel a bit desperate. He wanted to do something to help, but there was nothing to be done.

Quirk's eyes dropped closed and he fell into a deeper sleep. Griff rested his elbows on his knees and covered his eyes. Spindle. He still didn't know what a spindle was, exactly. And Quirk wasn't making much sense, but he was clearly worried about the thimble.

Griff reached into his pocket and drew it out. As always, the silver felt cold, not warming at his touch. It seemed to weigh more than it should. It was important, somehow, but he didn't know why.

As he continued his fall from the precipice, the wind rushing past him turned icy cold, and there wasn't any view at all. Only darkness.

HALFWAY THROUGH THE morning, and I was finally primped and powdered and dressed in yet another pink silk gown and uncomfortable shoes. My mother was asleep—she seemed to sleep a lot—and my father was busy with other things. So I was in a sitting room with Miss Amity and Miss Olive. They'd been *engaging in delightful gossip* for an hour. Disgusted with it all, Timothy had stalked out, saying she was going to find someplace to practice her sword work. I got up and paced to the window. The tiny panes of glass were thick and bubbled, turning the view into a smudge of green-brown ground that blurred into the gray sky above it. I leaned my forehead against the window frame, closed my eyes, and for just a moment was back in the cottage with Shoe.

Ah, Rosie, he would say, with his usual kindness. *You've been out rambling again, have you? I'm glad you're home.*

"I wish I was home, Shoe," I sighed, and opened my eyes again. I wondered what Shoe would think of Quirk, and even more, of Griff. He'd be appalled by the state of Griff's boots, I knew that much. He would like Griff himself, though. Shoe had been a wonderful talker; he would've had no trouble drawing Griff out of himself. I could imagine them, sitting on the front porch of our cottage in the clearing, talking, and then Griff would smile. . . .

"What do *you* think, Lady Rose?" called Miss Amity's shrill voice.

I turned. The Misses, both dressed in pink silk like me, were sitting on elegant chairs at an elegant table. "What do I think about what?" I asked.

Miss Olive leaned forward, clasping her hands under her round bosom. "We're talking about that new stableboy." She licked her lips. "He's extremely handsome, isn't he?"

"Oh, he is," Miss Amity agreed. "Don't you think so, Lady Rose?"

"Yes," I agreed promptly. From the moment I'd met him, I'd thought Griff was nice to look at. Now that I'd seen more of the world, I realized that he was . . . well, he was what Miss Olive had said. His hair had grown out a bit from its short Watcher's length, and it suited him to be a little rough around the edges. His eyes were watchful, but the gray didn't seem bleak to me anymore, but clear and keen. He had high cheekbones and a stern set to his mouth that changed when he smiled. . . .

"Look," Miss Olive said. "She's blushing."

I put my hands to my cheeks.

Miss Olive tittered. "She likes him."

"She can't *like* him," Miss Amity said chidingly. "He is a *servant*."

"Very nice to look at," Miss Olive agreed. "And perhaps to dally with. But not for anything more."

I opened my mouth to correct them—to tell them that Griff wasn't a servant, of course—but then I stopped. Maybe it was better if they thought he was. I knew that the ladies-in-waiting were really my guards, and surely Griff was being watched, too. If he was thought to be an ordinary servant, and not the trained weapon that he really was, he might not be guarded so carefully.

Keeping an eye on the ladies, I ambled around the edge

of the room, pretending to examine the faded tapestries that covered the black stone walls. "Actually," I said casually, "I am dallying"—whatever that meant—"with the new stableboy."

"Ooh," Miss Olive squealed. "Tell! Tell!"

As if confiding in them, I stepped closer to their table and lowered my voice. "I'm to meet him after lunch today. In the stable."

"The *stable*," said Miss Amity disapprovingly.

"Well, I can hardly invite him up here, can I?" I asked.

"That's very true," Miss Olive said. "She's quite right about that, Amity."

Miss Amity nodded in grudging agreement.

"Can you both keep it a secret?" I asked, to make it seem more like gossip, so they wouldn't take it seriously. "Just between us ladies?"

"Ooh, yes," whispered Miss Olive after a glance at Miss Amity, who nodded.

"And you'll cover for me if anyone asks where I am?" I ventured.

Miss Olive gave me wink. "Only if you'll tell us what his kisses are like," she giggled.

Oh, dallying was *kissing*.

The only other person I'd kissed before was horrible Tom from the village. Or, rather, I'd been kissed *by* him, and it hadn't been at all nice. But with Griff . . .

"All right," I agreed.

* * *

WHILE THE MISSES worked on their embroidery, I whiled away the time before lunch by examining the tapestries. They told a story, I realized, that began at the doorway and went around the sitting room, ending at the door again. The tapestries had an edging of entwined roses and brambles; the threads had once been bright, but their colors were faded now. One character was repeated in every panel—a tall girl with dark hair. The story seemed to begin with her father's death. Then she was in rags, with three women haranguing her. Then a lovely, silver-haired woman appeared, and the tall girl was transformed—there seemed to be bits of gold thread stitched into her dress to make it shimmer. Then something about a lost shoe? My own Shoe had never told me this story—it wasn't familiar.

Oh. It wasn't just a story, it was Story. I started again at the beginning, and when I'd gone around the whole room, the last panel by the door was the girl holding hands with a man who wore a golden crown. So the girl was supposed to end up with a prince of some sort, evidently. I wasn't sure how that ending gave power to Story.

"Isn't it nice?" Miss Amity called from across the room. "The tapestry? Such a nice story."

I looked up.

"Happily ever after," sighed Miss Olive.

Was that what it was? As I was scrutinizing the girl's face in the last panel of the tapestry, Dolly and Sally came in the door, carrying trays laden with our lunch.

"Ooh," Miss Olive squealed, and she and Miss Amity set aside their embroidery.

I pulled my chair up to the table and ate quickly. "Will you wait here, then," I asked them, taking a last gulp of tea, "while I go to meet Gr—the stableboy?"

Miss Amity nodded, and dabbed the corners of her mouth with a napkin. "We expect a complete report," Miss Olive added, with another one of her winks.

Blushing, I went out of the room and made my way outside. As long as I acted as if I knew exactly where I was going, none of the servants tried to stop me.

At the stable door, I peeked in. A big man with a pig-snouted face and tusklike teeth was slouched on a hay bale, eyes half closed. He'd been with Griff in the Great Hall before, when I'd met my parents.

"That's Arny," Griff said from behind me, then stepped past; I followed him into the stable. At the sound of our steps, a few horses put their heads out of their stalls to look at us. "I suspect he's supposed to be watching me," Griff went on, "and reporting in. But he's drunk most of the time."

"Oh," I said, fascinated. I'd never seen a drunk person before.

"Ready?" Griff asked.

"To fight?" I blinked. "I suppose so." I looked down at myself. Pink silk dress, thin slippers. "I'm not exactly dressed for it."

Griff shrugged. "Doesn't matter. Fighting's not about the

clothes. Or the weapons, either."

"What's it about, then?" I asked.

"Will," he said grimly.

"Will," I repeated. I had no idea what he was talking about.

Without warning, he moved. So fast. *So* fast. Grabbed my shoulders, shoved me until my back was against the stable wall, with his forearm across my throat.

For just a moment, I was back in the village with Tom pressing himself against me, his rough kisses, and I screamed and flailed against the memory.

Griff released me, stepping swiftly back.

I covered my face with my hands, shaking, gasping for breath.

"You've been attacked before." Griff's voice was steady, quiet.

Still hiding, I nodded.

He was silent.

Firmly I pushed the memory of Tom away and peeked out from behind my fingers. Griff was studying me.

"Because of that," he said. He reached out, as if to touch my face, but stopped halfway.

Yes. Then I found my voice. "He thought the beauty gave him permission. I tried to fight him."

"Like you tried to fight me just now?" he asked.

I nodded. "I was . . . I was lucky, I suppose. Merry—she

was an old woman I was staying with—she came in and stopped him, before . . ."

"You were lucky," he said soberly. He gave a half shrug. "But screaming isn't a bad idea if you're doing it to call for help, and not because you're panicking."

"Have *you* ever screamed before? In a fight, I mean?" I asked.

A smile lightened his eyes; then he turned away and took off his long coat, hanging it on a nail.

"I'll bet you haven't," I said.

"No." He started rolling up the sleeves of his ragged shirt. "Right, so the first thing is balance." He shifted to stand ready.

Kicking off my uncomfortable shoes, I joined him.

He explained what to watch for, demonstrated how to move, and showed me how my pointy, hard parts—elbows, the edge of a hand, the tip of a shoe—should strike out for my opponent's soft bits. I listened carefully to his instructions, and moved as he directed, but half of my mind was observing how intently focused he was. He was usually so silent, but he was very good at explaining the elements of fighting.

He told me that anything could be a weapon.

I laughed. "Anything?"

"Yes," he answered, with a sudden smile that made me feel happy all over. He looked around the stable. "Pitchfork is obvious. Oat scoop—" He picked it up and demonstrated how he'd use it to bash an opponent in the head.

"What about this?" I went to a hay bale and picked up a leather bridle and reins he'd been mending.

He nodded. "Toss it low to entangle your opponent's feet."

"Oh, very clever." I stood with a hand on my hip and surveyed the barn, looking for another potential weapon. Hmm. "What about a . . ." My cheeks flamed into a hot blush as I remembered that I was supposed to be dallying with him. "What about a kiss? Can a kiss be a weapon?"

He swallowed. Our eyes met. For just a flash of a moment I felt connected to him again, just as I had when he'd tried to lift my curse, and it was something beyond blushes and kisses.

Then he looked away. He seemed distracted as he taught me what he called the *City Kiss*, bringing my forehead down hard across the nose of whoever was attacking me. "Lots of blood with that one," he noted. "Gives you time to escape."

Yes, Griff, I thought. *Very useful.*

But that was not the kind of kiss I was talking about.

CHAPTER

21

GRIFF HAD NOTED ROSE'S PHYSICAL GRACE BEFORE, SO
he wasn't surprised to find that she had a natural sense of balance and a decided, confident way of moving, once she knew
what she was supposed to do. She was unexpectedly strong,
too, given her delicate appearance.

That was good. She would need to be strong if they were
to escape from Story's plot.

"Tomorrow we'll work on grappling," he said, when it was
time for her to go back to the castle.

She was sitting on the hay bale next to the sleeping Arny,
putting on her shoes. She grinned up at him, her eyes sparkling. "What's grappling?"

"It's . . ." He paused, gazing at her, forgetting what he'd
been saying.

Since she'd said the word *kiss* he couldn't stop thinking about it. Maybe it'd be better if they didn't get too close to each other. He changed the subject. "Do you want to visit Quirk?"

"Yes indeed," she answered, getting to her feet and shaking out her skirts. "Is he better? Will he be able to travel soon?"

"Not yet," he answered. He put on his coat again and led her across the courtyard, which was busy with servants going about their work, and into the castle. During the afternoon, when Griff had checked on him again, Quirk had been sleeping. He'd eaten something, though, the healer's assistant had reported, and the fever wasn't as high.

When he and Rose squeezed into the tiny closet, they found Quirk propped up in bed holding a cup of tea.

Griff felt a rush of relief; Rose went to her knees beside the low bed and reached out to hug Quirk. "Oh, you're awake." Her elbow knocked the tea, and Griff reached down to take the cup and set it on the floor so it wouldn't spill. Quirk smiled wanly up at him. It was easy to forget how small Quirk was, because he had such a big personality. But now he seemed strangely fragile.

Rose, still on her knees, gripped his hands. "How's your fever? You *are* better, aren't you? Not completely better, but you're going to be all right?"

"Yes, Rosie." Quirk smiled at her.

Rose blinked and then, for some reason, tears welled up

in her eyes. "Oh, Quirk," she said brokenly.

He patted her hand, and she leaned closer to kiss his pale cheek.

"Now, children," Quirk said, when she drew back again. His face turned serious. "I hope you've noticed that we're in some trouble here."

"Yes, we know," Rose answered, moving to sit on the edge of the bed. "Griff is teaching me how to fight."

"Hm." Quirk looked speculatively up at Griff, then back at her. "What you really need to do is get away."

"You're not well enough to travel," Rose said to him.

Quirk waved a hand weakly, as if dismissing her worry. "Doesn't matter. You should go anyway."

"No," Griff put in. He leaned a shoulder against the wall, folding his arms.

Both Quirk and Rose looked up at him. "Well, I suppose that's settled, then," Quirk said with a wry shake of his head.

"Yes, it is. We won't leave here without you." Rose patted Quirk's arm. "Quirk, you know a lot more about all of this than we do. I think you should tell us what's going on."

"Ah. Yes." Quirk was silent for a few minutes, thinking. "I assume you two and Timothy have realized that Story is at work here."

"Yes, we have," Rose said, with a quick glance up at Griff. "It's a story about me. I'm sort of . . . tangled up in it?"

"Yes," Quirk said. "Entangled is a good way to describe it." He turned Rose's hand, then ran his blunt fingers over the mark on the inside of her wrist. When Griff had seen it before, it had been a burn, but it had healed into a new shape, a softly pink rose in full flower. Seeing it, Quirk nodded, as if he'd expected it. "You were born for this story, Rose. Your curse will force you to play a role in it."

"I'm not a construct," Rose interrupted. "I don't have to be part of this."

"Rose, when Pen stole you away from here and brought you to Shoe, she was trying to stop the story from happening, but"—he sighed—"Story has a way of overcoming such efforts. It is extremely dangerous." He was silent for a long moment. "I'm not sure there's much we can do to fight it."

"We have to try," Rose said.

"Yes." Quirk closed his eyes, weary.

"What can we do?" Rose persisted. "My curse has something to do with a spindle, doesn't it?"

"The spindle." Quirk nodded and struggled to open his eyes. "The curse . . . it will draw you to it. If you prick your finger on the spindle, the curse takes effect."

Rose leaned closer to him. "What will happen?"

Quirk's eyes dropped closed again. "Sleep," he murmured. "Everyone in the castle will fall under a sleep spell. Must not happen. Story will triumph."

Rose patted Quirk's hand and looked up at Griff. "We'll have to find out what a spindle looks like." She climbed to her feet, and they stood looking down at Quirk, who seemed very small and pale in the bed.

Silently, she and Griff stepped out of the room, into the narrow hallway that led to the kitchen.

Rose turned toward him. "Griff?" she said hesitantly.

When Griff spoke, his voice felt rusty. "Yes."

"Will you . . . ?" A pink flush crept up her cheeks. After an awkward moment, she shook her head. "Nothing. Never mind. I'll, um, see you tomorrow."

Griff nodded. "Be careful."

"I will," she promised, and left.

CHAPTER

22

I found that I'd made a mistake not kissing Griff when I had the chance in the hallway outside Quirk's room, because as soon as I closed the door of the sitting room behind me, the Misses pounced on me and pressed me for details about dallying with the handsome stableboy, and I had nothing to tell them.

"Ooh, she's shy," Miss Olive said with a titter.

"No, I'm really not," I protested. "I just couldn't—"

"Kissing a stableboy is only dalliance," Miss Amity said condescendingly. "It doesn't *matter*. There is no reason for a lady like you, or like us, to feel sensitive about it."

"That's right," Miss Olive confirmed. "It's not as if we could actually *care* about someone we were only dallying with."

"Oh," I said faintly.

"You can go again tomorrow," Miss Amity pronounced. "But we expect details."

"Ooh, yes," Miss Olive said, and made kissing noises with her lips.

I resigned myself to more of their company as they talked about flirting with the castle's male courtiers, and practiced coquettish glances on each other. "More eyelashes, Olive," Amity counseled. "Put your chin down, and don't show your teeth." Olive contorted herself until she looked ridiculous, blinking her eyes rapidly, with a close-mouthed smile pasted on her face.

I tried to ignore them, passing the time pacing around the sitting room and worrying about Story, resolutely *not* thinking about Griff until the afternoon was over and it was time for dinner.

IN THE MORNING, when I'd been laced into yet another insipidly pink dress, Sally and Dolly ushered me to the sitting room. As always, the Misses were there. But no Timothy. She was off practicing with her sword, I guessed, or doing something more interesting, like spying around the castle. I stood in the doorway feeling desperate and trapped. How could I possibly spend another day just sitting around?

Strength, I counseled myself. Will, as Griff had taught me. Anything is a weapon, even patience. Quirk was still too weak to travel. Waiting until he was better was all I could do, for now.

I gritted my teeth as Miss Amity and Miss Olive fluttered gracefully to me, showering me with the same compliments they'd given me the day before, about my dress, and the color of my eyes. "And your new hairstyle!" Miss Amity exclaimed. "It is simply exquisite."

"No," I said blankly, pulling away from them so I could sit by myself on the window seat. "It's exactly the same as it was yesterday."

Unfazed, they seated themselves and chattered brightly to each other. Their conversation had no substance at all; I listened with half an ear, but it washed past me without making an impression. I looked out the window at the blurred sky and the empty expanse of low hills. I wondered what Griff was doing. Oh, I'd been so awkward when I'd said good-bye to him in the hallway outside Quirk's sickroom. I wasn't sure he wanted to kiss me, but I wanted it so much. Today I would do it my way. There would be no blushing, I promised myself, none of the flirtatious glances that Olive and Amity had prescribed.

I was quiet until lunch; when I'd finished eating four of the dainty sandwiches that Sally had brought us, I stood up from the little table and brushed bread crumbs from my skirt. "Well," I said briskly. "I'm off for my dalliance."

Olive and Amity broke off their conversation and stared at me for a moment; then they both tittered. "Remember," Amity said with a coy look. "We expect a full report this time."

"Yes, of course." Feeling enormously self-conscious, I went out of the sitting room, sure their whispers about me would begin as soon as the door was closed. Free of them, I hurried down the stairs, out of the castle, and across the courtyard. The air outside was cold, making me shiver and rub the goose bumps from my bare arms. Stepping carefully over the ice-slicked paving stones, I approached the stable and peered in the door.

The stable was empty.

As I stood there, wondering where Griff was and feeling a little bereft that he wasn't there to meet me, a warm hand clamped over my mouth, and an arm wrapped around me, roughly pulling me back against a long, hard body.

For just a second I stiffened, and all of Griff's instructions about what to do if I was attacked flashed through my mind. I raised my arm, preparing to strike. But then I relaxed and slowly turned to face the one who had grabbed me.

It was Griff, of course. He stared at me, wide-eyed, for a long moment. "You were supposed to fight."

I felt a little breathless; we were standing so close together. "I knew it was you." I tipped my face up. This was it. He was going to bend his head, and we would kiss.

Then he released me and stepped back. "How?"

"I just did," I said, and I couldn't help smiling up at him.

He blinked and moved abruptly past me; I followed him into the stable. Griff was pulling the sheathed knife from his belt.

"Grappling, you said yesterday," I reminded him.

He glanced at me, and then looked away, shaking his head. "No. Knife work."

And then he was all intensity and focus again, as he showed me how to hold the knife, how to keep it hidden until I was ready to use it, how to draw it quickly from the sheath and strike fast, without hesitation.

I knew I should be paying attention, but all I could think about was *the kiss*.

I found myself staring at Griff's mouth, at his finely cut lips. Every time he touched me, just a meeting of our fingers as he handed me the knife, or a brush of his arm as he showed me a move, my skin felt acutely sensitive. Would his lips against mine feel the same way? Or would it be awkward and strange?

Stop it, I chided myself. Olive and Amity were right, in a way. It was just a kiss. It didn't have to mean anything. And I needed to focus on more important things, like how we were going to escape from the castle—from Story.

Griff sheathed the knife and wiped his forehead with the sleeve of his ragged shirt. Rose seemed flustered, on edge. "That's enough for today," he told her.

"All right." She turned and went to the doorway. There she stood looking across the courtyard to the castle without speaking.

Which really wasn't like her. She probably didn't feel like

talking to him. It was his own fault, he berated himself. He shouldn't have grabbed her from behind. Surely she thought he was a brute, like the man who'd attacked her.

Working himself up to an apology, he joined her, feeling intensely aware of her, standing so near. She shivered as a breeze gusted in the doorway. The air had grown cooler as clouds had drawn in over the sun; a few pigeons spiraled down to land on the courtyard's paving stones.

"I don't want to go back in there," she said, nodding toward the castle.

Then just stay here, he wanted to say.

"My mother and father are fairly awful," she went on. "They ignore each other completely, and they seem to barely notice me. Even though they're part of Story, I still want to love them. But I can't. They're too . . ." She shrugged. "They're too blank." She shivered and wrapped her arms around herself. "Griff," she said musingly. "Do you miss your father at all?"

"No."

She turned toward him, leaning against the opposite side of the door. A smile played at the corners of her mouth. "One word," she teased. "Now you've only got nine words left of today's ration."

He wasn't sure how to answer that.

"I can see why you don't miss him," she went on, serious again. "He didn't seem very nice." Then she was silent, giving him room to respond.

His father. Griff looked down at the toes of his shabby boots. The weight of his father's disapproval, the depth of his coldness—he'd gotten so used to it. And now that he was free of it . . . "Being away from him is a relief," he said slowly, realizing as he said it how true it really was. "He's the Lord Protector first," he tried to explain.

"And a father not at all," she finished for him. She waved at the castle. "Like the man in there who is supposed to be my father."

They were silent for a long moment.

"I wish you could have met Shoe," she said. Her face brightened. "He was a wonderful father to me."

"You miss him," he noted.

"Oh yes, of course. Very much. I loved him. And he loved me."

The breeze swirled in the stable door, stirring the straw on the floor, and Griff felt its chill on the back of his neck. He wondered what it would be like, to love like that. To be loved. It wasn't something he'd ever experienced, and he didn't know how to imagine it.

Across the courtyard, a servant in a blue uniform leaned out the castle's kitchen door and lit the lantern. It had gotten late, not long until dinner, and the sun was setting behind the heavy clouds.

"They'll be sending one of my guards to find me soon," Rose said, straightening. "I'd better go in."

He nodded, feeling chilled by the thought of the long

stretch of time before he'd see her again tomorrow.

Instead of leaving, she turned toward him. "Griff?" she said hesitantly, and then put her hands to her cheeks.

The stable was growing dim with the oncoming night, but it was bright enough to see her face. Was she blushing?

"Can I kiss you?" she asked abruptly, her flush deepening.

His mind went blank. "What?"

"I could only get away by telling the ladies-in-waiting that I was . . ." She paused and huffed out a laugh. "That I was dallying with the new stableboy. That's you. Dallying is, um, kissing, and I'm supposed to report back to them, and I don't know what to tell them." She shrugged, and then went on in a rush. "And if I can't tell them anything I won't be able to get away again so you can go on teaching me how to fight. Because I've never kissed anyone before."

"But you were . . ." *Attacked*, he was going to say.

"Yes, I know," she anticipated. "But that was awful. That doesn't count as kissing." She stepped closer. "So can I?"

Completely at a loss for words, he nodded.

She reached up and put her arms around his neck and pulled his head down. At first it was awkward. He'd never kissed anyone before, either. But her lips were so soft. She smelled so good. His arms went around her, and he drew her closer, close enough that she must be able to feel his heart pounding in his chest.

And for just the briefest flash, he didn't have that sinking, falling feeling, that certainty that he'd stepped off a precipice and was plunging to an abrupt finish.

With a sigh, she pulled away and looked up at him, lips parted, face glowing. "I should have guessed that you'd be good at this."

He was? "I don't know," he said, his voice rusty. "I think I might need more practice."

"Oh," she said breathlessly. "Yes." She tipped her face up to his, and they kissed again, and she was right. A kiss could be a weapon. He had no defense against it; it left him shaking, and bereft at the thought that it had to end, and she would go away.

But it did end.

Still in the circle of his arms, she touched her lips with her fingertips, smiling a little. "I'd better go," she said softly. But she didn't move.

Griff felt like he should say something. All he wanted to do was kiss her again.

Rose took a step away, breaking their embrace. "They're wrong," she said, as if speaking to herself.

"Who's wrong?" he managed to say.

"The ladies-in-waiting," she answered. "They have absolutely no idea what they're talking about."

He shook his head, not understanding.

"Never mind," she said. "I'll kiss you tomorrow." Her face went scarlet. "I'll *see* you tomorrow, I mean." A last flustered smile, and she was gone.

* * *

Just after Rose had gone back to the castle, Griff was settling the horses for the night when he heard a quick step at the wide door that led out to the courtyard. Rose, he hoped. Sneaking out so they could spend more time together.

It was Timothy. She carried a lumpy burlap sack, which she dumped on the ground beside the door. "Watcher," she said with a nod.

I'm not a Watcher anymore, he wanted to say. Instead he brushed past her and picked up the wooden scoop he used to give the horses their nightly ration of oats.

She blew out a breath and watched him cross to the oats bin. "Have you figured out what's going on here?"

"Yes," he said briefly, and scooped up some oats. "This is Story's place. Rose is in danger."

"Very succinct," Timothy commented. "But you left something out. We're all in danger."

He nodded and carried the scoop of oats across the stable to the horses' stalls.

"But Rose is the one we really need to worry about," Timothy admitted.

He paused. "She never belonged to Story." He searched for words. "She's honest. And true." And when she was happy, she glowed with it, like a flame, warming everyone around her. She had glowed that way after their kiss, too.

"Yeah, I know." Timothy shrugged. "You see the beauty first. It's hard to see the girl behind it. But she's there, and she's not a construct. I'm not going to let Story have her."

"You'd make a good Watcher," Griff found himself saying.

"Ugh," Timothy said, with a mock scowl. "You probably think that's a compliment." She flopped down to sit on one of the hay bales. "So can we get Rose out?"

Griff considered it. That morning he had scouted the castle, avoiding the always-watching servants and courtiers. One of the things he'd found was an armory full of weapons that were sharpened, ready. Story's servants would be well armed if it came to a fight.

He had his patrol knife; Timothy had her sword, and Rose would fight, too, but one of them would have to carry Quirk. "No," he answered at last. "We can't."

"Yeah, that's what I thought." Timothy got to her feet again, as if she was too restless to stay seated. "I've spent the last two days collecting supplies." She picked up the burlap sack.

His stomach sank. "You're abandoning us."

"No," she said, with a flare of anger. "Stupid *Watcher.* I'm going for help."

"Who can help us?" Griff asked, surprised.

"I'm from outside the City, remember?" she answered. "I have friends, not too far away from here. Other Breakers. They knew Pen, and they've been watching this castle for a long time, ever since Story's latest Godmother came here and set this place up."

"The Godmother?" Griff interrupted.

"Yeah." Timothy studied him for a long moment. "You know how she did it?"

He didn't want to know the answer to that question.

"About twenty years ago Story found a new Godmother so it could escape from the City. Then she worked Story's will. She came here and had the castle built, and turned animals into the servants, and she brought Rose's mother and father here and took their memories away. She probably had to force them together to conceive the baby, since they obviously don't like each other very much. And how did she do all of this?" Timothy paused and then answered her own question. "She used the thimble."

No. He hadn't known that. The horror of it froze any words he would have spoken. His hand dipped into his coat pocket and drew out the thimble. It felt icy cold under his fingers.

"Yeah, that thimble," Timothy said. "It was hers. The Godmother's."

CHAPTER

23

OLIVE AND AMITY WERE SO COMPLETELY WRONG.

The kiss did matter.

I walked through the door from the kitchen, still feeling Griff's lips against mine, and the diminishing heat of the blush that had flashed from my head to my toes as he had kissed me. I was lost in thought, trying to hold on to that feeling, as I started down the finer passageway, intending to return to my rooms. There I encountered a cluster of people. At the center of the group was my father; trailing him was a servant with fur-tipped ears, and a few lavishly dressed courtiers.

Seeing me, they stopped. The courtiers stared at the beauty. It made me feel prickly. Uncomfortable.

"Daughter," my father said. Like when I'd met him

before, he wore a fur-edged mantle and his lordly gold chain. His face didn't change when he saw me; it was like a mask, bland and blank. "Why are you not with your ladies?"

My guards, he meant. I was not a very good liar. "I was . . ." I looked frantically around. Just the hallway, paneled in dark wood, lined with doors. "I was . . . I'd like to find a book to read." Good answer, I thought.

My father inclined his head. With a snap of his fingers, he summoned three of the courtiers, young men, who stepped forward and bowed to me.

I curtsied back to them.

"Accompany Lady Rose to the library," my father ordered. "Then see she goes back to her rooms."

So the courtiers were my guards, too.

"We will meet at dinner tonight," my father stated, and with a rustle of silks and satins, he and his entourage continued down the hallway.

"I am Sir Roland, Lady Rose," said the first courtier, with a sweeping bow.

The next bowed. "I am Sir Richard, at your service, Lady Rose."

"And I am Sir James," said the third, with a bow and a flourish of a laced handkerchief. All three of them were blandly handsome and wore colorful coats—light-green silk, peach velvet, blue satin—over embroidered waistcoats, and pale pantaloons with silk stockings and buckled shoes. They all wore narrow swords at their hips, too.

I couldn't help but compare them to Griff. They were sleek where he was shabby; they spoke smoothly, where he barely spoke at all. But . . . I eyed their mouths. Roland's was smiling silkily; Richard's was loose and wet; James's thin lips were chapped. I had absolutely no desire to kiss any one of them.

"This way, Lady Rose," said Sir Roland, and bowed again. That was three bows for Roland, two each for Richard and James.

I let them lead me to another part of the castle. It was deserted, silent, and chilly, but even more ornately decorated. All three of them stared at the beauty, which made me feel on edge.

"These were the Godmother's rooms," Sir Richard volunteered. "She only stayed here for a short time, but they are just the way she left them."

"Oh," I said, more alert, and continued down the carpeted passageway, stopping when Sir James opened a door with a silver handle.

I stepped into the room, which was lit by blazing candles. Tall windows edged by ice-blue curtains let in the last rays of the fading sunset. It was a library, all right, lined from floor to ceiling with shelves of books. I turned in a circle, trying to decide where to start. I missed reading. Shoe and I had told stories, but we also read them aloud to each other, and on every trip into the village he'd taken our old books with him and come back with new ones.

All the books on the Godmother's library shelves were bound with leather, the same ice blue as the curtains. I stepped closer to examine them. They were all the same size, all the same width. And on the spine of every book was the same title, printed in shiny silver letters. *Story.*

A frisson of worry shivered down my spine. I pulled out one of the books and opened it. On the page were printed the words

Rose pulled out one of the books and opened it.

I slammed the book closed, then dropped it as if it was hot enough to scorch my fingers.

"Oh," I breathed. The blue-covered book lay there on the blue carpet. It had to be a coincidence. I shivered and backed away.

"Are you all right, Lady Rose?" asked Sir James.

I turned, and they were still watching me without blinking; Sir Richard licked his lips and smiled wetly at me.

"I think . . . ," I stammered. "I'll go join my ladies-in-waiting."

They led me to the sitting room. At the door, they bowed again.

As before, Amity and Olive demanded details about my so-called dalliance with the good-looking stableboy.

I didn't tell them everything. Just enough. And I did it without blushing, which I considered an enormous triumph.

"Ooh," Miss Olive squealed. "*And* you've met Sir Roland and Sir Richard and Sir James. Aren't they handsome?"

Miss Amity sniffed and looked faintly disapproving. She was doing something ladylike with a thick needle and a bobbin and white thread. Her fingers flew, making loops and twists and braids, and a patterned web took shape.

Beside her, Miss Olive was holding a length of what looked like golden hair in one hand, and in the other a length of wood about the size of a pen, with a sharp end. She was twirling it to tease the hair into a thread, then winding the thread around the pen's base.

I got up and walked around the room, thinking about Griff, but also thinking about the library, and how strange it was. What would happen, I wondered, if I looked into another part of the book?

I shook my head. Better not to think about that.

But . . . I could almost feel Story in the air. A kind of heaviness. *Entangled*, I'd told Quirk, but it was more like *stuck*. Like a bee in honey.

We had to get out. Tomorrow when I went to Griff for my fighting lesson, we would have to decide our next move. Surely Quirk would be well enough to travel soon.

After walking around the room again, I sat down next to Miss Olive. "What are you doing?"

She nodded at Amity. "She is tatting. Making lace."

Oh, so that's what tatting was. One of the ladylike accomplishments, I remembered.

"And I am spinning the thread for the lace," Miss Olive added. She held up a stick wound at the top with a length of golden hair-like stuff. "This is flax on a distaff." She licked her fingers and twisted a bit of the flax around the wooden pen-like thing. "As you see, I draw it out with the spindle."

She kept talking, but I didn't hear her words. A roaring filled my ears, and I froze, suddenly frightened as something rose within me in response to seeing it.

Spindle.

Miss Olive kept spinning, pulling the threads, twirling the spindle between her fingers. She watched me. "Would you like to try?" She held out the spindle. It was made of smooth, dark wood, wrapped with the spun thread at one end. The tip at the other end was made of metal, and it was very sharp. Like a needle.

"No," I croaked, shaking my head, but I couldn't stop staring at it, enthralled. Against my will, my hand lifted. I could *feel* it. Story. It was so heavy, so powerful, and it wanted me to reach out and take the spindle into my hand; it wanted my finger to prick itself on the metal tip. There would be just one drop of blood. . . .

And now I saw what Quirk was afraid of. He had warned me. So had Griff and Timothy. *Be careful.* I hadn't realized.

But now I knew.

It hit me physically, like a blow; I shuddered, and black spots swam before my eyes.

I really was a construct of Story.

So were my parents; it explained why they were so blank, so empty. Story had made them, and it had made me. It had made me for this. I was nothing; I was hollow, and Story would fill me up.

I trembled with the horror of it.

My hand kept reaching for the spindle.

My heart pounded; I felt a scream rising in my throat.

And then I remembered what Griff had taught me about panicking during a fight. Fight. *Will.*

It took all my strength. My reaching hand clenched into a fist. Slowly, carefully, I got to my feet and willed myself to back away.

The Misses were watching me avidly, Olive still holding out the spindle.

"Come, Lady Rose," Miss Amity said, and her words seemed to echo in the room. "Take it. You know you want to."

"Take it," Miss Olive echoed.

I steadied myself, my back against the door to the stairs that led to the pink bedroom, my hand groping for the knob. "No, thank you," I said, surprised at how normal my voice sounded. "It's late. I think it must be time to dress for dinner. I don't want to keep my mother and father waiting."

My hand found the knob. Turning it, I fled, slamming the door behind me.

CHAPTER

24

"GRIFF," HE HEARD, A WHISPER. A HAND SHOOK HIS shoulder.

He jerked awake. The loft in the stable that he shared with Arny was dark. He'd been dreaming again about the fall from the precipice, listening to the wind whistling past, trying not to think about the ground that had to be rushing up at him, even though he knew it was coming. It would all be an awful mess when he landed.

"Griff," came another whisper. "It's me. Rose."

He sat up, the straw rustling, and rubbed the sleep out of his eyes.

"I need to talk to you," she said.

From not far away came the sound of Arny snoring, then snuffling and turning over.

He nodded, even though she couldn't see him. "Not here." He heard her bare feet pad across the floor; climbing out of his bed of straw, he followed her down the ladder to the main room of the stable, where he lit the lantern.

Rose was wrapped in a pink robe; her hair hung tangled around her pale face. "I'm not sure I'll be able to get away again," she said. "They're going to be guarding me more carefully." She looked around vaguely. "We should find Timothy."

"She's gone. For help."

"Oh. Good." She shivered. "But I'm afraid it might be too late for that. I found out about the spindle."

He nodded. He wanted to reassure her, to, maybe, put his arm around her for comfort, but he knew that would just make him want to kiss her again. And now that he knew about the thimble, he should stay as far away from her as he could.

"And . . . ," she added, her voice trembling, "I've learned more about Story."

"We should go to Quirk," he said.

"That might be best," she agreed. "He knows a lot more than we do about what's going on, and I think it's time for him to tell us. But maybe we shouldn't wake him up."

"It's all right." Griff had checked on Quirk after dinner, and his fever was almost gone. He took the lantern and Rose followed as he headed for the stable door. They crossed the paved courtyard and went into the shadowed kitchen, then down the hall to the closet.

As they entered, the light from the lantern spilled across

Quirk's bed, and he sat up. His straw-colored hair stuck out in all directions, but his eyes were bright and clear of fever. "What's the matter, children?" he asked.

Griff set the lantern on the floor. Rose stood, her face half in shadow, her hands clenched together, and looked down at Quirk.

"I'm really frightened," she said.

"What's happened?" Quirk asked sharply.

"Oh," Rose said, and it was almost a sob. "You told me about Story, and you told me to be careful, but I didn't understand."

"And now you do," Quirk finished for her.

She nodded. A blink, and a tear rolled down her cheek, shiny in the lantern light. "You were right," she said, almost inaudibly. "I am a . . ." She shook her head, and another tear fell. "A construct of Story. Just the beauty, nothing more."

"Ah, lass," Quirk said sadly. He patted the bed. "Come here."

Rose sat beside him and put her face in her hands; more tears leaked out between her fingers.

Griff felt frozen; he didn't know what to say to help her. But seeing her cry made something hurt inside his chest.

"Now, Rosie," Quirk said. "It's true enough. Story made you. But listen." He reached out to tap her hands. "Shoe made sure that you were more than that, didn't he?"

She shook her head, her eyes swimming with tears. "I don't know."

"He did," Quirk said firmly. "Shoe raised you to be good, and loving, and happy. A true, real person with her own story, not a clockwork doll. You can fight Story."

She scrubbed at the tears on her cheeks. "Can I? But I'm so entangled in it, I don't know how."

"Mm." Quirk was silent for a moment. "You're not the only one entangled here, lass."

"You?" Rose asked.

"No." Quirk pointed with a blunt finger. "Him."

The thimble, Griff thought, with a sudden lurch in his stomach.

"If Griff is who I suspect, he is part of this, too," Quirk went on.

"If?" Rose asked slowly. "Who is he, then?"

Quirk studied him, his green eyes clear. Then he nodded. "It's time to tell your story, lad."

Griff couldn't bring himself to speak.

"Everyone has a story," Rose said, her face so lovely in the golden lantern light. "Once upon a time," she began.

"Rose, I don't—"

"Once upon a time," she continued, "there was a baby boy born to the Lord Protector."

"He wasn't the Lord Protector then," Griff corrected. "That happened later, after the first Protector didn't return to the City."

"Pen," Quirk put in. "The first Protector was the Penwitch,

as you call her, lass. She left the City to steal you away from this castle, Rosie."

"Oh," Rose said with a blink. "That means our stories begin in the same place, almost, Griff."

Maybe they did.

"What about your mother?" Rose prompted.

He shook his head, and she and Quirk stayed silent for a few minutes, enough time for him to think it over. "The Penwitch left. . . ." He'd never told a story before; he wasn't sure what to tell them next.

"Telling a story is like putting beads onto a string," Rose said.

She had the same odd way of talking that Quirk did. Comparing things that were nothing alike.

"And once you've got all the beads together," she went on, "you've got something more than just one bead and another and another, you've got a necklace."

He frowned. "I don't know what you mean."

"Oh." She blew out a frustrated sigh. "It means the beads, all together, make a thing that's more beautiful than just a bunch of beads. It's the same with stories. When you tell them, they're not just words strung together. A story is more than a collection of sentences. It means something more. It helps you understand."

He'd always thought he understood things. But maybe he hadn't. "All right." He considered a bead. It wasn't easy. He'd been trained for so long to engage only with what was right in front of him. The beads, though. They required an unaccustomed effort to go back over things that had happened long ago, things he'd tried to forget. His mind felt rusty. "The Penwitch left, and the City had no Protector. But it was too late. Story had already seized its chance. In secret it had found a new Godmother."

He couldn't bear to tell them the next part. He'd never spoken it aloud before. His father had ordered him never even to think of it. "A new Godmother," he repeated. "She was . . ."

"Go on, lad," Quirk said gently.

The words felt like stones as he spoke them. "She was my mother."

Quirk was nodding, as if this confirmed something he'd suspected.

Griff blinked. "How did you know?"

"These things make a kind of sense," he said. "Go on."

He glanced at Rose, to see how she'd reacted to this new information. She regarded him gravely. "Tell," she prompted.

"She . . ." He swallowed. "My mother served Story. When I was still a baby she went away for a while—she must have come here to build Castle Clair—but then she returned. That's when the Penwitch left. Someone had to oppose the . . . the Godmother, so my father made himself the Protector. He created the Watchers, too. There was a battle in the citadel. It was still a castle, then."

And suddenly he could see it just as it had happened. Smoke had billowed from the castle's central tower and then, stone by stone, it had crumbled; the four spires had snapped and crashed to the ground. The air had smelled bitter, and a pall of ash had settled over the City. Everything green and growing had withered and died.

"After two years of fighting, the Lord Protector won the battle, the Godmother was killed, and Story was subdued," he said. "That was when the Forest moved to cut off the City from the rest of the world so that Story would be contained there if it ever tried to rise again."

"That's when I arrived in the City," Quirk said unexpectedly.

They both turned to him.

He gave them a wry smile. "Pen was busy keeping an eye on Castle Clair, so even though I wasn't even your age, Rosie, she sent me to see to things in the City. I got in right before the Forest made its move." He shrugged. "And I couldn't get out again. So I stayed."

"I was right," Rose said, mock glaring at Quirk. "You've always known far more about all this, haven't you?" She narrowed her eyes. "You clearly knew Pen, and Shoe, too. Who *are* you?"

"I was there, Rosie, in the cabin in the valley, when Pen brought you to Shoe." Quirk shook his head. "Such a tiny, squalling mite you were. I was thirteen years old," he said with a smile, "and I'd never had to deal with a baby before. I left it to Shoe."

"They were your *parents*!" Rose exclaimed. "Shoe and Pen? They were your father and mother?"

Suddenly, Quirk sobered. "Yes, lass."

Rose's face had turned sad. "You know that Shoe is, that he—"

"Yes." Quirk reached out with a small hand and rested it against her cheek. "He's been lost to me for a long time. And Pen, too."

They sat quietly together for a few moments. "Shoe was a good father, wasn't he?" Rose asked.

"The best," Quirk answered.

"Not like the Lord Protector," Rose added. "He never loved anyone. Not even his wife. Or his own son."

They both turned to look up at Griff.

"Tell what happened to the little boy," Rose said softly.

Griff found his place in the story again. Story had been defeated; the castle had fallen. "The boy was too young to really know what was happening. He didn't understand his father's new rules or where his mother had gone. Mostly he was alone, and he was frightened." He remembered going days without speaking to anyone; without anyone speaking to him, left to himself in his father's cold citadel rooms. Food had been scarce, and he'd been hungry all the time. "A few years after that, the Lord Protector discovered that the boy was a curse eater, and he started training him to become a

Watcher." And it had been such a relief to lose himself in that training until he barely noticed how coldly rational his father was, and he didn't remember the castle's fall, or the fact that his mother had abandoned him to serve Story.

"And here you are," Rose said.

He nodded. As Quirk had said, *these things make a kind of sense.*

"Well, that was one thing I wasn't sure about," Quirk said. "I didn't know that Griff's mother was a Godmother."

"The Lord Protector didn't let it be known," Griff said. "And we never spoke of it."

"Mm." Quirk looked speculatively at him. "The Lord Protector is very good at silencing the people he doesn't want speaking aloud."

When Griff didn't comment, Quirk went on with his part of the story. "As I said, Pen sent me to keep an eye on the City while she was gone."

"Why didn't you become the City's Protector?" Rose asked.

Quirk gave a wry smile. "Well, look at me, lass."

"Because you're small?" she asked.

"Exactly," Quirk said with a nod. "And I was very young at the time, as I said."

"I think," Rose said, narrowing her eyes at him, "it's more likely because you're devious."

Quirk smiled. "Anyway, I assumed at that point that Pen would return. The Forest would have let her through to the

City; it's always been her ally. I knew something had happened when she didn't."

"She sent letters to Shoe for a long time," Rose put in. "And she only died recently."

Quirk nodded. "I think she must have felt certain Story would find some way to rise here at the castle, and she couldn't leave."

"The Godmother lived here once," Rose noted. "The courtiers told me that today. I saw her library." She shuddered. "It doesn't have books, it only has Story." With nervous fingers, she combed through a lock of her hair. "What would the Godmother do to establish Story here? I mean, how did she do it?"

"Ah," Quirk said with a brisk nod. "Griff's mother acted as a true Godmother. She created the castle and the servants, and she brought a man and a woman here, took their memories, and forced them to become your parents. She was able to do all of that because"—he held up a stubby finger—"she had an item of power."

Thanks to Timothy, Griff knew exactly what Quirk was talking about. He reached into the pocket of his ragged coat and drew out the thimble. It seemed even colder and heavier than usual. He held it up.

"The thimble," Quirk acknowledged. "It was lost when the Godmother was killed, and then found again, as such things always are. It was held in trust by Precious, the leader of the Breakers. Storybreakers, they are, and their purpose has always been to fight Story. I assumed it would be safe with them."

"Why didn't you take the Godmother's thimble?" Rose asked. "You were the son of the Penwitch, after all, and you could have hidden it safely away."

"Nobody knew that," Quirk explained. "I never told anyone, not even the Breakers." He shrugged. "And I suspect, despite the Breakers' attempt to keep it safe, that the thimble has a way of finding its intended heir. Your mother, Griff, must have been related in some way to the previous Godmother. Just as the thimble found her, it found Griff. You can imagine my surprise in the Forest when the thimble wasn't working for Timothy and it seemed like we had no choice, that Griff would have to carry it. That's when I started to suspect who he was. At first I couldn't believe the irony of it: the son of the Lord Protector was also the son of a Godmother." He paused and studied Griff. "And even then, lad, I didn't know what kind of power the thimble would have over you. If you could wield it as a Godmother would."

Griff felt a sudden lurch in his stomach, a keen sensation of falling. A creeping horror.

But it was Rose who spoke the horror aloud. "He did use the thimble," she said slowly. "He used it to get us out of the Forest. He led us here, to the castle. Into Story."

"Now we come to it." Quirk gazed up at Griff, and his green eyes were so clear. "All along, Story has had a plan for you, Griff." His voice was strangely even. "You are the son of a Godmother. Not a curse eater, but one who can control curses. You are not a Watcher. You are Story's weapon."

Rose was staring at him. And he could see it in her eyes. Doubt.

The icy cold of the thimble crept over his skin, striking deep into his bones, freezing any word of denial he would have spoken.

And the wind rushed past him, howling in his ears. He hurtled through the last part of his fall, and his body slammed into the ground.

Strange, he found himself thinking numbly, as if from a great distance from himself. His landing hadn't made a mess at all. He must have been completely obliterated.

CHAPTER 25

It was hard enough trying to make sense of the fact that I had been born as a construct of Story, and still would be, if Shoe hadn't raised me.

But now I knew that Griff was Story's weapon.

And he had the Godmother's thimble.

But I had kissed him . . .

What did it all mean? The words were there, the sentences, but we didn't understand. Not yet.

I could still see his face as he'd turned and left Quirk's tiny sickroom. Pale, his gray eyes bleak, the way they'd been when I'd first met him. I'd wanted to leap up, to take his hands in mine, to warm him, but instead I'd sat frozen until it was too late.

Feeling bereft, I wrapped my arms around myself for

comfort. It was late, very late, and oh, I was weary.

Quirk, looking troubled, had leaned back on his pillows. He seemed tired, too.

We stayed quiet for a few minutes.

I didn't want to believe it. "Quirk, I was created for Story, but you said I could fight it. Why can't Griff?"

"Love, and warmth, and happiness are our greatest weapons against Story," he answered. "Shoe gave them to you, as he did to me. Story has a much harder time using someone who is truly loved. Griff wasn't raised the way you were, Rosie. He grew up in the citadel."

A prison, I'd thought the citadel when I'd first seen it. Cold, comfortless. "His father is horrible."

Quirk nodded. "From the sounds of it, his mother was worse." He was silent for a moment. "Griff is so quiet, it's hard to see what he is thinking. We can't know for sure what his motivations are."

"Why would he bring us here?" I asked. "I mean, we're in terrible danger, aren't we?"

"He wouldn't have known that," Quirk explained. "Story was using him."

Another silence. I knew we were both thinking the same thing: what if Story used him again? Would he be able to fight it?

"I don't know what to think," I said at last. We had to do something. "Timothy has gone for help, Griff said. Can we try to get away and join her?"

"No," Quirk said. "The servants would be ordered to pursue us."

"Unto death," I murmured.

"Yes," Quirk agreed. He rubbed his temple. "I have an idea. You're the one Story wants. If I left the castle alone, and quietly, I don't think the servants would come after me. There's something, if I can find it, that might help us. If I go, do you think you're strong enough to resist Story, to stay away from the spindle? It would only be for a few days."

"I think so," I said wearily.

"All right." Quirk settled into his pillows and pulled the blanket up to his chin. "I'll go as soon as I can. You'll have to be very careful. And stay away from Griff, too. Even without intending it, he could be a danger to you."

"I will," I said.

But that wasn't going to be easy.

AFTER I RETURNED to my pink room in the tower, I climbed into my chilly, lacy bed and lay awake in the dark. I was in danger. I missed Shoe, and our cottage, but I was glad to know that Quirk was his son. I shivered at the thought that Griff had the Godmother's thimble. Story had used him once. It would certainly try to use him again.

I knew he was in the stable; I knew he wasn't sleeping. He was alone, and probably in despair. My heart ached for him; I wanted to go to him, but I knew that was the last thing I should do.

In the morning, I was still awake. The room was dim, the bed curtains drawn; I heard a clatter followed by an unhappy hiss.

I sat up, blinking, then peered out of the curtains. The snakelike servant, Sally, was kneeling at the hearth, trying to light a fire. "Good morning," I said, and my voice sounded creaky. "Do you need some help with that?" Shoe had always left the fire starting to me; I was good at it.

"Sahhh," Sally said, and stuck a burned finger into her lipless mouth.

I climbed out of the bed and went to help, kneeling beside her. Sally hadn't put any kindling in; she'd been trying to light a log with a match. I started building a proper fire. "Where's Dolly?" I asked. "Doesn't she usually do this?"

"Ssshe . . ." Sally was usually so smooth, but now she seemed flustered. "Mousesss are all the sssame," she hissed. "Silly, sometimes."

"Silly?" I asked. "What do you mean? Hand me the box of matches, would you?"

Sally gave me the matches. Her fingers, when they touched mine, were cool and scaly. "She is slipping," she said.

I lit a match and got some wood shavings burning, then started adding bigger sticks. "Slipping," I repeated.

"Slipping backwardsss," Sally said, as if explaining. "Moussssing." She drooped, and her forked tongue flickered out to taste the air. "Snakeses like to eat mouses."

I sat back on my heels and studied her. Sally's neck was longer than it had been before, I realized. And scalier. If Dolly was . . . mousing, then Sally was snaking.

Something was wrong. The castle's servants were reverting to their animal selves—Story was slipping, somehow. Maybe we still had a chance to resist it.

ONCE I WAS dressed in yet another rose-pink silk gown, with my hair rather haphazardly braided, Sally brought tea and buttered muffins, and whisked the tray and plates away again when I'd finished.

The day stretched before me. My eyes felt heavy from my lack of sleep during the night. In the evening I would have dinner with my parents, but neither of them would show any interest in me at all. I felt caged, needing to act, and I was desperately worried about Griff, but the only thing I could do was stay quiet, unnoticed, until Quirk returned. It'd be ladylike accomplishments, then. With a sigh, I went down the stairs to the sitting room.

Strangely, my ladies-in-waiting were not waiting. The room was empty, the heavy velvet curtains drawn. A few golden threads in the tapestry glinted in the dimness. Just one sliver of light came in from outside, running like a line across the carpet, pointing to a small, round table.

My skirts rustling, I went farther into the room. On the

table, illuminated, was Miss Olive's wad of fluff, and a ball of thread, neatly wound.

And the spindle.

I stepped closer to see it better.

It was as dark as shadows, but the metal point on its end gleamed wickedly in the faint light.

"That's close enough," I whispered to myself, when I was four steps away.

The way the spindle was lined up with the crack between the curtains made it seem as if it was drawing all the light out of the world and into its own darkness. The air felt heavy. The room seemed to revolve around me. Shadows swirled in the corners.

I hadn't moved, but somehow I found myself standing next to the table.

I clenched my hands and put them behind my back.

With a huge effort of will, I fought to take a step away.

Quirk was gone, Timothy was gone, and Griff was not to be trusted, at least for now. I was alone in this fight. But I had my will.

No.

I would not touch the spindle.

ARNY WAS DRUNK again. He sat slumped on the hay bale, snoring heavily. His blue vest was stained with food, he hadn't shaved, and the bristly whiskers, added to the yellowed tusks that protruded from his mouth, made him look more like a wild boar than a man.

Griff's brain felt numb. He didn't know what he could do to help Rose and Quirk. Instead of doing nothing at all, he started the morning chores, mechanically mucking out stalls, carrying water to the horses, forking hay from the loft.

After his fall had ended and he'd been obliterated, he'd stumbled back to the stable. He'd sat in the darkness for the rest of the night. Rose was right to be horrified. *He* was horrified. All his life he'd been trained to fight *against* Story.

And now he was Story's weapon. He didn't have any choice about it. He knew from his training as a Watcher that this was how Story worked—it used people, entangling them until their will was destroyed and any action they took was warped until it served Story's purpose.

He wasn't sure what to do. Try to explain? Try to convince Rose and Quirk that he wasn't their enemy? He thought he wasn't, anyway, even though he'd been the one to bring them to the castle, into terrible danger.

Could he throw the thimble away? Somehow he knew it would come back to him. *The thimble has a way of finding its intended heir,* Quirk had told him.

He was the Godmother's heir. It explained his father's coldness and his enforced silence, didn't it? Griff had never thought about his mother—he'd been trained not to—but the Lord Protector must have decided that strict rationality would excise Story from his son, just as he'd burned the Story-mark from Rose's wrist.

As he worked, his eyes felt gritty. He hadn't slept at all. Maybe he'd never sleep again.

In the afternoon, he watched for Rose, in case she came for her fighting lesson. He watched, and waited, then cursed himself for being an idiot. Of course she wouldn't come.

Later, as Griff lugged a last bucket of water from the pump into the stable, Quirk came out one of the castle doors and headed across the courtyard. He stumped up and put his hands on his hips. "Well now," he said, looking Griff up and down. "You look a bit rough."

Griff set the bucket on the paving stones.

"Didn't sleep?" Quirk asked.

Griff shook his head.

"Right, well," Quirk said, after a silent moment. He frowned down at the paving stones, then back up at Griff. "Listen—"

He was interrupted as a door to the castle was flung open, and a clot of shouting servants spilled out into the courtyard. In their midst was a thrashing figure, a servant with gray-furred ears, yellow eyes, and a long nose. The other servants shoved him away, gathering around to watch as he snarled and snapped in a frenzy. With clawed fingers he started ripping at his blue uniform, scratching at his own skin until blood spattered on the paving stones around him.

Griff could only stare, but Quirk darted into the stable

and came out with a length of rope, then hurried over to the servants, issuing orders. "Grab him, now," he shouted, and when the wolf-servant was pinned to the ground, Quirk got him wrapped up with the rope. "A secure room," he ordered. "Keep him bound so he doesn't hurt anyone."

"Thin's is fallin' apart," Arny said. He'd staggered up to stand beside Griff, watching as the wolf-servant was dragged away, howling. The other servants, looking frightened, trailed back into the castle.

Quirk rejoined them, rubbing at a few drops of blood that had splashed on his gray tunic.

"Fallin' apart," Arny repeated, and burped. "We was made a long time ago."

"Ah," Quirk said with a nod. He looked at Griff. "Your mother used the thimble to turn them human."

Griff didn't want to talk about the thimble.

"Story's been waitin' a long time," Arny said, blinking. "Too long." Then he turned and shuffled back toward the stable.

Quirk watched him go. "I think he must be right. According to Story, Rose should have pricked her finger on the spindle on her sixteenth birthday. Months ago, I'm guessing." He frowned, then pointed at the castle. "And now the spindle has been revealed. Rose is in terrible danger, and there's nothing I can do to help her. As soon as it's dark, I'm leaving. I'm going to look for something of my mother's." He paused, and then went on. "Her thimble, as it happens. It has different powers than the Godmother's thimble."

Words rattled around in Griff's head. "Why . . . ?" he managed.

"Why tell you?" Quirk finished for him. "Yes. That is a question, isn't it."

Griff stayed silent.

Quirk paced in a tight circle, his hands behind his back. "Here's the thing, Griff. You know how powerful Story is. Rose is under enormous pressure to allow it to play out. She's strong, but I don't know how long she can withstand it."

"What if . . ." Griff cleared his throat. "What if she can't resist?"

"Her curse will rise," Quirk answered, "and Story will seize its chance, and it may not be possible to defeat it. There is nothing Rose and I could do after that, to fight it."

"I will," Griff grated. "I'll fight it."

"Yes, well." Quirk looked solemn. "You have the God-mother's thimble, and you've shown that you can wield it." He paused, as if waiting for Griff to protest. "Whatever happens, you must not put it on again. If you do, Story will seize its chance, and it will take you. Do you understand?"

Griff jerked out a nod.

"Good. Now, I came to tell you to stay away from Rose. Your intentions might be good, but your actions . . ." Quirk shrugged. "Whether you mean to or not, you would do what Story required of you."

His words were worse than a stab to the heart.

Griff stared bleakly at the grim, black walls of the castle. He knew there was no point in protesting. Quirk was right not to trust him. He couldn't even trust himself.

CHAPTER
26

HALFWAY THROUGH THE AFTERNOON, THE LADIES-IN-waiting peered into the sitting room. I was standing with my back pressed against the tapestry. I'd been there for a long time, long enough that the cold from the stone wall had seeped into me; my feet in the pinched shoes were numb. The light from the window had changed, and now the spindle was in darkness.

"Oh *here* she is," said Miss Olive, swishing into the room.

Miss Amity went to the window and opened the curtains.

After a keen glance at the spindle, Miss Olive sat down in a chair. "We're *so* excited, Lady Rose."

My head was full of fog; all I could do was blink at the afternoon light flooding the room.

"It's your *birthday* tomorrow," Olive went on.

"Oh," I croaked, and peeled myself from the wall. "How old am I turning?"

"Sixteen, of course," Miss Amity answered, and went to sit beside Olive.

"But—" I shook my head to clear the fog. "I turned sixteen months ago." In the early spring, Shoe and I had celebrated the sixteenth anniversary of the rainy night that Pen had brought me to him. I had baked brown-sugar cakes, and Shoe made a special dinner. Really, I was closer to seventeen than sixteen.

"Of course you haven't," Miss Amity said with a sniff.

"She's right," Miss Olive put in. "If you were already sixteen, how could it be your birthday tomorrow?"

"Because it's not," I said flatly.

"Turning sixteen," sighed Miss Olive. "The perfect age for a young lady, I've always thought."

It was like arguing with water. I shrugged and let the Misses' conversation flow around me.

The spindle was still sitting on the table at Miss Olive's elbow. I would keep an eye on it, I vowed to myself. So it couldn't take me by surprise.

"The seamstress will be here soon to fit your party dress," Miss Amity said.

"Ooh, the party!" Miss Olive leaned toward Miss Amity. "Will you wear your lavender?"

"The pink, I should think," Miss Amity answered with a nod to me.

"Oh, of course," Miss Olive agreed. "Rose pink." She smiled with sickly sweetness at me.

There was a knock at the door, and the Keeper entered, followed by the seamstress, who carried a sewing box, and Sally, who held what looked like a canvas-wrapped body in her arms.

"Ooh, the dress!" Miss Olive screeched.

"To the bedroom," Miss Amity pronounced, and we all trooped up the stairs to my round tower room. *So* much pink. It was like being in a mouth without teeth.

Sally pulled me to the wardrobe, where she stripped me down to my petticoats and corset, then added two more lace-edged petticoats. Reverently, the party dress was unwrapped from its canvas cover. It took Sally and the seamstress, with the Keeper's help, to lower the dress over my head. Sally pinned it up the back; for the party, the seamstress would stitch me into it.

I turned to look at myself in the mirror. My face was the same as always. The dress was . . .

Well, it was spectacular. It was made of rose-pink satin, with very full skirts gathered at the back into a cascade of pink and white silk roses and green silk leaves. It had a gauze overskirt spangled with tiny pink diamonds; froths of lace dotted with silk rosettes edged the neckline and the tiny capped sleeves, and there were more roses nestled in gauze at the waist.

"The shoes," Miss Amity said, and waved at Sally, who

presented a pair of pink satin shoes with diamond buckles, "and the jewels," she added, pointing at Miss Olive, who opened a velvet box to show a diamond necklace, hairpins, and bracelets.

"My goodness," I breathed.

"Nah, then," said the Keeper. "See to th' fitting."

With an obedient curtsy, the seamstress went to work, having me step onto a low stool, then crouching at my feet to pin up the hem, pausing now and then for whispered consultations with the Misses and the Keeper.

The dress looked as light as gossamer, but with the wide skirts and the extra petticoats, it was heavy. I tried to stand without drooping. Sally was sent to build up the fire, and the room grew hot, stuffy. My feet ached in the shoes that didn't fit me right. All of it made me feel light-headed, as if I was drifting away.

The Misses had settled on some chairs near the hearth, Amity with her tatting. Then Olive pulled out her ball of thread. I hadn't seen her gather up the spindle before we left the sitting room, but there it was. Seeing it was like being doused with cold water; I was suddenly wide awake again, my heart pounding. My eyes stayed fixed on the spindle. As Olive drew thread from her skein of flax, its tip flashed in the light. Almost like it was winking at me.

"Nah then," came the Keeper's soothing voice.

"Stand to thissss side," hissed Sally, and her cool hands seized my waist and turned me away from the spindle.

The seamstress adjusted the fall of the overskirt, then marked a few places at the bodice. All the while I was acutely conscious of Olive, sitting behind me, spinning thread with the spindle.

"Hold thisss, if you please," Sally hissed.

I held out my hand.

And . . . something pricked my finger.

The spindle.

I gasped and flinched and wobbled on my high heels for a moment, then fell off the low stool, tumbling to land on the carpeted floor, my skirts and gauze settling like a pink cloud around me.

The seamstress stood with horrified hands over her mouth; I heard Olive titter and Amity give a disdainful sniff. The Keeper stared down at me, eyes wide.

And . . . I opened my hand to see that Sally had given me a pincushion, with one pin loose. Not the spindle at all. There wasn't even any blood on my finger.

I let them help me back to my feet and onto the stool. The seamstress continued with her adjustments. After an eternity, the dress was ready; they took it off me and wrapped it again in its canvas cover, and hung it like a dead body in the wardrobe.

I let Sally put me into a dinner gown and lead me down to the dining room.

As on the other nights, my father sat at one end of a long, gleaming table, my mother at the other end, and I took my place halfway between them. A chandelier lit the room. We ate with silver forks from paper-thin porcelain plates, and drank from crystal goblets. The food was bland, but fancy, and served by footmen from silver platters.

My mother and father were not quite as blank as usual. My mother seemed to have finally come to understand that I was her baby, all grown up. She stared at me, fascinated, and ate nothing.

Between bites of poached fish and pastry, my father talked about the party. Sir Roland would be there, and Sir Richard and Sir James, and the other courtiers, and the cook was baking a special cake, and afterward there would be dancing.

I listened with half an ear, realizing that I hadn't seen what Miss Olive had done with the spindle. It could be here, in the dining room.

I glanced down at my plate, at the silver forks and knife and four different spoons, all gleaming in the candlelight. My hands trembled, and I folded them in my lap. My head was spinning, and my stomach roiled with uneasiness. My lack of sleep made my thoughts fuzzy. My father was still speaking, but I couldn't make sense of his words.

Neither of them noticed that I didn't eat and didn't speak. I'd been so hopeful that finding my parents would mean I'd also found my place in the world. But I hadn't. They had to know that it wasn't my birthday. They were so caught up in Story, they were more like paper cutouts than a real mother and father. If I tried to get away, they'd be the ones to order the servants to pursue me unto death.

When they had finished, I got up from my chair, curtsied to them, and went out. For half a moment, outside the dining room door, I considered rushing out to the stable to see Griff, just to talk to him. I knew that he was dangerous, that I wasn't supposed to miss him. But I did.

He was in the stable, alone—always alone—with the knowledge of what he was weighing on him. I wished I could help him carry that burden. It was easy to see, now, why he was so silent. There were so many things that he couldn't speak of. If I could, I would go to him just to feel his arms come around me, and then kiss him until he told me everything.

"Come 'long, Lady Rose," the Keeper said from behind me.

With a sigh, I let her lead me back to my pink room in the tower.

There, Sally silently undressed me, unbraided my hair, and buttoned me into my lacy nightgown, then curtsied and went out.

Wearily, I took the candle she'd left me and crossed the room. I reached out to set the candle on the table next to my bed, and froze.

The spindle was there.

It was like a snake, ready to strike. I couldn't move it. I couldn't even go near it. Which meant I couldn't sleep in my bed. What if I turned over during the night and put my hand on it, by accident?

Except that it wouldn't be an accident, would it?

Blowing out the candle, I sat on the floor, my back against the wall, watching the fire in the hearth crumble away to red embers, and then ash. The room grew dark, and then darker.

The entire mass of the castle, and everyone in it, weighed on me, pushing me. My story—*the* Story—needed to continue. It needed me to prick my finger, to be taken by the curse. And then what?

I would sleep.

Quirk had already left. We had made a mistake, I thought, not trying to get away together.

And Griff . . . he was awake, too, thinking of horrors of his own.

I shook my head. I didn't know what I could do to help him.

Tomorrow. As soon as it was light I would find a way to get out of the castle, to escape.

AT LAST THE gray light of morning seeped into my room. I hadn't slept at all. If fog had filled my head yesterday, today it was filled with glue. My thoughts felt slow and heavy.

A sound at the door, and Sally stepped into the room holding a tray. I climbed stiffly to my feet. "Good morning," I croaked.

"Sahhh," she said, seeing my undisturbed bed. She put down the tray and went to the wardrobe, then brought me my robe. "Sit," she ordered, and as I settled in a chair near the fireplace, she poured tea and brought me a steaming cup.

It was fragrant and sweet, and my cold hands warmed around it. Some of the heaviness in my head lifted. Silently I watched as she added more wood to the fire, then selected a dress and laid it out on the bed. Sally seized a brush from the dresser and started on my hair. I set down the teacup and closed my eyes.

The servants were all creatures of Story, I knew that. They'd all been created by the Godmother. But they'd shown me kindness, too. I wondered how much they knew about what was happening. "Sally, in the story, what happens to the girl after she pricks her finger on the spindle?"

"Sssahhh." The even strokes with the hairbrush stopped.

"You all seem to know about it," I said.

"Yesss." Another silence. Then, "She falls under a spell of sleep."

"On her sixteenth birthday," I finished for her. "Then what happens?"

"All sleep. Ssssleep for hundreds of yearsss."

I jerked around to look at her. "Hundreds?"

"Ysss." Her slitted eyes were opaque. "Then he comes. The prince. Ssstory sends him."

A prince, of course. Like in Story's tapestry, in my sitting room. "What does the prince do?" I asked, fascinated.

"He kisses her. He loves her. Only the kiss of true love can stop the curse and wake the sleeper. She awakens, the castle awakensss."

I blinked. "How can he love me if he's only just met me?"

"Love at first sssight," Sally answered. "A device of Story."

"And the girl loves him, too?" I asked.

"Of course." Sally set down the hairbrush and went to fetch my dress. I watched carefully to be sure she stayed away from the spindle beside the bed.

"I can't imagine falling in love with somebody I don't even know." I shook my head. "I mean, it's not very likely, is it?" It reminded me of being kissed by Tom, back in the village. He'd thought that he could possess me—or the beauty—and he'd done it against my will. Even more likely, the prince sent by Story would be like one of the courtiers. "What if I don't want him to kiss me?" I asked.

"She must. She is Story'sss. There mussst be a happily-ever-after."

I felt a sudden freezing chill. Story would do this. I'd become a doll—Story's clockwork doll—and I would not fight when the prince pressed his lips to mine. I'd be lost. "And . . . and Story gains more power, doesn't it, if this happily-ever-after happens?"

"Ysss. It escapesss. It spreads."

Fright fluttered in my chest. The only thing standing

between me and Story's victory was my will.

Will was the most important thing in a fight. Griff had taught me that.

But thinking about Griff, and the role he might be playing in all of this, was too painful. All I could do was try to get away. It might be enough to disrupt the inevitable.

Getting to my feet, I took off my robe and let Sally put me into an ordinary pink dress, not the one for the party. She returned to the wardrobe to fetch a pair of shoes.

"Not those," I said, peering around her. "Are my boots here? The ones I was wearing when we arrived?" I spotted them in a corner of the wardrobe.

"Sahhh," Sally protested as I dug out the boots and sat down to put them on. They fit perfectly because Shoe had made them with the best materials, with skill, and with love. Remembering him gave me strength, determination.

My heart beat faster and my fingers shook as I laced up my boots. It was still early morning. The ladies-in-waiting were late risers, and my parents wouldn't expect to see me until later, when the party started. I could walk a long way in Shoe's boots before anyone noticed that I was gone.

"Sally," I said briskly, turning to her. "I am going out for some air. I need you to wait here, and not speak to anyone, all right?"

"Sahhh." She bowed her head, obedient.

"Thank you." I whirled, went to the door of my tower room, and flung it open.

And there, waiting at the top of the stairs, were two footmen clad in ice-blue uniforms. They both had catlike whiskers, round yellow eyes, and furred ears.

I halted, and felt Sally's cold presence at my back. "They serve by seeing you're safe," she hissed.

"They're guards," I realized.

At my words, one of the men's ears twitched toward me. They were both very alert. They wouldn't let me set a single foot outside the walls of Castle Clair.

Slowly I closed the door. I took a few steps toward my bed, then stopped as I realized the spindle was pulling me in again. Resisting it, I headed toward the chair beside the hearth.

I sat, feeling limp with weariness and misery.

Tonight. It would happen tonight, at the party. I was entangled, and I would never get free.

CHAPTER

27

THE LADIES-IN-WAITING LED ME DOWN THE STAIRS TO MY sitting room and guarded me all day. I watched carefully; Miss Olive brought the spindle and kept it on the table beside her while she made dull, ladylike conversation with Amity. As they talked, all I could do was sit there like a lump, too tired even to think. I kept my hands gripped together and stared at the spindle. I wouldn't let it out of my sight. I wouldn't reach for anything in case I reached for it. Sally brought tea and then lunch, and then more tea, and I ate nothing and drank nothing.

At last it was time to get ready for the party.

The Keeper came, her broad face grim, along with Sally and two other maids whose names I didn't know, and the seamstress with her sewing box. They were ready, I thought, to wrestle me into the party dress if I tried to resist.

The Misses got to their feet, twittering excitedly about the party. I watched as Olive gathered up the spindle and thread, taking it with her when she left.

I was certain that I'd see it again later.

Docile, I went with the servants up the stairs to the pink room. They stripped me, put me into a bath, and washed me with rose-scented soap, then pulled me to my feet and dried me with a towel that had been warmed by the hearth.

I was so tired. So, so tired. My will had frayed to a thread; there wasn't much left of me to fight.

If Shoe could see me now, he'd be horrified. He'd fought all his life against Story, and here I was, trapped within it. I missed him so much; I wished I could ask him, *Shoe, what should I do? How can I get out of this?*

I missed Quirk, too, and his odd way of looking at the world.

And Griff . . .

If Story took me, I'd never see him again. I'd never kiss him again. I almost didn't care that he was Story's weapon. He was Griff, too, and I—

I gasped aloud. Oh no. I'd been so wrong about him. Griff had been raised with coldness and neglect and silence, and I'd left him alone. What had Quirk told me about our greatest weapons against Story?

"Here nah, Lad' Rose," said the Keeper, interrupting my thoughts.

"In a moment," I murmured. I had no sword, but thanks to Shoe I had something better. Our weapons were love, and warmth, and happiness. If I could give them to Griff, we could use them to fight Story. If I could get to him, I could save him. I looked around wildly. There were three people between me and the door.

"Here nah," said the Keeper, and taking my hand, she led me to stand near the wardrobe. My breath came fast. I had to get away, but I had to wait. Somehow I would find a chance. I stood there, my thoughts whirling, as the maids put the lace-edged petticoats on me, and the corset, and then the dress. Swiftly the seamstress stitched it up the back. While Sally did my hair, the other maids dabbed rose perfume behind my ears and put on the jewels. The bracelets weighed on my wrists, the diamond necklace was heavy around my neck.

They sat me down, and Sally crouched on the floor, pulling silk stockings onto my feet. Then she went to the wardrobe and brought out the ill-fitting satin shoes with the diamond buckles.

"No," I protested.

Sally froze and stared unblinkingly at me; the Keeper and the other two maids and the seamstress looked dismayed.

I got to my feet. "I'll do everything else. I'll go to the party, and I'll behave"—the words were bitter in my mouth—"like a lady, but I won't wear those shoes." I pointed with a shaking hand. "I won't," I repeated, feeling like a stubborn child. "I'll wear my boots."

The Keeper shook her head. "Nah, then, Lad' Rose, nah then."

"The boots," I insisted. I swept my hands down my wide skirts, which brushed the floor. "The dress is long enough; no one will see my feet."

They consulted in whispers, casting worried glances my way. Then the Keeper nodded.

I sat down again, and Sally put the party shoes away and put my boots on my feet and laced them up.

"Stand," hissed Sally. "Sssee."

I got to my feet and felt the Keeper's hands on my shoulders, turning me to face the tall mirror that the two maids dragged closer.

With the lack of sleep and the worry, my face should have been pale, haggard, my eyes shadowed.

But the girl reflected back at me was ethereally lovely, glittering in satin and jewels, with diamond pins in her blond hair and more diamonds sparkling at her neck and wrists. It wasn't me, really. It was the beauty.

Her every move graceful, the girl in the mirror reached down and raised her skirts just enough to see the toe of a scuffed brown boot, incongruous amid the lace and finery.

The girl smiled just a little. It was a small triumph, really. But the boots reminded her that she was not just the beauty.

She had her own weapons. She was not just Story's construct. She was more than that.

I hoped she was, anyway.

WHILE ARNY SAT on the hay bale with his jug, Griff got out his knife and went through his Watcher's drills until he was panting with exhaustion. Then he sheathed the knife and went to lean a shoulder against the frame of the stable door. The courtyard was deserted. The pigeons had gone to roost; the sun had set; its blood-red rays lingered behind a bank of heavy clouds. The castle loomed, its stone walls black in the gathering darkness, but every window was brightly lit.

All day, Griff hadn't spoken a word to anyone. He hadn't slept during the night, either, and his head was heavy with weariness. In his pocket, the Godmother's thimble was a heavy, cold weight.

What was Rose doing, right now? She was in danger, he knew that much, and it was his fault. He wanted to help, but Quirk had warned him to stay away from her. Maybe it was better if he did.

From the castle came the sound of laughter and, very faintly, music.

Arny heaved himself up from the hay bale and lumbered to the doorway, where he stood, blinking. "'S tonight," he said, and pointed with his chin at the castle.

Griff rubbed his eyes, which were heavy from his lack of sleep. He cleared his throat. "What's tonight?"

"Th' Rose's birthday party." Arny burped and scratched his belly. "Means it's time for her Story."

Griff straightened, suddenly wide awake. "Tonight?"

"Yep," Arny said with a ponderous nod. "'S what I said, innit?"

He checked the knife sheathed at his back, and, without thinking, took a step toward the castle. Then he stopped. Quirk had warned him that anything he tried would be warped so that it served Story.

Arny seized his arm. "Where you off to?"

He stared at the castle's brightly lit windows. It would be all over tonight if he didn't do anything. "The party," Griff answered.

"No, y'r not," Arny grunted, and pulled him back toward the stable. "My orders is, you stay here."

In a flash, he had the knife out and at Arny's throat. The bigger man's close-set eyes widened, but he didn't let go. "I don't want to hurt you," Griff warned.

Arny gulped. His grip on Griff's arm loosened.

Griff jerked himself free and headed for the castle.

"What're you going to do?" Arny shouted after him.

Griff didn't know. But he couldn't do nothing. He had to help Rose.

THE PARTY BEGAN with dancing in a huge ballroom with a shiny marble floor. My mother and father sat on brocade chairs on a platform at one end of the room; between them was a chair for me. Around them stood a few blank-faced courtiers, all dressed in glittering splendor. At the other end of the room were a few birdlike musicians playing flutes and fiddles. Three blazing chandeliers hung from the high ceiling; below them swirled dancing couples. I didn't know how to dance but it didn't seem to matter. I was dragged around the floor by Sir Richard, who had damp hands and a wet mouth and who talked blandly over the music, and then by Sir Roland, and Sir James, trading off with the Misses, who both wore pink. All three men wore narrow blades with golden hilts at their hips.

As a dance ended, I curtsied politely to Sir James and then headed straight for the ballroom doors. I was determined get to Griff. Before I'd taken three steps, Amity and Olive had clustered around me.

"Sir Roland is so handsome, isn't he?" whispered Olive, casting a flirtatious glance in his direction. Seeing it, he stroked his mustache and bowed. "Ooh," Olive squealed.

"Much nicer than that stableboy, don't you think, Lady Rose?" Amity asked coyly.

I felt a sharp longing for Griff, for the feel of his quiet strength beside me.

"Of course she thinks so," Olive put in with a titter. "I mean, a *stableboy*."

Without realizing it, I had turned and taken two more steps toward the wide double doors at the end of the room.

My feet, steady in my boots, knew where I was supposed to be. Not here in this cold, glittering ballroom, at any rate.

A hand on my arm stopped me. Amity. Olive took my other arm. "Ooh," she said, and her voice sounded shrill. "It's time for dinner."

"And then," added Amity, "birthday presents."

I knew what that meant. My mouth went dry with fear. I tried pulling against their grip, but they held me firmly, turning with me to face the room. My head spun. My mother and father had risen from their chairs; we followed them through another set of doors, into a dining room.

It held a long table laden with food: piles of sugared fruit, crystal bowls filled with peeled eggs speckled with flakes of gold, silver-scaled fish wearing their heads and tails and necklaces of herbs, tiny roasted birds with gilded beaks. The forks and spoons gleamed; the plates and bowls were edged with gold.

With great ceremony, my father paced up to me, seized my hand, and brought me to the head of the table. As I sat, two blue-coated footmen stationed themselves behind my chair. My plate was loaded with food and set before me. I couldn't eat. The sounds of talking and shrill laughter swirled around me. I felt heavy and hollow at the same time; desperate, but unable to move.

At last dinner was over. My parents rose from the table.

Aware of the footmen behind me, I pushed back my chair

and climbed to my feet. The dress was so heavy. The diamond necklace gripped me around the neck like cold hands; the bracelets weighed on my wrists like manacles.

I blinked, dizzy, and found myself sitting on the chair between my parents on the platform. Below us, all of the courtiers were staring avidly at me. My head pounded; darkness edged my vision. It was all happening too quickly; there was nothing I could do to resist.

My father said something, but my ears couldn't make sense of his words. I felt icy cold, too cold to shiver, colder than when Griff, Quirk, Timothy, and I had come through the Forest.

My father, his face a smiling mask, held out a gilded box.

Somehow I'd gotten to my feet again. I held the box; I felt my father's hands on my shoulders, holding me still.

I tried to drop the box so that it would smash on the floor and I could run away, but my hands were frozen around it.

Moving as if she was pulled by strings, my mother jerked herself up from her chair, came to me, and opened the box.

Inside it, the spindle lay on a bed of ice-blue velvet.

Seeing it was almost a relief. I was so, so weary. Sleep. If I just touched the spindle, I would be able to sleep.

My hand reached into the box. The dark wood of the spindle felt smooth under my fingers. I lifted it out.

Distantly, I was aware of a commotion at the double doors at the other end of the ballroom. But it was so far away; I could barely hear it above the roaring in my ears.

Light flashed from the spindle's sharpened tip, and pain lanced into my head.

I heard more shouting, the clash of blades.

Blinking, I looked toward the door.

Compared to all the glittering finery, Griff was like a crow with bedraggled feathers in his tattered black coat and his crest of dark hair. To fight him, Sir Roland had drawn a thin sword; Griff blocked the attack effortlessly with his knife; then he whirled and parried Sir Richard's sword thrust. Three blue-coated footmen carrying clubs converged on him. From behind, Sir James slashed with his sword; blood from Griff's arm spattered on the shiny floor.

There were too many of them. It was hopeless.

I rested the spindle's sharpened tip against the end of my finger.

"Rose, no!" Griff shouted. Looking up, I saw him flinch from a blow. But he moved, as ever, with the clean efficiency of a knife through the crowd of courtiers.

With sudden clarity I knew that I could never let Story take him. Or me. We could both fight.

The spindle was Story's weapon.

I would make it my own.

Carefully I turned the spindle until its glittering, sharp end pointed away from me. My father's hands still held my shoulders; I pulled out of his grip and brandished the spindle. "Let me go," I gasped. Distantly I heard the sound of fighting.

My blank-eyed mother reached for me, and I slashed, and

a thin line of blood opened across the palm of her hand. She staggered away, shrieking.

And then the curse fought back. The spindle writhed in my hand like a snake, and the sharp tip was its fang. I struggled against it. But my hand opened, and the spindle fell.

A moment later, my father held me from behind, pinning my arms. Miss Olive and Miss Amity swooped onto the platform.

Griff. I tried screaming, but no sound came from my mouth. Desperate, I kicked back with my boot; my father grunted, but didn't loosen his hold on me. "Her finger," he ordered, and his voice held the grinding inevitability of Story.

Miss Amity seized one of my arms; Miss Olive bent to pick up the spindle.

For just a moment, we stood in a bubble of stillness and silence. I felt Story's triumph as Olive brought the spindle closer and wrapped my hand around it. A wave of icy cold washed through me. Then she caught my other hand and brought my finger to the spindle's glittering tip.

No, I wanted to scream. The curse roared out. I was so cold, I didn't even feel it.

But a drop of blood blossomed at the end of my finger.

GRIFF WHIRLED AND elbowed a blue-clad footman in the face, then tensed, ready to meet the next attack, when the first of Rose's three curses howled past him, filling the room.

Everything went silent and still.

A spray of blood had burst from the servant's nose; the droplets hung in the air, arcing slowly toward the floor. The faces of the men frozen while lunging at him were feral, snarling. They weren't asleep—it wasn't yet that curse. They were aware, but frozen in place.

Fighting the weight of the curse, Griff straightened, gripping his knife. Drops of his own blood, from the cut on his arm, splashed onto the shiny floor. He didn't want to think about why the curse didn't affect him. Quirk had said it before—he wasn't just a curse eater, he could control curses. He belonged to Story.

That gave him a little room to maneuver, didn't it? The tiniest space. But he would use it.

He turned. Rose's father stood like a statue; between two ladies was Rose, holding the spindle. Her eyes were open; her skirts were frozen in a whirl around her.

Stepping past the unmoving footmen and courtiers, Griff leaped onto the platform. The curse roared around him. Shadows arose in the corners of the room, advanced across the floor, and lowered from the ceiling. The air grew heavy and chill. He only had a moment to decide, and then the next curse would rise and it would be too late.

Slowly he bent to set his knife on the floor. Then he straightened and stood before Rose.

She was heartbreakingly lovely. She was not for him, he

knew that. But he was hers. She would never know it, but he was. For just a moment, he let himself look at her and he could see past the beauty to her weariness and fear.

There was only one thing he could do to help her.

As a Watcher, he had lifted many curses at the command of the Lord Protector, but they had been paltry things compared to Rose's curses, which had all the relentless power of Story behind them. Only with the Godmother's thimble on his finger could he break the spindle curse. He knew what that meant for himself, but he would do it for her. For Rose.

His hand heavy, he reached into his coat pocket and let the thimble slip onto his finger. He drew it out. In the gathering gloom, the thimble shone. In its icy light, Griff could see Rose's curses, all three of them surrounding her, entwined like snakes made of shadows and smoke. The first curse disentangled itself from the rest, bleeding its heavy chill into the room. The spindle curse. Ever since they had arrived at the castle it had been drawing Rose to the spindle so that she would prick her finger and activate the second curse, which would plunge her and everyone in the castle into a deep sleep. That second sleep curse was too strong, too dark for him to break now. But he might have enough power to push it back before it took effect, and to hold the first curse until she got away.

Stepping closer to Rose, he focused on the spindle curse. He raised his hands, which felt surprisingly steady, and set them on either side of Rose's face, with the thimble resting at her temple. Blood from his cut dripped onto the bodice of her dress, staining the lace.

He had to trust himself. He had to hope that even with the thimble on his finger, he was acting for her, not Story. And he had to do it now, before the sleep curse had time to take hold. Bracing himself, he wrenched the spindle curse away from her. It slammed into him, and he staggered, then fell to his knees. The second curse writhed into an attack, and raising the thimble, he held it back, kept it entwined with the last curse. As he did so, his head filled with shadows; he peered through them, trying to get one last glimpse of her face.

Rose blinked, and she gazed down at him. The spindle fell from her fingers.

"I'll hold it," Griff gasped, as the spindle curse pounded at him. "Go. Get out of here."

Her lips moved, saying something he couldn't hear through the roaring of the curse in his ears.

"Go," he shouted.

She hesitated for another moment, then gave a determined nod and, gathering her skirts, jumped from the platform, carrying the last two curses with her. Shadows pursued her as she ran across the ballroom. One last glimpse of pink at the door, and she was gone.

He held the spindle curse for as long as he could, to give

her a chance to get outside the castle walls. It enwrapped him in coils of roaring darkness. Gasping for breath, he fought it with every scrap of his will, but it was relentless. The last thing he managed to do was pull the thimble from his finger and drop it; it tumbled slowly to the floor.

And then Story took him.

CHAPTER

28

I FLUNG MYSELF OUT OF THE BALLROOM AND RACED through the hallways of Castle Clair. Story had been weighing so heavily on me that, released from it, I felt light, scudding over the shiny floors like a leaf in the wind. Story pursued. I heard a hissing sound; casting a quick glance over my shoulder, I saw coils of bramble coming after me. They slithered through the hallway like serpents, their thorny tendrils groping after my fleeing feet.

I ducked around a corner, my shoulder slamming into the wall, then pushed myself forward. Story's brambles raced along the walls, then spread to the ceiling, trying to get ahead of me. The floors trembled under my feet; dust sifted down.

At last I reached the door that led to the kitchens. The brambles washed up against it; I thrust my hands past their thorns and gripped the latch, then pushed open the door. Like a wave, the brambles washed into the passageway beyond. The satin skirt of my dress shredded as the thorns stretched after me.

I fought my way through them and, at last, I stumbled through the kitchen and into the dark courtyard. Another quick glance behind showed vines twining from the castle windows and around its towers; more brambles snaked toward the walls. Sobbing for breath, I ran for the arched gateway. Its darkness closed in around me and for a moment I felt overwhelmed with fear, and then I burst out of the other side. A few brambles spilled from the gate, groping blindly after me, and I staggered away, into the night.

I FLED ALONG the narrow trail through the long grass until I reached the river that Griff and Timothy and I had crossed, with Quirk carried on Griff's back. There I crouched, shuddering, gasping for breath.

As my breathing steadied, I heard the rustling of the river over rounded stones. The air was cold; I wrapped my arms around myself and shivered. On the other side of the river, the Forest was a distant black wall. Still crouching, I turned and looked back at the castle. The lights from its windows were gone; it was a looming darkness against the darker night.

Shaking, I lowered my head and squeezed my eyes shut. Griff . . .

Come with me, I had said to him, but he had shaken his

head as if he couldn't hear me. *Go,* he'd said. I knew what he had done—he'd taken my curse on himself, freeing me. My head whirled with exhaustion. I couldn't make sense of anything.

I couldn't go into the Forest on the other side of the river. I couldn't go back toward the castle. My skirts were in rags; my arms were bare. A chilly breeze washed over me. Completely weary, I settled to the ground and curled into the long grass, which was like a nest around me. My eyes fell shut and, free of my curse at last, I slept.

WHEN I WOKE up, the sky was the gray of late afternoon; a rough woolen blanket was tucked around my shoulders. I sat up, blinking. A pin fell out of my head and landed in my lap, and a lock of braided hair slithered onto my neck. With cold fingers I picked up the pin. The diamond at its end glinted in the fading light. The necklace and bracelets still weighed heavily on my neck and wrists.

Standing with his back to me, hands on his hips, was Quirk. "Awake, lass?" he asked, without turning around.

"Yes," I croaked in surprise. I looked past him. In the distance, across the grass-covered plain under lowering gray clouds, was the castle. Or, what had been the castle. I could vaguely make out the shape of it, but it was completely enwrapped in thick, heavy ropes of bramble, the wall around it covered with the same thorny vines.

Slowly I got to my feet and went to stand beside Quirk.

He glanced up at me, his face grimmer than I'd ever seen it. "Are you all right?"

I wasn't. I glanced down; the blanket had slipped from one shoulder. The tattered lace and the silk of my dress was stained there with dried blood. "It's not mine," I said. "It's Griff's blood."

"Where is he?" Quirk asked urgently. He cast a keen look around us. He was on guard. Against Griff, I realized.

I looked toward the castle. "He's in there."

"Inside the castle?" Quirk shook his head, confused.

"Yes. He lifted the curse from me and took it on himself."

Quirk turned to face me. "Was he wearing the thimble?"

I remembered that heavy, long moment when the curse had taken me, its darkness, the weight of it on my shoulders, and then seeing Griff. His face had been pale and determined; he'd gone to his knees as the curse had slammed into him.

And yes. The Godmother's thimble had been an icy glow at the tip of his finger. I felt utterly lost. "Yes. He used the thimble."

Quirk said something under his breath and kicked at a clump of grass. "You know what this means, lass."

I crumpled to the ground again. I couldn't bear to hear him say it. Wordlessly, I shook my head.

"It means he's let Story in. It will break him, if it hasn't already, and use him again. It will send him after us."

"No," I whispered.

Quirk crouched beside me. With gentle hands, he pulled the blanket to cover my shoulders. "Rosie, Griff was born to a Godmother for one purpose. To serve Story. To be its weapon."

I felt an icy wash of desolation. Tears welled up in my eyes. Angry with myself for crying, I dashed them away.

Quirk sighed and stood, resting his hand on my shoulder. "Even though you were born for Story, lass, Shoe raised you, and that's why you are not a clockwork girl sleeping in that castle right now. All Griff has ever known in his life is grimness and grayness, and silence, and obedience to the Lord Protector's rules." He shook his head. "There's irony for you. It was his strict training to fight Story that made him most vulnerable to it."

I got to my feet, standing next to Quirk. A low wind gusted around us, making the grass bow down in waves.

I had to see for myself that there was truly no way into the castle. Clutching the blanket around my shoulders, I started back, marching along the path that led through the long grass. Ten paces away from where the main gate had been, I stopped. Quirk stood just behind me. The castle was completely wrapped in vines. I blinked. They were moving. The thick ropes of bramble were twisting, crawling over one another, growing upward, making the wall taller, thicker, insurmountable. A tendril of vine detached itself from the wall and groped toward where Quirk and I were standing. We edged back, and the vine wove itself back among the other vines.

Quirk was right. It was impenetrable.

"Come on," he said softly. "There's nothing we can do here. We'd better go."

"Go where?" I asked, still watching the castle.

"This is not over," Quirk answered. "The castle is still a threat, and so is Griff. We can wait a bit to see if Timothy shows up. Then we'll have to contact the other Breakers. And we'll have to decide what we're going to do with you."

My heart quivered in my chest. Were we really going to leave Griff behind?

I heard quiet footsteps receding down the path as Quirk started away.

The wind gusted around me, blowing through the tatters of my dress. I shivered. There was nothing I could do here. It was hopeless.

"I WANT TO show you something," Quirk said. We were following the merest sketch of a path that ran along the river. The castle was hidden behind a fold of the hills, behind us. The Forest had curved away on the other side of the river and was a dark blot in the distance.

With every step I took I felt as if I was making a huge mistake. I kept glancing back to see if something had changed, but it was the same long grass, the same gray sky.

Quirk stopped and surveyed the river that rushed below the bank where we stood. "This is the place," he murmured. A depression in the bank led down to the water's edge. It was shallower here, rustling over pebbles. On the other side, the path appeared again. Quirk led me down to the river. "Somebody made this path," Quirk said, and pointed back the way we'd come. "Why?"

"I don't know," I said wearily. I used the diamond hairpin to secure the blanket around my shoulders, like a cape, and its ends fluttered in the breeze.

"Come and see." Quirk stepped into the river and, raising my tattered skirts, I followed him across, the water no deeper than my ankles. On the other side, the path picked up again, leading away. All around us, the long grasses were tawny gray and brown, and the sky was gray. The air was damp and growing colder. The breeze smelled faintly of burned wood.

"Not much farther," Quirk said over his shoulder. "This was the place I was searching for when I left you at the castle."

The path led us around a low hill and down into a bowl-shaped dell. At its bottom were the charred remains of a little cottage.

"Somebody lived there," Quirk said. His face seemed oddly sad. "She wore a path between here and the castle. Keeping an eye on it."

"Oh." I finally understood. "The Penwitch."

He nodded.

"What happened?"

"Don't know." His face was grim. "I poked around a little. She wasn't in there when it burned."

"So you found what you were looking for," I noted.

"Not quite." A silence stretched between us. All I could do was stand there, my shoulders slumped. The charred wood of the cottage was sodden. Everything around me seemed gray and dead and sad. Night was falling. A quick look at Quirk, and I saw that his face was gray, too, and haggard. He had to be grieving for his mother and father.

I straightened. "We'll camp here, I think." I surveyed the dell. A corner of the cottage was still standing, with a bit of roof that overhung a ragged edge of what looked like a stone wall. "Come on." I reached down and gently took his hand and led him to the sheltered spot beside the remains of the cottage's chimney and hearth.

Wearily Quirk set down the pack he'd been carrying and settled onto the soot-covered hearthstone. After taking off the diamond necklace and bracelets and stowing them in a pocket of the pack, I dug around in the ruins, scavenging enough dry wood so we could have a fire.

When I came back to the hearth, I was covered with soot, my hands were black, and my hair hung in ropes around my face. Quirk was asleep. I built the fire and dug in the pack for matches. I found a pot and a pan, too, a packet of cornmeal and a few sausages, and salt, so after fetching some water from the river, I crouched next to the fire and set about making us some dinner.

The sausages hissed and bubbled in the pan, and smelled delicious. I hadn't eaten for a long time. My stomach was absolutely hollow.

Quirk stirred and opened his eyes.

"I expect you're hungry," I said to him, adding some salt to the cornmeal mush that I had cooking in the pot. "I know I am. I don't think I've eaten anything since before the spindle."

Moving stiffly, Quirk sat up and edged closer to the fire. He held out his hands to warm them. I put a sausage and a scoop of mush onto a tin plate and handed it to him. We sat eating quietly. I felt sad and weary and chilled, and I couldn't stop thinking about Griff, alone in the castle. I put down my plate and stared sadly into the flames.

"Well, well," came a hoarse voice out of the night. "If this isn't the sorriest pair of travelers I've ever seen."

I leaped to my feet. My eyes were dazzled from the fire, and I couldn't see anything but darkness. More deliberately, Quirk set down his plate and stood, picking up a length of burning wood from the fire and raising it like a torch.

"Going to hit me with that stick, little man?" the voice asked, and Timothy stepped over a pile of charred, broken wood and into the light.

"Huh," Quirk said, and tossed the wood back onto the fire. "I've been half expecting you, sweetheart."

I stared at her, noting that she had on rough traveling clothes now, not her pink dress from the castle, and then I stepped forward and flung my arms around her. To my astonishment, she let me hug her for a moment before pushing me away.

"That's enough of that," she said roughly.

"I'm so glad to see you," I choked out.

"Yeah," she said, and squatted by the fire. "And what about you?" She nodded at Quirk. "Glad to see me?"

He gave her a tired smile. "Always."

To my astonishment, she blushed. Then, with a shake of her head, she asked, "Got any more of that dinner? I could smell it a mile away."

Quickly I spooned some mush onto a plate and added two sausages, passing it to her with a fork.

"Ta." She took a bite. "I've got some information," she said through a mouthful of mush. "We're not going anywhere until morning. So sit down and let me tell you a story."

CHAPTER

29

GRIFF STRUGGLED FOR A LONG TIME AGAINST THE FREEZ-
ing darkness of the curse that enwrapped him. He was so
cold, and the air was so heavy, that just breathing was an
effort.

He was in the ballroom, he remembered. It was dim; the
candles in the chandeliers burned only faintly. Thorny vines
grew in the high windows of the room, twined about the ceiling and down the walls. Nearby stood the two ladies and the
lord of Castle Clair, Rose's father, eyes wide; her mother sat
in one of the gilded chairs next to him with her mouth open
in a silent shriek. At their feet, near where Rose had been
standing, rested the spindle, dark wood with a metal tip that
gleamed in the greenish light. On the needle end shone a
single drop of blood.

The thimble lay on the floor next to it. It shone with its own pale light, and the dark thorns etched around its base writhed.

He felt absolutely no urge to pick it up again.

Turning his head with a nearly audible creak, Griff checked the rest of the room. Two blue-coated, goat-horned servants were frozen with clawed hands reaching for him; three courtiers dressed in brocade coats had their swords drawn.

This wasn't the sleep spell. The courtiers, Rose's parents, all of them—they were awake, but immobile under the spindle curse. The second curse, which would have sent everyone in the castle to sleep—he'd forced that one down. It was still with Rose, along with the third curse, the one that was most tightly bound to her. If he could have freed her from them, he would have, but they had been too strong. No, this was still the curse that had drawn Rose to the spindle and forced her to prick her finger, and it was Story, too, with the castle and all its people in its grip. It would hold them, immobile, until it had decided what to do next.

Distantly Griff felt the wound on his arm, just below his elbow, where one of the courtiers had slashed him with the tip of his narrow blade. It was a shallow cut; as he watched, a few slow drops of blood soaked into the sleeve of his coat. He looked beyond the courtiers to the vine-choked door of the ballroom.

Rose.

She had fled the room, but had he held the curse long enough for her to escape the castle?

Straining every muscle against the weight of the curse, he picked up his patrol knife from the floor and climbed to his feet. A blink, and he felt the curse wrap cold, dark fingers around his throat.

"Fight it," he told himself. His voice sounded dusty, muffled by the dead air.

The thimble was on the floor at his feet. All he had to do was put it on his finger, and he could master the curse and escape the castle. But to do that, he knew, would be to give himself fully to Story. So he would have to fight with his will alone, and leave the thimble where it was.

Slowly he pushed himself through the curse. It was like . . .

What would Quirk or Rose say?

It was like trudging through mud.

Mud up to his neck.

By the time he reached the ballroom door, he was exhausted. Hours, he guessed, had passed since Rose had fled. And for how long before that had he struggled against the curse's immobilizing darkness? There was no way to tell. It could have been a day, or a year, or longer.

The curse weighed on him as he pushed himself through the thorny vines in the doorway and down the hall. A few steps, and he had to stop to rest, leaning against the wall. His hand dropped into his coat pocket.

And there, under his fingers, was the silver-cold touch of the thimble. Dismayed, he pulled it out. It gleamed with a cold light, and then winked at him. And there was something else. His fingers touched wood, and he pulled out the spindle.

No. This time he gathered all his will and hurled them both away, hearing the muffled tinkle of metal and the clatter of wood against the stone floor as they rattled down the hall.

He panted with the effort of it. The curse was so heavy, so cold. It wanted him silent and still. He had to rest, just for a moment.

The curse didn't hesitate; its shadows wrapped around him again, and dragged him down into the frozen darkness.

BEFORE STARTING HER story, Timothy dug in her pack, pulling out a little kettle, which she filled from a water bottle and set over the fire.

"So when I left the castle, I went to see my grandmothers," she began. "They don't live too far from here."

Quirk gave a sudden bark of laughter. "Oh, let me guess the next part of your story. They are famous Breakers. Templeton and Zel?"

"Exactly," Timothy said, adding tea leaves to the kettle.

"Oh," I said, my eyes wide. "Shoe told me stories about them, how Templeton rescued Zel from a tower by using her long hair to climb to the ground, and then fought off a prince." It had been one of my favorite stories, the true love between Templeton and Zel and their daring escape. Shoe hadn't told me that it was one of Story's broken plots.

"Yep, that's them," Timothy confirmed. "They wanted to come with me, but they're actually fairly ancient. I told them I could move faster without them. But they sent their greetings to you, Quirk. And something else."

"Ah," was Quirk's only comment.

After casting him a sharp look, Timothy went on with her story. "They live a few days' walk from here, guarding the castle from the other direction. I wasn't with them when Story made its move—they'd already sent me to make contact with the Breakers in the City. They told me that a few weeks ago, men came from the castle and killed Pen, and burned this cottage."

Was it really only a few weeks ago that I'd still been living with Shoe in the valley, with no idea of who I was or my importance to Story? It seemed like years. "They sent men to find me, too," I said.

"Yes," Quirk put in. "The pressure must have been building, when your sixteenth birthday came and went. That's when Story moved to find other ways to bring you to the castle."

"Story had been quiet for many years," Timothy said, frowning. "My grandmothers and Pen figured the beauty was safe with Shoe, especially after the date of her sixteenth birthday passed. It was stupid of them not to realize that Story was just biding its time."

Quirk nodded. "Yes." His mouth flattened into a grim line. "As long as Rose was still out in the world, and cursed, Story remained a danger."

"Hmm," Timothy said. "And now her curse has been broken, Story's trap has been sprung, and she's not in it." On the fire, the kettle boiled; she took it off and poured three cups of tea. "How'd you manage to escape it?" she asked, handing me some tea.

The tin cup felt hot under my cold fingers. "I escaped because of Griff." I realized the extent of what he'd done. "Story has no hold on me anymore." I should have felt light and happy at such a thought, but I didn't.

"He used the thimble to hold the curse so she could get away," Quirk explained further. He lowered his voice. "Griff is the son of the latest Godmother."

"*Is* he?" Timothy exclaimed, and then sat contemplating that revelation. After a few moments, she gave a satisfied nod. "My grandmas had wondered why a new Godmother hadn't arisen." A wry twist of her lips. "Tricky. They never would have expected the latest Godmother to be a boy."

"But he's not the . . ." I trailed off, shaking my head.

After a glance at me, Timothy went on. "Griff is in there now?" She jerked her chin in the direction of the castle. "With the Godmother's thimble?"

"Yes," Quirk confirmed.

"So he's dangerous," she stated. "It's just a matter of time before Story sends him after us."

Quirk frowned and rubbed his mouth, looking troubled.

No. This was all wrong. Restless, I set down my cup of tea, got to my feet, and stepped to the edge of the circle of firelight. I felt the warmth of the fire at my back, and the chill of the night on my face. Behind me, Quirk and Timothy were quiet for a few moments, and then Quirk got up and moved to sit at her side, and they started talking about the Lord Protector, and about the City and what Story might be plotting there.

Castle Clair was too far away to see, but I knew where it was. I took another step into the darkness, so I could think.

Griff.

Quirk and Timothy thought that Griff was a clockwork boy who was acting for Story. A kind of boy-Godmother. A danger to us.

But what about me? Somehow I hadn't been able to think clearly before, but now I could. How did I feel about Griff? I knew how I'd felt about him before I'd found out who he really was. I reached up to touch my lips. A boy who served Story couldn't have kissed me the way he did. And it wasn't just the kiss, either.

I closed my eyes and saw him again, in the ballroom, at the moment when he'd lifted the curse from me. He'd been intent, focused, determined, the same way he was when he was fighting. But as I'd opened my eyes, in the instant after the curse had gone to him, I'd seen something else in his face, too.

He'd been trained all his life to fight Story, but I knew there was more. There was another reason he'd taken on the curse.

My hands clenched into fists. I stared out at the night, toward the castle. He was alone there, trapped inside Story's vines and thorns. If he were left there, without love, without warmth, Story would take him. I was certain about that.

But Story had not reckoned with me.

I whirled to face the fire again, and another pin escaped from my hair and tumbled to the ground. Quirk and Timothy looked up at me, and their eyes widened.

"You're wrong." I pointed at Quirk. "And so are you," I said to Timothy. "Griff is not Story's weapon. He's good, and strong, and . . ." I shook my head. "I don't know the right words for it, but he's *true*."

"But he . . . ," Quirk started.

"No," I said flatly. "He does not belong to Story, and he never will. He is ours."

"I don't know, lass," Quirk said, shaking his head. "He—"

"Don't argue with me," I interrupted, glaring at him. "You're so worried about Story—you both are—that you can't even see Griff for what he really is. You said that all he's ever known is *grimness and silence, and obedience to the Lord Protector's rules*. But that's not true. He knows you, Quirk. You were his partner, after all. And he knows me."

I looked across the fire. Quirk's eyes gleamed, reflecting the flames.

"I suppose things have gotten as bad as they can possibly get," I went on. "The Penwitch is dead, and so is Shoe, and Griff is inside the castle imprisoned behind a wall of thorns. So yes, Story is hugely powerful. But we've escaped it, for now. And I feel as if, well, like I never knew what I was capable of before. Now I know that I can fight." I examined the tip of my finger. It was sore from the prick of the spindle. "I lost the first battle. But I will fight harder in the next one." I glared across the fire at Quirk. "There is going to be a next battle. We're not going to scuttle off and hide." I waved my hand in the direction of the castle. "I'm going to get him out."

There was a long moment of silence.

Quirk cleared his throat. "I want to believe that you're right about him."

"So you'll help me?" I asked him.

"Yes, lass," he said simply.

I turned to Timothy. "I know you don't like me, but—"

"Why would you think that?" she interrupted roughly.

My mouth dropped open. "The scowling?" I said. "The way you curl your lip every time you look at me?" I remembered another thing. "You even wanted to kill me!"

"Yeah, well." She shrugged. "I don't anymore." Then, to my surprise, she held out her hand. "Friends?"

My heart gave a thump. I put my soot-stained hand into hers. "Friends," I confirmed.

"Good," Timothy said with a nod. "Then we'll storm the castle together. And to help with that, my grandmothers sent presents for both of you."

ROSE WAS NOT free of Story, Griff remembered. She still carried two curses.

That was the first thought he had as he fought off the curse again, in the cold passageway outside the ballroom. Thorny vines had wrapped themselves around his ankles and one of his wrists, pinning him to the wall. Carefully he extricated himself and started making his way slowly down the corridor again.

"Three curses," he said aloud. A faint, grinding thunder echoed in his ears. He frowned and rubbed his aching head.

The second and third curses had gone quiescent in Rose, but they were waiting. Even if she'd escaped the castle, she was still in danger. She might not even realize it. She wouldn't realize it until too late, unless he escaped from the castle and warned her.

Grimly he trudged along the hallway, where a few blue-coated servants stood with blank faces, and finally stepped out into the courtyard.

The air was thick with greenish shadows cast by the wall of tangled, thorny vines that climbed up the outer wall and met overhead like a high ceiling, enclosing the castle. The castle itself was enwrapped in thorns, too, and loomed behind him like a vast storm cloud. Pigeons lay smashed on the courtyard's paving stones, having fallen under the curse while flying. All was still.

Trudging to the stable, Griff saw the horses in the stalls with their eyes frozen in mid-roll, their ears pricked. Arny leaned against a wall with his arms crossed, a dried trickle of drool at the corner of his mouth; his jug had rolled onto the floor, and drip by slow drip, the alcohol oozed out. At the corner of the stable door was a spider in its web, paused in the midst of sucking the juices from a fly.

There was no sign of Rose.

She must have escaped the castle. He sighed with relief and relaxed for just a moment, but that moment was long enough. The curse seized him, and as he was pulled into its darkness, he knew with wild certainty that he would not see the light again.

CHAPTER

30

"MY GRANDMAS LIKE WEAPONS," TIMOTHY SAID. THEN she grinned. "A lot." She brought me something long, wrapped in burlap, and tied with twine. "They picked this one for you."

I unwrapped the present. It was an ax with a wooden haft about as long as my arm; the head of it was blunt on one side, curved and sharp on the other. On its face was engraved a knot-work rose. I fit my hand over the ax's worn leather grip. It was just the right size, made for a woman's hands. Getting to my feet, I hefted it. The ax felt heavy, solid; I felt solid, holding it. I remembered what Griff had taught me about fighting. It was all about *will*. Well, it was about sharp edges, too.

"It's perfect," I said to Timothy. "Thank you."

"Huh," she said, as if I'd surprised her. She turned to Quirk. "If we're going into the castle, we'll need more than swords and axes." Reaching into the pocket of her coat, she pulled something out and set it on the sooty hearthstone in front of Quirk.

Still holding the ax, I leaned closer to see. Then I gasped. "The thimble?"

"No, not that thimble," Timothy corrected. "Another one. Pen had it on her when she was killed."

Silently Quirk studied it. Then he gave me a quick glance. "This is what I hoped to find when I left the castle, Rosie."

It looked just like Griff's thimble, except that among the etched thorns that twined around its base were tiny, perfect roses. Its untarnished silver shone softly in the firelight.

"There are two thimbles," Quirk explained to me. "One for the Godmother, who serves Story. One for the Witch, who fights against Story." He sighed. "Griff has his mother's thimble, obviously. It's associated with cold, and with forgetting, and silence, and with warping people and animals out of their usual shapes, and away from themselves. A Godmother can use it to act for Story in the world." He tapped the rose thimble. "This one belongs to the Witch. Its purpose is to thwart Story. It is associated with warmth and fire, and with strength and memory and truth. It was my mother's, and now it has come to me."

"Are you the Witch, then, Quirk?" I asked him.

All was silent, except for the crackle of our fire. I stood

beside Timothy with my ax and held my breath, waiting for Quirk's answer.

Finally Quirk reached out to take the thimble. "I am my mother's son, lass," he said quietly. "So I suppose I am."

THE THIRD TIME Griff dragged himself from the curse's grip, the thorns had spread.

He was standing in the courtyard between the outer wall and the castle. The thorns that had before only circled his ankles now twined up his legs and across his chest. Only one of his arms was free. With every breath he took, the thorns, as long as daggers and just as sharp, stabbed—shallow, stinging cuts that, as he fought free of the curse, started to bleed.

He held himself still against a rising tide of panic. His mouth was as dry as dust; the air was icy cold and still, almost crystalline. The curse receded, as if it wanted him ready. The grinding thunder grew louder in his ears.

Gritting his teeth, he reached for his knife with his free arm, and found his hand going instead to his coat pocket, where the thimble was somehow once again waiting for him, and the spindle, too. Leaving them both, he went for the knife, feeling the thorns bite deeper, his own blood flowing hot over his icy-cold skin.

In one desperate motion, he unsheathed the knife, its handle slick with his blood, and slashed at the vines that gripped him. The thunder grew into a pulsing roar in his head that sounded almost like laughter. With a wrench, he tore himself out of the thorns' grasp and stumbled away from them, dripping with blood, his coat in tatters.

A sharp pain lashed across his back; whirling, he used his knife to deflect a second strike from the whip of a thorn-studded vine. Another vine came at him like a thrown spear. He raised an arm to block it, and it shredded his coat sleeve, leaving a line of pain behind; at the same time, another vine snaked across the paving stones and around his leg. As he bent to untangle himself, a vine wrapped itself around his neck; another vine around his chest jerked him off the ground. He struggled, still clinging to his knife, and the vines gripped tighter, until a thorn laid itself like a drawn blade across his neck. He stilled, feeling its razor-sharp edge, a line of icy cold on his skin. It moved up, forcing his chin back, leaving him completely unprotected.

The vines continued to twine around his arms and legs, their thorns biting through his clothes, holding him still.

All fell silent except for the sound of his own harsh breaths.

The air grew darker. Outside the castle and its cage of thorns, night was falling. The sound of thunder started again, faint at first, then building to the grinding roar of mountains shifting. It was beyond sound; he heard it not just with his ears, but in his bones, and then it formed into a word.

Mine.

Story, he knew with a flash of terror. He clenched his eyes shut, hoping for the oblivion of the curse, but now that he wanted it, its darkness evaded him.

The thunder pounded at him. *Mine*, it repeated. *Mine, mine, mine, mine.*

His lips moved. A denial.

The roar of Story intensified. *Mine*, it insisted. *Alone. Alone, forsaken, unloved, alone. Mine.*

It kept repeating those words until he knew it was true.

He felt a tendril of vine probing; after a moment it encircled his wrist, dragging his arm up until he could see his blood-smeared hand; at the end of the tendril, within reach of his fingers, was the thimble.

It gleamed like the edge of a knife.

Take it.

Take it.

Take it.

Become what you were always meant to be.

He had no words left; he could not speak. But he had his will. And he had his memory of Rose. To give in to Story was to lose her forever. Slowly he clenched his hand into a fist—no. He would not take the thimble.

The thunder roared in fury; the thorns bit deeper.

With them came the cold.

All of his warmth was bleeding out of him, the thorns infusing him with a chill that turned his bones to ice and struck with a frozen dagger toward his heart.

The curse rose again, and this time he welcomed its cold emptiness.

But Story was there, waiting. It would offer the thimble again. It would offer blood, and silence, and ice. And next time, he might not be able to resist.

I WAS DESPERATE to get back into the castle to save Griff. Even before the sky turned pink with dawn, I woke Quirk and Timothy.

She had brought me clothes from her grandmas. I dressed in trousers and a warm red sweater knitted by Zel, and had my hair braided in a crown, secured with diamond hairpins. Shoe's boots were on my feet. We had tea and a little breakfast, and then we packed our knapsacks and took up our weapons: Timothy's sword, Quirk's thimble, my ax.

"There's something you need to see first," Timothy said.

"We don't have time—" I started to protest.

"We have time for this," Timothy said, without a trace of a snarl in her voice. "It's not far."

In the gray morning light, the Penwitch's burned cottage seemed small and forlorn as we left it behind. Timothy led us out of the dell. A few steps down the path was a low hill; at its top was a lone oak tree, a kind of outpost of the Forest, which was a dark cloud on the horizon. The tree's leaves had turned red, and its branches were spread wide, like embracing arms; below it was a long mound of turned earth.

"My grandmas buried Pen's body here," Timothy said, her voice gritty. She and Quirk, who had both known and loved the Penwitch, stood beside the grave. I saw Quirk reach up and take Timothy's hand; to my surprise, she didn't pull away.

I turned and let them grieve in peace, going to the edge of the hill and looking out. The oak tree's leaves rustled over my head; the breeze swept out from the hill and over the long grasses, making them bow down in waves. In the distance, from this height, I could see the castle on the other side of the river, a blunt shape overtaken by the thorny vines, almost as if they'd grown out of the ground and were pulling the castle back down with it.

Knowing that Griff was in that horrible place made my heart ache. He was a fighter, but he had no weapons he could use to fight Story. For all he knew, we'd abandoned him to the thorns and the cold and the silence.

He had lifted the curse from me. He'd done it knowing that it meant he'd be trapped in the castle. He wasn't some kind of evil minion of Story. No, he'd done it to free me.

"Why, Griff?" I whispered. "Why did you do it?"

I knew what I'd seen on his face as he lifted the curse. All his life, he had known nothing of love. Yet somehow . . .

He loved me.

I was absolutely certain of it. And oh, I loved him so much, I almost couldn't bear it.

Which meant I had a weapon even better than a sword or an ax, or even a thimble. I would fight Story with that weapon, and with every scrap of my will. "You can't have him," I said fiercely to Story. "He's not yours. He's mine."

And then I spoke to Griff. "Hold on," I whispered, gazing across the waving grasses to the castle in its shroud of thorns. "Hold on, love. I'm coming for you."

THIS TIME, WHEN Story dragged Griff away from the curse again, there was nothing but the unrelenting cold, and pain, and Story speaking in the stern, disapproving voice of his father.

It went on and on and on.

By the time Story let him alone again, he had his own, unmelting core of ice. He knew that the thimble and the spindle were in his coat pocket. He could barely remember Rose's face. And he was certain that she, like his father, despised him.

Story was everywhere. It was everything. He was nothing.

CHAPTER

31

We stood before the gate of the vine-covered castle.

I held the ax, a comforting weight.

Next to me was Quirk. Timothy had brought him a hat knitted from green wool with an incongruous yellow bobble on top, which he wore pulled down over his ears. It suited him, odd as it was. Timothy had her sword sheathed on its belt around her waist.

The castle was enwrapped with vines and shadows, a looming, dark shape against a sky turning pink as the sun rose over distant hills. Cold seemed to radiate from it; shadows seethed behind the thorns that covered it.

"So what's the plan here?" Timothy asked. Without seeming to realize she was doing it, she moved closer to Quirk and, almost protectively, rested a hand on

"I left Griff in the ballroom," I said. "Her.
straight across the courtyard to get inside."   e to go

"*If* we can get inside," Timothy muttered.

"We won't fall under the curse, will we?" I asked.

As an answer, Quirk held up his hand. He wore
Witch's thimble on a finger. "This should keep us safe."

"From the curse, at least," Timothy added.

Feeling grimly determined, I hefted the ax and nodded
to Quirk. "Let's go."

Thorns and vines clogged the gateway; as we stepped
closer, they shifted; a single vine tipped with a razor-sharp
thorn quested toward us.

With a hiss, Timothy drew her sword and hacked off the
end of the probing vine.

The other vines surged toward us; as Quirk raised the
thimble and led us forward, they recoiled, leaving us a dark,
heaving tunnel to walk through. A single whip of vine lashed
toward us, and I lopped it off with the ax.

My heart was pounding. We moved forward; the vines
closed in behind us, and the dark encroached. Quirk whispered a word, and his thimble started to glow. By its warm
light I could see that we were in a bubble of light edged with
writhing, snakelike green, studded with thorns. The air grew
heavier and colder as we went farther into the tunnel through
the castle wall. A sound grated at the very edge of my hearing, a faint, ominous thunder.

"...ke this," Timothy murmured, slashing at a stray vine...'t either.

...last the tunnel lightened, and we stepped through to ...re open area. The shrouded castle loomed before us; ...rny vines slithered toward us across the courtyard. Quirk ...aised the thimble higher, and some of the vines were pushed back, but a few hissed and struck past him at me. The ax was a clean arc of silver as I brought it down on one vine, and then another. Holding the thimble, Quirk looked almost heroic, except for the bobble hat.

"There, lass!" he shouted.

I whirled, ax at the ready.

He pointed. Then I saw him. Griff. Wrapped in thorns, just ten paces away.

"We'll hold them off," Quirk shouted, as Timothy swatted a questing vine out of the air and held it down with her foot as she hacked it to pieces.

I eluded a vine that was trying to loop itself around my ankle, and raced across the paving stones to Griff.

He was held in the grip of the thorns, his feet several inches off the ground. Blood stained his shirt and his tattered coat; a daggerlike thorn lay across his throat. His eyes were closed. His face was so pale. One of his hands was clenched into a fist; the other held his long knife.

He hadn't been lost under the curse. He'd been fighting.

"Oh, Griff," I whispered, and my heart ached for him.

Setting the ax on the paving stones, I stepped onto a loop of vine, stretching to reach him. I set a shaking hand against his cheek. Cold. So cold and still. But not dead. He was breathing. My relief was so intense, it made me dizzy for a moment.

Carefully I pulled the thorn away from his throat. It left a line of blood behind it, just a scratch. But the other thorns had cut deeper.

Story. I could feel it, a heavy dread in the air, the faint rumble of thunder, a pressure against my ears. It had done this, trying to force him into its service.

From behind me, I heard Quirk and Timothy fighting the vines. "Get on with it, Rose!" Timothy shouted.

I reached up and put my arms around Griff's neck, pulling him closer. It was time to use my most powerful weapon against Story.

When I was learning to fight—when I'd been falling in love with Griff—he had taught me that anything could be a weapon. A sword, an ax, a pitchfork, an oat scoop.

A kiss.

The maid Sally had given me the key. *Only the kiss of true love can stop the curse.*

So I kissed him.

At first it was cold. I shivered. Then, faintly, his lips warmed to mine. My love for him whirled up in me, making me feel elated and terrified at the same time. I had missed him so much. I wanted to feel the length of his body pressed against mine, and feel the pounding of his heart as he kissed me. I was his, completely. And he was mine. I deepened the kiss, pouring all my love into it—into him. Story hadn't expected this weapon, and it capitulated at once, and like sand running out of an hourglass, the curse drained from the castle. All around us, the light grew brighter as the vines around the castle withered and shed their leaves. The brambles fell away from us in limp coils, leaving us standing on the paving stones.

I trembled in Griff's arms, clinging to the front of his coat, and he leaned in to me, as if he was exhausted. My heart felt as if it was about to overflow with joy; I thought I must be glowing with it, like the sun on a glorious day. We'd done it. We'd broken the curse. We were free.

A shudder passed through Griff, into me. His eyes blinked open. Just for a moment, as he gazed down at me, his eyes almost silver in the morning light, I was sure that I'd been right, and he loved me just as much as I loved him.

Then slowly, horribly, his face turned bleak and he raised the knife and held its sharpened edge against my throat.

"No," I whispered.

I felt the chill of the blade against the thin skin of my neck, and then he flinched away from me, stumbling back and taking up a defensive stance. I drew a steadying breath. "Griff?"

He stared at me for a long moment, as if he didn't recognize me. Dead, wrinkled leaves that had fallen from the vines drifted through the air and settled onto the paving stones around us.

There were noises coming from the castle, the rustle of the vines withering away.

"Rose!" Quirk shouted. The burning glow of his thimble had faded. "We have to go!"

"Something's wrong," I told him.

He looked past me, to Griff. "You all right?"

No answer. Griff stood clinging to his knife with a blood-stained hand. Blood oozed from other cuts on his arms and chest, soaking into the tatters of his shirt and coat. His other hand was still clenched into a fist, as if he was holding tightly to something.

The Godmother's thimble. I knew it. "No, he's not all right," I answered for him.

"No time to see to him," Timothy said. She was watching the castle, every line of her body tense, her sword drawn. "The curse is broken, right? So what's going on in there?"

"What?" Quirk spun to face her.

She nodded toward the castle. "Somebody's issuing orders." There was more shouting. "The Godmother's servants are going to come after us," Timothy went on. "Can't you feel it? Story's not defeated here."

I pointed at Griff. "But he's with us now," I protested. "We broke the curse. We're free of it now, aren't we?"

When Quirk spoke, his voice was sharp and low. "You should be."

Timothy sheathed her blade. "We can't stay and fight. There's too many of them. Let's get a move on before they get organized."

"Horses," I remembered. "We can take the horses from the stable."

"Good thinking," Quirk approved. "Let's go."

WE FLED FROM the castle, Timothy holding Quirk on the saddle before her, me on a horse I had no idea how to ride, and then Griff on a horse that had tried to bite me when I'd approached it. I clung to the reins and the mane and bounced in the saddle. Looking back, I saw blue-coated servants issuing from the castle gate; there was a glint of light on metal—they were well armed. The horses seemed to sense our urgency, so our flight was swift, and we'd loosed the other horses from the stable so the servants couldn't ride. But they would pursue on foot.

Unto death, I knew.

"We'll have to try for the Forest," Timothy shouted over her shoulder.

We rode hard, and the Forest grew closer, a wall of trees with leaves turning the yellow and brown of autumn. I had to focus on staying in the saddle, but I kept a worried eye on Griff, who rode beside me. He still hadn't spoken. He hadn't looked at me again. The knife was sheathed at his back, and he wasn't clenching the thimble in his fist anymore, but I was certain that he had it in the pocket of his tattered coat.

With every thud of my horse's hooves on the ground, my heart gave an answering thump. Something was so wrong here. I had broken the curse with my kiss, but the fight wasn't over yet. Story still had a hold on him.

We reached the shallow river and the horses slowed, splashing through the water, their hooves crunching on the sandy gravel on the other side. There, Timothy pulled her horse to a stop, and my horse and Griff's staggered to a halt, sweating and blowing hard through their noses.

"We can't bring the horses into the Forest," Timothy said, swinging down from the saddle. "Without a path, they'll never get through. And they're too tired, anyway." She reached up to help Quirk from the saddle.

I climbed gingerly down from my own horse, and Griff got off his, then wrapped his arms around himself as if he was cold.

I longed to move closer to him.

But he kept his face turned away, as if he couldn't bear to look at me.

Timothy was having trouble with Quirk. "Get your foot out of the stirrup, curse it," she growled.

At the word *curse*, Griff's head jerked up. He stared at me intently.

Quirk and Timothy were still talking, but I ignored them, taking three quick steps, the long grass brushing at my knees, closing the distance between me and Griff. "What?" I asked. "What is it?"

He didn't move, didn't answer.

I glanced back in the direction of the castle. I could see nothing but the rolling waves of the plains.

Quirk, off the horse at last, came over to me, wading through grass that came nearly up to his chin. "I'm hoping the Forest won't let Story's servants in." He pointed at Griff. "But listen, lass. It might not let him in, either."

I felt as if I'd been slapped. "What? Griff grew up in the City. Why wouldn't the Forest let him return to it?"

"Rosie. Look at him."

I did. Griff stood silent, watching us. He was so pale; I wondered if my kiss back in the castle had warmed him at all. With trembling fingers, I reached toward his face—and he flinched away, pulling his clenched hand out of his pocket. He was holding the Godmother's thimble.

I wanted to tell him that it was all right—but it wasn't. He wasn't.

Looking closer, I could see that, in addition to the blood that had seeped through slashes in his coat, his eyes were deeply shadowed with weariness, and his face was lined with pain. Story had done that to him.

"I shouldn't have left you," I whispered.

He didn't answer. His usual silence was deeper, colder.

"He is the son of a Godmother," Quirk said from behind me. "He possesses a thimble just as powerful as mine. Story had over a day to work on him. He is Story's weapon."

"No," I breathed.

"All this time, lass, Story has been in the City," Quirk said. "It was quiet, and subtle, but it was there, watching, waiting, keeping Griff in reserve for when it needed him. The Lord Protector's methods against Story were never completely effective. All he and his Watchers could do was hold it at bay. Not even the Breakers could eradicate it. Now that Story has been thwarted at Castle Clair, it will almost certainly try to rise again in the City." He held up his own thimble. "I've revealed myself to it—it knows that I am the Witch and the City's true Protector, and it knows that I am coming. I can't bring . . ." His voice faltered. "Rosie, I can't bring Story's weapon into the City. Not now."

But we couldn't leave Griff behind. I stepped closer to Quirk and knelt so I could look right into his eyes. His face was so serious under his ridiculous green cap. "I love him."

"Ah, lass," Quirk sighed.

"And he loves me," I insisted. "I won't leave him. We have to come with you." I felt a knot of desperation tighten in my chest. "I don't know what else we can do."

There was a long silence as Quirk considered it.

Timothy had finished unsaddling and setting free the horses; she swished over to us through the long grass. "Less talking, more running away," she said brusquely, with a wave toward the Forest. Almost as an answer, we heard a distant howl—the castle's servants, in pursuit.

"Hurry," I told Quirk. "You must decide." The howls and shrieks of the servants grew even closer.

"It might be enough," Quirk said.

I knew what he meant. Love was one of the most powerful weapons for fighting Story. "It will have to be," I said.

"It's a risk." Quirk released a weary sigh. "But we don't have any other choice. That's how Story works, Rosie. It narrows our choices until we have no options left except to serve Story, whether we will it or not."

"And now our only option is to run," Timothy said, with a worried glance toward the sounds of pursuit. "Go!"

CHAPTER
32

GRIFF FOLLOWED THEM. AS HE WALKED, HE HEARD NOTH-
ing but a low, grinding thunder, saw only shades of gray, as
if all of the color had leached out of the world, and he felt
nothing but pain from the thorns and the ice in his bones.
His mind turned, gear-like, obedient.

Story drew him onward. Story willed that he stay with the
son of the Witch and with the girl, who remained under two
curses. The castle had fallen, but she still had a role to play;
she was still a thing it could use. Story had plans for her, and
for him.

He would go with them to the City, where Story had
invested most of its power. It had once ruled there; it would
rule again, though to ensure its rule it needed the son of a

Godmother, with his thimble, and with the spindle that he carried in his coat pocket.

All of the Godmothers who had ever served Story had, like him, carried ice in their bones. They had given up their will and their warmth, and in return they had received power.

But . . .

He hadn't given up his will, not entirely. It was bound, but he still had it. His warmth had been ripped away from him, but he still had a bit of it left, too. Just a spark.

And . . .

Distantly, he remembered a kiss.

Story's construct. The girl. He had loved her. Hadn't he?

The thunder in his ears resolved into words.

Mine.

Mine.

Unloved.

Alone.

Mine.

Shards of ice lanced into his temples as punishment for his rebellion, no matter how momentary, and his vision went dark. He stumbled to a halt.

Then he felt a faint warmth; peering through the darkness, he saw that the girl had taken his hand.

Her lips moved, but he couldn't hear what she was saying.

Before, when he'd been a Watcher, he'd been able to

sense curses. Now that he could see with Story's vision, he saw her two remaining curses, covering her like a shroud made of shadows.

With numb fingers, he felt for the edge of the curses. It frayed at his touch, and dissolved like smoke.

And then he felt the weight of Story, and the curses' threads reknit themselves. More curses gathered in his hands, heavy as stones; if he tried again to lift her curse, he would burden her with them. He couldn't risk it.

The girl had started running again, holding his hand, pulling him along with her.

He was a danger to her. She should let him go; she should leave him.

Yet he clung to her hand. He had a spark left of his own will; he focused all of it on her hand, because it was a point of life and hope.

Their flight was a whirl of exhaustion and pain, and cold far deeper than the chill he'd felt when walking to the castle with the thimble on his finger. He'd been carrying Quirk on his back. And Rose had been with him.

That was her name, he remembered.

Rose.

THE FOREST LOOMED closer. In the distance, we could hear the howls and shouts of the castle's servants pursuing us. We'd wasted too much time talking.

Quirk led the way, with Timothy, and I followed, pulling Griff along with me.

"There," Quirk panted, pointing.

Ahead there was a scattering of trees and, farther into the Forest, the beginning of a path. Quirk picked up the pace, using his arms as if he was swimming through the grass. I took one quick look over my shoulder, past Griff, to see how close the servants were. I could make out their blue coats. Some of them were running on all fours.

When I turned back, the path leading into the Forest had disappeared, and so had Quirk and Timothy.

"Quirk!" I shouted.

There was a snarl and a series of barks from the servants. They raced toward us, leaping through the long grass. They were close enough now that I could see foam spraying from their mouths as they panted, and blood running from their noses.

I dodged a tree, pulling Griff along with me, and looked frantically for the path. "Quirk! Timothy!"

"Here, lass," he called, and stepped from the Forest's shadows. He raised his arm, as if holding a door open, and there it was, the path. Griff and I stepped onto it, and Quirk followed, with Timothy, and the Forest closed in around us. Five steps later, and the sounds of pursuit were silenced.

I caught my breath. The four of us stood in a clearing not much larger than we were. Tree trunks were like a wall at our backs. Branches arched overhead, blocking the daylight; dried leaves rustled underfoot.

"You all right?" Quirk asked, peering up at me through the gloom.

Relieved, I nodded. I checked Griff. He seemed completely exhausted. His hand, in mine, was very cold. "We're safe for now, Griff," I told him.

He blinked and focused on me. "Rose," he said, his voice rough.

"He spoke!" I exclaimed.

"So he did," Timothy said dryly.

"That's a good sign, don't you think?"

"Story is weaker here, in the Forest," Quirk said, then jerked his chin in Griff's direction. "And look at him now."

I did. Griff took a breath, about to speak again, then went even paler. His eyes clenched shut, and he gritted his teeth, as if he was in pain.

Story wanted him silent, I guessed. "It's all right," I whispered. "You don't have to talk." I looked down at Quirk. "He needs to rest."

"All four of us need to rest," he said grimly. "But can you smell that?"

As he spoke, the wind shifted a bit, and I caught a whiff of smoke. "Yes," I replied. "What is it?"

"The Forest won't give them a path, so Story's servants are hacking and burning to come after us," Quirk said. "We'd better get deeper into the Forest before we can rest. I know a place where we can camp; we'll be safe from them there. Do you know it, Timothy?"

"Yeah," she answered. "Come on."

They led the way, and I followed, not taking my eyes from the yellow bobble on top of Quirk's hat, pulling Griff along with me.

The Forest seemed to dislike me and Griff. Where the path was smooth for Quirk and Timothy, we kept stumbling over roots that appeared under our feet, and being swatted by branches. I kept my eye on the bobble and trudged on.

A tree with smooth, silver bark appeared in our path. Quirk and Timothy went to the right around it, and without thinking, I led Griff onto what seemed to be a wider path around the other side of it, and two steps later, the path ended and we were facing a tangle of golden leaves and ferns turning brown at their tips. I stopped and shouted for Quirk.

He responded from a surprising distance away. Calling constantly, we fought our way through densely packed trees and sprays of bramble until we managed to find each other again.

"Well, that's enough of that," Quirk muttered. Digging in his tunic, he pulled out the thimble and put it onto his finger. "A path, curse it," he ordered.

Almost grudgingly, the Forest offered us another path.

"Not much farther," he assured me.

We went on as the evening shadows gathered. There was

no more smell of smoke on the air. We'd been traveling since before dawn, and I was tired; Griff's shoulders were hunched, as if he was carrying a heavy burden, and he walked with his eyes closed.

Finally we reached a cliff. It stood across our path, as high as the treetops, rosy in the last of the afternoon light, and crusted with moss and ferns that grew on little ledges.

"See?" Quirk asked, pointing.

I looked, and saw, high above us, an opening in the cliff—a cave.

"It's an old Breaker hideout," Quirk said. "A safe place."

"How do we get up there?" I asked wearily.

"There's a trick to it," Timothy told me. "Watch."

The cliff had seemed steep and unclimbable, but she was right; there was a path of sorts. She scrambled up it first, bringing the knapsack, and then she came back down and with her on one side and me on the other, we led Griff from one handhold and foothold to the next, up and into the cave's opening. Quirk followed.

Inside it, we found a ladder, which we climbed down into darkness, standing on what felt like a sandy floor, the last of the afternoon light like a window at the cave's opening, above us. The air was chill and musty.

Quirk whispered a word, and his thimble glowed. Its light reflected from rough, sand-colored walls. The cave was huge, and along one wall there were boxes and barrels, and there was a fire pit in the middle, already set with wood.

Quirk went to it, bent, and a spark fell from his thimble. In a moment, a merry fire was burning. Then he and Timothy went to the boxes at the edge of the cave and started opening them. "There's a spring back here, too," she called.

I sighed with relief. "Come on, Griff," I whispered, and led him closer to the flames. He sat, wrapping his arms around his drawn-up knees, and I sat close beside him, lending him my warmth.

Quirk came from the boxes with another, smaller box. "Physician's kit," he said, dropping it on the sand next to me. Then he went back to the supplies, and he and Timothy started setting out blankets and preserved food.

I turned to Griff. "If you take your coat off," I said, "I can bandage up the cuts you got from the thorns."

He shook his head. "No," he said, his voice rough.

My heart lifted. "You're feeling better, aren't you?"

He looked around at the cave. "It's weaker here."

"Story, you mean," I said.

Quirk had brought a kettle and was hanging it on a hook over the fire. He nodded. "This cave has long been a place hidden from Story. We're safe. For now."

Griff nodded, and rested his forehead on his knees.

"Eat something," I told him, "and then you can sleep."

He lifted his head again. "I won't sleep."

"Oh." I looked at the flames.

Quirk was setting out a frying pan, and mixing up flour and oil. "Did you find the dried berries?" he asked, and in answer, Timothy tossed him a paper package tied with string.

It wasn't exactly comfortable, but it was a respite. I dredged up a smile. "This reminds me of our cottage, mine and Shoe's." I glanced aside at Griff, who watched me, his face sober. "Every night we ate dinner, and then we read stories to each other, or told them."

Quirk poured out tea and passed me two cups; I gave one to Griff. He held it in his hands, warming himself. I set my cup in the sand beside me, and leaned on Griff's shoulder. "I'll tell you the story about the time the goats got out of their shed and met a wolf."

Timothy settled on the sand next to Quirk. "Oh, this sounds exciting."

"There was the occasional wolf in the valley," Quirk remembered, pouring the batter he'd mixed into a pan and setting it over the fire.

I nodded. "In the winter they'd come down from the heights to hunt. Mostly they left us alone, but this one time . . ." While we drank our tea and ate the pan-cake that Quirk had made, I told the rest of the story. Quirk laughed at the parts that were funny, and Timothy rolled her eyes when I told about the stupid thing I'd done. "And then . . . ," I said, and paused. Griff was gazing at me, listening. I smiled. "But maybe you don't want to hear the end of this story."

"Let me guess," Timothy said. "The snow kept falling and the wolf ate the goats, and you and Shoe had no milk or cheese for the rest of the winter."

"No," I scolded. I turned to Griff. "Do you want to know what happened?"

He frowned, studying my face.

"Not all stories are Story," I said. "Sometimes it's just goats and a wolf and a silly girl in a shed on a cold, snowy night."

"Story will have its ending," he said in a voice that grated almost like the grinding of gears.

The sound made me shiver. "We can make our own ending," I told him.

He shook his head. "Rose," he started, then took a steadying breath. "Your curse."

I nodded. "We broke it when I kissed you."

"No." He rubbed his head, as if it ached. "The spindle curse has been broken. But there are two others. The sleep curse. And one more."

I felt a twist of terror in my chest. "Two more curses?"

He nodded, then reached over and took my hand; turning it, he pushed up the sleeve of my sweater, exposing my wrist. With a cold finger, he tapped it. "You are still marked by Story."

My rose had faded slightly, but he was right. It still bloomed on the pale skin of my wrist.

"Can you break the other two curses?" Quirk asked sharply from across the fire. Timothy stared at us over the rim of her mug of tea.

"No." There was a long silence. When Griff spoke again,

his voice was brittle. "If I try, Story will use me to burden her with more curses."

Trembling, I gripped my hands together. "What are the other two curses?"

He studied me. "The sleep curse is one. I don't know what the third one is. But I can see both of them." He lifted his hand, and did something strange, tracing a shape around me, but not touching me. "They cover you," he said grimly. "Like a shroud. I think one might be death."

I WASN'T FREE, after all. Story was coiled in me, and in Griff, and it was pulling us toward the City. During the night, I lay next to the fire wrapped in a blanket, but I barely slept. Possibilities kept turning over in my mind, but none of the threads of thought that I followed led anywhere. We couldn't go back; we had to go on.

As the night ended and the cave opening brightened with the morning light, I sat up, so weary, nearly despairing.

Griff was on the other side of the cave, where the sandy floor was smoothest, doing his Watcher's drills. I watched him, the shift of muscle over bone, the flick of the knife, the block, the turn, the flow into an attack. His face was focused, austere.

As the cave lightened, Quirk sat up from his blankets, his blond hair tousled. Timothy slept on beside the fire, oblivious. Seeing me, he nodded. "Didn't sleep?"

I shook my head. "I don't think he did either." I pointed at Griff.

"No. He wouldn't." Getting to his feet, Quirk yawned and stretched. Then he poked Timothy with his toe.

"What?" she mumbled without opening her eyes.

"Time to go," Quirk said to her.

"I'm still asleep," she said, and pulled the blanket over her head.

"Not at her best in the morning, apparently," he said to me. "I'll have to remember that." He crouched beside her. "Come on, Timothy. I'll make tea."

She peeked out from under the blanket. "Will you put sugar in it?"

"Aren't you sweet enough already?" he teased.

She mock-glared at him, but she got up.

After we'd eaten, we prepared to leave the cave, to push on toward the City. I saw how Griff gritted his teeth, steeling himself to bear the weight of Story again. By the time we got to the bottom of the cliff, he was pale and silent.

Timothy seemed on edge, and Quirk was quiet, too, deep in thought. He knew that Story was forcing us back to the City; he knew that we'd all be in danger there. How the danger would arise, we didn't know.

We walked all that day. In the evening, when we stopped, Griff sat down and fell at once into an exhausted sleep. But after a few minutes he jerked awake again, his eyes wide. I knew why. Story was waiting for him in sleep.

The next day we continued. As we set off, Griff pulled away from me when I tried to take his hand. Then he led us onward. Quirk and I exchanged a look—something had changed. But Griff still didn't speak. When we took a break, he paced, restless, and ignored my attempt to share my food with him. We went on, and as we walked, brown leaves drifted from the trees along the path. Autumn was advancing; soon it would be winter. Evening fell, and we reached the clearing not far from the City where the leader of the Breakers, Precious, had her cabin.

Timothy ran ahead to open the cabin door. After putting her head in, she came back to us, frowning. "Abandoned." There was no sign of Precious or any of the other Breakers.

Quirk shook his head and led us to the river's edge. The water flowed past, swift and dark in the fading light.

Too tired to talk, we set up camp. I huddled close to the fire with a blanket wrapped around me. A few paces away, Timothy and Quirk had their heads together, discussing something in low voices. Griff stood with his back to us, looking upstream, toward the City. As night fell, its lights stained the sky. We would be there tomorrow.

I ached with the need to be with Griff, to kiss him one more time. I got to my feet. "Griff?" I asked, taking a step toward him.

His shoulders stiffened. He didn't turn around.

Sorrow, sharp as thorns, gathered in my chest. "What are we going to do?"

Quirk came to stand beside me. He was turning the thimble in his fingers; I saw it glint in the firelight. "We'll decide tomorrow."

"All right," I said.

But in the morning, they came for us.

CHAPTER

33

THE CLOSER THEY CAME TO THE CITY, THE MORE CLEARLY Griff saw his path before him. Story was rising to power there, and it drew him. It had received a setback at Castle Clair, when the beauty had not fallen to the spindle curse, but it had found a way to turn the situation to its advantage. There was no escaping it. It was too big, too powerful. Even the Forest could not resist it. He was Story's weapon, and it wanted him at hand.

And so he made himself into a blade. Sharp, cold, emotionless.

He was awake when they came.

The two girls and the Witch were asleep. The sky to the east was gray with dawn, but the shadows of night had not yet lifted.

At the river, he heard the men sent from the City. The splash of paddles in the water, the low growl of an order. The scrape of wooden keels over rock. They were black outlines climbing out of their boats, lurching up the steep riverbank.

He got to his feet. The thimble, a cold, heavy weight, was in his hand; the spindle was in his coat pocket. He had his knife, sheathed at his back, but he knew he wouldn't need it. The fire was behind him; he knew that he was a looming shadow to them. Four of the servants gathered in the darkness just beyond the circle of light from the campfire.

"Hold there," Griff said quietly.

"Well, if it isn't the errant junior," came an oily voice from the shadows.

Luth, the leader of the prison cohort, edged into the light. With him was another Watcher in gray, and four of Story's blue-coated servants from Castle Clair, two with the long snouts and fangs of dogs, two with furred faces and the hulking shoulders of bears.

As he had expected, the servants had found boats and gone down the river to reach the City before him. Despite his carefully honed rationality—or maybe because of it—the Lord Protector would have been easy prey; without the City's true Protector to save them, he and his Watchers would have fallen to Story and joined with its servants. All was in readiness.

"Seize them," Griff ordered, and pointed toward the

banked fire where the Witch and the Breaker and the construct were still sleeping. With a howl, the servants leaped to
obey. He heard a scream, and a scuffle; there was a brief flash
of light and the sound of a blow. He did his best to ignore it.

"Ran away, did you, junior?" Luth taunted, easing closer.
"And now you've come back."

Behind him, he heard another shout and the sound of a
blade being drawn, and more Watchers and servants emerged
from the darkness, ready to seize the two girls and the Witch.

"Some of us are *very* glad to see you," Luth said, and
stepped forward to grab Griff's arm.

"No," Griff said, slipping the thimble onto his finger.

"But—" Luth protested.

The thimble was heavy with power. Griff raised it slightly
and fixed Luth with a cold eye.

Luth faltered and fell silent.

Griff turned as the blue-coated servants came to report.
Two of them held the beauty by the arms. Her braids had
come unpinned and hung loose around her face; her eyes
were wide with fright.

"Griff?" Her voice trembled.

He didn't let himself respond. "Where are the others?"
he asked.

"They slipped 'way," a servant answered, with an uneasy
look at Luth. Then he bowed his head deferentially to Griff.
"The little one used magic, sir. We c'n go after them."

"No," he ordered. "Leave them. I will take the girl to the citadel."

I COULDN'T STOP shaking. Partly from the cold—the air near the river was dank and chilly—but even more because of Griff. As he gave orders about binding my hands, his eyes skimmed over me as if he didn't see me.

His vision had once been so keen. I wondered what he saw now. The beauty? Story's construct? The shroud of the curses that lay over me?

The horrible Watcher, Luth, tied my hands in front of me. "Taira and I missed our chance with you before," he said, jerking the knot tight. I shuddered and tried to pull away, but he took me by the chin and leaned closer as if he was going to force a kiss. "Frightened?" he crooned. "Good. I like that."

And then Griff was at his shoulder. "She is not for you."

Scowling, Luth released me, stepping back.

For a moment I was relieved; then I saw the glint of the thimble on Griff's finger. It meant he was saving me for something else.

"Put her in the boat," he ordered.

Rough hands seized me and dragged me down the steep riverbank, and thrust me onto a seat with my back to the bow of one of the boats. After a moment Griff climbed in and sat, facing me. Watchers and servants shoved the boats away from the bank, leaped in, and started paddling upstream, toward the City. They hadn't found Quirk and Timothy; I felt some hope, knowing they'd gotten away.

The dawn had advanced; the sky was white, with an edge of red to the east where the sun was coming up. In the dim light, Griff's eyes were the gray of old ice and deeply shadowed with weariness. He still had on the bloodstained, tattered black coat; our hard days of travel had pared him down to bone and lean muscle.

I was shivering. My hands were bound, so I couldn't wrap my arms around myself for warmth.

The Godmother's thimble, Quirk had told me, was associated with cold, with forcing people away from their true selves, and with forgetting.

"Griff," I started, then steadied my voice. "I think you must remember me. I'm Rose."

A flicker of a glance from the ice-gray eyes. But even that was better than Story's blankness. It gave me the will to keep going.

"I know," I said, with a rueful shake of my head. "Shoe used to tease me about how chattery I am. Even at a moment like this, when everything is awful and I'm so frightened, and Story wants us to be miserable, and isolated from each other, and obedient to its . . ." I paused and lifted my bound hands. "Its plots and its plans for us."

He didn't comment.

That was all right; I didn't expect him to.

I leaned closer, so only he could hear me. "I love you," I whispered.

He stared at me.

"And you love me," I went on. "It's all right, you don't have to say it. I know that you do. We love each other, and that is definitely not part of Story's plan." I grew more certain. "Story has made a mistake."

When he spoke, his voice was rough. "Story does not make mistakes."

"Yes, it does," I insisted. "Here's the irony of it, Griff. We can be certain that we love each other because of Story, because we broke the spindle curse. According to Story's rules there's only one way to break a curse like that." My voice softened. "And that's with a kiss of true love."

He frowned.

"You are mine," I finished. "And I am yours."

There was a long silence, long enough that I started to wonder if he was going to acknowledge my words at all. Finally he spoke. "No," he said quietly. "The kiss of true love is only a device of Story."

"Not this time," I told him. I remembered the moment when my love for him had surged up in me. "Our love is much more true and real than that."

"No," he repeated. "You belong to Story, just as I do." Then he turned his face away. I understood what that meant: he would not listen to anything more that I had to say.

In the distance, I heard a deep rumbling sound. For a panicked moment I thought it might be Story, but then I remembered the waterfall, how it fell from the cliff at the edge of the City. I turned to peer over my shoulder to see if I could see it yet. The boats had just entered the wide lake from which the river flowed. At the other end of it, I could barely make out the dark wall of the cliff. Then it was veiled from my sight.

Fog seeped from the Forest, creeping from the shore over the surface of the water. Damp tendrils encircled us, and, a moment later, the other boat had disappeared and we were completely enveloped in a white cloud.

The sounds of oars splashing in the water, or knocking against the side of the boat, were louder; the roar of the waterfall was louder, too, and the air grew heavy with dampness.

When we reached the end of the lake, the fog lifted. The waterfall pounded down, spraying us with cold droplets. The other boat was gone.

I realized that the docks were deserted; there were no other boats or rafts or barges on the water. They should have been waiting to send supplies up the lift or receive finished goods to take down the river. The Forest had taken them all. The lift itself was silent, a dripping metal skeleton.

Without Griff's thimble, it might have taken our boat, too.

The City, I realized, had been completely cut off from the outside world. It belonged to Story, alone.

There was no help here. No hope.

The keel of the boat grated on the graveled edge of the lake. A muted order from Griff, and the Watcher Luth pulled me from my seat and over the side of the boat; it scraped against my hip, and then I was standing on the shore. I was shaking with a combination of fright and cold; I could barely stay on my feet.

Griff gave some orders in a low voice, and I was taken up to the City and through its silent, deserted streets, to the citadel.

GRIFF'S FATHER, I knew, had been Story's enemy, the City's Lord Protector. Any hope I had that he was resisting Story's takeover of the City was extinguished when I stepped through the door of his office in the citadel.

The room was as bare and cold as it had been the first time I'd been brought there. The Watcher Luth untied my hands; then he and two of Story's servants went to guard the door. Griff stood at my back.

The Lord Protector sat behind his desk. As the door closed, his head jerked up. Seeing Griff, his face didn't change; it stayed still and cold, and I realized why Story had found it so easy to corrupt him. It had probably been using him for years, without anyone's knowledge. He had no warmth in him, no love; he wasn't even glad to see his own son. "Ah," he said. "We have been awaiting your return." There was a hint of criticism in his voice.

Griff stepped around me. The weariness that I'd seen before was gone; he was all sharpness and metal now. "The Forest has made its move. The City is cut off. It is time."

"Time . . . ," the Lord Protector repeated. "Yes. All is ready."

"On your feet," Griff ordered. "Have her taken up."

Like a clockwork man, the Lord Protector stood up from behind his desk. His head bowed as he acknowledged Griff's command.

"What are you going to do with me?" I asked. My voice sounded thin and desperate.

Neither of them seemed to hear me. Clawed hands gripped my arms and dragged me out of the room. The guards' footsteps were loud on the stone floors as they pulled me down empty hallways and then up darkened stairs to a huge room at the very top of the citadel. They thrust me into it and then slammed the door, leaving me alone.

The room was bare, high-ceilinged, and made all of stone. The air was dry and cold. I could feel the heavy weight of Story here. On one side of the room was a wide opening, a window without glass; chilly air blew in. Shivering, I went to it and looked out over the City.

The sky was gray. The City was gray; the Forest beyond it was muffled in fog. There was no color anywhere. Quirk was out there, with Timothy. I hoped they were all right, that they had escaped. There was nothing they could do to help me. Desolate, I wrapped my arms around myself. "Oh, Shoe," I whispered. "What would you say if you could see me now?" He had raised me with love and happiness, and he had tried to save me from Story. But I didn't think there was anything

I could have done to keep myself from ending up right here.

There was a noise at the door; I turned and saw Griff enter, then close the door behind him. He had changed out of his ragged coat and now wore the plain gray uniform of a Watcher.

I started across the room toward him. He came to meet me. We stopped in the middle of the room. I saw the glint of the Godmother's thimble on his finger.

"Beauty," he said.

"Rose," I corrected.

He frowned.

The floor shifted under my feet; I looked down and gasped. Gray, thorny, leafless vines were growing from the stone. They twined around my feet, holding me in place. Shadows gathered in the corners of the stone room. A faint thunder ground away at the edge of my hearing.

"It is time for you to sleep." He pulled something out of his tunic pocket.

With sudden horror, I realized what was in his hand. He must have brought it with him from the castle. "No," I breathed.

His gray eyes fixed on me. He held out the spindle. "Take it."

I tried to pull away, but the vines held me in place. The air grew heavy; the thunder grew louder. "Griff . . . ," I panted, desperate. "I can't. Please don't let Story do this."

"You are cursed," he said quietly. "You must take it."

He held up the spindle. Its point was stained with dried blood. My blood.

The spindle curse had been broken, though. It had no power over me now.

Griff knew this, and he knew he still needed to use the spindle to activate the second curse.

He reached out and took my hand, and his hand was so cold, as if he was made of ice and gears. I could hear the weight of Story shift. He turned my wrist to expose my birthmark, my faded rose. I knew what he meant by it—I was marked by Story; I belonged to it.

I used the only weapon that I had left. "Kiss me," I whispered. But it was too late.

Griff brought the needle-sharp point to my fingertip. A single bead of blood, warm against my icy skin, and the second curse washed like a dark wave over me, pulling me down to drown in the roiling depths of sleep.

THE CITY SLEPT UNDER THE CURSE.

Story's weapon stood guard over the beauty. She slept on a bed of woven vines in the middle of the stone room. She lay as still as death, the curse her shroud. Her face was pale, colorless, framed by the muted gold of her hair. Her long lashes rested on her cheek, and her mouth was relaxed, almost smiling.

She would sleep for a hundred years. Story would have its dominion over the City, growing in power as the years passed, until its chosen prince arrived to break the curse with a kiss. After that, not even the Forest would be able to contain it.

He was Story's weapon. He would wait, alone, on guard, as the City slept around him.

He couldn't bear to look at the beauty, sleeping, so he stood looking out over the City. At its outer wall, a second wall grew, a high barrier made of thick, gray, leafless vines woven together.

The sun rose and set behind a heavy blanket of clouds. Days passed. Weeks. Snow fell. The City slipped into the long darkness of winter.

Beauty's guard welcomed the clarity of the cold. It froze his thoughts. His heart stilled in his chest. The cold struck with gleaming shards of ice at the odd spark that he held within him.

Kiss me, she had said.

And on the boat, as he'd brought her out of the Forest and into Story's City. *I love you.*

He paced, restless.

The beauty slept on.

IN THE CITY, something shifted.

The angle of the light had changed. The long, dark winter was ending. Icicles dripped along the edge of the opening in the wall. One by one, as the air grew warmer, they broke off and fell, shattering on the stones far below. Snow melted and flowed into the gutters of the City streets. The river grew swollen, and the roar of the waterfall grew louder.

The guard's thoughts became troubled.

Kiss me.

He circled the room, the sound of his footsteps muffled

by the dust that had settled over the stone floor.

I love you.

He shook his head, dipped into the pocket of his tunic, and took the thimble into his hand. It was a heavy, cold weight, and it steadied him.

"I love you."

He froze and looked toward the bed. Had she spoken?

No. She lay quiet, still. Too quiet?

He stepped closer, studying her. To his relief, her chest rose and fell as she took a breath. The sleep curse that lay over her had thinned to a veil. At a touch, it would dissolve.

And under that was the beauty. He went to his knees beside the low bed of vines. Story gathered in his bones, making him feel heavy, slow. At the edge of his hearing, its thunder awakened. Her beauty should have made her simply a construct of Story. A false, hollow person.

But she wasn't. She was vibrant, alive, warm. Herself.

Rose. Her name was Rose.

"Go ahead, lad," came a half-familiar voice from behind him. "Kiss her."

He whirled away from the sleeping beauty, leaping to his feet and drawing his knife in one smooth motion.

The Witch—Quirk was his name, he remembered— stood inside the doorway; the young woman, Timothy, was just behind him with her sword drawn, ready to defend him. Other Breakers waited outside on the stairs. He hadn't heard their footsteps; he hadn't heard the door opening.

The Witch wore a green hat with a puff of yellow yarn on top of it. He had a long scratch crusted with blood across his cheek. He was unarmed.

Except for his thimble, which glowed with a warm light on his finger. "We had to fight our way through the thorns to get here, Griff," the Witch said, his voice tense, "and I can only hold it for a moment more."

Story, he meant. He could hear its rumble, feel its fury building. The walls of the stone room trembled; dust sifted down from overhead.

The Witch's face turned gray and drawn. "If you're going to kiss her, lad, you'd better do it now."

Kiss her?

Lowering his knife, the guard turned back to the beauty. The Witch said something else, but he didn't hear him.

He sat on the edge of the bed and set down the knife. She sighed, deeply asleep. Her lips parted.

Kiss me.

His arms went around her, and he pulled her closer, and after a moment that stretched almost to breaking, he lowered his lips to hers. Their kiss filled him with heat and light until she felt like a lick of flame in his arms, trembling. Her hands moved to cling to his shoulders. She gasped, and they broke the kiss.

"My goodness," she breathed.

He looked down at her. She gazed at him, her eyes luminous. She sighed, and reached up to run her fingers along the edge of his jaw. At her touch, his whole body awakened to an awareness of her, her nearness, her warmth. It spread through him, until he could feel his heart beating again. Somehow tears had gotten onto his face. Pulling back a little from Rose, he wiped them away with the palm of his hand.

"When ice melts," he heard Quirk say dryly, "it makes a terrible mess."

Rose was smiling at him. "Kiss me," she said softly. "Kiss me again."

And he did.

CHAPTER

35

ALL AROUND US, THE STONE WALLS OF THE CITADEL WERE
shaking.

"I think we'd better get out of here," Quirk said from
behind us, interrupting our kiss.

Griff nodded and pulled me to my feet. I should have
been stiff after sleeping for what seemed like a long time, but
I felt free and alive, and like laughing and crying at the same
time.

Timothy was saying something to Quirk, who nodded.
Other Breakers were there, too; some of them turned and
started hurrying down the stairs.

"Story's power here is breaking," Quirk said, beckoning
to us. "Come on."

The floor trembled under my feet as Griff and I, hand in

hand, left the room; the shaking turned to shuddering and the grinding of stone over stone. We broke into a run, pelting down the stairs. The building was awakening around us; gray-coated Watchers fled, as did animals that had once been servants of Story, all of us rushing out of the citadel doors, spilling into the courtyard and then out into the City's streets.

I could hear shouts and screams and the rushing of water as the river surged out of its banks. The air tingled and the late afternoon sun burst brilliantly through the clouds. Still holding hands, Griff and I stumbled to a halt. From where we stood, we had a clear view down the main street that led to the edge of the City.

Quirk climbed onto a chunk of stone to see better; Timothy stood beside him, steadying him so he wouldn't fall. "Careful, sweetheart," I heard her say.

Behind us, the citadel was crumbling; there was a roar of stone collapsing, and dust filled the air. At the City wall, gray vines were melting away. As we watched, the wall itself fissured. For just a moment, the grim gray of the City seemed frozen, waiting.

A flash of green caught my eye. "Look!" I said, pointing.

A single blade of grass had appeared in the dust at our feet. Its vibrant green was very bright against the gray of the road.

As we watched, the Forest flowed over the crumbling wall and into the City. It advanced as moss spreading and ferns uncurling at their tips, while young trees forced themselves up through the cobblestones. The air turned warm and moist, and rich with the smell of dirt and growing things.

As night fell, the clouds drew together over the City, and a gentle rain sifted down.

QUIRK AND THE Breakers established a kind of headquarters in one of the big, dilapidated houses that edged what had been a hard-packed, empty square and was now a park seething with new growth.

I had only been awake for a few hours, but I felt suddenly exhausted, and ravenously hungry. I couldn't seem to go more than a step away from Griff. He was quiet, but watched everything keenly. He said a few words to Timothy, who nodded, and then found us a quiet spot in a dusty attic at the very top of the house. We sat wearily down together. One of the Breakers brought us bread and cheese and a plate of salted potatoes. It was all I could do to take a few bites.

As my eyes were closing, I jerked awake, suddenly remembering the third curse—had it been broken when Story was broken? I said something incoherent about it to Griff.

"It's all right, Rose," he said, and I felt his arm come around me.

I knew I was safe with him. I put my head on his shoulder and fell asleep.

A FEW HOURS later, when I woke up, he was gone.

I yawned, stiff from lying on the hard attic floor. As I stretched, the sleeve of my sweater fell back, exposing my wrist. My birthmark was still there, just the faintest outline of a fading rose. Despite Griff's assurances, its lingering presence remained a worry. And where was he?

Climbing to my feet, I made my way down the stairs, dodging groups of frightened people who had come to see the City's new Protector and hear from the Breakers the story of how Story had come to fall.

In a hallway I found Timothy, wearing a sword, giving orders to a few Watchers dressed in gray.

Hearing my footsteps, she turned and grinned at me. "So you had a nice nap?"

I rolled my eyes, but couldn't help smiling back at her. "It was a bit on the long side."

"People are already talking about how it ended," Timothy said. She stepped closer and slung an arm across my shoulders, pulling me with her down the hallway. "You know, it wouldn't be a bad idea to kiss that boy some more," she said. "Just in case."

I blushed. The Breakers were spreading our story throughout the City, and it would be told and retold. I knew that our kiss, the kiss that had broken Story, would be remembered for many years to come.

"Before you find Griff, you should talk to Quirk," she said, pointing to a doorway.

Speaking of Quirk . . . "Timothy, did I hear you call him *sweetheart* before?"

"Oh, no," she said, stepping back and holding up her

hands. "We are not doing this, Rosie. We are *not* gossiping about a man."

"But that's what friends do," I assured her.

"Even if that's true," she said dismissively, "he's way too old for me."

"No he's not," I said. She was about twenty, I guessed, and Quirk couldn't be more than thirty. "He calls you *sweetheart* all the time."

"He doesn't mean anything by it," Timothy said, but I could see that she hoped he did.

"I think he does," I assured her. "I think the two of you could be very happy together."

She stared at me for a moment. She opened her mouth, and then closed it again.

A laugh bubbled up in me.

"Stop it," she said, trying to hide a smile. "Go on." She shoved my shoulder and pointed at the door again. "Go and talk to my sweetheart, or whatever he is." With another grin, she left me there.

I stepped into a room crowded with Breakers and Watchers, and a few ragged people from the City. Quirk stood on a chair; he was obviously in charge. The City's Protector. I paused, watching him. He was pointing at a map that covered a table and issuing orders about making sure the people of the City were safe, and clearing away the debris from the fallen citadel, and opening up trade on the river so that food and supplies would start coming in again.

Looking up, he saw me and nodded. He said a few words to a big man—Bouchet—and then clambered down from the chair. He came over to me. He looked tired, but also like he was doing exactly what he was meant to be doing.

"Let me guess," he said. "You're looking for Griff."

I blushed. Again. "Yes."

"Ah, lass," he said, shaking his head. "Pen would have loved the irony of it, you know."

"What?" I asked.

"That the two people who were made to serve Story," he answered with a gap-toothed grin, "were the ones to defeat it."

I smiled back at him. "It's really defeated, then?" I asked.

He cocked his head. "For now." Then he amended his comment. "For a long time, I hope. Story can never be completely destroyed, Rose. But this time we'll fight it a different way." Somebody from the table called his name. He glanced over his shoulder and answered, "Coming." Turning back to me, he said, "You'll find Griff at the citadel. Or, rather, what's left of it."

"Thank you," I said.

"His father didn't make it out," Quirk added as I turned to go. "His body was found an hour ago."

I went out of the new headquarters of the City and into the dark, humid night. While I'd been sleeping, the rain had stopped and the clouds had drawn off. A full moon hung low in the west, filling the streets with its pale light. There was a sense of big things moving in the night. Growth, change, the Forest settling in. The people of the City should have welcomed it in long ago, instead of forcing it outside the walls. The new Protector, Quirk, would let it stay. There would be love, too, and warmth, and happiness. Now that those weapons were established here, Story would have a much harder time rising again. As I went along the street toward the citadel, I could see that trees had grown up already. Springy moss was underfoot; as I went around a corner, fern fronds brushed my knees.

I found Griff sitting on a mossy chunk of stone near where the citadel had been. Nothing remained of it but a moon-silvered jumble of stone and broken wood. As he heard my footsteps, he got to his feet and came to meet me.

He was the perfect height for kissing. Not too tall. We kissed, and then we stood with our arms around each other.

"Griff," I whispered.

I felt him shift, and knew he was listening.

"There is one more curse," I reminded him.

"Yes," he said. "I know."

SHE LAID HER hand flat against his chest. Then she turned her arm to show him the fading rose on the inside of her wrist. "Can you break the last curse?"

He nodded.

With a sigh, she pulled away to stand before him.

He could see the veil of the third curse covering her,

glinting in the moonlight.

"What is it?" she asked.

With a fingertip, he traced the delicate arch of her eyebrow. "It's the beauty."

"Oh," she breathed. "Of course." Her lips quirked into a smile. "What if I'm a toad, underneath?"

The question caught him by surprise. He laughed. "You won't be." Gently he reached out. The edge of the beauty curse frayed under his fingers. It was only the faded remnant of a broken story. A pull of its threads, and it was gone.

She stood gazing up at him. Her face had changed. A few freckles were scattered over her nose. Her mouth was a bit wider, her eyelashes not quite as long, her hair not so golden blond. She held up her wrist, and it was smooth and unmarked. She was not the beauty anymore. She was just Rose.

"Well?" she asked.

"You look just the same to me," he said with a wry smile.

"Oh, sure I do," she scoffed, but she was smiling. "I suppose it doesn't change how you feel about me."

"No, it doesn't," he said soberly. "I love you."

She sighed happily and leaned into him, resting her head in the angle where his neck met his shoulder. She fit perfectly there. He put an arm around her.

For most of his life he had been so sure of who he was—a Watcher. And then he'd met Rose and left the City, and he hadn't known who or what he was, and it had felt like falling.

After that had come the sick certainty that he was Story's weapon. Now he was something else. He wasn't sure yet what he would become now that Story was over, but it didn't feel like falling. He was with Rose, and it felt more like flying.

"Look." With his other hand he pulled the thimble from his tunic pocket. He held it out to her. She reached for it, then hesitated. "It's all right," he said.

She took the thimble and held it up, turning it in her fingers. It gleamed silver in the moonlight.

"Oh," she said softly. "It's changed."

It had. Around its base, where before only brambles had been engraved, there were now roses among the thorns.

The End.

ACKNOWLEDGMENTS

THANKS TO

My always-amazing editor Antonia Markiet and the rest of the A-Team, Abbe Goldberg and Alyson Day.

To my most excellent agent, Caitlin Blasdell.

To the wonderful team at HarperTeen who turned the words into a beautiful book: senior production editor, Kathryn Silsand; production manager, Lillian Sun; my design team, Joel Tippie and Amy Ryan; and my marketing team, Nellie Kurtzman and Jenna Lisanti.

To my Goat Heaven buddies, Jenn Reese, Deb Coates, and Greg van Eekhout.

For information about burns, Erin Cashier. For horses, Jennifer Adam. For spindles and spinning, Sarah Goslee.

To Luke Reynolds for all his book-love and for snark about Pin.

To John and Maud and Pip for being the best family ever.

And for all the excellent copy editors, Stet is for you.